NOVELS BY DAVID POYER

THE CIVIL WAR AT SEA

That Anvil of Our Souls
A Country of Our Own
Fire on the Waters

TALES OF THE MODERN NAVY

The Command
Black Storm
China Sea
Tomahawk
The Passage
The Circle
The Gulf
The Med

THE HEMLOCK COUNTY NOVELS

Winter Light
Thunder on the Mountain
As the Wolf Loves Winter
Winter in the Heart
The Dead of Winter

THE TILLER GALLOWAY SERIES

Down to a Sunless Sea
Louisiana Blue
Bahamas Blue
Hatteras Blue

OTHER NOVELS

The Only Thing to Fear
Stepfather Bank
The Return of Philo T. McGiffin
The Shiloh Project
White Continent

A
COUNTRY
OF OUR OWN

A NOVEL OF THE CONFEDERATE RAIDERS

DAVID POYER

SIMON & SCHUSTER PAPERBACKS
NEW YORK LONDON TORONTO SYDNEY

SIMON & SCHUSTER PAPERBACKS
Rockefeller Center
1230 Avenue of the Americas
New York, NY 10020

First Simon & Schuster paperback edition 2005

SIMON & SCHUSTER PAPERBACKS and colophon are
registered trademarks of Simon & Schuster, Inc.

For information about special discounts for bulk purchases,
please contact Simon & Schuster Special Sales at
1-800-456-6798 or business@simonandschuster.com.

Book design by Ellen R. Sasahara

Manufactured in the United States of America

1   3   5   7   9   10   8   6   4   2

The Library of Congress has cataloged the hardcover edition as follows:
Poyer, David.
A country of our own : a novel of the Civil War at sea / David Poyer.
p. cm.
1. United States—History—Civil War, 1861–1865—Naval operations—Fiction.
PS3566.O978 C68 2003
813'.54—dc21   2003045435

ISBN-13: 978-0-684-87134-9
ISBN-10:   0-684-87134-3
ISBN-13: 978-0-671-04741-2 (Pbk)
ISBN-10:   0-671-04741-8 (Pbk)

ACKNOWLEDGMENTS

Ex nihilo nihil fit. My heartfelt thanks to Miles Barnes, David Bartle, Marian Booth, Ina Burch, Mary Catalfamo, James W. Cheevers, Bill Cogar, John Coski, Rosie Crichton, Mark Danziger, Claiborne Dickinson, Ed Finney, Alan B. Flanders, William M. Fowler Jr., Herb Gilliland, Frank Green, Glenn Augustus Gossett, Preston Haynie, Angela Herbert, Jane Herman, Alice Hershiser, Julie Holcomb, Bob Holcombe, Roger Hull, Phil Hunt, Pam Innes, Robert Kelly, Jeff Kuller, Jodi Lamagna, Gary LaValley, Ivan T. Luke, Katty Mears, Paula Mills, Joseph C. Mosier, Shannon Murphy, Ethel Nepveux, Jack Ordeman, Tara Parsons, Naia Elizabeth Poyer, Nancy Richard, Isolde Sauer, Sandra Scoville, LeRoy Sealy, Shayne Sewell, Prabha Shah, Bruce Smith, Greg Starbuck, Bill Thompson, Bob Thorp, Darren Thurman and *Tramontana,* Ann Vosikas, Robert Walsh, Allison Wareham, Mary Warnement, Tom Wescott, and many others who gave unstintingly of their time and expertise to help bring this book into being.

Above all, let me express my gratitude to two remarkable women for their oft-tested support and indulgence during the writing: Marysue Rucci, editor of these volumes, and Lenore Hart, my wife.

Thanks are also due to the National Archives, The Marshall W. Butt Library at the Portsmouth Naval Shipyard Museum, the Naval Historical Center, The Eastern Shore Public Library, The Navy Department Library, The Port Columbus Civil War Naval Center, The Chrysler Museum of Art, The National Maritime Museum of Greenwich, the Piers Park Sailing Association, The Bostonian Society Library, The Royal Naval Museum Library, The United States Coast Guard Barque *Eagle,* The Pearce Civil War Collection at Navarro College, the Division of Cultural Resources, Boston National Historical Park, the Northumberland County Historical Society, The Nimitz Library Special Collections and Archives Division of the U.S. Naval Academy Library, The U.S. Naval Academy Museum, The Central Library Record Office, Liverpool, The National Science

Museum at New Kensington, The Virginia War Museum, the Northampton Free Library, The Museum of the Confederacy, The Institute of Marine Engineering, Science, and Technology, The Mariner's Museum, and the Joint Forces Staff College Library.

As always, all errors, inaccuracies, and shortcomings are my own.

CONTENTS

8. And Abraham said unto Lot, Let there be no strife, I pray thee, between me and thee, and between my herdmen and thy herdmen; for we be brethren.

9. Is not the whole land before thee? separate thyself, I pray thee, from me: if thou wilt take the left hand, then I will go to the right; or if thou depart to the right hand, then I will go to the left.

10. And Lot lifted up his eyes, and beheld all the plain of Jordan, that it was well watered everywhere, before the Lord destroyed Sodom and Gomorrah, even as the garden of the Lord, like the land of Egypt, as thou comest unto Zoar.

11. Then Lot chose him all the plain of Jordan; and Lot journeyed east: and they separated themselves the one from the other.

—Genesis 13

PART I

Virginia, May 10–June 10, 1861.

1

A Stolen Pistol ♦ Dawn in Richmond, Attended by Ravens ♦ A Messenger
from the Navy Department ♦ Disappointing Conversation with Commodore
Rousseau ♦ Arrival of a National Dignitary

T HE first thing Ker Claiborne realized that morning was not that
this was the day he was to fight a duel, but that his monkey was
no longer in the bed beside him. The sheets still smelled of ape,
but the animal wasn't there.

Rubbing his eyes, peering across the room in the vibrating grisly light
that preceded dawn, it took him some seconds to make out the furry
shape of C. Auguste Dupin, holding one of his master's pistols. And even
then sighting down the barrel at him.

Fully and suddenly awake, he threw the coverlet back. Then froze,
hearing the ratcheting click of the hammer being pulled to cock. Remembering how intently the beast had observed him as he cleaned, oiled, and
loaded the finely crafted Bertrand & Javalet. How he'd watched his master extend the weapon, aim, and squeeze.

Hurling himself from the bedclothes, Ker cuffed the pistol aside just as
it went off. The washbasin exploded, showering him with water, bits of
Wedgwood, and jagged splinters off the corner of a carved oak Bible box
dated 1709, when the Wythes had arrived in the New World. Then all
was pandemonium in his father-in-law's house. Screams came from the
other bedrooms. His own was a reeking box of sulphurous smoke. The

howling, chattering ape ricocheted along the baseboards like a squirrel with its tail afire.

—Ker, are you all right in there?

The voice outside his door belonged to his father-in-law, old Thomas Wythe. —Quite all right, sir, Ker called.

—What's that?

He raised his voice. —I said, thank you for your concern. Only an accidental discharge, while loading my sidearm.

Ker lunged, collaring Dupin by the nape with one hand and scooping up the weapon with the other. He replaced it in the case and set the lock, then remembered he'd done exactly that the night before. The monkey tried desperately to sink its teeth into his arm. Really, he could see why his wife had lost patience with it. She'd found it in their nursery, holding their toddler upon the windowsill. She'd told him in no uncertain terms that if he was going to Richmond, it was going with him.

A knock. He opened the door to find Wythe and his young cousin Harker Bowen in rumpled nightdress. Wythe's pepperbox revolver was pointed at the floor. —Rather early to be loading a pistol, Ker, he observed.

—I have an early appointment, sir.

—May I ask what sort of appointment?

—The kind which requires a loaded pistol. He met the older man's gaze and saw he understood; saw also he ached to ask more. But of course could not. Ker bowed. —If you'll excuse me.

—Certainly, said Harker. Down the hallway, his mother-in-law, dressed only in a loose cotton volante, turned away too. Only Wythe lingered. He pressed Ker's arm. —Who?

—A man of no consequence to you. A naval acquaintance.

—If he is of no consequence, why, you need not take the field.

—I wish it were avoidable, but it is not. I left letters in the Bible box for Catherine and Robert. Will you make sure they get them? If necessary?

His father-in-law blinked, stroking a graying mustache. —Of course I will. You're wearing fresh linen, my boy?

—Yes sir.

—Then God be with you, son, and may He have mercy on us all.

When Wythe had gone downstairs Ker stropped his Canton, then guided the razor around mustache and small Vandyke. He combed his hair, which he'd allowed to grow out to cover his ears, and threw on his one presentable suit of civilian clothing, a brown sack, with an embroidered vest, black cravat, soft-brimmed hat. Dupin gibbered to himself in the corner, turning over the shattered pieces of crockery.

As he drew on yellow kid gloves Ker's amusement faded, replaced by a cold rawness to reality, to each passing second, as if his nerves had been skinned. This could be the day he died. Perhaps it was as well he'd left his wife and son in Norfolk. If the worst happened . . . too late to think of that. No gentleman could neglect a challenge. He could face death. To lose one's honor . . . for their sake as much as his, *that* one could not contemplate.

A small, cased ambrotype of a dark-haired woman stood on the sideboard. Ker looked into Catherine's eyes for a moment, kissed the cool glass, then folded the case with a snap and pocketed it. He tucked the pistol-box under one arm, and the struggling ape under the other. At the landing he handed Dupin to a startled servant, along with a silver coin that closed her open mouth.

The sun had not yet risen. As he turned his gelding's head for the river, the hills were taking shape from misty darkness. The sloping land carried him easily down toward the James. To his right rose the church spires and tobacco warehouses of the city, crowned by the Parthenon-like Capitol. A repeated, metallic clanging rang from the Tredegar Ironworks. The tap of drums began in the distance, reveille tattooing from the militia encampments on Chimborazo Plain and Maddox Hill. As Aquila neared the river its voices rose to meet them, the rush and chuckle of rapids and the groaning of mill wheels.

As he rode, his thoughts slipped back to the decision that had brought him here. U.S.S. *Owanee* had returned from Africa to find the country splitting like a rotten stick. Every Southerner in the Navy had to make a decision. Stay with the old flag, or follow his home country into an unimaginable future. Ker had revered the Stars and Stripes. It meant government by consent of the governed, freedom to strive and live according to one's own lights.

Only gradually did he realize that the Lincolnian victory had given it a different import: shackling unwilling states into a union now hostile to an entire society. Till at last he'd acknowledged, heart like cold stone, that it was not for him to divide prudence from folly, right from wrong, and loyalty from treason. Virginia had seceded, and he as much as any Spotsylvania farmer was bound by that sovereign act.

Lieutenant Henry Lomax Minter had seen his gradual process of decision in a different light.

A hail; his mount shied, and Ker gentled it, patting its neck. He called in a low voice, —Good morning, Jennings.

Obadiah Jennings Wise was tall and dark, and sat his horse with the grace of a rider from childhood. He too was in civilian clothes, a tweed coat and hunting breeches, though he was in the Light Infantry Blues. Wise was the passionately secessionist editor of the Richmond *Enquirer* and a dedicated duelist. Jennings, as his friends called him, had been with Ker in the bar of the Spotswood Hotel when Minter had passed insulting words.

Wise indicated the box under his arm. —You needn't to bring your own, you know.

—I'm sorry, this is my first time. They're not unknown where I grew up, but they're rare. And of course, in the Navy—

—Prohibited?

—Very much so.

They cantered toward a silver-rose glow nestled within gradually bleaching darkness. Lofty shadows resolved themselves into ships off the City Dock, awaiting their turn to take on flour and tobacco. —Shall I review the formalities, then?

—Please do.

—I met with Mr. Valentine last night. He engaged as Minter's second, you will recall. We attempted to settle the matter before proceeding to the ground. Unfortunately, we were unable to reach an honorable conclusion. Unless, of course, you wish to drop the challenge?

—It was not I who challenged.

—It was you who gave Minter the lie.

Ker cleared his throat, obscurely irritated by the punctilio, the forms. —Not so. It was he who lied, in his intimation I remained with the Union too long, and for base reasons.

Wise said briskly, —Then the quarrel is irreconcilable, and we must proceed to the ground. Once there, we will dismount, see to the weapons and make our final dispositions. Remember, to take more than three seconds aiming is ungentlemanly. Let us canter; the morning is growing bright.

He urged his mount forward, and they rode down out of the cover of the oaks that shaded the grounds of Hollywood Cemetery into the sloping open that ran along the edge of the canal. Beyond, the James burned with the steadily focusing light of the incipiently rising sun.

Two silhouettes, horses and men, spurred forward from behind a stone-built canal house. Ker recognized Valentine, and beside him a clean-shaven, freckle-faced young firebrand whose red-blond hair fell nearly to his collar.

Henry Lomax Minter's piercing green eyes examined Ker, then Wise as the latter rode up to them. Wise lifted his hat, a salute the others returned.

Ker sat his horse, listening to the denial of ravens as they discussed the oncoming day. The poetry of a man he'd once met returned to him. His lips moved, whispering the word. Nevermore to see his wife. Nevermore dandle his son. Nor see the sun rise, nor heed the dark music of the night sea.

He drew a slow breath, dismissing regret. No choice remained to him but to fight. For this was what honor meant: to back one's conduct with one's lifeblood, and to demand of others the same accountability. Without that base, that rock, beneath the relation of man and man, what sort of society could exist? Some things were worth a life. So be it!

Valentine and Minter separated, and the latter swung down to the dew-laden grass. Ker dismounted too. A black boy ran from the cottage and caught up their bridles. He felt in his purse and tossed the servant a dime, conscious, as he did so, that each commonplace act might be the last. The thought gave each moment a significance beyond itself. The raven-croaking dawn, the silver shimmer of the river, the hoarse panting of the gelding as it was led away, seemed to carry a message beyond words that he could almost for a moment interpret. The very leaves seemed to tremble with sympathy and, yes, with *joy*. If this were his last day, by God, it was a lovely one!

—Mr. Minter, he said. —I trust I find you well this morning.

Minter bent the brim of his hat but did not extend his hand. —Very well indeed, Mr. Claiborne. Somehow his lazy-voweled Mississippi speech sounded both carefree and menacing.

—You persist in saying I behaved dishonorably?

—I only state the truth, sir. You captained a vessel for the Republican scum, even after Sumter. For the pay, or due to a sluggish liver—does it really matter why?

—We should have no more speech, said Wise, striding up to them. He thumbed out his watch, then glanced at the sun, which had just appeared as a stamped-out disc of heated iron above Chimborazo Hill. —Once met upon the ground, principals may only exchange greetings. Mr. Valentine and I have charged my pistols single load and single shot, on our honor and in each other's presence. Is this ground acceptable?

—Uh huh, Minter said, squinting at the sun. His manner was cool, his expression ironic, but as the light grew Ker saw he looked pale. Ker agreed too, feeling detached from the proceedings, as if he were watching from the far bank of the river.

Jennings's big single-shot pistol dragged his arm earthward. The ball would be deadly at close range. He'd watched men die of sepsis, of stomach wounds. He swallowed, suddenly terrified. Not of death, but of dying. *Lord, forgive this act of folly; forgive us both.*

—The principals are ready? said Wise. —Back to back, then. Ten paces, to march at my count; then turn and fire. Ready.

Straightening his shoulders, lifting hollow steel to the brightening clouds, he felt Minter's back against his own. In a moment he'd try to kill this other man. This former shipmate. No Southern gentleman could have acted otherwise. Why then did it strike him suddenly as inexplicable, as uncanny? Could it be, he suddenly wondered, that Minter might be right? That some subterranean motive, like a deep-buried spring beneath reason and explication, had made him delay for a reason darker than he admitted even to himself?

Even now, did he not yearn for reconciliation with the flag he'd served so long?

At that moment he heard distant thunder. He did not move or look. He waited, pistol raised, thoughtless and at peace, for the command to pace, and turn, and fire.

The thunder resolved into hoofbeats, growing closer, louder.

—Lieutenants Minter and Claiborne? called an unfamiliar, peremptory voice. —These proceedings are against military law and regulation, and are declared null and postponed until the cessation of hostilities. By order of the Honorable Stephen Mallory, Secretary of the Confederate States Navy. You will both accompany me at once.

They dismounted a block west of the Capitol, before the four-story brick pile that had till a week before been the Mechanic's Institute. Now the War and Navy Departments of the new government divided it between them. Early though it was yet, workmen in canvas trowsers and red neckerchiefs were carrying lumber and paint buckets, and hammers clattered deafeningly in the stairwell. Climbing to the second floor, Ker could not help contrasting plain new desks and chairs, bare floorboards and freshly whitewashed wainscoting with the decaying carpets and general fustiness at Main Navy in Washington. He'd left his card here without response. Now, it seemed, they'd pulled whatever string demanded attention. He wished he was in uniform. —Can you tell us the nature of this summons? he asked their escort again, a dandyish, barely civil young fellow who'd introduced himself as Mr. Quoddy.

—I told you, I'm only the clerk.

—We're to see Mr. Mallory, is that what I'm to understand?

—Oh, hardly. Quoddy paused at a door and put his ear to it. He rapped, then shooed them inside. —The Secretary is occupied with important matters. You're for Commodore Rousseau.

Ker's heart sank. Lawrence Rousseau, chief of the Bureau of Orders and Detail, was a snarling bruin of the old school. Minter stood aside for Ker—he was senior, or had been when they'd both written USN after their names. He came to attention before the mahogany schoolmaster's desk. —Lieutenant Ker Claiborne, reporting as ordered.

—Lieutenant Henry Minter, reporting as ordered.

Before him, not so much manning as overwhelming the desk, sprawled a bulky, white-maned old man in dress blues. Ker had known Rousseau was very senior, but was not prepared for decrepitude. The Commodore's long hair was white and silky, and his skin, where it was not mottled by age, almost transparent. His hand trembled as he handed a paper to Quoddy, then blinked up with vague, wandering, watery eyes.

—These are the young gentlemen who were playing at a duel? he demanded sharply.

Behind him Quoddy grinned. Minter said nothing, so Ker had to respond. —Yes sir.

—Claiborne and . . . Winter?

—Minter, sir.

—Academy whelps, no doubt.

—I am class of '56, sir, Ker said. —Mr. Minter is my junior by a year.

Rousseau searched tremulously through his papers. Holding a sheet of foolscap before his glasses, he glanced over it. —Your current status, if you please?

—Lieutenant, Virginia Navy, commissioned the first of this instant, Ker said.

—I am currently on the rolls of the CSN, as of the twenty-seventh of April, said Minter.

—Then you are both under military discipline. There will be no such foolishness as dueling until our new nation's independence is secure.

—Beg your pardon, sir, Ker said, —but I had already applied at this office for a clarification of my assignment.

Rousseau rattled the foolscap like a snake's warning. —What have you been doing to date, young sirs?

Ker reminded him that during the interval between Virginia's secession from the Union and her admission to the Confederacy, the Commonwealth had organized her own navy. Since only two or three ships were in commission, though, he'd been posted to Fort Powhatan, an earthwork battery below City Point. Minter's tale was even shorter; he'd been in Richmond a month, without orders or employment.

Rousseau tapped his finger on the table, then applied it to his brow as if pondering some transcendental mystery. —A hundred and twenty officers resigned from the United States Navy. A praiseworthy display of loyalty. However, the Congress at Montgomery has authorized an officer corps to a total of only thirty-eight. Four captains, four commanders, and thirty lieutenants. The single resource we possess in superamplitude is junior officers. Fortunately, we shall not need them. The petty tyrants in Washington may strut and threaten, but their rodomontade cannot be carried so far as war.

—What do you suggest for us, then, sir? Minter said. —We are as desirous of serving our country as those senior to us.

—To those who feel they must serve, we suggest the Army, said Quoddy, behind the commodore. —Several of our former sea-officers have found billets with the volunteer units now being formed.

—And what of *Merrimack*, sir? Ker asked Rousseau.

—What of her, sir?

—I called on the new commander of the yard in Norfolk. He has set his men to raising her. Will she not require a complement, when she is refloated?

—I simply cannot employ you, said Rousseau, tone final. —There is talk of enlarging the Navy List, but even if that eventuates, I can offer no hope of preference. There simply are no commands to be had.

Minter said, —If that is so, sir, why did you interrupt our duel? We could perhaps have reduced the supply of superfluous lieutenants for you.

This got a frosty look from Rousseau and a disbelieving stare from Quoddy. Ker decided he might as well terminate the interview. —I will leave my town address, sir; please consider me ready at any time to render service, should the situation change.

—That I will do, Lieutenant, that will I do. Rousseau extended a palm soft as old doeskin. —Thank you both for coming by.

Outside, on the street, Valentine and Wise threw their cheroots into the trampled mud of Ninth Street. —What news? Wise said, lifting his hat to a passing lady. —Good, I hope?

—I fear not. Ker explained, and they stood glumly for a moment before Valentine said, —Well, perhaps a libation will set things in order. Unless you wish to resume your quarrel.

Ker looked at Minter, who hesitated, then shook his head. —We've been placed under interdict.

—Excellent, excellent. Suddenly both their seconds were in good humor, the awkwardness was gone.

They were adjourning to an oyster-house for breakfast when Ker heard his name called from above. He looked up to see Quoddy motioning him back from an upstairs window.

—The commodore wondered if you have had any acquaintance with twelve-pounder boat-howitzers, Quoddy told him at the top of the stairs.

—Rather intimate. Both at the Academy and in active service afloat.

—Where?

—In West Africa, during the uprising at Kisembo. Is there a purpose to this quizzing, sir? What's the commodore want?

—We just got authority to commission twenty officers in the artillery of the Confederate Army. Your response to be given tomorrow.

—I do not believe that I—

—Tomorrow, sir. If you truly wish to serve.

Ker nodded, contemplating orders that were not orders, a suggestion that he leave the Navy, presumably forever. Looked up into Quoddy's red-cheeked, smirking visage once more. Then left without a further word.

He was looking for the others when a heavy gun went off down by the river. Followed, at measured, even intervals, by more, one after the other. Ker counted them in growing puzzlement. Thirteen. Fourteen. After fifteen detonations the guns fell silent, followed by a distant roar he only gradually realized was the thunderous cheering of an unimaginable multitude.

2

THE city had expected the president's train for days. The telegraph had traced its triumphal progress across the South. At each stop, the *Dispatch* and *Enquirer* and *Whig* reported, he'd been thronged and feted, speechified and dined.

Now cannon roared as the green-and-gold-shining locomotive bringing Jefferson Davis to his new capital chuffed out jets of smoke and steam, rumbling out onto the trestle that curved across the rapids. Ker guided Aquila around and urged him to a canter. But people were streaming into the streets like a tide-run, and after a few blocks the gelding shied. He slowed to a walk, and at last dismounted, hitched the horse before an oyster-bar, and took to shank's mare.

By the time he had walked to the Richmond & Petersburg station, the train had come to rest amid a mass of humanity that stretched west to the brick-spired walls of the State Armory, far up Byrd Street, down toward the Millrace and the City Dock, and past the paper mill toward the flat brown water where the Kanawha canal boats lay along the loading quays. Beside the platform three brass bands competed with "Hail the Conquering Hero Comes" and the jaunty new minstrel walk-around "Dixie." The city tugs reinforced the din with steam whistles. Ker slid past gentlefolk and working-class waving kerchiefs, troops in the varied and colorful plumage of the militia regiments, as well as a sprinkling of the city's numerous free blacks. The sun brushed gold leaf down the wake-creased river, to where an erect spare figure was even now descending with slow dignity from his car, lifting a hand to acknowledge the rising roar. Cheers erupted as he stepped into a handsome carriage drawn by four matched bays.

A squad of cavalrymen with drawn sabers spurred up Fourteenth. Steel struck sparks off cobblestones. They swept past Ker in a clamor of dust and a sting of horse lather wet and warm on his face, followed by a new eruption of huzzahing and the crash and bray of the band in a new composition out of embattled Maryland. The words roared from a thousand throats.

> *Hurrah! Hurrah!*
> *For Southern rights, hurrah!*
> *Hurrah for the bonny blue Flag,*
> *That wears a single star!*

For one swift moment, as the carriage slowed to turn onto Main Street, Ker examined the president at close range. Tall, pale, Davis looked much like the wood-cuts of Uncle Sam. Graying hair fell over his temple. He was tailored in a broadcloth morning-coat with a bow cravat. One hand tilted his beaver to the encompassing crowd. Bouquets flew through the air, landing in the carriage or falling to be crushed beneath the wheels. Outstretched hands offered letters, flowers, New Testaments.

Davis smiled through it all, a courteous bending of thin, tightly compressed lips. Ker noticed that the left eye was filmed and dull, curtained from sight. Where had he seen a dead orb like that before? Oh, yes. *Owanee*'s half-savage steward had always seemed to see more with the blind eye than with that endowed with light.

Then the carriage was past, high wheels weaving and jolting over the cobbles, and a rearguard of cavalry clattered after. The throng surged back, like the sea resuming its place under a steamship's counter. Ker let the hurrying press of the crowd carry him after the carriage.

By the time he reached the Spotswood a new crowd had converged, or had been waiting; a more substantial gathering, frock-coated men, respectable women in bonnets and crinolines that scribed a forbidden circle about them; and of course many more soldiers. The bands were still playing down by the waterfront, their brassy strains echoing up the hill. The talk was louder here, punctuated with the snap and powder-smoke of firecrackers from boys on the fringes of the crowd. They quieted as a black-clad gentleman of impressive girth appeared on the balcony above. He spread his arms wide, then intoned, —Ladies and gentlemen: The President of these Confederate States.

Davis looked down for a moment before beginning. Then the voice, resonant, penetrating, every word clearly enunciated, rang out over the throng.

—My friends and fellow-citizens.

—I am deeply impressed with the kindness of your manifestation. I look upon you as the best hope of liberty; and in our liberty alone is our Constitutional government to be preserved. Upon your strong right arm— and here he bowed to the ranks of the soldiery —depends the success of your country. In asserting the birthright to which you were born, remember that life and blood are nothing as compared with the immense interests you have at stake.

Here the crowd burst into renewed cheering. Ker raised his voice with the rest, inspired not so much by the words as by the erect dignity of the man above him. Davis raised his hand for silence, then continued.

—It may be that you have not long been trained, that you have much to learn of the art of war. But I know there beats in the breast of Southern sons a determination never to surrender—a determination never to go home but to tell a tale of honor.

—Never! Someone shouted from the crowd, and other voices took up the cry. Ker joined in the applause.

—Though great may be the disparity of numbers, give us a fair field and a free fight, and the Southern banner will float in triumph. The country relies upon you. Upon you rest the hopes of our people; and I have only to say, my friends, that to the last breath of my life, I am wholly your own.

Davis bowed and the crowd burst out with a prolonged roar of applause, handshaking, and embraces, helped out by gunshots; and the bands blared anew like beasts with lungs of metal. The president bowed once more, waved to them all, and retired within.

Ker stood pondering after he'd vanished into darkness. Then wiped his brow—the sun was growing warm, the air oppressive—and made his way back toward his horse.

He cantered back to Church Hill lost in thought, letting the gelding find his way. The uphill streets boiled with wagons and tradesmen, tobacco-barrows muscled by brawny sweating Negroes, carts of flour and goods, and here and there the carriages of the quality, returning home like him.

As he shot between the iron gateposts of Wythe's Rest, the city roar and heat and dust stepped back. At the big house a stableboy came running. Ker tossed him the reins and went up the steps, stripping off gloves and spurs.

They were still at table, in the breakfast room. Ker bowed to his mother-in-law, to the rest of the family. —Good morning, all.

—You were out very early, Ker, said Lutetia, louder than she usually spoke.

Thomas must have told her his destination, Ker saw; she looked both frightened and, now, relieved as he bent to kiss her cheek. —Yes, Mother. An early ride, to clear the head.

—I trust all went well? Wythe hid behind a napkin and a cough.

—Events were interrupted by a messenger from naval headquarters. My friend and I were reminded we are under military discipline.

—So you didn't get to fight him? said Harker, who was immediately glared silent by his seniors. He flushed, looking into his tea.

—I thought I heard cannon fire, Lutetia went on, shaking her dark side-curls and frowning.

—President Davis arrived today, Mother Wythe. He spoke at the Spotswood. There was quite a crowd.

Harker groaned and clutched his head. Ker smiled, remembering the despair of a youngster who's missed some excitement. His mother-in-law said primly, —A crowd? I can imagine. My heavens, I'm sure it's an honor, but I can't say I'm entirely happy. There will be such a lot of new people in town now, to be sure.

—I have seen some of them about, said Aunt Miriam. —Many do not appear to be of the better sort. Wherever they come from.

The ladies fell to discussing Varina Davis, who had not yet arrived but who was known by reputation in the city. Aunt Miriam said in an undertone that she was rumored to be rather, well, *dark,* and in her behavior more like a man than one could wish. A servant bent with sliced Smithfield ham. Another poured tea, and Ker set to, only half-listening as around him the morning conversation went on.

As soon as he had done, and a glance from his father-in-law signaled he too was finished, Ker excused himself. Thomas rose too, and they went out into the garden. An aged gardener raked feebly at the pebbled path as they crunched slowly along.

Ker opened. —Sir, may I assume you have acquaintances in the new dispensation?

Thomas Wythe fondled a rose, carefully stroking a new bud with a fingertip. —Though I am no longer a judge, I know many members of the bar who serve both in the city and in the state. The which, of course, is at your disposal. Have you need?

—I most possibly may. As a mockingbird tried out its repertoire, Ker laid out the situation. —The upshot being, Commodore Rousseau recommended I consider the Army, in particular the artillery branch.

Wythe patted his balding head, glanced back toward the house. Ker saw Harker's face at an upper window, forehead against glass, staring hungrily down. —I can make inquiries. Our cousin George Randolph is with the Richmond Howitzers . . . but I know you would rather serve at sea.

—I hesitate to place my predilections before the defense of my country.

—I daresay there'll be opportunity to demonstrate your patriotism in either venue, said Wythe. He sighed and turned back toward the house. —May I impart a bit of hard-won wisdom, my boy?

—I should be grateful for any advice.

—Follow your heart. I am old, Ker. And what I regret most is not what I did but what I dared not do. I placed other responsibilities before my heart's desire, and have regretted it ever since.

Ker wondered what "heart's desire" the old man meant, but it seemed forward to ask. —You are a man of substance, sir, and greatly appreciated by your family and friends.

—*Néanmoins* . . . what the Testament says about where your treasure is . . . well, enough of that. Perhaps I can put you in the way of something.

By now they were in the study, where a servant silently set out decanter and glasses. Wythe searched his desk, handed a tract or brochure across. —I received this last week.

Illustrated with a wood-cut of a jaunty-looking schooner flying the new Confederate flag, the flyer advertized for seaman and sea-officers for something called the Richmond Volunteer Navy Company. A letter of marque had been granted and a vessel engaged; the only article wanting, apparently, being the manning. Ker glanced up to see Wythe consulting an account book.

—The *Sentinel* has carried reports of captures made by volunteer men-of-war out of Charleston and New Orleans. Should you desire to join the company, I should subscribe for part of the capital stock.

—That's very generous of you, sir.

—Shall I write them a note, indicating our interest?

—Thank you, sir; I should be grateful for that kindness.

—I have observed you for some years now, Ker. My daughter chose well. I wish she could be here with us, but perhaps one day . . . I venture to say you will acquit yourself well in whatever you undertake. Wythe clicked open his watch, then motioned to the tray. —A bit early, but will you join me in a sherry?

The afternoon passed pleasantly. He read the reports in the *Examiner* of Davis's arrival. Jennings's editorial, much as he valued the man's friendship, seemed to protest too much, to threaten and revile. Ker could not fully accept his picture of Northerners as abolitionist demons intent on obliterating the Southern way of life. He found most Yankees hard to take. They were ignorant, somehow, of things Southerners knew without knowing they knew; how to receive a guest or a favor, to win with a careless smile or lose with a jest. They had only the most rudimentary sense of honor, and when confronted with one who truly valued it seemed torn between astonishment and ridicule. He'd served with too many to doubt their courage. But he no longer questioned that North and South had grown apart into two peoples. If, indeed, they'd ever truly been one.

When the first course at dinner had been served and consumed, he excused himself. He deliberated briefly in his room, then belted on his sword. The family jeweler had transformed his Federal full dress to the new pattern with a simple alteration to his epaulettes. The dark blue cloth was the same hue that marked the naval profession the world over. His sword too was the U.S. Navy pattern of '52 he'd purchased at Annapolis. He wound black silk round his neck, hooked the collar, and placed his cocked hat just so. Looked himself up and down in the pier glass.

—Your boots, sir? Romulus, eyes downcast. Ker nodded and the boy knelt with boot-brush and blacking. Ker told him he was only stepping downtown, not to a review. The servant leapt up instantly and held the door, head lowered as his master passed through.

The Spotswood was lit so brightly it might have been afire. The doors stood wide and a throng pushed in and out, almost entirely male, but sprinkled here and there with brightly costumed and painted females as well. Snatches of avid talk, of commissions and postmasterships, told him what this locust-swarm hungered after. The reddened drunken faces, the slickness of expectorated tobacco underfoot repelled him. He thrust his way to the entrance only to spy a card advising that the meeting of the Volunteer Navy Company would take place next door. He turned aside, but was halted by a hand on his arm. A planterly looking fellow, with check trowsers and long linen frock coat, stared insolently down a cheroot. —I beg your pardon, said Ker, glancing pointedly at his hand.

—What d'ye mean in that there suit?

—I beg your pardon? said Ker again. He felt instinctively for his sword, but found himself pinioned from behind. A stench of breath bathed his face.

—Comin' here in a Union uniform.

—For your information, this is a Confederate Navy uniform.

—We don't have no fucking Navy.

—'N if we did they wouldn't wear no fuckin' Northern blue.

—I assure you we have. Take your hands off me, gentlemen. Now.

A hesitation, then they released him. As he shrugged his coat back into shape his interlocutors muttered apologies.

At Ettinger's he was handed a glass of port and conducted to a private room. Some dozens of businesslike men stood about conversing beneath a whale-oil chandelier. As he came in heads turned, and two gentlemen made for him. The elder, distinguished-looking in embroidered waistcoat and silk neckerchief, introduced himself as Mr. Wolff. His friend he introduced as Mr. Colcock. —And you would be Thomas Wythe's son? Wolff asked him.

—I have the honor to be Mr. Wythe's son-in-law, Ker Custis Claiborne.

—Of course. We are in receipt of his note. The committee was most impressed.

—Thank you, said Ker, wondering what exactly Thomas had said, but of course one did not ask about the content of private communications.

—I understand you're interested in our venture?

—I've heard only a sketch of it as yet.

—Of course, of course; but you would not be here if you had not found it of interest, not so? Wolff did not wait for an answer, but lifted his head as the note of a spoon on a water-glass rang through the murmur. —Will you sit with me, Lieutenant?

Ker pushed back his sword and sat as Colcock went forward; the assembled men scraped chairs and reached for wine bottles.

Colcock rapped for attention and began. —My friends, we celebrate today not only the arrival of an esteemed statesman of great personal bravery, but the striking off of shackles that have bound the growth of a bounteous land.

Ker relaxed, sensing the onset of a stem-winder. He could not contemplate entering the Army with any eagerness. Unless and until the North showed fight, perhaps the best thing to do was return to Norfolk. He could spend some time with Catherine and Robert; time they deserved with their so-often-absent husband and father. Only gradually, as Colcock reached tariff policy, did his attention return.

"Why has wealth fled from the South, despite our monopoly of the brown leaf that soothes, and of the fleecy staple that clothes the world?

Why the pressure for money in our productive land, and the frugal habits of our race pushed to self-denial? Because under the heel of federal legislation, nearly the whole of government income derived from those same exports. The ledgers show that Virginia, the Carolinas, and Georgia defrayed three-fourths of the annual expense of supporting the national government, and of this immense stream of revenue, little or nothing returned. It flowed in a broad and uninterrupted flood northward, to the protection of Northern manufactures in New England and Pennsylvania. When the black Republican Mr. Lincoln was asked "Why not let the South go?" he replied, "Let the South go! Where then should we get our revenue?"

—We are justly free now of this tribe of spoliating cormorants. Yet they are not content to let their erstwhile bondsmen depart in peace. Instead they utter claptrap about "treason to the flag" when it is they who have deserted and insulted the memory of our forefathers, who established a regime of constitutional democracy.

—In respect of which our President, His Excellency the Honorable Jefferson Davis, first President of the Confederate States of America— Here he was interrupted by patriotic cries and yells, whistling and hammering of bottles on tables —Has opened wide areas of action for us in responding to these bellicose threatenings by signing for us the letter of marque and reprisal displayed near the door. It is one of many signed in the last weeks. As we speak, armed vessels of Southron patriots have sortied from Hatteras Inlet, New Orleans, Charleston, and other points throughout the South, which I may liken to a shaken hornet's nest. As the poet has it:

> *For* they, *'twas* they, *unsheathed the ruthless blade,*
> *And Heaven shall ask the havoc it has made.*

Colcock inclined his head, then cried in a rising intonation, —I therefore announce to the world the formation of the Richmond Volunteer Navy Company, officered by the association you see before you, and dedicated to the destruction of Northern arrogance, the patriotic defense of our Southern system, and the individual enrichment of our shareholders.

I thank you . . . I thank you . . . please hold your applause. I will now introduce Mr. Thaddeus Wolff, a gentleman of substance of this city, who will acquaint you with the specifications of the case.

He sat, and Wolff rose from beside Ker. After avowing his pleasure at their company, he explained that the association, desirous of responding to the national call, had made arrangements with a certain Northern shipowner for the purchase of a fine new paddle-wheeled steamer, two years old, of 1,650 tons, mounting seven guns, and taking a complement of twenty officers and two hundred and twenty men. It was currently fitting out in Delaware, ostensibly for Federal service, but in actuality for delivery to the Company. The Company would provide officers and crews upon the vessel's turnover at Ocracoke Island, North Carolina, at which point the Confederate flag would be hoisted for a cruise into the rich shipping lanes between New York and Europe.

At this point Wolff made a grand flourish in the air, ending with his arm outstretched toward Ker, still seated.

—She lacks only a bold and fearless captain; and if I am not mistaken, we have the genuine article with us today. May I introduce Lieutenant Ker Claiborne, young, energetic, enterprising, native of our fair Commonwealth's Eastern Shore, recent commander of the steam sloop of war U.S.S. *Owanee*, and currently lieutenant without portfolio, Virginia Navy. A sea-rover who faced savage warriors during his cruises on the Africa Station, and was promoted for heroism; who has evinced the warmest interest in the success of our endeavor, and who moreover has connections with the highest social circles of our fair city.

Ker was taken aback, and not pleased at being unexpectedly thrust into the limelight. But courtesy demanded he rise, bow, murmur a word of thanks, and find his seat again.

Wolff went on, —With such a commander, our undertaking cannot but meet with success. I will now throw open the books of the Company for your generous subscriptions.

With the flourish of a riverboat faro dealer, Colcock was opening ledger-books on a table and setting out a cashbox. With the audience's attention diverted, Ker said to Wolff, who stood gripping his lapels, a broad smile wreathing his face, —Sir, I have not yet made myself part of your enterprise.

—I am aware of that, sir; nor did I say you had.

—I believe you conveyed that impression.

—If I took a liberty, sir, pray accept my apologies; it was in the service of our country. Which I assume you are as ready to serve as I.

—That is not the point at issue.

Wolff murmured, not looking directly at him, —I have not yet discussed with you that the voyage is to be conducted on shares.

Ker thought this through quickly. He understood shares, had in fact participated in the distribution of prize-money when *Owanee* had fallen in with the infamous slaver *Arachne* off the Guinea coast.

The practice had been inherited from the Royal Navy. A prize's value, as determined by a court ashore, was divided into twenty parts. The commander received three, the lieutenants and master divided two among themselves, the marine and warrant officers another two, and so on down to the seamen and rank-and-file marines, who disposed of seven shares among themselves. As captain, he would thus stand to receive fifteen per centum free and clear of the value of any prizes they made, and that included both ship and cargo, and armament if any.

But in his next mental breath he realized privateers had to run on a different system, one that recompensed the capitalists who financed them as well as those who faced storm and battle at sea.

—Need I outline the possibilities of personal enrichment? Wolff persisted. —Half the proceeds to the investors, half to captain and crew; the latter to be divided according to the usage of the sea. There will also be two thousand dollars in pay.

That dropped his share to seven and a half per centum. Still, one or two rich merchant vessels . . . It was an attractive offer. He couldn't help comparing it to the fifteen hundred dollars he'd had to keep a house and family upon, as a lieutenant in the U.S. Navy.

—Well? said Wolff, at his side. —There are other candidates for the position. A Mr. Minter, whom I understand you know.

—I know him, Ker said. The trader was taunting him; no doubt Wolff knew he and Minter were at odds. Still, privateers were making fortunes, if the reports could be trusted, sailing from New Orleans and Charleston. Why shouldn't he?

It was then, as he hesitated, Wolff's urging arm close round his shoulders, that he caught sight of Mr. Quoddy. The clerk stood inside the door, searching the room. When he spotted Ker he began pushing his way toward him. —I've been after you since dinnertime. This from the commodore.

Ker broke the wax seal. Within was a hastily penned scrawl.

Lt C.—
Word has reached me of a projected descent of the Yankee on the sacred soil of Virginia. Do me the favor of reporting to me at once.
    Your Servant,
    Como. Rousseau.

He folded it carefully, tucked it into his hat, and extended his hand to Wolff. —I must respectfully decline your kind offer, sir.

—Damn it, what is it? Another company? Let us make it three thousand. We must have a captain. The prospect appeals, sir, I could read it in your expression—

Ker interrupted courteously, —I must wish you success without me, sir, and a very good night. I'm sorry, I'm called away. I have no doubt Mr. Minter will give entire satisfaction in your venture.

Taking his leave with a bow, he followed Quoddy out into the raucous night.

3

THE next dawn found him nodding on a hard box seat thirty miles
north of Richmond. A hundred and forty troops dozed on and
under worn pine bench-seats, and two cars back, griped down
with chain and canvased under heavy tarpaulins against dust, locomotive
ashes, and rain, rode a battery of bronze twelve-pound boat-howitzers on
field carriages.

The hastily coupled train had left the Central Depot on Broad Street
after a night of such confusion, threats, frenzied desperate effort, and out-
rageous mummery he had been divided whether to laugh or weep. Truly,
if the Federals landed disciplined troops in the face of what the Confederacy had scraped and hurried to meet them with, this mission was already
a failure. Still, he'd accepted it. His commission was still stuffed into his
cocked hat—he'd not had one moment during the night past to even
think of changing his uniform. Only a hastily scribbled note via an Irish
urchin from Rocketts had fetched Romulus from the Wythes' with valise,
pistols, and a change of linen. Also with Monsieur C. Auguste Dupin; the
servant said Missus Wythe had insisted he must go too. The monkey now

slept uneasily behind Ker's neck, nails digging into his scalp as if dreaming of its mother, now unutterably far away.

His arrival at Mechanics Hall had found Rousseau pacing the floor. Announcing himself, Ker had a yellow telegraph-chit thrust into his hand. —Read, the commodore ordered.

The message was from General Beauregard. A Northern force was embarking in Annapolis for Smith Point, at the mouth of the Potomac.

Ker thought this through. Virginia's secession in April had placed the capital at Washington in a vise. The federal capital ate and lived by river traffic, up the Potomac from the Chesapeake Bay. Holding the southern bank, Virginia troops had quickly erected batteries, closing the river to merchant vessels. Union troops had occupied Point Lookout, at the north end of the river-mouth. That, however, was in Maryland, which was at least for the moment still within the Union.

Only days before, though, three Federal regiments had suddenly occupied Alexandria and the heights of Robert E. Lee's plantation home, Arlington. That had been their first step south, the first invasion of Southern territory, as opposed to Sumter, Ship Island, and Fortress Monroe, federal outposts before the separation. It also put the upper Potomac in Union hands. If Smith Point were occupied as well, Confederate forces would find their occupation of the central portion of the river untenable. It would push the South's boot off Washington's windpipe.

It was also an invasion of the soil of Virginia. And though he found much of the bombast so liberally dispensed of late about the Sacred Soil excessive, he saw quite clearly that they had to resist outright aggression. If the new Confederacy didn't make that plain to Lincoln, Cameron, and company, there'd be no hope of peace.

—Till now, we have not met force with force, Rousseau said. —We didn't defend Arlington. We let Alexandria go, and the only hand lifted was that of a hotelkeeper who was shot on his own property for flying his flag. If we meet this attack at the outer gate, and drive them off in confusion, there will be no wider war. Will you do that for your country?

And Ker, of course, had said he'd do his best.

The railway carriage jolted abominably, but they were maintaining their speed. They were bound north, past Hanover Junction, to where a bend in the track brought them as close as a railroad would get to the headwaters of the Rappahannock. From there, some fifty-eight miles, they'd have to haul the guns overland. Passage by water would have been faster, but the danger of interception by Union blockaders had ruled that out. They had to go by land, and they had to reach Smith Point, object of the impending raid, before the Yankees got there by sea.

Ker blinked sleepily out at dense forest, snarls of undergrowth, undulating hills with mist curling in the hollows like white smoke. His eyelids sank. But only for a moment, as the monkey began scratching itself vigorously. He grunted and sat up, and across from him Romulus smiled uncertainly. Ker yawned and stretched, looking past the servant at the others who filled the car.

The command setup was confusing, and he wasn't sure he liked it. He owned the guns but not the crews. They were volunteers, apparently just the troops nearest to the railroad station last night, scraped up and thrown on the train with no more warning than he'd had.

The Second Tennessee, which the men told him was called the "Bate regiment," after its colonel, was from Sumner County. It had been organized on May 6 and mustered into Confederate service at Lynchburg. Company "I" was commanded by Major William Driver, whom Ker had met the night before, loading guns and mules and men. Ker and the officers were of an age, but the troops were boys. Few had uniforms and not all even weapons. Driver had told those without rifles to report to Ker.

Dupin was awake now, chattering angrily at Romulus. The colored boy stared with shy fascination. —What he saying, Mass' Claiborne?

—You don't understand monkey talk, Romulus? He's saying, I want my breakfast. Ker winked and drew a biscuit from his map-case. The animal seized it and leaped straight up into the wooden baggage racks. It took a bite, spat angrily, and whipped the rest down into the face of a sleeping private.

—Who threw that? Joe, you son 'a a bitch—

Ker had had only the briefest meeting with his crews last night. In a few hours they'd be on the road, racing the Yankees steaming down the bay. They might be in action the moment they reached Smith Point. But not one of them knew the first thing about working a gun.

The troops were awake now, and clamoring for coffee. Then the sergeant came through with the good news. Their rations were still sitting back on the platform in Richmond. —No point bitching, ya might's well shut up and take it like men. The boys groused loudly, but soon cards came out and they spread blankets and settled on the floorboards, coughing as smoke, dust, and pine pollen blew in the open windows. Ker hooked his collar and rose. After a brief ablution from a canteen, he lit his first segar of the day and went in search of the major.

The heavy planks of the ballast-truck vibrated and swayed under his boots. A stiff wind streamed his hair back. Ash and hot cinders fell smoking from the cloud that streamed out behind the brass-trimmed balloon-stack. Ker handed his cocked hat to Romulus. All in all conditions were no worse than on deck in a moderate sea, and he didn't have to worry about spray.

They were passing through open fields north of Hanover Junction, the fields green with new wheat, the men fortified with hard bread and sliced salt ham contributed by the station buffet, and Ker had the tarpaulins off two of the howitzers.

John Dahlgren had designed the naval twelve-pounder in the 1850s. It was light enough to be hoisted to a frigate's foretops for service in repelling boarders, or as a boat gun, mounted on a sliding sea-carriage. An iron land-carriage made it useful ashore as well. The gun itself was simple, a tapered bronze tube with sights and a percussion lock after Hidden's patent. But loading and firing could be confusing, even dangerous.

—Man number one, he called, pitching his voice above the rumble of rail trucks. From the knot of men sitting farther back on the rocking flatcar ten troopers rose unsteadily, some spitting on their hands as they approached.

Ker placed each in his respective station, from the gun-captain, behind the breech, the number two or primer man, right-muzzle, left-muzzle, wheelmen, ammunition-passers, and assistants. He explained each man's duties, then ran them through the drill as a team. Sponge. Load. Point. Fire. He was most particular about number two covering the inserted primer with his hand, and closing the vent once firing had been completed.

When they grasped the rudiments he nodded to Sergeant Gostin, who took two privates and headed toward the rear of the train. They returned lugging one of the hundred-and-forty-pound ammunition boxes. Ker surveyed the passing countryside. Open land, woods a mile distant, plowed fields verdant with new corn between.

The initial loading went slowly, as he preferred. One didn't encourage young men to be slapdash with gunpowder. When charge and shell were loaded, fuze cut, rammed, and primed, he conned the passing fields once more. A paintless house, laundry hanging like white flags. Beyond it a ghost-oak, girdled long before and left to die. He waited till the house was past and pointed out the tree. The gun-captain spun the elevating-screw and directed the wheelmen on the trail. Ker checked the restraining tackle again, then raised his hand and brought it down. —Fire, he shouted.

A dragon-tongue of red flame leapt out, succeeded in no perceptible slice of time by a thunderclap and a denseness of yellow-white smoke. He raised his field glass to track the flight of the projectile. Caught it as it struck the earth and exploded, flinging up a gout of black dirt and young corn fifty yards from the tree.

They fired through the morning, turn and turn about, until at last Driver advised him they were approaching their offload point. Ker secured drill, had Gostin return charges and primers to their boxes, and set the men to readying the battery for mule-towing. Unfortunately the boat-howitzer hadn't been designed for it, and it seemed the mules hadn't either; they eyed the guns with alarm and suspicion, and kept making breaks for the near woods. There were eyelets on the axles, and drag ropes for man-towing, but for a lengthy overland march they'd have to improvise. He sent men to a nearby farmhouse for reins, rope, and carriage-shafts, and started jury-rigging.

By the time the battery was more or less in marching order it was past noon. More hard bread was issued, water served out from buckets toted from the farmhouse well, and at last they stepped off down a country road. The rest of the troops had set out long before, and their dust hung like a dry yellow fog in the hot motionless air, coating the clothes and tongues of the makeshift artillerists who trailed behind, cursing the mules and splicing traces when they snapped. Loblolly and longleaf crowded close along the road. At the infrequent and tiny settlements the locals, both colored and white, turned out to watch them pass. They raised thin cheers and waved kerchiefs, and small boys and barking dogs ran after them till they lagged back and gradually vanished in the dust.

They camped that night on the banks of the Pamunkey. The rations still hadn't caught up. When the battery wheeled in the rest of the Tennesseans were off in the gloom, hunting or splashing in the stream, trying to catch fish with their hands. Ker found Major Driver by a fire. Driver introduced Captains Bate, Tyree, Charlton, and House. They were clerks and brokers from Gallatin, civilians, so far as he could see. They quieted as the major spread a map on a log.

—Gentlemen, we have a piece to go and not overmuch time. We've done fifteen miles today by my reckoning. Forty-five more will see us to Smith Point. We must make the most of each day and not let the men lag back.

Tyree said it was hard for troops to march without rations. Driver nodded, face clouding. —That's my fault. I should have checked with the quartermaster. One expects that he would have . . . anyway, I've telegraphed for rations to be ready for us in Heathsville. The Northumberland County militia's mustering there too. He looked at Ker. —You're keeping up with us pretty well.

—Your boys have spirit. I wish I could say as much for the mules.

—You'll have to drive 'em. We can't take the Yankees without artillery.

Driver uncorked a canteen and splashed corn whiskey into their cups. Then came the sighs of tired men pulling off stiff new boots, grunts as they settled for sleep. And at last, only the crackling of the fire and snoring and the slow spiral of smoke up through the silent watching of the stars.

The next day they scow-ferried across the Pamunkey, two strong ferrymen heaving them along the heavy hemp with padded leather gloves, the cable gliding back into the river like a serpent seeking shelter. Landing on the far side, they pushed hard toward Dunkirk and then Clarksville, taking to ferries again at Tappahannock. A mule panicked in midstream, kicking his driver into the water. They camped on the north bank of the Rappahannock, but Driver had them on the road again before dawn, pushing on via Warsaw Courthouse.

They got to Heathsville just as the tops of the pines pricked the falling sun. By then everyone was exhausted. The fine dust choked them when it was dry, and when it rained turned to a sticky, clinging mud that weighted feet and hooves and wheels. Driver had bought pone with his own money. Ker too had spent what he had to relieve the distress among the men, and of his own stomach. A farmer along the road contributed a wagonload of dried peanuts, and they cracked and ate as they marched, littering the rutted dust with crisp thin shells and raising a crackle among the ranks as of a grass fire. But other locals looked away, or stood silently in their fields watching the troops slog past.

He was both utterly weary and ravenously hungry as they turned in to bivouac in a rye-field next to Hughlett's Tavern. He was sitting on a stump watching Romulus build a fire as Driver and Charlton rode up, accompanied by a bearded man in a chip hat whom Ker didn't know.

—Lieutenant, you might want to come along with us.

—Sir?

—We're going up to scout out the shoreline. This here's Captain Cundiff, Company C, Fortieth Virginia. Heathsville Guards, they call themselves. Just mustered and started training at Fairfields.

As the men prepared meager meals of beans and ground corn, the officers rode out a little sandy track the last two miles to the beach. The last screen of trees fell away, and as they rode up over a ridge of sandy hummocks the wind met their faces, fresh and cool, and the horses neighed, hoofing the sand and sniffing curiously at the sea-wrack underfoot as Driver reined in.

The wide Bay-meeting mouth of the Potomac spread before them. Gray-green swells rolled in to break on the brown sand in a grating hiss. Ker shaded his eyes. He could just make out the far white speck of Point Lookout light. As Driver rattled his map open in the sea breeze he twisted in the saddle, inspecting the shoreline that fell away to west and eastward, receding into the fading distance and gathering darkness.

He needed no map, nor any chart. As a boy he'd coasted across here from the Shore, beating across the Chesapeake south of Tangier. Past the Rock and the Lumps. Over the shallows where the oyster-boats lingered by day and by night the distant sidelights of Baltimore-bound clippers and ferries plodded like voyaging stars. He'd sailed up the Potomac as far as Georgetown, the great river thronged with shallops, sloops, schebecs, punts, tobacco-boats, schooners, flats, shad-galleys manned by singing blacks, longboats stacked with cordwood, flatties, oyster-brogans, pungy-boats, black-nancies, bugeyes, and the sturgeon-skiffs that hunted the great armored fish, fourteen feet long, that lurked in the deep holes of the river. Many a time he'd anchored under the point opposite, snuggled close in the curved protecting arms of Cornfield Harbor.

He raised his glasses and scanned the Potomac again. It looked deserted now. To the west, past the Fredericksburg bend, lay what was now, how strange to think it, the capital of his country's enemy. To the east, the open sky and open water of the Chesapeake.

—I don't see the light-boat.

—Some of our boys rowed out to it, Cundiff said. —We took in all the marks this side of the river. Snuffed the lighthouse too.

Ker nodded. Then straightened in the saddle, tucking his elbows to hold the glasses steady.

—What is it? said Driver.

—Smoke.

The major raised his own glasses, but lowered them a moment later, saying he saw nothing. Meanwhile Ker studied a stain sifting above the horizon. At last he made out three mast-tops, tiny and distant but perfectly clear, rising above the curve of the bay.

He said, —It's the Federal fleet, Major. They'll anchor off during the night and land after a dawn bombardment.

—Good God, said Charlton.

Driver rose in the saddle, peering again. —I really can't see what you're looking at, Claiborne. Are you sure?

Ker studied the pinpricks again. Merchants did not steam in close company. They were still distant, north of the Middle Grounds. Ten or perhaps fifteen miles off the Point. But dark would be on them in minutes. He said, —They're warships, all right. They'll feel their way in, anchor when the lead shows shallow water, and land their force at dawn.

Driver tried his glasses again, after glancing doubtfully at Ker. Then said to the captain, —Lycurgus, ride back and rouse the men. I want them on the road immediately they have eaten. Cundiff, I will be grateful if you will join your men to my command.

The captain of militia said he would do so gladly, and they galloped off. Driver looked worried. —How close in can they come?

Ker considered. The distant tops were hard to classify, but if he had to he'd guess the tallest as a sloop-of-war. That meant *Pawnee* just now, as he was unaware of any other in the Bay. The same *Pawnee* that had so frightened the residents of Richmond a few weeks previous. —If she's the ship I think, they'll have to stay a mile offshore hereabouts; farther out if they approach from down toward the point. There's a shoal pokes out there.

—Where would you land?

—That's hard to say. You could put men ashore in boats anywhere along this stretch. He turned his head, feeling the wind first on one cheek, then the other. —If this wind holds, it'll be hard for the oarsmen to row back out, though. They might figure it'll be easier to round the point, and land south of the inlets.

Smith Point was remarkable in that two small channels exited to the Bay just at its tip. There really was no high ground, such as at Lookout, opposite, or Old Point Comfort, or most of the named points on the western shore. The channels themselves were awash at low tide, so Ker didn't think they'd use them as entrances. But the invaders would expect nothing more than local militia in opposition. The home guard the Commonwealth had called up a few weeks earlier, farmers with shotguns and squirrel rifles.

Driver had been watching him think. —Well, Lieutenant?

—You think the men will stand?

—Oh, they'll stand a brash. These are good boys, they are.

—The enemy will shell the beach first. Before they land.

—I said, these are good boys. They're hungry, but they haven't marched all this way to be driven off without a scrap. What worries me is there's no high ground, said Driver tentatively.

—No sir, said Ker. He looked along the coast, then back at the distant ships just as they merged with the blue evening. —There's no high ground. But maybe we can make some.

―――――

The bombardment opened at the first hint of light, a ripple of booms and flashes that lit the black sea. The first shell whined low over the beach, and burst behind them with a concussion that shook the ground. The sleepy calls of waking songbirds stopped abruptly with that first detonation, succeeded by a hoarse excited cawing back in the woods.

Ker stood smoking segars with Driver near the oystershell mound they'd decided on as their "fortress." During the night the troops had thrown up a rough log palisade around an old brass four-pounder the militia had brought up on an ox-wagon. Great fires of driftwood had given light for their trenching and piling.

And seeing those fires, and the bobbing torches of the working parties, the Federals had accepted the challenge. Spaced out across the near horizon lay four black silhouettes. Ever and anon guns flashed, and he watched the reddish comet-trail of the shells. They were firing with medium charges, so the projectiles would not bury themselves in the sand before exploding. But they were firing long, the shells moaning overhead to burst in the marsh and forest. When the sun rose, their aim would be more exact.

—Fall back, Sergeant Gostin shouted. The men shouldered their weapons and streamed into the woods as another shell howled over. Ker stayed with Driver, watching as the other ships joined in to start the play in earnest. Several hundred yards down the beach the Guards settled into their entrenchments, grooves scraped in damp sand, marked by no flag.

For the same reason, he'd left his battery back on the road. A farm track, at times little more than a deer path, but it paralleled the beach five hundred yards inland, covered by the woods. The clop of axes echoed between the booms and thuds of incoming fire. His gunners were improving the traces to the beach.

—You're damned exposed here, Major, Gostin said, riding back up to them. Driver said nothing, just watched the ships. Ker felt the first trepidation as the shells kept coming, faster as the light grew. Now and again one plowed into the beach, tossing up sand in a fanning spray from which blue haze cooked for a few seconds before dirt and logs fountained upward. It wouldn't be long before some sharp-eyed gunner would pick them out, and aim more particularly.

The smells of powder and raw earth mixed with the pine resin and leaf mold of the Virginia woods, the smell, for him, of home. He'd grown up in this kind of country: low, sandy, infiltrated by water. It seemed right to fight for it. What didn't seem right was who they were going to fight against. It made him both uneasy and, because he was uneasy, suddenly angry. Why did they have to keep something alive that was dead? Why couldn't they just accept that the South had had enough? The washed blue sky was innocent of cloud. Light the color of rubbed copper stole over the water gradually, silently. Ker tapped ash off his segar and shaded his brow as the first phosphorous glint of full sun ignited like a flare on the horizon.

—Where'd that monkey of yours get to? Driver said, exhaling smoke, looking around.

—I left him tied to one of the guns. Auguste reacts badly to fire.

—He will not profit by your example?

—Unfortunately he only imitates my worst features.

—Where'd you get that thing anyway?

—Africa. Ker drove smoke into the wind and watched it fray and thin and disappear. —Our crew took a dozen of them aboard in Porto Praya; the fruit vendors sell them to the sailors as pets. But as we were sailing home they started to vanish. One by one. Every day there were fewer monkeys. No one could figure out why. Then one night the after lookout saw Dupin here pitching one of the little ones overboard to watch him swim.

The major smiled. —How'd you end up with him?

—His owner lost interest, he attached himself to me . . . he was easier to acquire than to dispose of. You would not perhaps care to add a mascot to your regiment?

Driver grimaced and shook his head. He quickly looked seaward again. —How long you reckon before they land?

Ker raised his glasses again. Smoke lay low on the water, shrouding hulls and masts like sea-fog. Through the murk he glimpsed a boat being swung out, others riding beyond the firing line. He counted them, multiplied by what he knew to be their capacity in troops; the sum doubled that of the Tennesseans and Virginians. A shell slammed into the woods behind them, throwing a tree down with a crash. He waited for the detonation, but none came. —They will fire for at least an hour. Their purpose being to reduce the fortification and demoralize us before landing troops.

—Should we reply?

—We must offer them honey if we wish them to land on our flower.

He followed Driver down the mound toward the four-pounder, the smooth bones of oystershells slipping and grating under their boots. The sun was full now, the hot red-golden light glaring flat along the water. He made out the men-of-war plainly now. One was indeed *Pawnee*. The others were smaller, paddle-wheel steamers—maybe ferryboats. All flew the Stars and Stripes, oversized battle flags streaming in the steady wind. Seeing them he felt again that disquieting mix of unease and anger. But if they *would* invade. . . .

A projectile screamed low and he nearly ducked, then caught himself; the men were watching. Another burst in the surf, tossing up spray that drove down over them. He licked salt from his lips, relishing the taste after so long ashore.

The men got up from around the old brass gun. —She primed? Driver asked them.

—She's all ready, Major.

—Claiborne, will you drive our first shot?

Ker pulled his attention from the ships to see Driver offering him the lanyard. Without reflection he set his boots, leaned, and pulled. The antique went off with a bang and a great cloud of white smoke. He doubted the shot even reached the anchored line, but immediately the Federal fire freshened and concentrated. The Tennesseans worked furiously at the little gun and Driver touched off the second round.

Now all the ships were firing, bringing their broadsides into play. He admired how rapidly they found the range. Now each shell landed within a narrow band of a hundred yards to seaward and just behind the top of the dunes. Cracks bracketed them to left and right. A shell buried itself in the earthwork, boosting up soil in an eruption that heaved them off their feet. Fragments pattered as they struggled up again.

—Sounds like they mean biz, Sergeant Gostin said.

—It is growing hot. Time for you to decamp, the major yelled into Ker's ear.

—I can stay yet a while.

—Go back and organize your battery. Listen for my signal.

Ker looked toward *Pawnee* again. When she found the exact range her heavy shells would sweep this beach clean, dig it up, and overturn it like a farmwife turning her truck-patch. He debated telling Driver this, then realized from the set of his lips that he knew. He touched his cap, and headed up the dune.

He was almost to the woods when a wall of sand knocked him down. He lay stunned, ears ringing, the earth swinging as crazily beneath him as if it rolled in heavy seas. But by some miracle he seemed to have lost nothing more than his wind, and he forced himself to his feet and trotted the last few yards to cover. He crouched there, breathing hard, before he realized he'd lost his hat. He gathered his courage and walked slowly back down to retrieve it.

Inland his Tennesseans waited by the howitzers. The mules stood flicking their ears and snapping at flies with big yellow teeth. Ker slipped his watch out. The bombardment would continue for a while yet, attempting to destroy what they took for a fort. At some point, though, the boats riding out would turn and make for the shore. They would not head directly for the Confederate trenches. They'd land to one side and assault them in flank, with covering fire kept up from seaward.

He looked at his men again, then motioned them down. Over the continued rumble that came through the trees he called, —Fall out and rest. We'll wait for the signal.

It did not come for some considerable time. The men sat about, some whittling, others boiling coffee over small fires, still others simply staring with fixed eyes in the direction of the firing. Ker himself lay down on a bed of Virginia creeper in the shade of a large maple, arm thrown over his eyes against the sun. But he couldn't get his mind to stop spinning. On the bay the guns were slamming like huge iron doors. Besides, flies kept landing on his face. He wasn't afraid, exactly, but he still dreaded the idea of firing on men who'd been comrades and countrymen only weeks before. Still, he'd accepted his commission. There was no point reconsidering the matter now. He only hoped he could do his duty. More than that was in God's hands. He wished he'd had time to write to Catherine. He wished he'd had time to go home.

He'd seen her naked body once. A few months after the wedding. He'd come into the bedroom as she was picking up her nightdress to slip it over her head. She'd turned away, but not before he'd seen. Her pale flanks and breasts, still engraved with the reddened marks from her stays, had imprinted themselves on his memory with the timeless motionless fidelity of a daguerreotype. He ran a hand over his face to erase it. He didn't want to go into battle with this image in his mind. He tried to think of nothing, nothing at all, and it must have worked because not long after he was unconscious.

He woke to Gostin shaking him. The sergeant looked anxious. —Sir, the cannonado's lessening.

—Thank you, Sergeant. He sat up and brushed bits of leaf and twig from his uniform; clicked his watch open: seven minutes to nine. In the distance the firing had slackened, though an occasional *boom* still rolled over the woods, echoing from tree to tree. He got up quickly and looked for Dupin.

His heart sank when he picked up the frayed rope-end. Chewed through. He spied the ape at last above him, its wizened visage glaring down from high in the maple. When it saw him looking it chattered angrily down at him. He called, then whistled, the signal he'd trained it to associate with food. But as he had none in his hands, the monkey simply jabbered more angrily. A shell cracked close by and it flinched, then began whirling around the branch like a mechanical toy, screaming at the top of its lungs.

—Auguste. Auguste!

One of the Tennesseans stepped forward, cocking his rifle. —Want me to bring it down for you, Loo-tenant?

—No! Don't shoot it. It's a pet.

—A pet! Why the hail would you keep somethin' like that fer a pet?

—I often ask myself that very question.

The men stared up as it whirled the branch again, screaming. —Sure's hell sounds mad, one fellow observed.

—Has anyone a piece of hardtack?

After some discussion a chunk of pone made its appearance. Ker left it under the tree and stepped back. Dupin cursed them but at last made his way down the bole. But when Claiborne stepped forward he darted to safety again, the crust gripped in a tightly curled paw.

—We need to get the men moving, sir, Gostin observed.

—You hear the signal?

—Yes sir. Don't you?

Ker cocked his head. Yes, he did, the cracked-bell note of bayonets hammered on rifle-barrels. He looked up at Dupin again, frustrated, and told Gostin, —Very well, Sergeant, get them on the move.

The guns creaked and jolted, the mules snorted, the battery began rumbling out. Ker eyed the beast again. He'd just have to leave him here. Then one of the men said —I've a notion, sir. Give me some more of that pone.

This time when Dupin ventured down the soldier hurled a ball of cloth at the trunk above him. A moment later a shapeless mass struggled and shrieked beneath the capacious folds of the raglan. Ker sprang forward, and a moment later had the animal fast. He thrust it into his saddlebag, getting a savage bite on the web of his thumb for his pains, and tied the flap down. Then swung up into the saddle, and was off.

Now it was a footrace. The clatter-clang from seaward marked men running along the beach, paralleling the progress of the pulling-boats a few hundred yards off. The battery column, inland and hidden by the forest, toiled along trying to keep pace. The forest track was too narrow for more than one gun to pass. It dipped into sloughs filled with inches of leaves on top of sticky black tidal mud. Swarms of green-headed flies buzzed viciously, pulled in, apparently, from this whole wooded neck. Each time they landed blood trickled down necks and faces. Gun barrels dipped and swayed, wheels hung up on saplings, limbers slid off at crazy angles. When they stalled men put their backs to the iron wheels; when they surged forward suddenly men screamed, holding broken hands or hopping on feet crushed by the narrow iron. Trees and brush cut off the wind, and it was dreadfully hot. Ker rode ahead, trying to select the least unnavigable route that would keep them in shouting range of the beach. They fought the guns along like this for something over a mile, men and mules swiftly losing breath and strength, before a musket banged. Several more succeeded it before settling down to a steady crackle.

The musketry found him fifty yards ahead of the lead gun. He hauled Aquila's head around and kicked him toward the beach. Ducking under heavy limbs and letting the lighter ones whip him across the face, ignoring the shrieks and chattering from his saddlebag, he fought his way through a region of scrub to the dune-line.

He reined atop it, looking out at one of the grandest and most chilling scenes he'd ever witnessed.

The militia had kept pace with the landing party, and were drawn up now along the beach to receive them. To seaward, riding the wind-frayed waves a surprisingly stiff easter was gusting landward, the invaders were coming in. Ship's launches and cutters, so close he could make out the pancake caps of the crews. At each dip of oars white froth spattered up and was driven back into the boats by the wind. And in the boats, the troops, a mass of dark blue and spiky bayonet-bristle, though many hung over the gunwales, paying tribute to Neptune.

Only a moment's glimpse, but so grand—the spread of sea, the wind-driven surf, the disciplined line of small craft inexorably converging on the few grim-looking men who stood loading and firing old muskets, squirrel rifles, even shotguns—that he knew it would be many a year and a day before Time, man's nemesis, could wipe it from his memory.

Then he turned and spurred his way back to where he could hear, from the crashing and shouting, the outraged braying and the cursing of exhausted men, that his guns were approaching the beach.

4

U RGING Aquila through the woods, Ker pulled up to point a direction of deployment to the lead gun; then kicked the gelding,
which was heaving its flanks like a bellows in the close heat, on to
the midpoint of the column. The rest of Company I was streaming past
him. He pulled the horse's head round when they reached the third gun,
pointing his sword where he wanted them. —Refuse your line from the
beach at a forty-five-degree angle. Load at once with shell and stand by to
fire. He caught a moment's picture of Captain Charlton leading his men
in a jog-trot through the underbrush, bayonets swaying before them like
the probing antennae of some exotic and aggressive species of insect.

A shell snapped through the treetops, dropping boughs, then crashed
inland as he negotiated another ducking, weaving, branch-whipping passage back to the beach. His throat was clogged to the point of vomiting
with the sifting dust. His sight tunneled, to compass only the yards of leaf
and wait-a-minute directly before his mount's pounding hooves.

So that when forest floor turned to sand again, vine and creeper to low
salt-defying wiregrass, he whipped his hat off and dragged sweat off his
forehead with the wool of his sleeve. God, it was hot. Only the onshore
breeze brought any relief.

He spurred Aquila over the dune, the horse digging quickly to counter the sagging sand, and saw that the same wind brought them Yankees too.

More small boats had joined the oncoming line, emerging from behind the steamers. They carried troops as well, though he'd guessed only the sloop-of-war would have had room enough to embark a land force of any size. Whoever commanded, looking on from *Pawnee*'s rolling deck, was holding nothing in reserve. The cannon still spoke from seaward, more deliberate as the crews tired, but still tossing shell after shell crashing along the beach. They burst in white wreaths of cottony smoke, sending shards of hot iron ripping through air and foliage, dune and surf.

He shaded his eyes, fastening his gaze once more on the gridiron flag that streamed and rippled at each masthead. And remembered suddenly how he'd felt to see it streaming out one morning above an African bay. They'd been on an expedition upriver, and barely made it back after weeks of fear, heat, disease, and the ever-present danger of the Arab slavers and their native allies. He smoothed his beard, blinking. How wonderful that same flag had looked to him then.

Now he had to kill those who fought beneath it.

Pulling himself from doubt and regret like a man fighting free of a slough, he twisted in the saddle. He had to get the howitzers forward. But though he heard frenzied shouting and the crackling of breaking brush they were not yet in sight. He faced front again, noting the militiamen reloading and aiming. A popping came from their ragged line, and splashes leapt up around the lead boat. But their motions were jerky, uncoordinated. Already they were glancing back longingly at the woods.

A flag snapped down on the sloop-of-war's halliards and, ship by ship, firing ceased. After long seconds the last detonations rolled back from the Maryland shore, an ominous drumroll like faraway thunder. The lead boats were creeping across the line of fire. Ker watched their prows rise and fall as the surf steepened, oars reaching and straightening, reaching and straightening. He licked his lips, tasting a metallic sharpness, like sucking nails. Felt his heart pounding.

He bowed his head, alone on the strand, and sought what he always asked for before facing death, at sea or ashore.

Lord, let thy will, not mine, be done.

He opened his eyes, and began to plan the battle.

The bottom here shoaled gradually, then suddenly surged upward, shallowing to five or six feet a hundred yards out. His eye picked out where driving waves changed color, from a clouded green, dull yet opalescent, to the murky tint of stirred-up sand. The lead boats were entering that zone of transition. They yawed and wavered, one nearly broaching to before its steersman swung the bow once again toward the beach.

Now their motion changed. The rising surf lifted their sterns and sent them scooting for swift yards before dropping and cradling them in the trough. The boats were well handled. The men at the oars would be New Englanders, bred to the sea. Most U.S. Navy enlisted were from Down East. Their officers would be more mixed, especially since so many had come South. Volunteers, most likely, like the fellow from New York who'd reported aboard *Owanee* just before Sumter. Green beginners. Completely at sea, so to speak.

He shaded his eyes, but couldn't make out the troops who rode stolidly, facing backward. He only caught solid blue, from which flashed out an occasional sparkle of polished steel, bright and instantaneous as a photographer's flash-powder.

A crunch and grate of iron grinding sand, gasps of breath and blasphemies, the deep hawing protests of fed-up shit-scared mules. The first howitzer was coming up at last. It reached the dune-line and promptly stalled, wheels sinking deep into the white cascade. The mules snorted, eyes rolling. They kicked in the traces as the ground slumped away beneath them, as the lashes of the drovers licked down on flanks and necks. The second team halted at the woods' edge as its sweating cannoneers eyed the quicksand struggles of the first. Aquila danced about, nervous both at the untenable ground and the continuing rackety-bang of musketry.

Gostin came slogging through the sand, cheeks livid, white mustaches bristling like a hostile dog's rump. He waved a carbine and shouted —Never mind that! Unhand it. Cut those fuckin' mules loose. All you men, up forward on this one. We'll carry the bastard if we have to.

Ker looked to the beach again. The militia were wavering, falling back. The Tennesseans were moving up to stiffen them, scooping out shallow rifle-pits with driftwood and tin cups and rifle-butts. Ramrods thunked as they loaded.

The lead boats were barely a pistol-shot off. Ker saw a wisp of wind-weaved smoke as a trooper fired shoreward, doubtless against orders. He could make out individuals now even without the glasses.

On the beach Charlton lifted his saber, held it aloft, and let it drop. A ragged volley spurted from the kneeling men, and in the boat a figure stood suddenly, as if moved to object to the proceedings. A rifle cartwheeled into the sea.

Ker jerked his attention back to the lead Dahlgren. A dozen troops had fisted on to it now, boots kicking collapsing holes in the sliding sand as they braced shoulders and arms under its weight. The Navy had designed the howitzer to be manhandled from boat to shore-carriage; had trimmed off every frill and decoration, even dispensing with trunnions. But it was still eight hundred pounds of bronze and more of iron-carriage, bogged deep in dry, loose white sand. Ker cast a despairing glance at the approaching boats, the outnumbered defenders in their grim waiting line.

He shouted down to Gostin, —Trip the fighting-bolt, Sergeant.

—Sir?

—Unfasten and withdraw the bolt. Carry the tube and carriage up separately. You'll cut your weight in half.

—You heard the lieutenant. Pull that fucking bolt there, Harry.

A bullet hissed close and Aquila reared. Ker fought him back down, wishing he had a mount accustomed to fire. Below him the bolt rasped, the tube came free. The men swarmed it, twenty hands on the dark metal length, a swarm of ants wrestling a twig. And as he watched some slipped and fell and the barrel dipped but others held grimly and began setting their boots sidewise in the sand. The bronze cylinder climbed. The men who'd fallen struggled up from the sand and seized the carriage. The disburdened wheels turned, and they were able to push it to the top of the dune and then, at Ker's shouted command, downward toward the beach.

Satisfied matters were in hand here, he kicked the horse down toward the frothing line of surf. The lead boat was backing water. Not a clever move in the face of the crackling fire the Tennesseans were directing at it, but obviously the invaders had orders to maintain a beaching line. The boats following were rowing hard, the men bending their backs to catch up.

A flag shook out in the guide boat, the bright new colors licking out to snap in the breeze like live flames. He wondered what unit this was, from which state the men came who were preparing to assault the Old Dominion. And how they'd feel if it was their own home being attacked.

As he galloped behind the digging riflemen, his doubt ebbed, replaced by reluctant acknowledgment. Commodore Rousseau was right. If they held here, Washington would think long and deep before another landing in the South.

The problem was, far more men filled the oncoming boats than Driver had to stop them with.

He pulled Aquila up as he reached the right flank. Here his gunners had piled enough driftwood, hacked down enough brush, to harden a ramp up the dunes, which were also less steep in this quarter, declining in the direction of a marsh-choked inlet farther east. The lead guns were already in position. The crews were loading, the staffs of the rammers plunged in and out like the staves of butter-churns. The last two howitzers wheeled around to point down the beach. He repositioned one masked by a rise in the ground, reminded the men to hold fire until his command, and spurred back toward the Confederate left.

Halfway there he made out Driver up at the woods-line, motioning him in. The major was standing behind the center, his men below lying on their bellies, watching the approaching boats. —Is your battery in position? were the first words out of his mouth.

—Half are taking position on your right flank. The ground on the left is proving rather more difficult to negotiate.

—I intend to meet them with a musket volley, then fall back and permit you to direct your fire until either your guns are taken or they reach our rifle-line. Can you winnow down their numbers for me?

—I shall endeavor to do so to the best of my ability.

—They must not gain a foothold. If they do, we'll lose the whole Northern Neck.

—The militia? Ker glanced shoreward, saw the locals were already scattering. Picking up fowling pieces and ancient muskets, dropping back from the river's edge toward the rifle-pits above.

Beyond them, driven on by wind, sea, and hard-bent oar, the assaulting boats were swiftly covering the last yards to shore. As he watched, a petty officer hurled a kedge-anchor from the stern of the lead launch, the one bearing the flag; obviously that of the landing force commander. The anchor astern would make it easier to back off in the face of this onshore wind.

—I have instructed them to stand as long as they can, then retreat and form a second line behind us. For an untrained body, they have done well so far.

—Perhaps you should induct them into your ranks.

—There are a few boys down there I shouldn't mind having beside me. Captain Tyree, finger to his slouch hat. —Sir, enemy's beaching.

—Very good. Have the men cap. Driver nodded to Ker. —You're on your own, Claiborne. Remember, you must winnow them down.

Ker flourished his sword in the salute. Driver returned it with a gloved hand, then turned back to the beach.

Aquila reared as Ker heeled his flanks, then charged up the bank. Ker bitted him as they reached the crest, and hauled around to face the Chesapeake.

From here he could see both flanks, see his gun-captains watching him tensely. They stood stiffly at each gun, rammer propped erect to signal readiness to fire. The crews knelt by the wheels, or stood back by the ammunition chests, cradling the next charge.

—Point, he shouted as loudly as he could.

His voice sounded faint to him against the wind, yet the crews bent instantly, slewing the sights to bear. The gun-captains squinted down the bore, then straightened, lanyards in hand. Ker pressed his elbows to his ribs, not giving them anything they might take as a signal to fire, and raised his eyes again.

The day was dazzling bright now, the downward glare of sun augmented by its rippling glitter up again off the waves. The whole hemisphere of the gray-green bay opened before him. The distant violet crayoning, looking like islands from here, that marked Piney Point and, closer in, a darker hue, Point Lookout. The great sweep of the river, with far off one tiny gaff-sail making its way in on who knew what errand—a pungy, perhaps, with a hold of oysters tonged off Tangier or Smith Island. And then the line of sloops and gunboats riding at anchor, helpless now to affect the outcome. All creation seemed to draw a breath, then hold it.

The oars left the water and swept upward in ragged unison to point at the blue zenith. The prow of the guide boat rose suddenly, grounding, then yawed as a following wave shoved the stern around. A tall officer vaulted the gunwale, planting his boots in the surf. A stride behind him followed a husky trooper with a great spreading blond beard, bearing the flag proudly aloft.

Men in blue rose in a sudden wave of their own and spilled, leapt, fell, lurching and staggering as they searched for footing beneath the frothing surf. The color-bearer made for the front, grasping the varnished staff from which the red and white and blue surged. The recoiling militia turned. Rifles barked. Men flung out their arms, making sudden Ys against the surf, and fell back to float face upward as their uniforms, billowing pockets of air, held them up. But only a few. The mass still came on, breaking into a floundering run as they cleared the surf for tide-hardened sand.

Just at that moment, the flap of Ker's saddlebag jerked upward. He reacted too slowly. By the time his hand clapped down, feeling for the brass catch, the ape was gone.

Cursing, he drew his sword. The blade shone in the sun, reflecting spangles of light that wavered over the sand. He felt the focus of eyes from all along the beach. A puff of white from one of the boats. The heavy minié ball thudded to a stop five yards short. Dirt spurted up, spraying him with stinging sand.

Suddenly Dupin was screeching in his ear, climbing his shoulder from behind. Ker swung at it, tried to shake the beast off him. It clung doggedly, chattering invective.

The line of blue formed ragged as the surf-wash as it raced forward over the sand. A hoarse command, echoed by other voices, some shrill, some confident. Rifles rose, then leveled, tipped with glittering steel.

Then they charged, and simultaneously with their hoarse shout, their uneven huzzah, a sheet of red flame and smoke flared out from the shallow pits, the men lying at full length or kneeling on the beach, on this embattled hundred yards of sandy ground. As the bullets struck the Federals spun and fell, collapsed where they ran, staggered out of line clutching breasts or stomachs. But the blue line itself came steadily on, bent low now, like men walking into a hailstorm.

Ker blinked sand from his eyes, lifted his saber higher, waiting for one breathless moment; looking down at the men who waded, walked, ran toward him. Then brought the blade down.

—Fire, he screamed into the soundless din.

The howitzers banged out one after the other, out of order, uncoordinated, but the twelve-pound shells sickled down men as they exploded. Hit sand and rebounded, leaping through the air with irresistible momentum. They knocked men down and smashed off arms. A body pinwheeled along the sand. When the crumpled form came to rest it was headless.

Ker jerked his eyes away and tried to shake the monkey off again, but it clung, riding his back. Screaming with insane rage, right into his ear. He wheeled Aquila to the right. He'd ordered the first round loaded be shell, in case matters began in a duel with the ships. But the range was closing. —Reload with canister, he bawled. The gunners elevated their staffs to signal they heard. He spurred back, passing the order to the furiously sponging crews on the left flank.

Below him the Tennesseans fired steadily, arms pistoning, ramrods an iron clatter, shots a crackling racket like popcorn in a copper pan. Auguste screamed even louder, clawing its way up his neck from behind, throttling him with leathery paws. The leading Federals came steadily on, and a terrible glitter of polished steel rippled along their front.

Now the Tennesseans were leaving their pits. Scrambling up, stopping to let off a round, then running for the shelter of the woods. Some made as if to stay, and were pulled bodily up by Gostin and given a lick with his carbine to set them going.

The Union line swept up the beach, the men leaping and stumbling over the fallen. Ker was surprised to see the blond-bearded giant, the color-bearer, still leading them. Then they were among the pits, and the line slowed, bent around the entrenchment.

Only a stone's throw below him now as the gelding pranced uneasily. Ker caught the eye of a tall officer in blue, a leveled sword, rifle-barrels foreshortening toward him. The next moment came a deadly sizzling in the air, a multiple thwocking of lead into green wood behind him. Something kicked at his boot. Beneath him the gelding flinched, then steadied, panting as he leaned forward to gentle its neck.

The crews completed their loading and stepped back The gun-captains laid their sights, crouched, and yanked the lanyards.

Canister was buckshot for cannon. Ker stared, steeling himself against all human feeling as it mowed down the officer who'd pointed him out, the soldiers who'd fired, and the men behind them, wilting and blasting down a dozen at once as if the breath of the Angel of Death had passed over them. One moment they were on their feet, the next blue lumps on the tumbled ground. The howitzers pinned them in enfilade: each vomiting forth of iron passed down the length of the Union line, not crossing it from the front, but from both sides.

The Dahlgrens banged into steady firing, losing synchrony as one crew loaded faster than another. Smoke rings spiraled outward, then melted into a thickening bank of sulphurous yellow-white. Detonations rolled out to seaward, reechoed from the anchored hulls, no more now than impotent witnesses to the slaughter. As was he, but at such close range he watched men's blood burst forth, heard the sound, like a carpet being beaten with iron rods, of canister-shot striking human flesh. And always, through the din, a prolonged, endless screaming he only gradually realized was that of the ape clinging to his back, its claws digging through thick wool and cotton undervest.

Aquila suddenly went to his knees beneath him. Ker kicked stirrups free and swung awkwardly off the saddle as the beast shuddered, then rolled to lie helplessly panting. Blood bubbled at its nostrils. Its eyes, blown open in fear and pain, stared into the sun. His searching fingers found the ragged edges of a wound beneath its neck.

A puff of smoke, the howl of a shell from the river. It drove overhead and exploded to the right. But the sea-commander couldn't stop the slaughter. Ker's batteries were too close to the landing zone. And the warships' decks were rolling, the long axes of the hulls parallel to the surf. The sights would be rolling too, making it impossible to aim with any degree of precision.

One of his men came huffing up from the right flank. His words were lost in another ragged huzzah as the second Union wave beached. Ker cupped his ear. —Your pardon?

—Said, we're about out of powder, sir. Two more rounds per gun.

—I don't believe that can be correct. We should have plenty of ammunition.

—The second wagon bogged down in the woods. Boys couldn't shove it out of the mudhole.

Ker couldn't believe what he was hearing. Half the ammunition left behind? To riverward flags tumbled as another storm of canister boiled white water. The still-living stumbled over the suddenly dead through scarlet-stained surf. The ships thundered again, a renewed bank of smoke sweeping in toward the beach. Shells burst in white-wreathed fury, but too far off to sway the battle. The howitzers stamped out smoke rings that sailed out over the beach, again, again, but the bluecoats were still charging. God, he thought, even after this slaughter, this shambles, still *charging* . . .

A crashing, then a high yipping yell behind him. Ker turned to see Driver, saber lifted, and behind him scores of his Tennessee boys break from the woods. The tallest carried a pike, and something caught in Ker's throat as he saw what streamed from it. Fluttering out in the sea-wind, uncased for the first time. The white purer than smoke, the red brighter than blood, the blue so deep as almost to be black; the circle of gold stars gleamed in the sun with a glory that rivaled its own splendor.

The major whirled his blade above his head, and shouted —Charge!

Ker fumbled for his sword and ran forward with them to meet the last remnants of the first Union wave, some few of whom were still staggering forward from the ruin behind them. A tall marine in scarlet-striped trowsers lurched forward still, though gore encrimsoned the front of his tunic.

Ker blinked in disbelief. The man had no jaw. A heavy canister-slug had sheared it off as by some massive cleaver; his mouth was a bloody hole, upper teeth visible to the back molars as his head tilted back, gasping air in and out through a bubbling scarlet horror that gaped and sucked closed, gaped and sucked closed. He held his Springfield clubbed, but instead of swinging it hesitated, staring incredulously at Ker's head. Ker sabered him down, as much from mercy as from enmity, the impact of blade on bone jolting his elbow and arm with a tingle like a galvanic shock. Too late, he reminded himself to lunge rather than slash. In close quarters, you could saber the comrade behind you as readily as the foeman in front.

Then he stopped dead, fighting as claws came round his head and went for his eyes. The Tennesseans streamed by, ululating yips and howls as Ker struggled with the terrified monkey. At last he got it by the scruff of the neck and flung it off into a blood-soaked patch of sand. For a moment the beast lay stunned. Then came to its senses, sitting up and gripping its head for all the world like a little old man roused from a night of popskull. Then a shell burst above them, veining blue air with smoking, zinging iron, and it bounced to all fours and tore off across the sand, tail high, screaming into the din.

Thuds and cracks stitched across the beach like the treadled steel needles of some monstrous sewing machine. The howitzers had let loose again, double-canistered now. Sheets of sand flew up. Metal harrowed live bodies and dead alike.

A moment later the gray line and the blue collided in a crash of screams, shots, the flash of sharpened steel. Men threw up their arms and fell. A few attempted retreat, but the boats had backed water on their stern anchors and lay now outside the surf-line, crews silent and watching, lying on their oars.

The two lines wavered together, merged, a dozen melees going on at once. Men bayoneted each other. Swords flashed. Discharged rifles became clubs, pikes, quarterstaffs. Pistols were held at arm's length, recoiling in puffs of blue smoke.

Till the blue line staggered back. But could only run a few steps before being confronted with the impassable river. And at last a gold-braided figure turned, at bay, laid a blade gracefully across a forearm, and bowed.

The word flew from mouth to mouth up the beach. Quarter. The invaders had asked for quarter.

Ker panted down almost to the water's edge, conscious as he did so of the frowning mouths of the howitzers to either side. He would not have relished charging into them.

Perhaps two score federal troops still stood, surrounded by the Confederates. Every mortal yet erect looked insane, consumed, cheeks blackened with powder-smut and streamed with sweat. A diminutive officer with the insignia of a captain offered his saber to Driver over a crooked arm. The major returned a tired bow, and croaked to Gostin, —It's over. Gather the arms and stack them in the woods, Sergeant. Detail guards. And let us do our best now to succor the wounded.

Ker limped across the bloody scuffed-up sand, only now feeling a wet squishing inside his boot. No pain yet, but it was on its way. Each step took all his determination, all his strength. His gaze moved emptily across the fought-over ground. Paper cartridge-twists, copper glints of fired rifle-caps, discarded packs, broken rifles, boots, and above all bodies. They lay in every conceivable attitude, but most, it seemed, on their faces in the sand, hands clawed under them. As if they'd died trying to mole them-selves beneath the remorseless cross fire. At close range canister did not kill gracefully. The wounded stirred in slow agony, like crabs dismem-bered by vicious children. The sun illuminated all so brilliantly he had to shade his eyes. He was astonished to see it still below the zenith. The sky seemed infinitely larger than he had ever seen it before.

When he lowered his eyes a man was sitting upright before him, hold-ing a shattered arm. Splinters of yellowish bone protruded between his fingers, but oddly enough there was only a trickle of blood. His dilated eyes followed Ker, who suddenly realized he was still carrying a bloody naked blade. He got the point into the scabbard-hole on the fourth try and knelt, patting the man's good arm. —The battle's over, friend. You need not fear us now.

—Thank God for that.

—What unit are you from?

—Weah the Massachusetts Eighth.

—You sailed from Baltimore? A nod. —I'm sorry about your wound. You'll be going home, I should say.

—Wisht I was to home right naow. One ahm or none.

Ker reassured him he'd be taken care of, then rose and walked on. He recalled that his collar was still unbuttoned. He hooked it, and straight-ened his cocked hat. Brushed dust and sand from his sleeves, from the breast of his tunic.

Driver was still with the little Union captain who'd surrendered to him. Ker returned the latter's crisp salute with a lift of his cap.

—You are a naval officer, sir?

—That is correct. I am responsible for those howitzers, under the ma-jor's command.

—You have gained the field, sir. I only ask fair treatment for my dead and wounded.

—You're among Christians, Driver said. —We'll honor a flag of truce, should your commander request it.

—I believe one is in the offing, Ker said, pointing.

Pawnee's launch was coming in. A seaman waved a white banner in great curling swoops. An officer in epaulettes and braid sat in the stern-sheets. Ker recognized Captain Stephen Rowan, commanding *Pawnee*. He did not care to stay for what promised to be an awkward interview, so he raised his cap to Driver. —Permission to see to my men, sir.

—Certainly, Claiborne. Please convey my appreciation. They have carried the day.

—Without those guns we should have swept the field, the captain said. —I had no idea where they came from. How many of those have you got hidden around here?

—Two hundred, as well as considerable of larger bore, Ker said with a straight face. —I should not advise another landing hereabouts. Aside from a large militia force, we have garrisoned with a full regiment of regular troops from Richmond.

He trudged back up the beach. Here and there walking wounded were being helped to their feet. It was a victory, but he saw now not all the dead wore blue. Some were Confederates, most of the latter bearing the marks of the bayonet. The Yankees had shown unquestioned courage at the charge. They had not surrendered until the alternative was useless annihilation.

We have been very lucky here today, Ker thought. He hoped with all his heart the result would be peace. Another such morning, he did not care to see.

He was looking up the beach when his boots caught on something half-buried in the sand. He stooped and brushed at it, revealing a varnished pole, a ragged, shot-gnawed cloth.

He shook the sand from the flag. The varnished staff was sticky with blood. The crimson and white stripes were spotted with a darker stain.

—Put it down, a voice murmured.

The wounded officer lay at full length, half-covered by kicked-up sand. From his waist downward, though, the earth was dark red. His wounds were not visible, but from the waxen paleness of his face and the death-dew on his forehead, they were mortal. His shoulder straps bore the gold oak leaves of a major.

Suddenly Ker recognized the officer who'd stepped ashore with the Viking-bearded color-bearer. He propped the butt of the colors in the sand and went down on a knee. Found a canteen and rattled it.

—Would you like water?

—Go to hell.

The hate in the light blue eyes struck him like a heat-blast from a stoked-up furnace. The bloodless lips moved again, barely whispering. —You spat on the flag. I spit on you.

—You invaded our home. It was the greeting you deserved.

—You're a damned Secesh traitor. I hope you cook in Hell.

Ker said evenly, —I should anticipate you will arrive there ahead of me, my friend. Before the Grand Assize, your curses will harm yourself more than me. I will attempt to obtain medical care for you.

—Damn you and all your traitorous spawn.

The blue eyes regarded him, steady and filled with contempt; then slowly fixed, and the spasmodic motion of the chest ceased. When Ker rose again they no longer followed him.

Suddenly he felt both hot and cold. His hands shook so he could hardly grip the staff. He finally drove the sharpened iron spike at the butt into the sand, leaving the draggled banner stirring in the breeze. He inspected the batteries, complimented the crews, but as some far-off observer, not as himself. He could hardly drag one foot after the other. He knew he should pull his boot off, assess the damage, but kept putting it off. He didn't want to see how bad it was.

When he slogged back down to where Rowan and Driver stood together, the major turned. —Captain Rowan, let me introduce my artillery commander, Lieutenant Ker Claiborne.

—I believe we have met before, Captain.

They exchanged cool salutes, Rowan noting his uniform. —Former Navy, Lieutenant?

—Formerly commanding *Owanee,* sir.

—Oh yes. I have heard of you, sir. You took her into a Secessionist ambush, and abandoned her helpless there.

Ker felt himself flush, had to steady his voice before he replied. —You have been misinformed, sir. She was out of danger when I parted from her.

—I had heard that you betrayed her, sir. Rowed ashore in the middle of the night.

Ker burst out, —That is a damned lie, sir. Do you dare repeat it?

Driver intervened hastily. —We have arrived at a cartel, Claiborne. Wounded to be taken off by boats. The dead to be buried in the woods, on land cleared for the purpose.

—And the captives? Ker forced himself to ask. Still haunted by the memory of those hate-filled eyes. The words that had struck straight to his own misgiving.

—I'm open to parole. I feel no need to be vindictive to brave men.

Rowan bowed stiffly, and they parted. Launches and cutters were already making for shore. The wounded were gathered at the tide-line, lying on blankets. Confederates and Unionists moved among them, doing what they could.

Ker stood without occupation for the moment. He slowly became aware of a raging hunger. He'd missed breakfast, had been riding or running almost without cease since the morning of the day before. His foot flamed with pain. He limped up the shore to where the dead gelding lay. Flies rose as he approached, then settled again to the bloody sand, to the motionless eyeballs.

Then, making him jump back, a brown shape darted out from the bushes. He gathered the ape up and held it close, rocking it, crooning a wordless reassurance. Stroking the coarse fur over and over as it burrowed its face into his breast, whimpering with affection and relief.

5

---

16 Freemason Street,
Norfolk, Virginia,
June 2, 1861.

Dearest Ker,

I received yours of the eighteenth today. The mails are quite slow now in the unsettled state of the country. You will recall Mr. Rice, the postmaster? He refused to take the oath to the new authority and was dismissed. Mr. Cosgreave is still our postman, however, so we are greeted with a familiar face each morning, for which I am grateful in these unsettled times!

I conned over your letter only briefly, but it is unsettling. You mention that you anticipate the possibility of events changing very swiftly. You must tell me at length what you mean by that. I am glad you are staying with Mother and Father on Church Hill. I will enclose a separate letter for them, please hand it to Mother.

Little Rob is well and misses his Da. I am great and quite outgrowing my stays. I eat whatever is in sight and send Betsey for more. Really it is shameless and I shall be as stout as Aunt Lily if I do not rein in my appetite. Yet I fear stinting the child if I do. And also the larger the babe the more difficult the passage. You recall what a long and painful time I had with Rob I fear to think of it as bad again yet God's will be done. The markets are full though there is some scarcity of currency, the farmers no longer accepting bank notes from north of the Potomac, or haggling like Hebrews over the discount if they do.

The new Silver is giving me much satisfaction. I cannot help contrasting it with the old worn spoons which I have put away for playthings for our new son or daughter. We are making progress in our domestic establishment, little by little. I can bear much from day to day if we are building our means and our home by the way.

It is disheartening to hear you say there is no call for Sea-officers by the present government. It seems to me we should be driving every effort to building up our Fleet if it is true we have none. But if there is no opening in the military way perhaps this would be the time for you to think of going into the shipping line. There is not much going on down at Water Street just now as the Federals are not letting vessels by, but as soon as a settlement is reached Captain Sterett says trade will rebound and they expect to do very well out of the half-interest in their vessel.

I am very glad you have the freedom of our new Capital in these exciting days and I so wish I could have joined you. But Rob's illness and then the interruption of transport up the Bay make it impossible to consider just now. I will enter the period of confinement shortly and perhaps it is for the best. If they truly have no need of you perhaps you will be able to take leave and come here and be with us.

Suddenly just now Mrs. Morey rapped on the back door and holding out the newspaper toward me said all in excitement, "Read it, you must. It is all about Ker, our first fight and he has won a signal victory." So I did and before I was done Mrs. Sherrie and Miss Tennant were rapping at the front door and I had to send Betsey to put on the tea. Really, Ker, I was so torn between surprise that you were not in Richmond in comfort as I thought but enduring the deprivations & dangers of the field, and pride in you and fear—the temerity of woman—at what it recounted. The ladies were very impressed and kept mentioning "dispatches." I had no idea what they meant until they explained what an honor it was. But to lose your horse, and to be wounded—though the report said it was slight, which relieved my heart after a horrible start—and to render such comeuppance to so many of the invaders, and force them to surrender their swords and return to their ships in ignominy and failure! It is scarcely to be credited to the gentle "preeux cheavalier" I know. But then the next moment I tremble—knowing you have been in danger and in battle even though you are out of it safely now—it is merely the troubled imaginings of a lonely Female.

More callers at noon. This News has quite redeemed me in the eyes of the ladies of the Circle, the which had as you recall regarded us with some coolness back when you had indicated we might stay with the Union. I am very glad to feel in what high regard you are held justly due to your bold Exploits. Yet be not too bold, do not run risks for the sake of advancement. I should a thousand times rather be the wife of a Lieutenant than the widow of a Commodore. And also take enough rest, make as good board as you can, wear the flannel smallclothes I made for you, they are recommended by the doctors against recurrence of all Fevers.

I know we must defend our soil against the imposition of those who, presuming on former acquaintance, seek to advantage themselves of our momentary weakness. How can they imagine former circumstances give them the right to trample down the rights of others? The Union is but the compact of States, it was made by the States and can be no more without them. To preserve unity by force is the figment of a diseased brain, which I am told afflicts Mr. Lincoln. If these "Republicans" are so concerned about our servants, let them study how well they are treated here with us, rather than gaping at stage-plays and other such lies by that woman whose name I will not sully my page with. At any rate you have shown them the toll to be paid should they presume to violate our borders again. All here say there will be no more such incursions and peace will speedily come. I pray it may be so.

The news a few days ago from Alexandria about the death of Col. Ellsworth and Jackson, the proprietor of the hotel there. Did you read the address of Ellsworth to his hirelings before leaving New York about the riches of the men of the South and the beauty

of the Women? If ever a leader of renegados merited death it is he.
Let them send us no more such, they will find our response,

> *"This rock shall fly,*
> *From its firm base as soon as I."*

Samantha Pember was married the night before last, rather
more swiftly than her family expected. The groom, a Captain
Trulove from Portsmouth, is in a cavalry company and his troop
will be leaving town today for Manassas in Northern Virginia. Mr.
McBlair is at Craney island constructing a battery of eight-inch
guns taken from the Naval Yard here. I told Mrs. McBlair yesterday
of the part you played in the burning of it, she laughed and said
you had taken care to leave us the guns intact. I have seen Hettie
and her poor crippled little boy. I told him he might have a spoon-
ful of sugar & afterwards found the entire bowl quite empty. Yesterday went to Evening Prayer and saw Dr. Taylor, Mr. Upshur, the
Leatherburys, the Bosses, Miss Katty Mears, and the others you
know. Reverend Crandall's homily was very much to the purpose
as usual, applying the Lesson with its singular coincidence to present events, and sent us all home musing over the way Scripture
speaks to us in these troubled times. Mr. Upshur told us during fel-
lowship something I can scarcely credit, that Capt. Buchanan is
making exertion to return to the Federal Navy, but that the Lincolnian hirelings wrote back that they had no need of the services
of someone they <u>could not trust</u>. Can this be possible after the high
regard you said all had for him in the Service? He being from
Maryland, and all here say that State will follow ours out of the
Union shortly and join in our "Cousin Sam"—that is, our Southern Confederacy. Of course the Sinclairs, the Farraguts, and the
Barrons have made their choice long since.

I will now close to place this letter in the post today with thanks
for your preservation—and pride in what is reported so widely of
you. I can hardly believe I am the Wife of such a Hero. I cherish
perfect confidence in you and those brave men who served with
you, Tennesseans the reports say, they are a far way from home are

they not, I wonder what they think of our country. I hope and pray all may be right and the enemy, as I suppose we must now call the northerners, see the error of their ways. But all that we little pigmies propose must be undertaken in faith and confidence in that source of all good that is the Divinity. Take care of yourself.

Remember the flannels.

Truly Thine,
C.W.B.

6

––––––––––◆––––––––––

THE aftermath of an engagement ashore was quite different from
that of one at sea. Land had to be negotiated for from local farmers, brush hewed down, and graves dug. An unarmed Federal
shore party plied shovel and mattock alongside a fatigue detail from the
Second Tennessee.

When he let Romulus remove his boot, Ker found that the minié that
had killed his gelding had only scored across the upper part of his own
foot bone. With the wound washed out with seawater and then brandy,
he judged he had nothing to fear.

As dusk approached, so did the country people. The farmers' wives
had lined their cart-beds with baked and salted hams, sea-pies, hunter's
beef, veal à-la-daube, corn muffins, oyster-loaves, and pitchcocked eels.
Slaves spaded up a barbecue pit, and the aromas of hickory smoke and
roasting shoat, burnt-sugar glazing and mushroom-catsup sauce rose like
the incense of sacrifice. Beyond the main tables lay puddings, jellies, rice
milks, puff-pastes, mincemeat, flummery, and jumbal cake soused with
butter and molasses. For washing it all down, a head-numbing applejack,
hot orgeat, spring-cold molasses beer, or throat-scorching cherry brandy
that Ker, after the first sip, had to tip unobtrusively into a bush. One

woman had even made ice cream; the Tennesseans complained it was too cold to eat, and put it in their canteens to warm up for later.

Before long the troops, stomachs shrunken by the days of thin rations, lay about on the sward holding their guts in happy repletion. The Yankee captives sat wistfully regarding the banquet, until Gostin decided they'd suffered enough and let them tail on the line. When dusk turned to dark, strapping, busty country girls paired off with this trooper and that, disappearing into the darkness that pulsed with the flaring, drifting stars of lightning bugs.

One of the Yankee captives nursed a tin cup of cider by the fire, a curious circle of farmchildren, white and black, close around him. By this time the men from both sides were on better terms, the festive cup and the prospect of parole having taken the edge off enmity. On Ker's greeting he got hastily to his feet.

—Pray seat yourself. I only wished to ask where you were from.

—Brainerd, sir. Massachusetts.

Dupin snatched the cup out of his hands and drank, cider running down his fur. He seemed to have grasped the fact that the men in blue were prisoners, and delighted in snatching tidbits from men who could not resist. The Yankee said, —That yer monkey, sir? He sure is full of the old Nick.

—He is indeed. Do you like monkeys? Capital company. Never a dull moment.

—No sir, you can keep him. No offense, sir, but they give me the creeps.

—You're a militiaman?

—We're volunteers, sir. Joined up after Sumter.

—No regulars among you?

—Not a one, sir.

—Well, I must congratulate you on the resolution you showed in the charge. And ask a question which has puzzled me. If I may?

The trooper nodded, and Ker put it to him straight: Why would the grandsons of men who loved liberty, as the Minutemen had back in '76, impose themselves on the liberty of others? Was it for hire? The Yankee frowned, then said quietly, —No sir. It's to defend the Union.

Ker leaned back on the grass, fingers locked behind his head. The desire to sleep circled like a wolf; he yawned, determined to keep it yet at bay till he'd satisfied his curiosity. —But that Union has been dissolved. There is no point in trying to bring us back to a condition which no longer exists, which cannot be re-created.

—Oh, the Union and flag still live, sir.

—On your soil, perhaps, but not on ours. The Union was created by a compact of the states, correct? Well, we Southrons have dissolved that compact, and returned to our former condition.

—I don't see how that can happen, sir.

—Let me try an example. Two merchants have a partnership. One decides he'll dissolve it. Can the other say the partnership still exists? Can he force his former associate to continue to cohabit with him, and do business on the former ground?

—Plainly he cannot.

—So you see how ridiculous the argument descends. The only question that remains is for their employees to decide which to follow to a new situation. As for myself, though I loved the old flag, I had to go with Virginia.

The solider said stubbornly, —No state can leave the Union, sir. It is indissoluble.

Ker told him this was an interesting position for him to take, as it was Massachusetts which had threatened to withdraw from the Union over the Louisiana Purchase, and the New England states which had actually sent a deputation to Washington to secede over the war with Britain in 1815, to find when they arrived that peace had already been declared.

—I'm no historian, sir. But it ain't right.

They both sighed, staring into the fire. Finally Ker asked, —But why did *you* volunteer? And the other boys? Is it the colored? Our "peculiar institution"?

—Some of 'em say so. Me, I personally figure we got no business telling you what to do with them. It's not that. It's just the Union.

Ker tried again to make the fellow see reason. The New Englander admitted at last that Ker might even be right, in a theoretical sense, but that he'd volunteered to save the Union, and no amount of argument could make him abandon that simple and stubborn insistence.

The night passed quietly except for occasional cries from the woods. The anchored ships offered no renewal of hostilities. Ker noticed, however, that one gunboat had departed during the night, presumably to carry to Washington news of the misfiring of the enterprise.

The next morning boats brought those wounded who had not survived the ships' surgeons back to be buried with their fallen comrades. The prisoners signed a parole, which Major Driver had written out, and filed aboard. The pickets reported black smoke making from the fleet. Ker rode out in time to see them churning with clouds of inky-black smoke directly into the wind. Headed, he judged, for Point No Point and the day's passage back up the Chesapeake.

When he rode back disagreement had developed among the Tennesseans as to where their own dead should lie. Certainly it could not be alongside their enemies. The local Methodist congregation at last offered a shady corner of their graveyard. Driver accepted with thanks.

Meanwhile he set the Tennesseans, the local Guards, and fifty black hands tendered by the county to work half a mile down the beach. At the major's request Ker surveyed the point and staked out a fort near the old lighthouse. The quadrangular redoubt would dominate the Potomac entrance, with clear fields of fire in every direction in case of attack by land. All that day shovels flew and the ramparts rose. Civilians from the Neck came out to watch. Occasionally a well-dressed gentleman would descend from a carriage, take his turn with a few spadefuls of dirt, and retire, dusting gloved hands with a look of well-earned satisfaction.

One plain young woman, taller than Ker, rawboned, freckled like a spring fawn, with large, slightly protuberant blue eyes, attached herself specifically to him. She asked if he'd draw his sword for her, and raised the naked blade to her lips reverently. Gazing soulfully into his eyes, she declared her willingness to do *anything* for one of the brave heroes of the Battle at the Point. He had only to voice his boon, and it would be granted.

Ker wavered, then decided such patriotic fervor could not be denied. He sent her off with a parcel of his laundry.

Suddenly he had nothing much to do. He decided to elevate his foot, which throbbed beneath the bandages with an insistent pain. Seating himself atop the parapet with a field desk borrowed from Captain Charlton, he indited missives to Catherine, to Judge Wythe, and then, to the length of three foolscap pages, an official report of the action. Driver had informed him that his superior, and hence Ker's, was Brigadier General Daniel Ruggles. However, he was still in the Navy, and the action seemed significant enough in its outcome—Confederate forces were now fortifying one of the premier points of the lower Bay—for the attention of Secretary Mallory.

Indeed, it opened strategic possibilities. Ker hoped the landing's repulse would quench any desire Lincoln and Seward had for war. But if hostilities continued, the Confederacy could seize Tangier Island. With a couple of small armed steamers in the Pocomoke and Tangier Sounds, they could hold the whole lower third of the Chesapeake. The next step would be to reduce Fortress Monroe, opposite Norfolk, and clear the approach to Richmond. All these considerations he noted for the lucubrations of the secretary.

At midafternoon the picket reported a warship offshore. Ker examined it minutely through his field glass. It was schooner-rigged, side-wheeled, with gaff topsails. Already stern to when he first viewed it, it dropped slowly below the horizon.

The next day he woke weak and dizzy, with no appetite for the sausage and hoecakes Romulus had ready. He dragged himself out of the tent nonetheless and swallowed some bitter coffee. Made himself more or less presentable, considering his soiled and sweated clothes, and hobbled down to the fort to direct the digging of a bombproof magazine. His men struck water five feet down. Fresh water, welcome for drinking, but not for powder storage. He redesignated it the fort's well.

At lunchtime a boy came running, informing him a Miss Simpson was waiting for him on the coast road. Ker recalled no such person, but limped up at last to find that the woman who'd clung to his arm and assured him of her willingness to serve had returned.

Today he saw that what he'd dismissed as too great a height to be commensurate with womanly attractiveness was a stately carriage, and that her plainness of feature was mitigated by a liveliness of countenance that lent much charm. Dressed in a light summer day-dress, a bonnet cut forward, and a parasol shading her complexion from the burning rays, she bore not only his beautifully starched shirts and smallclothes, but a picnic hamper and the suggestion they address it together on the beach.

At this he felt uneasy. He cleared his throat. —I must forestall any misapprehension, Miss Simpson. I am married, and my heart belongs to my wife.

Freckled cheeks flamed. Her eyes dropped, then rose again, and it was like watching a battery unmask. —You do me an injustice, sir. I have brought you the heartfelt tribute of a Southron patriot to those who bled in defense of our new-minted flag. Is a gross insult to be my recompense?

Ker felt his cheeks burn. She was right; he'd made an assumption he had no right to make. He bowed, and apologized with all the abjectness of which he was capable.

At length she permitted herself to be mollified, and they walked, he limping, past the abatis toward the shoreline some hundred yards distant, this being low tide. When they reached a level patch of sand she bent to spread a checked tablecloth. Then placed both hands flat on the front of her crinoline, collapsed it, and sank gracefully, yielding only the most transient glimpse of a patterned stocking.

Miss Olivia Simpson was not from the Northern Neck, she said, but from Petersburg. She had come to the shore for her health, and resided at a private home with pretensions to a spa. Her father was the Reverend Doctor Theodore Simpson, of the Tabb Street congregation of Presbyterians. Her mother's family were the Brockenboroughs, of Nottoway County. In turn, he acquainted her with some details of his upbringing and relations on the Eastern Shore. The basket held harrico'd mutton, fried potatoes, and a batter-bread he'd not encountered before, which she called apoquiniminc cake. There was also a stone jug of cider, most refreshing in the noon sun. So refreshing, and so sleepy the midday heat, that he soon had to rouse himself from near unconsciousness. Miss Simpson was saying, —You and your men have thrown up this fort so swiftly, the folk hereabout are much astonished.

—An expedient fieldwork, no more. Heavy guns would soon make it untenable. Do you object to the stupefying weed? He held up a segar.

—Not at all. You were saying, about the fort?

Ker popped a lucifer on bone-bleached driftwood and puffed tobacco into a comforting coal. Beyond the earthworks one of the laborers struck up a tune on the banjo. As voices, white and colored, joined in, he pointed at the earthworks. —Major Driver has recommended to Richmond that they forward heavy guns to augment our twelve-pounders. The boat-howitzers are capital for quick maneuver, but not suited for defense against serious attack.

Ker gestured out to sea, and his sight snagged on an irregularity on the horizon. He sat up, shading his eyes, and glanced again toward the fort, to observe the sentry looking in the same direction. Standing, he could bring a bit more of the visitor over the sea-curve. He took out his watch and frowned at it.

—What is it, Lieutenant? Miss Simpson, shading her face with her parasol.

—A ship.

—The enemy, do you think?

—Yes, but don't worry; one gunboat could not disturb us here. She is beating north and south, tacking across the tidal flow. To monitor the approaches to Washington, no doubt, which we will threaten, once our heavy guns are in place.

His face must have betrayed his thoughts. Her glove pressed his arm. —You miss the sea.

—I will admit that to you.

—What then are you doing here? Should not you be employed with our fleet?

—Unfortunately we have none worthy of the name. No ships, and no facilities to build them . . . at least until the Norfolk yard is back in operation. I see now that Captain Trezevant was right.

—And who was he?

—My former commanding officer, at the time of Sumter. He sounded me out then as to whether, if the country was divided, the fleet ought not to be divided as well. Had not the Southern states purchased the half of them? Many of our officers came south. But not one brought his ship with him. Nor did I, when I commanded *Owanee*. It seemed to me dishonorable. Akin to theft. But I see now prescient he was.

Miss Simpson drew a fan from the hamper and snapped it open. —What are you saying? That you should have taken the boat?

—I could have arranged its capture. He looked moodily toward the distant speck, now receding again, as it had come, over the great blue bowl of the bay. The sun flashed off the water. When he looked back it was gleaming off a red-golden sheen of fine small hairs he had not before noted on the nape of Miss Simpson's neck. It traced barely visible silhouettes beneath the thin cotton sundress.

He averted his eyes as soon as he noticed himself staring, disturbed and wondering at his own response. There were paths down which he must not wander. But a few moments of polite conversation, a civilized meal . . . Surely there was nothing wrong in this. It was a welcome change from the rough men's company of the last few days.

But with this thought came a swimming dizziness whose meaning he knew only too well. It was not the applejack, nor the heat, though his blues were sodden with perspiration—one did not unbutton one's collar in the presence of a lady. Then suddenly he was not warm at all, but cold to the roots of his hair. His scalp felt as if it were being bathed in ice water. His legs began to shake.

—I must beg your indulgence. Can you . . . can you help me up?

Her eyes widened. —Is it your wound?

—I fear I am subject to an old fever. It recurs when I overstrain myself. Which I am very much afraid I . . . have been doing for the last few days.

He leaned on her as they made their way back up toward the fort. But with each step the weakness gained on him. Before he reached the rampart, the blackness fell, like a curtain, ending the play.

PART II

C.S.S. Montgomery,
June 21–September 9, 1861.

7

KER'S fever was gone, but his foot was still swollen. Limping onto the platform, jostled by the other passengers at the station buffet, had been so painful he'd had to support himself on Romulus's shoulder. The steamy hell of a Louisiana summer didn't help. As he settled back into his seat the pain was like a nail being hammered into his leg. He considered more laudanum, then decided to put it off, what with arrival in New Orleans in prospect at last.

His first attack, after the punitive expedition against the renegade slave trader Abdul bin Abdullah, had put him down for weeks. Like that first time, he seemed again to be tied to some great yardarm, through which he hurtled at terrific velocity first up, then to float suspended. And then plunge downward, through the insufferably hot dark. Over and over he traveled on this same dizzying ride, first up and then down at vertiginous speed. But this time, pummeled down by quinine, the fever abated after six days. It left him faint and nauseated but his head perfectly clear as he lay in freshly laundered sheets, looking out a farmhouse window at chinaberry bushes nodding and swaying outside his bedroom.

In those hours alone he'd revisited the battle. How bravely the Yankees had advanced. How desperately the contest had been fought on both sides. He hoped this was an end to the matter, that whatever aggression the Republicans designed, cooler heads would prevail.

If they did not, the possibilities were too horrible to contemplate.

During his fever-attack, Miss Simpson had wanted to nurse him in the guest house where she resided. Ker had declined. As a pastor's daughter she might place Christian charity above her reputation, but no gentleman could take such advantage of an admirable weakness. Instead, he sweated and shivered through it with Romulus and Dupin. Since the battle the ape whimpered if Ker so much as left the room for a visit to the necessary. Still, Simpson visited every day, feeding him jellies and reading him newspapers. That was how he got the telegram. Olivia—he'd resigned himself to using her first name after learning she'd sponge-bathed him during his delirium—had brought it, and hovered as he opened it.

Brief to the point of incivility, it directed him to repair to the Navy Department in Richmond to receive his commission as a lieutenant in the Navy of the Confederate States, and to report from there for duty to the war-steamer C.S.S. *Montgomery,* presently lying at the Port of New Orleans.

When the train pulled in, the clatter of rails succeeded at last by a shriek of escaping steam, the New Orleans, Jackson & Great Northern station was thronged with soldiers, ladies, and prosperous-looking civilians. French and Spanish mixed with the drawl of the Bayou. Ker instructed Romulus about their baggage, then limped to the freight agent's to make arrangements to hold the flatcar carrying *Montgomery*'s deck guns, in company of which he'd traveled since Richmond. He bought a *Daily Delta* from a hawker. Stephen Douglas had died in Illinois; Tennessee voters had officially approved that state's secession. There were also many column inches about local privateers, and from the advertisements for shipbuilders, fitters, and riggers, the yards hereabouts were busy with more.

Romulus returned with two middle-aged porters, and not long after they were on their way to the St. Charles Hotel.

His first order of business there was to be barbered, a pleasant interval of lying full length while his beard was trimmed, mustache curled, hair pomaded, coat and hat brushed, nails scraped, boots blacked, and cheeks dashed with Pinaud's—in short, completely renovated after the dust and sweat of the cars, and all for fifteen cents in spondulicks. He bought clean collars and new kid gloves. At the dining table, a gentleman who said he was "in hemp" informed him *Montgomery* was lying at Algiers, across the river. Ker went to bed at seven, and was at the ferry house at dawn.

He'd last seen the most prosperous city in the Southland in the summer of '58. Then the nine miles of Mississippi levee had been a solid park of shipping—no surprise in a port that vaunted itself as the terminus of thirty-three steamship lines and the transshipment point for the unimaginable sum of five hundred million dollars of trade. He'd listened to deepsea chanteys as anchors hove around and topsails sheeted home with a rattle and bang, as cotton-droughers cast off for the Balize and Massachusetts and Manchester. Cotton was New Orleans's white gold, and the great wagons and their teams of panting animals stood waiting for the lading, and loose cotton blew about the quays like snow, and wary cunning pigs and coarse-haired goats rooted in the gutters for spilled sugar, and the sky was black with coal-smoke and wood-smoke from steam presses. The smells of green leather, whiskey, French perfume, pig shit, and slave sweat mingled with the swampy stench of the river, and the riverfront saloons and bagnios had resounded with a hectic music and the laughter of men and women intoxicated with the day, unconcerned with yesterday, and thoughtless of the morrow.

Now the levee lay empty, and the streets vacant as if the dread Yellow Jack had returned. Only the broad brown passage of the river, serene in the sun, was the same, and the only sound of life the thud of drums from the direction of the Metairie Racecourse; infantry-drill, he guessed.

They pulled round the bend into sight of a steamer, a shear-barge moored alongside. Smoke and the clatter of caulking tools came from the shore. As they made up on her, the ferry needing only an occasional thrash of her stern wheels as the river moved them steadily on, Ker threw an eye along her black-painted length.

Could this be the cruiser? She was a side-wheeler, and no larger than the gunboats that had shelled Smith Point. Three-masted, and rigged as a topsail schooner—that is, schooner-rigged except for yards on the foremast. Her masts were raked, which he liked. The yards would lift as they swung outboard, making her less liable to trip in a sudden blow. A pennant signaled that her captain was aboard. He made out only one gun, at the bow. Of course, her principal armament lay back at the siding. The Stars and Bars flew at her stern. A wisp of brown drifted from a guyed smoke-pipe, then a heavier puff that whirled slowly over the placid river. As they neared he saw axes swinging in the cabin structure. Splintered paneling littered the river. Barge laborers were at work on the shears, which were swinging yellow-hewn beams inboard.

The ferry made for the unengaged side, and he stepped onto a crowded and busy deck. Save for the quarterdeck, every square inch of dirty pine was covered with iron plates, rails, spar bodies, dunnage, boat-falls, girt-lines, lightning conductors, and slush buckets. Shark-mouthed wind-sails fed air down the hatchways. He stepped over a euphroe and lifted his cap to a smooth-faced youngster natty in a white linen coat and wide-brimmed straw hat. He looked comfortable indeed to a man sweating in blue wool. —Permission to come aboard.

—Permission granted. The boy settled his cap carefully back on golden curls. —Midshipman Gustavius Dulcett at your service, sir.

—What class, Mr. Dulcett?

—I was an oldster, sir; would have been Class of '62, but I left the Academy when Mississippi seceded. I am from Hattiesburg. And you, sir?

—Lieutenant Ker Claiborne, with orders. Enter me in the log, if you please. My servant will wait with my trunk. May I send my card to Captain Trezevant?

—That will not be necessary, sir. He left word to show you in. Mr. Harrison! Take the lieutenant to the captain's cabin, if you please.

Picking his way aft, keeping an eye out for hazards aloft as well, Ker was greeted by several men he knew. He returned their salutes with gravity, knowing that to acknowledge them too warmly might give way to suspicions of favoritism later. Or, equally damaging, to resentment, if he had to send them to mast.

Harrison, another midshipman, told him the ship had been in hand for a month, but little had been done till the captain's arrival two weeks

before. She'd been built for the Gulf trade, and had been running between New Orleans, Mobile, Pensacola, and Havana till the state of
Louisiana purchased her the day war broke out. Her name had been
Icarus, after that Greek lad who had flown too near the sun. Disliking
that cognomen, Captain Trezevant had at first intended to name her
Calhoun, in honor of the great defender of Southern rights. Finding that
name taken for a privateer, his second choice had been *Montgomery,* after
the then-capital of the Confederacy. Though the seat of government had
shortly thereafter moved to Richmond, C.S.S. *Montgomery* she had remained.

—Mind your head on the after-companionway. In fact all her decks
are pretty squinchem.

—So I see. Ker took off his hat. A few paces aft Harrison tapped at a
louvered door, then opened it. Ker ducked in and came to attention.

Captain Parker Bucyrus Trezevant had not changed greatly in the
months since they'd parted. Long and spider-armed, he could be said to
outwardly resemble the new president of the United States. The resem-
blance ended there; he was a slaveholder without apology. His skin was
darkened by thirty summers at sea. His hair, dark and shaggy, sprang up in
back despite the liberal application of hairdressing. Ker had sailed with him
on the antislavery patrol, and what he knew of courage and seamanship
had come from watching Trezevant. As he entered the captain was leaning
his chin on a fist, listening somberly to an officer seated across from him.
As Ker reported himself the captain rose, hand extended. —Claiborne,
Claiborne, welcome.

—Happy to serve under you once more, sir.

—My boy, it is my pleasure as well. But what sort of 'longshore-
toggery is this? And you are limping?

—A close shave from a Yankee minié, sir; fortunately not serious. As
to my clothing, I'm afraid I have outrun my trunk.

—Well, well, you are welcome nonetheless. Doubly so, since I see you
are no longer accompanied.

—Accompanied, sir?

—By that damned ape you used to keep. Got rid of him, did you? The
beast was nothing but trouble.

Ker coughed into a fist. —Actually, sir, Dupin is still with me. I tried to leave him at home, but my wife would not have it. He is on deck with my man.

Trezevant looked taken aback, then cleared his throat. —And as well; the scamp's gambols will be capital amusement for the lads. Let me introduce Mr. Aeneas MacDonnell, who up to now has acted as my First.

The other had risen too, and stood regarding Ker. MacDonnell was tall and broad-chested, with a black bushy beard, heavy eyebrows, and small, constantly blinking eyes of a sparkling blue. Ker bowed. —Mr. MacDonnell; I am pleased to make your acquaintance.

—How d'ye do, sir.

—English, sir?

—No sir.

—Bob-Stay, as he is known among us, is a native of the Antipodes. From Sydney. Finding himself resident in New Orleans with the coming of war, he entertained a desire to strike a blow for liberty. Trezevant paused. —You do not shake hands?

Ker extended his at once. MacDonnell grasped it, but there was no friendliness in his eyes, and the clasp was dropped at once. Trezevant let it pass without comment. —Ah, he said, turning in his chair. —Here are our refreshments.

Ker turned his head too. And the same chill rode up his spine as ever when he encountered that strange being with whom Parker Trezevant roamed the world.

Ahasuerus was a Kroo, that tribe who by common consent were never made slaves; they were too useful as canoemen and guards for the slavers' shore-factories. His elongated skull was ebony, prickled with a ghost of silver hairs. A purple line split his face from brow to nose. A triangular mark, an arrowhead, or perhaps the fin of a shark, was tattooed on either temple. He wore green baize slippers and a rusty, out-at-elbows coat. The old African smiled slowly, demonstrating yellow teeth that had been filed short, long, short. The filed ones had turned black with rot. He did not speak, for he had no tongue. His own tribe had done that to him. They'd blinded one eye too.

—Wine, Trezevant told him. The African bobbed his head and shuffled into a recess, returning with a decanter and three glasses on a tin tray. Ker lifted his solemnly as Trezevant said, —To our enterprise.

It proved to be a palatable madeira, but the captain did not allow them to linger over it. Before many minutes Trezevant was unfolding a plan of the ship. —She gives promise of a sea-boat, but considerable alteration is necessary. I am making improvements to her sail-plan and quickwork topside, as you can see.

—What of her engines, sir?

—There you have fingered our weakest spot. I will leave it to Mr. Kinkaid to acquaint you with the details. Trezevant gestured to MacDonnell. —Bob-Stay has made himself useful in revising our belowdeck spaces.

The lieutenant said unwillingly, —She were set up for passengers. We left the officers' quarters in place aft and torn out all the other cabins down to the framing. We're laying pine and fardage for coal-bunkers, and extending crew's berthing aft twenty feet. That give us thirty more hammocks.

—Where are you placing the magazine and shell room?

—Here, protected by the coal-bunkers.

Ker nodded, seeing the Australian had redrawn the limited hull space into something approximating the requirements of a warship. But the man obviously resented Ker's coming, supplanting him as second in command and senior among the ship's lieutenants.

Trezevant interrupted. —I was told you'd bring the bulk of our battery.

—Yes sir, I left four thirty-two-pounders until called for in town. I should not trust them there long. Some gentlemen were casting covetous eyes at them when I left.

—Privateers, no doubt. They've fitted out several craft from this port; *Calhoun, Ivy, Music, Webb.* They have done well for themselves, though now the U.S. Navy has shown up on the Passes I misdoubt they'll have such success in future. I had intended to install Mr. MacDonnell as my gunnery officer. If you will inform him where you left the guns?

Ker handed over the freight agent's receipt. Trezevant then wished MacDonnell good day. The lieutenant took a moment to grasp he was being dismissed, then stood. His black brows signaled his anger, but he simply said, —Aye aye, sir. I'll take it in hand. A perfunctory bow in Claiborne's direction, and the door closed behind him.

Trezevant eyed the decanter, than poured another half-glass each. He tilted his head as heavy footsteps passed overhead. A gimbaled sea-lamp danced, sifting a fine dust. Ker recognized his expression; a weighty topic, and one not entirely to his liking, was about to be breached. Before that, he would temporize, putting the moment off at some pretext. True to form, the next words out of the captain's mouth were, —Will you join me in a segar? I find the shops hereabouts still well supplied with the Havana product, despite what the Ape-Man is pleased to call a blockade.

—I would be happy to, sir.

When they had clipped and lit, Trezevant leaned back. He said, —I am pleased to see you made the right choice at last. But damn me, you took your own good time. Is it true, you accepted *Owanee* from Welles and Paulding?

—Sir, I did.

—I have heard tales about your leaving her. I will not disguise from you, sir, they do not reflect to your credit.

Ker felt himself flushing. How much longer would this canard dog him? He said angrily, —May I enquire as to particulars?

—They allege that you attempted to give up your ship, through taking her under the batteries at Fort Norfolk; then abandoned her in a row-boat. Also, that you have never officially resigned from the United States Navy. I understand circumstances have changed many of our understandings about duty. And that I myself once asked you, if we ought not to include as our divorce settlement, as it were, some part of the fleet. Yet still . . .

Ker had to compose himself before explaining, as dispassionately as he could. —In the first place, sir, she was clear of any batteries, shoals, hostile forces, or dangers to navigation. I understand she came under attack from a fire ship after I debarked, but I had no foreknowledge of such in the vicinity. By then I had turned over command to Mr. Duycker, with instructions to see her safe under the guns of Fortress Monroe.

—Nick being up to that responsibility, I should think.

—My judgment as well, though I thought him tyrannical to his juniors; but we have all known sea-officers of that ilk. At any rate, I turned over command to him, with a formal letter, with particular instructions to forward it to Mr. Welles in Washington.

—That was your resignation?

—Yes sir; along with a personal note thanking him for his trust and explaining why I found it impossible to continue to deserve it.

—And why was that, Claiborne? When we parted you were still inclining to the Unionist persuasion. In fact I recall your words. Trezevant closed weary-looking lids. —You thanked me for the compliment of asking you to join me, but stated you could not accompany me South. Pray tell, what altered that resolution?

Ker could no longer meet his captain's eyes. His gaze sought the porthole, through which the shoreline smoked. —I am hard put to answer.

Trezevant urged the decanter forward. —Do me the favor of attempting it.

—I am a Virginian.

—That I knew. But pray go on.

Ker took another breath, trying to frame the conundrum. —I loved the old flag. My tenderest sentiments were wrapped up in its folds. And I was disabused of any predilection toward Hamitic Slavery on the Coromandel Coast.

—Your family owns servants, do they not?

—We do, though our circumstances are reduced. Yet I cannot reconcile the institution to the teachings of our Savior. Would we submit to the loss of our freedom, to become chattels of another? Plainly not. Are we not, then, trespassing against others, in depriving them of it?

Trezevant said quietly, —I am not in the presence of an abolitionist, am I?

—Sir, I do not flatter myself to have any ready answer for a question that has vexed cleverer men than I for generations. But I am attempting, sir, to disburden myself of my deepest sentiments.

The man opposite inclined his head. —Then please proceed.

Ker eyed the porthole again. —When I reported to Washington, I encountered suspicion from Hiram Paulding, yet acceptance from Secretary Welles. Rather to my surprise, he confirmed me in command. But during the burning of the Norfolk yard I was approached by a party of local residents. They pointed out to me the folly of destroying the yard, and necessarily much of the town. It is difficult to say why, but I realized that night I could not make war on my home, my state, my family . . . I had thought myself a citizen of the United States. I found that I was not that, or not entirely. Not to the point of turning my hand against the land of my birth.

—Yet some of ours have chosen that course.

—You refer to Captain Farragut?

—And General Winfield Scott.

—I respect both, but I cannot join them. The Confederacy may be misguided in defending the peculiar institution. But as Stephen Decatur said on a different occasion, right or wrong, it is my country. When war became a reality, there was only one side on which I could in conscience range myself.

—I read the newspaper account of your fight at Smith Point. I will not disguise from you that until that time, I would not have been easy in my mind in relying on you. Trezevant eyed him through the segar haze. —Yet after reading those accounts, I requested that you be sent to me, if available. I can see we differ on certain points. I myself regard the institution of servitude as divinely ordained. No European can pick cotton, or hoe tobacco, with the sun pouring his rays down at a temperature above a hundred and twenty degrees. The Negro not only can do so but is happy with the bargain; his food and drink provided for, no necessity for strife or worry; all is furnished for him by a kind master. It is the only possible relation of white and black. But I believe you and I can work in harness again.

—That is my most earnest wish, Captain.

Trezevant shifted in his chair, a signal, Ker knew, that one subject was exhausted, he was ready for the next. —It is unfortunate a sectional party has determined to rivet chains upon the larger portion of the land. But the cloven foot has been shown in the matter. It is a conflict between the Puritan and the Cavalier.

—I have not heard it represented as such, sir.

—Unto, unto, sir; it is as plain as the nose upon your face. The original Puritan fled to the rock-ribbed shores of New England that he might, as he averred, gain religious and civil freedom. But when another man lays claim to the same right, he visits on him persecution, imprisonment, the charge of heresy.

Trezevant's eye rested upon him no longer; he was declaiming. —Now that gloomy Puritan has seized the reins of government, and determines to bring us to task for our alleged sins. He will reform everyone but himself! No, no, we have always been two different countries, sir; and I do not admit any moral inferiority to these hypocritical preachers whatsoever. We have elevated the black man from ignorance and superstition to the discipline of agriculture and the light of Christian teaching. When the Garrisons and Stowes have filled the mouths of their own paupers, I will hear their reproaches anent slavery.

Ker ventured, —Well, sir, the die has been cast.

—As far as war? I believe their threats are empty. Your purebred Yankee is a merchant, not a warrior. They may enlist ignorant foreigners, and bribe city scum to fill their ranks, but I do not believe the better part of the people will follow them into a design of conquest. If they do, we shall see such carnage as the world has not heretofore witnessed.

Ker nodded, rather to acknowledge the vehemence with which his senior had held forth than in agreement. He'd heard such speeches in Richmond, and found them less entertaining since witnessing the effect of canister at close range. He tried to steer Trezevant into a more clearly marked channel. —Can you enlighten me as to our command here in New Orleans, sir?

—The army forces, militia in training at Camp Adams and the forts downriver, are under Major General Twiggs. I have called on him in the city. Our naval commander is Captain Rousseau. Whom I believe you know.

—I called on him when he was in Richmond, sir. Before the engagement at Smith. And what is the status of the blockade? I read in the newspapers it had been declared as of the twenty-fifth of May.

—That is correct. A paper blockade, though, has no force in international law.

—Are you saying there's no one out there, sir?

—Not exactly. But so far we know of only two ships. U.S.S. *Brooklyn,* twenty-two guns, under Commander Poor, was cruising off Pass à l'Outre at last report. Lieutenant David Porter, in *Powhatan,* has arrived from Mobile and is warning neutral vessels off the Southwest Pass.

Ker recalled from his midshipman days the distinctive conformation of the exiting Mississippi into the Gulf. The fanlike spread of the Delta, built up of mud and silt brought down over the six thousand years since Creation, divided at Head of the Passes into four more or less navigable outlets to the sea. The Southwest Pass, the South Pass, and Pass à l'Outre, which itself separated into a northern and southern egress and passage. Beyond that he was not clear as to which were navigable and to what depth, where the lights and pilot vessels were situated, the locations of the bars, the state of tide and currents, and the hundred other details he'd need to know as the first lieutenant. Details that might make the difference between a successful sortie and ignominious capture by one of the Union blockaders, either of whom would overwhelm the weight of metal *Montgomery* could bring to bear.

They were interrupted by a tap at the door. It was Midshipman Harrison, begging the captain's pardon, and informing him the officers were gathered in the wardroom.

—Give them my compliments, and ask them to delay the seating for ten minutes.

Harrison vanished, and the commander took a turn round the cabin, trailing smoke. —I will not disguise from you, this cruise will carry certain risks. Item, President Lincoln has issued a proclamation declaring any Confederate molestation of a Federal vessel on the high seas, piracy. If we attack their commerce, they will treat us as enemies of mankind. I need hardly remind you of the deserts appertaining to same.

Ker nodded. The penalty for piracy was the same the world over: a drumhead trial and a swift hanging.

Trezevant placed his fingertips together. —I do not declare myself fit to predict if such penalties will actually be applied. One would anticipate them to be levied rather against privateers than commissioned cruisers of war. Nonetheless, the threat has been uttered. Even with the additional bunker space MacDonnell has cleared, we will have short legs under steam. There are also questions of our legal status so far as the countries of Spanish America and Brazil are concerned, in consequence of treaties signed by the United States with those governments.

—Do those treaties bind the Confederacy?

—That is the point at issue. The proclamations of neutrality by France and Britain are particularly troubling. They purport to be fair-handed, but if we cannot send prizes into their ports, as their proclamations declare, what are we to do with them? It is still possible we may be able to deal with Spain and Holland. At any rate, first we will have to slip by Poor and Porter. That may or may not be difficult, depending on the results of our speed trials the day after tomorrow.

—What is *Montgomery* represented to make, sir?

—Estimates differ. The seller mentioned twelve knots under full steam; Mr. Kinkaid, our engineer, estimates her at nearer eight. If it is the latter, we will not cut a noble figure at sea.

—How are we fixed for crew?

—We are two-thirds manned at the moment. When I arrived the docks of Pontchartrain were full of discharged seamen, the result of the drying-up of trade. I wanted to recruit then, but the Department would not approve shipping a complement so far in advance of sailing. Since then the privateers have absorbed the greater portion and the army the rest. We are competing for what remains with Captain Semmes, who is outfitting *Sumter,* and with Captain Huger, who is preparing *McRae.* We shall require forty more hands to touch the pen before we sail. Engaging them will be your responsibility, of course.

Ker took out a memorandum-book and began taking notes as Trezevant went on about their preparations for sea. The captain passed from head to head without hesitation. Ker knew that after this he'd be expected to have every bit of the information at his fingertips, and to proceed with energy all along the line. This was the domain of the exec, man of many cares and concerns, from feeding the crew to acting as the captain's second during battle. He felt the familiar carapace of official worry sealing down on him, like the shells of a slowly closing oyster.

—Will you favor me with a discussion of our cruising-plan, sir? I don't need our exact itinerary, but it would be useful to know if we will be in cold or tropic regions, how long we will be at sea, and so forth.

—I will trust you to the extent of my own knowledge; you must keep the confidence.

—Yes, sir.

—I plan to sortie from Head of the Passes at the earliest possible date, before our friends are reinforced by other blockaders. I will cruise from the Gulf into the islands. From there we may range to Martinique, crossing the track of the enemy's East India ships bound for New York and

Boston. From there, Africa, perhaps, or Brazil. You may lay your plans for an outing of a year's duration.

The creak of hinges, and Ahasuerus looked in. Trezevant rose, putting his segar aside. —Will you join me.

The wardroom lay down a passageway, a paneled room lit by sconces on the bulkheads and a glassed skylight, propped open for ventilation. Through it sunlight illuminated those who stood waiting. Ker nodded to MacDonnell, and gave his hand as the others were introduced. A Mr. Kinkaid, whom he recalled Trezevant mentioning as engineer. Mr. Gibson, the paymaster. Harrison and Dulcett, the midshipmen. Mr. White, the ship's sailing-master. A white-mustachioed officer of marines named Earl Wescoat.

—And you will recall Doctor Steele, the captain said. —To complete the ruination of our constitutions on this insalubrious coast.

Ker bowed to the heavyset, rubicund-faced old gentleman. —Dr. Steele. I'm glad to see Maryland has sent us her delegation, sir.

—I am pleased to sail with you again, Lieutenant. It will be a remarkable voyage for us all, of that I am sure.

The captain pulled out his chair, waving to his right for Ker. The others took places in descending order, the midshipmen at the far end, where they began scuffling and talking in low voices. Ahasuerus entered, bearing a tureen steaming with the aroma of fish. Ker shook out his napkin, looking about at the worn planks, the mustached, sunburnt faces, feeling the warm breeze wafting down the skylight. Conscious of a sudden sense of challenge, of danger, but also of being, in a strange sense, exactly where he had always belonged.

8

THE next few days vanished in the myriad details of readying a ship for sea. But unlike his previous such experiences, this time they were not lying alongside a navy yard, with pursers and storekeepers dispensing government issue from well-stocked warehouses. Here, each shoulder-block or hogshead of salt beef required cunning, bargaining, and at times near-theft. It didn't help that two other cruisers were readying themselves for the same mission, and all raced against the steadily falling Mississippi. More than once Ker found himself forestalled by his counterpart aboard *Sumter*. And then one day he called at a shop on Moreau Street to see about water-tanks.

When he was shown in the proprietor was going over a set of plans with a gentleman in civilian clothing. Ker's eye sharpened on the latter, an aging but still dandyish fellow whose graceful fingers endlessly drew out a mustache and goatee of Napoleonic proportions. As their eyes met the man paused in his speech, rose as elegantly as at a dancing academy, and swept off his hat in a bow that crossed the boundary from elegance into affectation. —Lieutenant Ker Claiborne, I presume.

—And I believe you are Captain Raphael Semmes, sir, whose acquaintance I have long hoped to make.

They shook hands with a combination of affability and wariness. The proprietor, a little Irishman, looked nervous, glancing around as if calculating the damage to his office from an altercation. And indeed it appeared *Sumter*'s captain had been trying to persuade or bully the tradesman into completing his tankage rather than *Montgomery*'s. Reading his man, however, Ker decided to take the high road. He politely proposed the coppersmith hire additional workers and speed his delivery of both orders, dividing the limited supply of metal sheeting. Semmes made as if to protest, then gave a Gallic shrug and smiled disarmingly. The business settled, Semmes invited him to step around the corner. Ker consulted his watch—the steamer's launch was laying by for his return—and assented, but with the caution he could spare only a few moments.

—You quite disarmed me, Mr. Claiborne. Semmes inspected a faultlessly polished boot toe, preened his mustache, and took a sip of whiskey. Suddenly Ker understood where his Service nickname, "Old Beeswax," had come from.

—I, sir?

—I am fond of an argument, should the opportunity present itself; yet you proposed compromise with such calm goodwill I could not but agree. A most unfair tactic. Are you a student of Lavater, of Spurzheim?

—I fear I am but vaguely acquainted with the science of physiognomy.

—I recommend it; what one discovers only gradually in the acquaintance one may discern instantly from the length of a cranium, the molding of a brow. Our Celtic coppersmith, for example, will do us both in.

—You predict this from . . .

—The shape of the jaw, sir; it shines forth, he is not to be trusted save to line his own pockets. The goateed commander smiled tightly over his whiskey. —Although it's true they're all playing us off one against the other. Cy Trezevant, myself, and McRae. They know we are all determined to get to sea as soon as possible, and they're making us bid against each other for the service. What are you paying for a hundred pound of biscuit?

—Rather over six dollars.

—It was three-sixty last time I bought it in Philadelphia, but they are holding me up here for six dollars and fifty cents. Giving as their reason that you have put in an order for seven tons.

Ker nodded, unsure where one of the highest-ranking officers in the new Confederacy was going in the discussion. Semmes went on, —And why are we permitting these gouging prices, not just in our provisions but in every bolt and bucket of caulk? Headquarters should be buying in bulk and hammering down the price. Instead we spend our days chasing about the waterfront and spend twice as much of the government's money.

—I see no alternative, sir. We are not a permanently based squadron. Once we cast off, most likely it is the last we shall all of us see of New Orleans.

Semmes arched his eyebrows with surprise. —You expect capture?

—I did not mean that, sir, no. I simply meant our paths will lead us to far seas, far ports. I doubt we shall return to the levees, unless of course it proves impossible to sortie.

—What do you draw?

Ker debated a moment, then told him, though in an undertone: ten feet. None of the others at the dirty bar seemed to be listening, but he'd heard enough important information bantered about over a glass that he was wary of adding to it. A good many of New Orleans's inhabitants had been born at the North.

Semmes mused, —You can sortie through either the Southwest or Pass à L'Outre, then. As can we; but we had best none of us tarry. Without the usual traffic, the lack of dredging-effect of the screw- and paddle-wash will allow the mud to build up.

Ker was loath to leave; he had heard much of this flamboyant and fiery officer. He would have liked to hear Semmes's account of the sinking of the *Somers* off Mexico, but he had much yet to do that afternoon. Begging the captain's pardon, he drained the heel-tap and rose. —With the best wishes for your cruise, sir. I hope we will meet again.

Semmes raised his glass and smiled sweetly. —Your servant, sir, and good hunting.

The weather continued fine, warmer days punctuated by the drift of a rainsquall, turning the river a stony black under swiftly passing clouds. Ker completed his quarter, watch, and fire bills; caught up on the rest of his correspondence, such as witnessing allotments for such men who were married or wished to contribute to the support of their parents; and began sequestering himself with Gibson, going over provisions, slop-clothing, and small-stores. He also made a point of inviting himself one day to the engine spaces belowdecks.

Frank Kinkaid, a laconic, fortyish Pennsylvanian from York, had married a Georgia girl and had five boys at home in Port Columbus. He introduced Ker to his oilers, stokers, and second and third engineers, and at last sat him down in the cramped iron maze of the boiler room. Over the clang and scrape of chisels he told Ker the weak points of their mechanical arrangements.

Icarus had been built with English side-lever engines and Scottish boilers. Except for a buildup of scale on the boiler tubes, caused by insufficient blowing, the engines, condensers, and boilers were in reasonable steaming shape, though the engineer suspected their coal consumption in service would be higher than the seller had represented. He went into detail on salometers, water- and steam room, rod-bracing, and return-flues, from which Ker gathered that the boilers were stoutly constructed and the safety valves in operating condition. The weak point of the arrangement, Kinkaid said, was the paddle wheels.

—I had understood wheels to be satisfactory means of propulsion, Mr. Kinkaid.

—The fashion nowadays favors the screw propeller for a ship of war. One shot through a wheel and we can only steam in a circle.

—I see your point.

Kinkaid had worse news, however. At some point during her service, the shaft to the starboard wheel had fractured, either by a flaw in the original forging or a blow such as from a tug or barge running into her. It had been repaired, not by replacing the shaft, but by bolting a heavy iron sleeve over the weakened section. His men could strengthen the repair, but it could never be fully remedied short of laying the ship up and replacing the shaft itself. Till then, each revolution of the paddles brought them closer to failure, and Kinkaid could not predict when it would come. He himself would not have recommended the purchase of a ship with such a defect, but since the deed was done, he would do his utmost to keep the plant running as long as possible.

—Does Captain Trezevant know this?

—I've told him about it. Yes.

—His response?

—I'm to tell him if I note a worsening of the fracture or any working loose of the sleeving-bolts.

Ker thanked him, looked in on progress in the coal-bunkers, and then went topside, shaken and disturbed at the knowledge of such an Achilles' heel.

He'd delegated interviews of prospective crew to the boatswain, a former high-seas sailor and sometime riverboatman named Boileaux, a Cajun of small stature and enormous facility of swearing in English, Cajun French, and Choctaw, but he made it a practice of being present when new men signed articles. Ker's own visit to the naval rendezvous ashore had yielded little more than a string of excuses from the recruiter. The boatyards hired anyone with nautical experience. Most fit men were going into the army. And so forth.

So when the ferry eased alongside, sending a creamy wave rocking across the muddy stream, he was gratified to see five hands file up the boarding-ladder. When Midshipman Dulcett passed the word "boatswain to the quarterdeck," Ker strolled closer.

Only one was in seaman's toggery, white duck trowsers capping heavy brogans, a striped shirt, a straw hat. The others were dressed like laborers in denim trowsers, except for the last, a slight, pale fellow in a slouch hat with a leather band. He wore a tolerably good sack suit, and stood apart from the others, hands locked behind him.

—Clear the quarterdeck, Mr. Dulcett. Move them aft to the taffrail.

—Aye aye, sir. Come on, move your bones aft. Bo's'n! Some *gentlemen* to see you.

The boatswain greeted them warmly, shaking hands, welcoming them in Cajun and English and what Claiborne suspected to be Erse. The Jack Tar said he was from Cornwall, had served in the British navy aboard *Growler*. Boileaux clapped him on the shoulder and was easy and intimate; a pose, Ker knew, that Jack would see the obverse of the first time he fell afoul of Boileaux on deck. Another claimed service as head stoker on a riverboat. Boileaux sent a boy for Mr. Woodson, the assistant engineer. Ker was about to turn away when the boatswain suddenly caught at the pale-faced fellow's hand, turning it palm upward with such force he grimaced in pain.

—This hand, she seen no sailor work. Nor stooking neither.

—I had hoped there might be some other position available.

The voice was strained, as if the speaker had the croup. Something about it seemed familiar. Ker peered again at the man's face. Round and soft, with a blondish mustache and rumpled hair falling to his collar.

—Sorry, this here's a warship, *ami*. Got us enough officers already.

—I write a fair hand and am good at sums.

—We don't want no fucking ledger clerks. Need gunners, deckhands, and topmen. Just turn yourself around and—

Ker drifted closer. —Bo's'n? I could not help overhearing. You might ask Mr. Gibson if he has need of a purser's mate.

The fellow was staring openly at him, lips parted. Again Ker had the feeling he'd served with him before. —Your name, son?

—Simon, sir. Oliver Simon.

His eyes were so very large, and so very blue. But the name rang no bell. —Very good, Simon. I promise nothing, but we'll see if there's a place for you. He turned to the others, who stood shuffling their feet at the sudden confrontation by an officer. —Welcome aboard the Confederate war-steamer *Montgomery*, lads, from the decks of which we intend to strike for the Southland and defend our rights as free men. I am Lieutenant Claiborne, the first lieutenant. If the bo's'n and your petty officers pass you, we will have articles for you to sign this afternoon. A bonus of fifty dollars and, as you know, a share in all prizes taken and all Yankee warships destroyed. If you know of others in want of a place, we have a few spaces on the muster that remain to be filled. Have you any questions?

They had none, and as Gibson and Woodson were waiting, Ker stepped away, back to supervising the swaying aboard of a thirty-two-pounder onto an improvised carriage.

As she grew familiar, Ker realized the former packet was even less well fitted for her new role than he'd thought. Her small size and limited space belowdecks was only part of the problem. Her decks were quite weak.

MacDonnell had determined on reinforcing them with nine-inch timbers, but Ker was not convinced this would suffice to support the twenty-eight thousand pounds of carriages, gun tubes, and crews of four loaded thirty-two-pounders, to say nothing of bearing the recoil as they were fired. Workmen were already at work sawing away bulwarks and piercing her for the guns. Ker was even more disturbed when he estimated how the added topside weight would affect stability. In fact, he was so alarmed he sought an immediate audience with Trezevant.

He found the commander studying a letter. He turned it facedown as Ker tapped on the open door, and asked rather curtly whether the gig would be ready for his call on Commodore Rousseau that evening. Ker said it would be, its crew was just then returned from boat-drill in the river, but that he had come on a different matter.

—Speak out, sir; what can I do for you.

Ker began explaining his doubts about the guns' weight, but was dismissed with the statement the captain felt the margin of safety was adequate.

—Sir, I must say I don't agree. It's not the weight alone, but its effect on stability.

—Unto, unto, sir; this vessel has more than enough beam for a few thirty-two-pounders.

—It is not a matter of beam, but of their height. She will be dangerously crank, especially under sail.

Trezevant eyed him suspiciously, and Ker recalled the older man, trained purely at sea, had not had the benefit of a mathematical education. He said as deferentially as he could, —I will submit my calculations for your review, sir. But in my estimation, it would not be safe to put to sea with so much topside weight. At first all might seem well, but as we consume stores and water, at some point we will pass the margins of safety.

—What would you have us do, First?

—Sir, I recommend leaving one gun behind.

Trezevant did not look pleased. He lay down his pen and leaned back. —Indeed.

When he added nothing more Ker continued. —That would leave us with the pivot forward, a twenty-four-pounder stern-chaser aft, and two thirty-two-pounders in the waist. If our mission is commerce-raiding, that should be adequate to overawe any merchant.

—What are the dimensions of our forward hatchway?

—Twelve feet by twenty, sir.

—And the length of the gun tube on our thirty-twos?

—A trifle over nine feet, sir. Ker saw where his mind was tending.

—But in the event of an emergency, setting up the necessary purchases to strike the guns below would take a good deal of time.

Trezevant nodded, but said, —I have never heard of a side-wheeler capsizing, except under conditions where she would have sunk in any case. We will retain all four thirty-twos.

—I beg your pardon, sir; perhaps I did not make myself as clear as I might have. Should we encounter a beam sea of the right periodicity, there might be very little warning.

Trezevant picked up the letter again, and his brow contracted with annoyance. —Unto, unto; I understood you quite well, and have rendered my decision in the matter. You are dismissed.

Ker hesitated. Then discipline reasserted itself, and he bowed.

Standing in the passageway, he stood for a moment more, struggling with doubt. He raised a hand to knock again, but at last did not. The captain had spoken. Trying to dismiss the matter from his mind, he went forward.

9

TWO weeks later, just before sunrise, Ker leaned against the rail on *Montgomery's* new bridge, a hastily built hurricane deck of pine stanchions and planking that ran athwartships between the wheelhousings. He looked out across the river, gauging the current and the wind.

The latter had been westerly since midnight, but barely a breath; just enough to cool a sweating face. The heat had grown steadily, accompanied by a plaguey of mosquitoes. Not as bad as the Gulf of Guinea, where torrents of hot rain grew mold on boots and scupper-leathers overnight. But hot enough that loading ammunition at the naval arsenal had caused men to fall out in a faint; hot enough he'd not been able to sleep, even shrouded by a mosquito bar, and had to swallow a second cup of coffee before he felt alert enough to appear on deck. Where he'd been since the midwatch, supervising the preparations for dropping down the river.

A slim shadow, saluting, a confident young voice. —Sir, four minutes till sunrise. The music is up. Dawn gun standing by.

—Very well, Mr. Harrison. He shaded his eyes against the growing light, evaluating how the steamer set against her anchor. The current was a constant three knots near the onshore bend. But the Mississippi's placid surface was hearted with countercurrents and eddies, great circling swirls of fluid so laden with mud it seemed an intermediate element between earth and water. At its bends—such as those they'd have to negotiate before reaching Head of the Passes—the current would set an unwary helmsman crossriver on the banks if he didn't correct for it in advance. This he had gathered from the idled captains ashore. They also said he'd need a pilot for the last leg out to sea. But the last few ships downriver had had trouble with pilots, in some cases, leading to stranding for weeks.

Well, they'd just have to see.

A rounded sliver of sun gleamed sluggishly out from downriver, as if dragging itself into the sky by its nails. A moment later a drum rattled, and the boatswain's pipe sounded "hammocks up."

Some half-hour later Trezevant climbed the bridge-ladder. Behind him tagged the new purser's mate, carrying a portable writing desk. His copperplate Spencerian had proven so fair and his orthography so impeccable Trezevant had begun relying on Simon for his official correspondence. Despite the heat, the young man wore a crisp white shirt and a loose bow tie. A pen was stuck behind his ear. Ker raised his cap as the captain cast a gloomy look around. —Good morning, sir.

—Are we prepared to get under way?

—We are secured for sea, sir. Chafing-mats rigged, booms and boats secured, gratings and tarpaulins ready to put over. Mr. Kinkaid reports twenty-five pounds of steam up and both wheels ready to turn. We are unmoored, and hang by the bower anchor only. Muster is complete, all hands present and accounted for save for Seaman Denson, from the foretop.

—Any idea where he is?

—Two of his messmates reported he appeared to have a drop in his eye last night.

—Intoxicated?

—Yes sir. He expressed reservations about sailing with us. I suspect he slipped overboard and swam ashore.

—Place that in the sailing report, Trezevant said to his writer. Simon unclipped the pen, dipped it into a portable font, and began scratching. —List him as absent without leave.

Ker continued, —All other departments ready to get under way.

—Are the lightning conductors rigged in?

—I will find out, sir. Mr. Harrison, make certain they are.

Trezevant looked searchingly up and down the river. —It does not look as if we shall have to worry about crowding.

—Indeed not, sir.

The captain seemed to be considering the foreyards. Ker had thought them squared, but in full daylight there might be some question as to their absolute perpendicularity. But Trezevant merely cleared his throat. —Put her in the stream, then. We shall pass down the city levee, at a distance of not more than three hundred yards, and fire a parting salute with all yards manned.

—With the yards *manned,* sir?

—Well . . . no. Now that you mention it, perhaps we had best not test this crew aloft just yet. At least hoist the fighting colors, if you please.

Ker murmured his aye aye, used to this offhand passing of responsibility. Trezevant had long ago off Africa delegated to him the routine ship handling, though he would still take personal command in tight situations. He passed the word about the colors to the quartermaster, gauged the wind once more, looked out over the broad tan surface of the river, glittering as cat's-paws reflected the sun rising behind them. Then crossed the bridge to give the starboard bell cord one sharp tug; took a step to port, and rang that wheel slow ahead as well. Leaning over the rail, he called down to an expectant-looking Boileaux, swarthy face turned upward like some maleficient sunflower, —All hands unmoor ship. Bring in the bower, Boats, and cock-bill it ready to run out.

—Bring in the bower to cock-bill, aye sir. Backs to it, boys, and march away. Fiddler, strike up "Challo Brown."

The boatswain roared the first chorus himself, and the men joined in, pulling with a will to the stamp and music, the clank of dropping pawls and the thump and strum of taut-vibrating chain rode as the anchor began walking in.

> *She is a bright mulatter,*
> *Challo, Challo Brown,*
> *She hails from Saccarappa,*
> *Oh Challo, Challo Brown.*

By now the wheels were coming up to speed, taking the strain off the cable. By crossing to the side Ker could just see, through the black-painted sheathing of the wheelhouse, the paddle-buckets plunging slowly one after the other through the surface of the river. The groan and clank of the wheel-shafts and crank-arms mingled with the thud of the engine. Looking up he saw their smoke-plume towering up like a mountain, thinning only a little as it streamed off to the southward.

Toward the hunters, he thought. Still many miles distant, but he could not shake the image of the blockaders as watchdogs, waiting for the badger to venture from his hole.

As Raphael Semmes and *Sumter* had on the thirtieth of June, sending Trezevant into such a rage he'd ordered Ker to cancel the coppersmithing and ship their water in hogsheads. Less convenient, and it would reduce their endurance, but so the captain had ordered and so he had done; quoined bung up and bilge free in the forward hold slept forty heavy butts of cypress-hued liquid from Lake Maurepas, warranted potable for three months, making, with what they held in their original tankage, a total of ten thousand gallons of water.

—Anchor's aweigh. A shout from forward as ring and stock surged out of the stream, running a black pulsing blood of mud and water and hanging grass. The blast of a whistle, and the sudden loft of the Stars and Bars, a glory of hot scarlet and pristine white, the circlet of stars glowing as if minted new that morning.

Ker glanced shoreward to see the Patterson levee slipping ahead, the church steeples and housetops closest to him moving against those farther away. He touched the bell again for half ahead. Eyed the starboard wheelhouse, remembering the weakened shaft; then gave the helmsman south-southwest.

Montgomery's head swung gradually to point toward the idled shipping at the foot of Canal. At Ker's call MacDonnell took his hands out of his pockets. —Mr. MacDonnell? Prepare the stern chaser with a saluting charge, if you please.

—It's already laid.

—Then stand ready, if you please. Ker faced forward again and noted the sprit still swinging, compass-needling past the smokestacks of the cotton press on Perdido and Carondelet.

Trezevant was dictating to Simon. He finished, —That will do, my man; add the usual compliments and let it go. We'll drop our last mail at Fort Jackson. After that we shall be incommunicado until we touch at some neutral port. His pale amanuensis poured sand, then folded paper into a wedge and licked a patent seal. Leaning, he dropped it into the waiting hands of Uncle Ahasuerus. The Negro glanced at Claiborne with his one good eye and turned away, treading heavily toward the bow.

Ker studied the chart again as his ear registered the shout of the leadsman, reporting by the deep six. South of Pontchartrain the Mississippi sprawled eastward in looping bends. They'd be steaming northerly and even at times westward as they made their way south and east. The river was deep, swift, and clear of obstacles between Algiers and Head of the Passes. Once in the Delta, though, the positions and depth of the bars shifted constantly.

He flinched at the report of a gun. A perfect ring of smoke flew lazily out across the river. The crew swung their caps, raising a cheer that bounced back from the levee. The bright petunias of ladies' dresses clustered near the statue of Jackson. Handkerchiefs and parasols waved, and huzzahs came across a quarter-mile of river, over the steady splash and thump as they propelled along. Their path drew out behind them, marked by rocking shoals of foam, and by the widening train of waves that gradually diverged till they were lost in the rosy distance and the shimmering heat. The spires and smokestacks of the city grew gradually smaller. Jackson and Versailles passed and were lost in their turn as the Mississippi commenced its great clockwise wheel.

—Captain's left the deck.

—Very well, Ker murmured. He glanced at the climbing sun, wiped sweat off his brow, and told the boatswain to rig the midships awnings.

They steamed downriver through the forenoon. Ker kept the wheels ticking over just enough to give steerageway when the river tried to broach them beam to. No point burning coal while the Mississippi swept them between two endless lines of deep green that gave way near shore to stands of black oak and cypress, alternating with flat fields of young cotton. This was the richest land in the world, and plantation homes, much grander than those of the Shore or even the James, shone white along the river. Now and then the vista opened at a stretch of marsh, flat expanses of lighter green over which hovered clouds of birds. The sky arched blue as Chinese porcelain, and the sun turned every iron part on which its rays fell cookstove-hot. As dusk drew on Ker sent word down that they were passing Bolivar Point.

Trezevant came on deck, blotting his lips with a napkin. The lowering sun, a handsbreadth above the river, quivered a path of molten bronze as Ker pointed out what he took for Fort Jackson on the starboard bank.

—We'll anchor under their guns, Trezevant said, looking over the chart. —Prepare my gig, if you please, and put the mail into it. I'll call on the commandant. There may be some late information as to the activities of the blockaders.

Next up was the boatswain. —Permission to splice the main brace, Boileaux said, fingering his silver pipe.

—The captain has just instructed me we will anchor under the guns of that fortification you see ahead to starboard. I should anticipate about forty fathoms of chain. Bower anchor only, with the second bower ready to drop at command. The captain to go ashore as soon as we are anchored.

—Aye sir. And the spirit call, sir?

—We'll hold that until after the captain returns.

—Sir, but we should have plenty of time to up spirits before—

—I have already told you we will wait, Boileaux. And another matter. It is unnecessary for you to prolong your pipe-calls to such a length. We are all impressed by your lung power, but you need not imitate a steam calliope.

Boileaux flushed. For a moment Ker thought he'd argue. Instead he touched his cap and left, shouting orders hoarsely.

—The bo's'n did not enjoy your reprimand, Trezevant remarked.

—I have no patience with these prolonged calls. They simply add to the din, and by the time he has finished, one has forgotten what the pipe is about.

—You are right, of course. In fact, there is entirely too much noise and chatter on deck.

Ker's turn to flush; the captain was rebuking him for not maintaining the standard of a well-drilled crew. Trezevant looked toward the fort once more, then said he was going below to see to his dress. Ker bowed, and turned to getting the gig overside and streamed.

They were under way again the next morning under a light rain that drifted down from clouds the color of an old woman's hair. Past the forts the land changed. Cypresses gave way to palmetto scrub, then to marshland, and occasionally past the tidal grasses they glimpsed white sand.

Climbing to the foretop, wrapping an arm around a topmast-shroud, Ker made out the Gulf as a turquoise band beyond the narrow barrier that still confined the swiftly flowing river. The transient darknesses of clouds marbled the rippling almost-sea of the marsh.

On the chart the Mississippi made a topsy-turvy flower, blossoming as river met sea at last. They were in the stalk now, drawn like sap inevitably toward the bloom. The deck was another world far below. Behind him the stern drew a vee across eddying brown, dotting it with the foamy paw prints of the paddleboards. He searched ahead, but could see nothing of the blockaders. And in fact, and this he realized only after he was back on deck again, no sail nor any smoke at all had interrupted the whole curved expanse of sea his glass had traversed.

At noon the river widened ahead, and took on the appearance of a cul-de-sac. A few stunted junipers rose on higher land, spaced about a protected roadstead perhaps three-quarters of a mile wide. At its southern extremity a few board-and-batten houses clustered on the lavender-green of marsh.

This was Head of the Passes, and Pilot Town. Through the glass Ker made out that the houses were built on pilings. Catwalks cantilevered between them, and a haze of cooking fires hovered. *Montgomery*'s wheels, one ahead, one back, beat the muddy water into scud the color of molasses, gyring her in her own length. Ker brought her head to the stream and dropped the bower at short stay. Trezevant ordered the jack hoisted at the fore and told the quartermaster to escort the pilot to the bridge as soon as he arrived. Then he turned to Ker. —Will you join me in my cabin, sir? We have matters to discuss.

———

The captain's cabin on *Montgomery* was little altered, Ker guessed, from when it had been the master's cabin on a packet. He inspected a painting of the steamer in a stiff breeze, all sail set. The sea was clumsily handled, the waves lifeless. But somehow the artist had captured a hurricane sky, and the amber light one encountered only in the eye of the storm.

—A glass with me, First?

—I'll join you, sir.

Trezevant counted out a small key from his watch-pocket. He unlocked a teak cabinet and poured the wine himself. Ker wondered where Ahasuerus was, but didn't ask. Trezevant allowed him a sip, then reached below the table, into a cunningly contrived chart-stowage, and unrolled a hand-drawn sketch-chart.

—As you know, there are six passes leading from here to the sea.

—I had known of three, sir.

—Only two are commonly used, the South West and Pass à l'Outre. That is why our friends have blockaded them.

Trezevant tapped his lips with long fingers, humming to himself. Ker could not make out the tune. Then pointed to the westernmost pass.

—Do you know Lieutenant Porter?

—I know of him, sir.

—Son of the Commodore Porter who won fame in the war of 1812, grandson of the Revolutionary war commander, but for some reason still only a lieutenant though he is nearly fifty years old. And he does not like it. Part mountebank, part resourceful officer. The push and cheek of your pure-blooded Yankee, but withal an accomplished seaman.

—An interesting character?

—Decidedly. But of note to us at present is that he was with the Coastal Survey on the Mississippi. Meaning, he knows the passes much more intimately than Captain Poor.

—Poor is at Pass à l'Outre in *Brooklyn.*

—Correct; and Porter at the Southwest Pass in *Powhatan.*

They had both seen that ship in New York before the commencement of the war, but to refresh their memories the captain fetched down a copy of Stuart's *Naval and Mail Steamers of the United States.* The frigate, a bark-rigged, paddle-wheel steamer, was one of the largest vessels in the Navy, launched in '51 and serving since in the Japan expedition.

—The most interesting statistics are her draft, here given at nineteen feet six inches fully loaded, and her speed, nine knots. That is under steam alone; I have heard she does a knot or two better when carrying sail. She carries three ten-inch shell guns on pivots and six eight-inchers in broadside. At least three times the weight of metal we can match against her, and from more modern guns of higher velocity.

Ker waited. Trezevant said, —So that while she can by no stretch of the imagination get at us here, we can neither expect to outrun her nor stand up to her. Nor can we hope to outwit Porter by slipping through some side channel. I am sure he has a rod in pickle for us, and lookouts posted at all exits within his visual range. The word from the fort's commander is that he has anchored no more than a mile off the outer bar and does not budge from that position. The cat is watching the hole.

—You are making a good argument for Pass à L'Outre, sir.

—Commander Semmes intended to take Pass à L'Outre.

—That may be, sir. But if we should sortie together, should not each ship have a better chance? Against a single pursuer?

A discreet tap at the door. —Enter, Trezevant called.

It was the boyish passed midshipman, Gus Dulcett. —Sir, permission to strike eight bells on time.

—Make it so, make it so. Trezevant waved him out, frowning, and reached for a cheroot. —I do not follow in Semmes's wake, sir. Let us match our wits with Porter. With luck, both of us will escape. Let the Yankee flag officer explain that to his superiors. A lucifer flared and he puffed smoke angrily, still staring at the chart.

Ker said, —This calls for careful consideration.

—Unto, First; exactly what I have been doing for weeks just past. But I must confess the solution has so far evaded me.

Trezevant twisted suddenly in his chair. He peered out the porthole, then looked at the brass-mounted sea-clock above it. —Damn me; where is that pilot? Go on deck, find out what's delaying him.

Checking with Mr. White, who had the deck, Ker found there'd been no answer to their pilot flag. None of the boats among the pilings was stirring, nor had anything been seen from where the pilots habitually moored. No notice at all was being taken of their arrival. He sent one of the ship's boys down to the captain with this. Trezevant was on deck not three minutes later, spiky hair on end with rage.

—I had heard in New Orleans there might be difficulties obtaining a pilot, but had not anticipated this sorry welcome. Trezevant took out his watch and shook it. —Nearly an hour we've lain here.

Ker proposed firing a gun as signal, but the captain shook his head impatiently. —They know we're here. Call away my gig, and arm the crew.

Ker did not like to classify men as to their accents or antecedents. He'd been on the receiving end of that sort of thing. But it was difficult to ignore the hostility that surrounded him as he entered the smoky cabin of the little pilot-schooner that lay bowline to a cypress a mile down the Southwest Pass. And impossible not to link it with the Bostonish accent he heard declaiming loudly as he descended the companionway.

Five men regarded him stonily from around a dining table. Two held segars but most of the smoke came from a dish of punk smoldering on a sideboard. Ker made the eldest a short bow. —I presume I am addressing Captain Forbes.

—Yah sahvant.

The New England accent was identified. Yet Forbes, a weather-beaten fellow in preacher's black, did not rise. The cabin was silent, save for the drone of the mosquito, the creak and sway of cabin joinery as the schooner rocked to the afterwash of the gig's arrival. Ker cleared his throat against the smoke. He'd prefer the attentions of the skeeters rather than breathe this murk.

—I am Lieutenant Ker Claiborne, Confederate States Navy; first lieutenant of the war-steamer C.S.S. *Montgomery,* now lying at Head of the Passes. I have come to request the services of a pilot, none having answered my flag-signal.

Forbes's gaze roved the table. The others sat like waxen mannequins. —I'm afraid none such are on duty just now, young man.

—Then I suggest you rearrange your duty bills to accommodate us.

—There are no writs in law that force a pilot to accommodate pirates.

His tone was contemptuous. Ker's first impulse was to slap the cold face before him. His second, to draw his sword. Instead, he disciplined himself to a calmer response. —You are mistaken in your assumptions, sir. We are neither pirate nor privateer. I stand ready to demonstrate a copy of our commission, if you like. It is your plain duty to provide us a pilot, and I ask you one final time to do so.

One of the younger men, at the far end of the table, seemed to be trying to catch his eye. Ker did not meet it. He waited for Forbes to speak. But when he did, the older man said only, —I have said we have no one available.

Ker put his fingers to his mouth. His ear-splitting whistle nearly deafened him. In a moment armed sailors had spilled into the cabin, ranged themselves along the bulkheads. Wescoat, the marine, presented a drawn saber. —The deck topside is secured, sir.

—Very well, Mr. Wescoat. Ker faced the men at the table again. Not one had moved. Then, with a sudden start, the youngest stood, a mustached, alert-looking fellow with tousled brown hair.

—Sir, I will help you put to sea. Clemens, sir. A Missourian, and not unfriendly to your cause.

—Thank you; it is well to find one virtuous man in Sodom. But I am not here to ask for volunteers. Captain Forbes.

—Sir. The elder pilot had flushed, was looking up at Wescoat. The marine scowled back, fingers caressing his saber.

—You are commissioned pilots, gentlemen. As such, your duty is clear. If you do not feel it incumbent on you to give us the benefit of your professional knowledge, it is evident to me you are not fit for your responsibilities in the state of Louisiana and the sovereign territory of the Confederate States of America. In which case I will arrest you and send you upriver for a hearing which, I have no doubt, will end by the state board of commissioners relieving you of your licenses. Do I make myself clear?

—Perfectly clear, sir. Forbes rose at last. He swallowed, face so red Ker wondered if he was not subject to apoplexy. —I owe you an apology. At any time you wish to proceed to sea, you have only to send for one of us. My word on it.

—That is no longer satisfactory, sir. Your demeanor has convinced me that all of you must accompany me on board *Montgomery*.

The others began to protest, but Ker gestured peremptorily. Glancing at the armed sailors, they began shuffling topside.

He looked after them, consumed by sudden doubt. He might force them to serve. But could they be trusted? The labyrinth of bars and shallows, marsh and shoal through which the Father of Rivers sought the sea was a dangerous place. Aground, *Montgomery* would be a sitting duck for a boat-raid from the more heavily manned blockader. Ambitious, tireless, resourceful, this Porter did not sound like a man to trifle with.

Wescoat, atop the companionway. —Sir? The gig's ready to cast off.

Ker looked around the empty wardroom once more, listened to the whine of a Delta mosquito. Saw it dancing, blundering, toward the chimney of the hanging lamp. Then, with a faint, singing flash, it was gone.

10

THE next day they dropped down to Southwest Pass. The barrier between fresh and salt shrank to a ribbon of marsh, rippling to a northeasterly wind. Herons hesitated along its verge. Gulls wheeled. From the masthead the Gulf looked near enough to touch. Yet its flat greens and murky emeralds told Ker how shallow it was out there.

When Ker descended from aloft Trezevant stood with fingers locked behind him on the starboard bridge. The pilots were gathered on the port side. They stared glumly at the passing shore. They were not manacled, nor otherwise physically restrained. But they were prisoners none the less.

Trezevant had received them coldly, and listened to Forbes's explanation with a forbidding expression. After the pilot-captain's apology had come an awkward pause.

At last *Montgomery*'s captain had observed that although as a gentleman he placed the greatest confidence in the captain's change of front, it was his charge as a commander in time of war to act with prudence. In view of the doubts their conduct raised in his mind, he could not be certain which if any of them he could trust with his ship. Lacking which certainty, he must take them all, and determine from their deportment en route what confidence he could place in their loyalty.

And so he had. They'd been courteously treated, given dinner and wine and the use of those hammocks in crews' berthing nearest the hatchway. But they were still prisoners, and their silence on the bridge-wing reminded Ker of the engraving of Napoleon aboard *Bellerophon*, gazing on the coast of France as he left it behind forever.

In the pensive mood that thought inspired, he dropped down the ladder from the hurricane deck and went forward. He inspected the forward pivot with the gun-captain. He inspected anchors, chain, and pelican-hooks. Then proceeded aft, checking boat-falls, bedding, and running rigging. Observing too the demeanor of the men, the alacrity or lack of it with which they came to attention as he neared. Romulus was scattering grain into the fowl-coop. He snatched off his cap as he saw his master, and waited, eyes on the deck. Ker told him to carry on, and was rewarded with a flash of teeth in the dark face.

The second lieutenant lifted his cap on the afterdeck. The Australian's initial resentment seemed to have dissipated as they worked together; Ker guessed him too expansive of heart to cherish enmity. —Mr. MacDonnell. I assume we're prepared for action?

—I weren't ordered to beat to quarters yet, sir.

—I was referring to your preliminary preparations. It is likely we will be engaged within twenty-four hours. Or less.

—With *Powhatan*, right? Who both outweighs and outranges us. Will the captain fight?

Ker raised his eyebrows. —Why should he not?

—Caught by an enemy of superior force, some would be willing to strike their colors.

—Not Captain Trezevant. We'll swim before he surrenders. Have you seen to the curtains in the magazine?

—Vessel in sight off the bar, floated down from the mast-top. Ker glanced up, had his hands on the ratlings when he recalled his place was not aloft, but at the commander's side.

He reached the bridge again to find Trezevant examining distant topmasts through the deck glass. When he handed it to Ker that was all that was visible: three tiny vertical lines, an indistinguishable pennant, and above them the faintest possible haze.

—*Powhatan?*

—One assumes so. Trezevant rubbed his cheeks and studied the chart. Ker stood back, waiting for orders. He didn't need the chart. He'd memorized its every cove and bearing. But at the mouth, only empty space washed across the paper. And the words: *Consult local knowledge. Variable depths and shoals.* The pilot from Missouri, Clemens, said bars and shoals and even whole sandy islands rose and moved and melted away from year to year and even from season to season when storms pounded in or freshets augmented the outward flow.

Trezevant glanced toward their unwilling guests. Ker read his doubt. Porter knew the Mississippi. He'd sent boats probing up the Pass, had burned the telegraph office. Had he corrupted the pilots? Most were Northerners anyway. The South had neglected her merchant marine. Priding herself on her plantings, she'd left her carrying-trade in the hands of strangers. Now she was paying the price.

—Mr. Forbes? It is time for you to advise me, if you would be so kind.

At Trezevant's address the pilot-captain came alive. Stepping forward, he explained how in the first weeks after Sumter, the rush of shipping to sea had resulted in a fearsome pileup at the Southwest Pass. Dozens of ships had gone aground on the sticky mud of the upper bar, some so close together their rigging had fouled. Since then they'd dug their way clear, or the river had cut them out. Only one remained, a brig from Bremen that had its flying jibboom over the bar while its stern was still stuck fast. The only navigational mark remaining was the lighthouse, far out on the tip of the shoal to the north. It had been extinguished by local Confederates, but Lieutenant-Commanding Porter had placed a new lamp in it for the blockaders to hang on to at night. South of that was nothing but miles of fret and turbulence, ranging at low tide from six-fathom holes to wet mud.

—You mentioned the upper bar. There's another?

—Yes, sir, uppah and lowah. The upper being the limiting draft for the pass, just now; though there are other shoals and snags between the two.

—Is there an anchorage? In case we should be forced to wait?

Forbes said there was a hole above the upper bar with five fathom and hard sand bottom. However, it was open to any storm-wind from due southerly to west by northwest.

Trezevant looked out to where topmasts pricked the sky above the passing marsh like far-off bayonets. —How far from where *Powhatan* is now would this anchorage be?

—Ha'd to tell from this angle, sir, but I believe she's about two miles south of the lighthouse. If you anchor within the upper bah you'll be about three miles from the highest point she can reach, I should judge.

—The effective range of a ten-inch Dahlgren, Mr. Claiborne?

Ker said, —Seventeen hundred and forty yards at five degrees elevation, sir. Somewhat more than that at eighteen degrees.

—But not three miles?

—No sir. We should be safe at that range.

—The depth of this upper bar, Captain Forbes? Which you said was the limiting draft for the pass just now, I believe?

—Yes sir. About fourteen feet at high tide.

Ker knew what Trezevant was thinking: the nineteen feet, six inches full-load draft recorded for *Powhatan*. The Yankee frigate had been off the Pass for some weeks. Her coal-bunkers and provisions would be depleted, but still she could not possibly pass a fourteen-foot bar. If, of course, Forbes was not humbugging them.

—Rocket, two points off the port bow.

All followed the lookout's arm. Far out on the blue a white trail corkscrewed toward zenith, bearing at its apex a point of fire. Which meant not only that Porter was waiting but that he'd stationed a picket, on some shoal or in a ship's boat, to extend his view across the miles-wide pass.

And now he knew *Montgomery* was within.

Trezevant cleared his throat. —Will you guide us to this anchorage, Captain?

—I will be most happy to; asking only that you put a leadsman ahead, to guard against any misapprehensions.

—Lower the cutter, Mr. Claiborne. Leadsman, spare lead, and two riflemen.

Ker passed the word down to one of the boatswain's mates, Boileaux not being in sight at the moment. Trezevant passed several other commands preparatory to close maneuvering. Meanwhile the war-steamer passed slowly out from the last screen of scrub and marsh, and the whole sea-horizon opened before her.

The Mississippi met the Gulf in a scene both beautiful and desolate. From the elevation of the bridge Ker could see for miles. To his right a long shoal of black mud, edged with a cream that might be either shell mounds or sand hills, stretched far out to sea. A distant structure must be the lighthouse Forbes had mentioned. Closer, some half mile to the south-southwest, the remains of a brig, hard aground, masts leaning and yards scandalized.

And stretching out to the limits of sight, the eddy-strewn, coffee-brown waters of the debouching Mississippi. Its shallowness was evident in irregular reefs of snags, toppled and dragged-along trees. Torn from the banks of thousands of miles of the Missouri and Ohio, wheeling slowly downriver for weeks, here they found rest in rotting islands. In most waters, the eye could distinguish deeper from shallower water by subtle clues a seaman learns to read. Wave patterns. Turbulence, where tide-runs churned. The gradual shading from brown to green to the violet all-but-black of deep water. But here all was the same muddy churn. He could make out nothing that resembled a navigable channel. Clouds of birds rose against the amethyst blue and combed cotton of a late June sky.

And lying off to the westward, a solid-looking, flush-decked hull almost without sheer. The curved cutwater of a U.S.-built war-steamer rapiered to a sprit prolonged until it seemed to vanish into the air. Three-masted, but with mizzen smaller than foremast and main, painted white and nearly invisible. A squat stack emitted a faint brown smoke that streamed slowly off over the sea. Her paint scheme masked the large paddlehouses, but Ker could just make them out.

The kiss of the glass to his eye-socket, and she leapt into focus and memory. He'd last seen her in Brooklyn the April previous. Had in fact dined aboard, guest of one of the lieutenants who perhaps watched from those distant decks. A cutter was hoisted to the rail forward of the paddlehouses. A touch of white still farther forward puzzled him, till he realized they were wind-sails rigged at the hawseholes. He made out stowed bedding along the rails and then men. One was lifting a rifle. No, a long glass, the sunlight flashed off the lens. Could they see him as clearly? He had a momentary urge to wave his cap to those who'd been comrades not so long ago.

—*Powhatan,* Trezevant murmured beside him.

—Most definitely, sir. Alert and ready for us. Ker swung the glass around the horizon. He found the source of the rocket, a cutter riding a mile to the south. There seemed considerable activity aboard, and after a moment he saw they were rowing hard, directly out to sea.

—Afraid we'll fire on them, no doubt, the captain mused.

—We could possibly touch them with the chaser, sir.

Trezevant waved his fingers in mild rebuke. —Unto, Mr. Claiborne; that is not how one makes war. Let the poor fellows regain their floating home. It is of more interest to me where we will anchor.

Ker had been eyeing their own cutter, manned and lowered now. Oars flashing in the sun as they emerged from the river, it kept pace with the steamer's progress. The youngest pilot, Clemens, stood in the sternsheets, communicating with Captain Forbes with rapid graceful movements of his arms. Trezevant stood with his own folded over his chest, watching Forbes as he issued rudder-orders and engine-bells in rapid succession. On the passing mudbanks herons cocked crested heads. At one point he threw the engines back. Ker braced himself, awaiting the soft deceleration as she took the ground. But she pivoted in time, Forbes kicking her around with the wheels with surprising skill, and at last pointed to a patch of smooth water two hundred yards ahead. —There is your anchorage, Captain.

—Mr. Claiborne?

—Cables are bent and ranged; both bowers ready to let go, sir.

Trezevant nodded. Ker took that as an order, and ran in to a flying moor. He dropped the port bower first, then ran ahead to twice the cable range. The starboard roared out in a cloud of rust and dust, heart-stoppingly close to the swirls that betrayed another mudshoal beneath the impenetrable surface. Loons laughed in the marsh as Boileaux's men reeved away on the lee-ward cable, then heaved in on the weather side. They clapped on service, then began clearing up the decks. At this Trezevant nodded again and descended the ladder, vanishing below.

When the decks were clear Ker told the quartermaster to hoist the recall signal for the cutter. As it made for their quarter Forbes touched his cap. —I hope that was satisfactory.

—We did not touch, at any rate.

—I will leave Mr. Clemens heah with you, as you seem to trust him more than the rest of us. He'll give you satisfaction the rest of the way to sea. Forbes looked at the cutter. —Then we shall be indebted for the use of your boat back to Pilot Town.

—I'm afraid only the captain can release you, sir.

—Nonsense, my man, we have accomplished our part of the bargain. The Bostonian blustered, but Ker only resocketed the glass. *Powhatan* seemed so close now as to be berthed alongside. Could that be Porter, with the black beard? The side ports had been lowered aft and he could make out the mouths of the guns. A darker plume jetted suddenly from the stack and drifted southward. She was stoking her fires. He bowed to Forbes, lifted a hand to Harrison, on the deck below, and slid down the ladder.

The afternoon wore away in the routine of duty at anchor, varied only by orders from the captain to send down the topmasts. This had just been completed when a squall bore down from Deltaward. Ker ordered the hammock-cloths laid in, but it passed them by, leaving them only a sprinkle of glittering mist, fine silvery particles that fell slowly, bringing a refreshing coolness.

Shortly thereafter a thud and flash resounded from their dark warden. MacDonnell appeared at Ker's side as if by sorcery. They looked over the mudflats at their enemy. A second gun boomed out, the sound expanding in a visible wave over the calm water, through the thick humid air.

—Target practice, the Australian said. —They're at putting the wind up us, the larrikins.

—To intimidate us, you mean? My thought exactly. Mr. Dulcett! Inform the captain *Powhatan* is conducting firing practice.

MacDonnell said, —Two can play at that. Shall I call away the gun crews?

—I think not, Bob-Stay. If I may call you that?

—I don't mind.

—She's better provided with powder than we are. You might exercise the men at drill, though. Ker looked to the sun, which rode lower on the western horizon than he'd expected. —And charge for the night with canister. In case our friends should call upon us after dark.

Dulcett, panting from running up ladders, brushed a lock of flaxen hair self-consciously from his forehead. —Captain's compliments, sir, and he requests the favor of your presence in his cabin along with Mr. White and Mr. MacDonnell.

—Very well, I believe I saw the master going aft a short while ago. Please inform him. Ker looked once more at the frigate that lay like a wall between them and the sea; then went to see what his commander wanted.

Trezevant was in shirtsleeves, and Ker at once knew why. Even with windows swung wide, at anchor the stern-cabin had no advantage of the breeze. It was a sweltering crate, with mosquitoes singing through it like plucked wires. The captain waved toward a box on the sideboard. Ker selected a dark Havana, clipped and lit. What solace there was in tobacco . . . Shortly thereafter the sailing-master arrived, the second officer with him. Trezevant directed them quietly to close the door.

When they were seated the captain drummed his fingers on the table. —Well, gentlemen, we are down to cases. Unless Mr. Porter can be persuaded to step aside, we shall have to go under, over, or through him. I have asked you here to beg counsel as to which. First? What have you concluded?

—Sir, I had about accepted we'll have to fight our way out. The only alternative is to attack *Powhatan* from our own boats, at night, and hope for surprise to carry her deck.

—A bold plan, sir. Especially considering the odds. Is there no alternative?

Ker knew what Trezevant wanted. Merely to glean ideas, and to weave attractive ones into whatever plan he himself had already conceived. —Well, sir, we could try our heels with her, but that arithmetic lies against us. She's faster than us under steam and no slower under sail. We might hope for some failure of attention or seamanship. But given Porter's reputation, such does not seem likely.

—I must agree with you there, Trezevant said quietly. —Unfortunately.

Ker pulled at his cheroot again, then went on. —There remains the choice of returning to Head of the Passes, and reconnoitering down to Pass à L'Outre. We may have more luck on the far side of the Delta.

The captain's expression did not invite further exploration of this approach, and Ker went on. —But if we're committed to the Southwest Pass . . . There remains the possibility of slipping out under cover of night, or of some meteorological event, such as a blinding fog. I understand from Mr. Clemens there are such hereabouts, during the summer. They sometimes follow an evening thunder-squall, and are quite impenetrable. But we might have to lie here for weeks waiting for one. Even if such occurred, it seems unlikely we should succeed in navigating out in night or fog without going aground between the upper and lower bars. Even a pilot needs to see. Once we're fast, Porter can shell us into submission at his leisure.

Ker fell silent. Trezevant rested his head on his fist, lips pursed, eyes distant. For some time the only sound was the shout of commands from above, the deck-shaking rumble as thirty-twos ran out. At last he said, —Well, if we had been a privateer, I admit our shares would be rather at a discount just now. MacDonnell? Have you any ideas as to the means of our escape?

The black-haired giant stirred. —Nawt beyond what Mr. Claiborne were proposing, Cap'n.

—Unto, sir, unto; he has proposed nothing, only glossed the situation. Trezevant eyed the master next. —Mr. White, if you have anything to propose I should be glad to hear it.

—I have received one suggestion of interest, the sailing-master said.

—That is?

—It was voiced by Hercule Boileaux. It seems our bo's'n's occupied himself now and then as a smuggler. He has considerable experience evading sea-guards and the Revenue Service, both here and on the coast of the Havana.

Trezevant asked him to continue; and after hearing several sentences, sent one of the cabin boys in search of the boatswain, to explain himself in person.

Montgomery lay at her mooring all the next day. At dawn the Union warship lowered a cutter, which rowed across the wide mouth of the river and took up station southeast of *Montgomery*'s anchorage. While the cutter and the gig left the latter, and while one explored mudflats and bars and shifting channels between her and the lower bar, the other rowed back up into the marshes that lined the lower pass. And not long after, the pop of a duck gun echoed back over empty miles.

That evening Ker offered the pilots the freedom of the wardroom. The feast began with oysters, pulled fresh that day, and continued with boiled duck with cream onion sauce and Phipps's ham. For side dishes there were curries and potato balls, fried up with egg yolk and bread crumbs, and cabbage with onions. A very good Médoc passed from hand to hand with increasing liberality as the meal progressed. Trezevant made himself agreeable, and served out the henrietta pudding with his own hands.

A discreet knock. —Ah, the captain said, pushing back his chair. —That will be our postprandial entertainment.

Boileaux, in a bright red neckerchief, a battered violin tucked under his arm, entered. The boatswain seemed subdued in the wardroom, but recovered sufficiently to render several Arcadian airs. He had a rough but by no means displeasing voice.

By now some conviviality had developed, even among the New Englanders, assisted by Uncle Ahasuerus's circulation with a box of especially fine Impérials. Captain Trezevant kept urging Dr. Steele to take brandy. The surgeon protested that he seldom indulged, but was at last persuaded to take what he called a "squirrel-load of Hermon's dew." Before long he launched into several tales he'd picked up on a cruise to Turkey in the old *Yorktown*.

Amid laughter the table was cleared and fresh candles lit. There was no piano, so Ker could not play, but he rose, announced his intention, and launched into the melancholy but surpassing sweet air of "Aura Lee," the tune he thought the most beautiful of all he'd ever heard. They gave him the first chorus, then joined in at the second.

> *Aura Lee, Aura Lee, maid of golden hair,*
> *Sunshine came along with thee, And swallows in the air.*

He finished to no more than polite applause, and many a hand raised to dash away a surreptitious tear. Ker feared he'd less entertained than reminded them of those they'd left behind, perhaps forever.

Fortunately the next entertainment was less lugubrious. Accompanied by waxed-paper mirlitons, bones, and Boileaux's violin, the midshipmen made the grand entrance in burnt cork blacking, oversized shoes, and frock coats big as tents. Kinsie carried the tambourine, Harrison a violin made out of cardboard, and the usually elegant Dulcett, as Mr. Bones, a banjo. They seated themselves—Brudder Bones! Brudder Tambo!—cracked timeworn jokes —Yassah, on dat cruise all de food was gone, so we lived on eggs. —On eggs? Where you get de eggs? —Well, de wind rose so high, ebry night de captain, he laid *to*. And at last settled to play. At first there was doubt as to their command of their instruments. But Dulcett strummed with such deadpan earnestness, whilst singing "Hark from the Tomb, that Doleful Sound," that by the time the *Montgomery* Minstrels finished an enthusiastic breakdown and three curtain calls, even Forbes hammered his hands in glee, tears of merriment running down his cheeks.

Ker visited the heads in the paddle-wheel housings. Bats flitted through the rigging as he took a turn around the deck. The crew had the evening's freedom, and shouting and fiddle music spilled over the river as one of the English tars "came the double monkey" with hands behind him and cap tilted back, prancing the hornpipe so rapidly his feet could hardly be glimpsed.

Across the water, *Powhatan's* lights burned brightly, as if to advertise her readiness for battle. The moon was a sliver of horn, just above the sea; by Ker's calculations it would disappear in another hour. He made certain the forward lookout was on the qui vive. Were he Porter, he'd be tempted to try out a boat attack. Received with double-canistered thirty-twos, the carnage would be frightful, but enough men might gain the deck to give them a chance of victory.

Then he remembered what they proposed to do tonight; and shivered in the warm and fecund breeze off the Delta.

When he returned, the light and smoke, the smells of lard oil and brandy struck his senses with redoubled force. Captain Trezevant asked to be excused, and retired. No one else seemed to want to leave, though. The pilots began setting up for old sledge at the side-table. Ker flipped his watch open, then sat in for a few hands.

At two o'clock, White came down with the word all boats were rigged and manned, the anchor was at short stay, *Montgomery* was trimmed down by the bow, and the moon was touching the western waves. Ker rose and nodded to the pilots. —Gentlemen, we enjoyed the chance to show you our hospitality. If you will now repair to the boats, we shall soon, I hope, all be quit of one another.

In his cabin, Romulus had blacked his boots and laid out clean underclothes and a freshly brushed uniform. And along with that, the worn-out shirt his master had requested.

He watched as the boats melted into the darkness. Invisible from *Powhatan* as the moon dipped her horns in the sea, five of them, each with a pilot, an armed petty officer, and a leadsman, were rowing through the mudbanks toward the lower bar. Within the hour each should be at its assigned position.

The last rays of the satellite showed him the sails being cast loose, the deck being cleared for action, galley fires put out, fire hoses rigged. Trezevant had ordered the guns cast loose but not primed, nor were side ports to be dropped. Not a light showed about the deck. Quartermaster Grice stood before the wheel. Ker went to the side, forward of the wheelhouse, balled the shirt, and dropped it into the river. The patch of white was just visible in the near darkness. It hesitated, then drifted sluggishly aft.

Ker placed the breeze on both sides of his cheeks. It had veered southeasterly over the past twenty-four hours. Not a brisk wind, but they could sail with it. He glanced at the masts, their unaccustomed stumpiness, as if lopped short by some giant with a stick. As the topmasts had been struck, there'd be no gaff-topsails, nor any flying jib to set. He had doubts about this, but the captain's instructions had been explicit.

A whiff of stack-gas reached him, curled forward by some trick of the wind. He snagged a passing ship's boy and sent him below for Kinkaid.

A spare, dark figure stood at the rail: Trezevant. Ker identified himself and waited for orders. None came. The captain seemed occupied in looking first toward the waiting frigate, then out toward the bar. Ker ran his eyes above the horizon. He could make out only one spot of darkness,

perhaps one of the pirogues the cutter had brought back from its visit to
Pilot Town the day before.

—Shall we hazard this tombola, Claiborne?

—It is our only recourse, sir.

—I agree, though we may spend some little time on the anxious
bench. The night-glass, if you please.

The moon was now very low, only an upper oval visible above the
waves, like a thumbnail gripping the western horizon. Trezevant studied
their distant watchdog. Ker made out a faint glimmer from the stern
quarter, as if Porter were working late. —I see no evidence of alarm.

—If there is, I fear we can do little about it.

The chief engineer reported in a low voice. Trezevant said, —Do you
understand our tactics tonight, Mr. Kinkaid? We shall not require your
engines, nor most especially any visible evidence of them, except in case of
emergency. At which time we will require full power at once.

—My fires are banked, sir, and precautions taken against flame from
the chimney pipes. We have fresh river water in the boilers and so will not
require to blow off for some time. For immediate power, I have placed
buckets of hot stuff next to the boilers.

—"Hot stuff," Mr. Kinkaid?

—Sulphur, resin, spirits of turpentine, and coal-oil, sir. To make a
sudden and diffusible heat of high caloric value.

Trezevant nodded and dismissed the engineer. He studied the frigate
once again, as Ker rechecked the moon. It trembled on the skyline now,
yellow-red, ringed in the humid air with a subtle light that radiated out
several diameters.

Then slowly trickled out of sight below the horizon. Leaving only the
faintest silver outlining of the sea, the stars, a brilliant Jupiter, and patches
of darkness that were clouds.

—Have you our first mark in sight, Mr. Claiborne?

Ker opened his eyes wide and caught a spark far ahead. Then another
blinked on, much closer. —I believe so, sir.

—The current?

—Near slack low, she may be making slightly.

—You are certain of that, sir?

—The opinion is from observation, sir.

—Jib and main, then, if you please, and board-sheet them both.

Ker passed the order to the sailing-master. He heard the squeal of blocks, a creaking aloft as the gaff-booms took the canvas weight. Trezevant spoke to Grice in a low tone, and the helmsmen hauled the wheel around until it was hard astarboard.

—Jib and main, sir, sheeted hard a-taunto.

—Commence bringing in the anchors, First. Stand by me with your watch, if you please.

Ker had done his share of ship-handling in restricted waters. This, however, would take a high order of skill. The captain was proposing to sail out against the tide, with the wind against him, in a channel too narrow to tack in. Not only that, he was not used to the ship yet, nor did any of them have a clue as to her handling.

—Anchor's aweigh, sir, said Dulcett, in a low voice. Trezevant said very well, and gave his first helm order as the bow fell slowly off to port. He told Ker to commence timing when they passed the first light abeam.

Montgomery began ghosting ahead, her motion unnoticeable as the dark absences of her masts circled among the stars. Watching that first light walk closer, Ker had to admire the concept, soldered together from suggestions from several sources, at which the captain had arrived. There being no marks at night, and no visibility, he'd stationed a pilot in a boat at each turning point. One lay by where the upper bar was deepest, and the next where they'd have to come right to avoid the abandoned Bremener. Six hundred yards later, the pilots had agreed, came a sharp left, taking the ship's head from north by northwest to almost due south. Another four hundred yards, threading between shoal patches, and they'd come right again.

The last turn, the last light, and the last pirogue would be just before the lower bar. By then they'd be fairly sure of passing over safely, as it lay deeper than their draft nearly the whole of its length. But that would also be their closest point of approach to the Federal sloop-of-war; well within sound-range of a human voice, a lifted steam valve, even the scream of a tail-trodden monkey on such a quiet night. Which was why Dupin had been dosed with laudanum and locked in Ker's cabin.

The skiff lights, of course, would be visible not only to *Montgomery* but to *Powhatan*—and that was where Boileaux's smuggling experience had come in. The boatswain said that in his career dark lamps had come in very handy for signaling at night. They could only be seen at certain angles, and although there were only two such lamps aboard, others could be improvised from biscuit tins and isinglass.

This solved the problem of guidance, but did nothing to assure them the guidance was correct. It would be all too easy for one of the pilots, simply by locating himself fifty yards off the channel, to lead them into the same trap the Bremener had fallen into. Where dawn would reveal them helpless within easy throw of Porter's heavy guns.

All this time the guide-spark had been drawing closer. *Montgomery* was walking forward through the darkness, bow canted to port of her direction of travel, it seemed, or perhaps that was only an effect of the night. It was hard to keep his bearings with nothing but the stars, and the faint glimmer of distant candles, strung out in an undulating chain. Ker walked to the starboard side and marked when the first bobbing light passed the wheelhouse. He could of course not make out the hands of his watch, and he did not dare show a light; so he began counting seconds under his breath. —First mark's abeam, sir.

—Very well. Mr. White, take those men aboard, if you please.

The splash of oars; the grunt of a seaman heaving a line. The clatter of hemp on oak, and moments later a darkness under their quarter. Another clatter as of a Jacob's ladder being dropped, and then the scuffle of feet.

For that was the second insight: to trust men one could not be sure of, they had to keep a noose around their necks. Not only did each pilot, at each turn point, have a bayonet behind his back. He also knew that once the Confederate steamer passed, he'd come back aboard. Only when they were sailing free would Trezevant put Forbes and the others off for shore. In case of trickery, Trezevant promised them the one responsible for *Montgomery*'s stranding would wear a hempen necktie to his last dance, this same night, at the end of her yardarm.

Which accounted for the difficulty the men from Pilot Town had had in joining in the gaiety that night.

The second light lay nearly still on the water. From its very lack of motion Ker knew it lay cupped within the point of half-awash land that marked the petering out of the riverbank. The turn would be sharp. He craned forward, anxious to see how Trezevant would negotiate it.

—The count, First?

—Three minutes, sir.

—Cease counting as we come abreast, and pick up when we begin making way aback.

—Aback, sir?

Then he saw, and held his breath in admiration and misgiving.

As they swept past the second pirogue Trezevant began rapping out commands. Wheel hard astarboard. Haul taut on the starboard head-braces. Haul up the spanker, and the jib sheet flat aft. The bow yawed left, sprit moving amid the stars. The lines sailed out, heaved by brawny arms, and the second boat's crew scrambled aboard and cast off the pirogue to bob astern, an inchoate blotch that slowly receded and was lost to view.

—Rudder amidships.

—Amidships, aye.

The wind came now from starboard, from south by southwest; for a moment the ship seemed not to move. Then she did, rocking, gathering way, but going astern now, quiet as a shadow, the only sound the sigh of breeze in the backed and flattened sails.

—Helm alee a trifle . . . steady as she goes. The captain's voice was soft in the darkness. *Montgomery* gathered sternway, passing the black mass of the Bremener, aground and immobile where she'd fall apart and rot. Ker looked to see the light of the third boat, at the point where they must alter course to due south, quickly moving toward them.

—Time, Exec?

—Four minutes and a half, sir.

—You may cease counting, I have her measure now . . . hands to the lee braces and jib sheets, Mr. White . . . leave the spanker sheets as they are. All hands to step lively, or this could be dicey. Ready with the heaving line. Take charge aft, Mr. Claiborne.

Ker ran, threading barely visible gun-carriages, past air-scoops and smoke-pipe, skylight and the boxy darkness of the fowl-coop. Other pounding feet paralleled him down the windward side, the boatswain, with the heaving line. They reached the stern just as the third boat coalesced around the pinpoint of candle flame under their counter. They were bearing down on it swiftly, and though Ker heard the creak of the yards coming round forward, he could see they'd gathered too much sternway. They were going to run the boat down, and there was nothing he could do about it.

But then a fresher breath exhaled from the night, and the hull leaned to it. He felt her fall off, felt her slow. Saw the light quivering just under their stern.

—Heave, for God's sake, he muttered, and heard the rush as the hempen monkey's-fist hurtled over the dark water. The clatter as the line fell over a thwart. Then the boat was alongside, the hands were swarming up the ladder, and *Montgomery* was easing ahead, gathering speed as she pointed up into the wind once more.

Walking forward, he collided with the captain near the mainmast. Trezevant quieted his apology with a barely audible murmur. —Unto, sir; we are nearer her with each fathom to windward. Are we sheeted tight aft and forward? See to it, sir, see to it.

By the time Ker reported back the fourth light was fine on their starboard bow. It was picking up the rise and fall of the Gulf swells. They were nearing the lower bar.

Lifting his eyes, he saw the lights of the Federal sloop off the starboard beam. Shining in the night, shimmering on the undulating water, they seemed the epitome of reflective calm. But he remembered those frowning iron muzzles, couldn't forget the solidity of their discharge. Even at three miles it had felt like a blow to the chest. *Montgomery* had been built as a packet, not a warship. Her light framing and thin sheathing would shiver to heavy shot like a bushel basket caught under a dray. And still, paddle blades removed, she slid with the faintest hiss through the dark water.

A disappearing jingle from aloft. And next to his ear, a murmur that after a moment he identified: Boileaux's. —That's de main a-luffing, sir. Better to ease off.

—Port your helm. Half a point more . . . that will do, hold that.

For with no spark of light from moon or binnacle, the great sails aloft were only shadows, and how could one steer by a shadow? How to gauge how close to the wind an unfamiliar ship could run? The sails' luffing warned of swinging into irons, losing way, falling off onto the mudbanks to leeward. But without vision, how to know?

By Boileaux's "honey-fogle." An old smuggler's trick, he said. With light chain whipstitched to the luffs of main, spanker, and fore staysail, they could hear a sail lose the wind. Ker stood spellbound, contemplating the needle they threaded, the narrow bridge they walked. On one side, shoal. On the other, Federal guns.

A clear note across still water. Four bells . . . Ker's fingers closed around his sword-hilt. In ten minutes they'd be free, or on their way to Hell. All it would take was a lookout to glimpse an eclipsing star, to sense a black absence moving across the night.

—Sheet out, all. Stand by for boat to starboard.

The fourth marker boat clunked into the bow, scraped and then somehow, as the last man levered himself onto the Jacob's ladder, rolled free and drifted aft. Whispered curses and thrusts with boathooks followed it, but it kept drifting back in, thudding and scraping along the blackstrakes. Then it wedged hard into the starboard paddle wheel, beneath the skirting, and began dragging along. Ker leaned out over it, lips drawn back. The rush of water seemed loud as a millrace.

But it was lessening. The yards were creaking around again. The luffing chains jingled uneasily. Judged by *Powhatan*'s lights, perhaps a mile astern now, they'd lost way. The wind whispered messages from the dead. From his parents, perhaps, lost at sea so many years ago.

Main topsail aback, after sails backed, she drifted more and more rapidly astern. Ker watched the last light grow in the dark from a pinpoint, to a star, to a candle flame a rod off. Then the riffle of bare feet, the sigh of indrawn breaths. The creak of sheetblocks as the yards squealed around.

The light aft winked out. The cruiser drifted alone in an inklike blackness. Suspended below the stars, she seemed to move not at all. Only rolled, very slightly, as if swinging from the starry void by the tips of her masts.

Boileaux, staring down toward the still-jammed pirogue, —This *imanukfila iksho* boat! I'll put a man down, kick it free.

—I believe it's moving, Boats. Maybe it'll work adrift now we're making sternway.

—What if we need the wheels?

—Then things will be dark indeed. Give it a few more minutes. Then send your man down, but keep a line on him.

—Mr. Claiborne, Cap'n wants you.

He explained the problem with the skiff to Trezevant. The captain grunted, pointing aft. Ker looked, to see a light rising on the Federal's afterdeck, a bustle along her bulwark.

—He's lowering a boat. We must get clear before it puts out in this direction. Trezevant glanced astern again, muttered a helm order; the steering-ropes creaked. —We have one marker crew remaining. Once they're aboard I shall put directly across the bar, then make all sail.

—Tops as well, sir?

—No; but full sail and stays'ls fore and aft. Ship's boats must come aboard fast and in perfect silence. Do I make myself understood?

Ker said aye aye, and passed the orders. Shortly thereafter Trezevant filled again, and their forward motion resumed, steering due south. With a glance he saw *Powhatan* bow on now, within easy gun-range. A light showed them the picketboat, getting ready to set out for its station.

The leadsman's runner relayed and a quarter, four. Forbes, breathing hard. —You are approaching the lower bar now, Captain.

—Very well.

They stood waiting, floating through the dark.

—By the mark, three. In a whisper, from Harrison. Trezevant acknowledged with an outstretched hand.

Ker stood hardly daring to breathe. Then Forbes turned his head, looking back along their path. Taking his bearings from the stars, or the just-barely-visible outline of the coast against them.

—And a half, three.

—You're over the bar, Captain, and free to proceed.

—Thank you, Captain. Lay your pilots aft. Exec, you may—

Just at that moment, with a faint grinding, *Montgomery* coasted to a halt, leaning forward as she did so. The masts groaned in their sockets. Gear rattled aloft. Boileaux muttered wild curses in Choctaw and Spanish.

—Mr. Forbes? Were we truly past the bar?

—I believed we were, sir. I'm sorry. It must be a snag. A mess of trees, waterlogged and sunken. You have to believe—

—I do, sir, I do; compose yourself, if you please. Trezevant turned, checking the Federal. The light had parted from her waist, was setting out in their direction. —But what are we to do now? Will forward power help?

—The branches interlock; more power will only force the forefoot deeper into the trap. The only way out is to back.

Trezevant rapped out commands, backing the fore topsail, then the after sails. —As soon as sail handling is complete, all hands aft. Mr. Claiborne; ascertain, if you please, whether our port wheel is still fouled.

Ker ran to peer. Returned in a moment to report the fouled boat had either cleared or sunk; it was no longer in sight. The wheels were free to rotate, though of course they were missing three of their eight paddleboards. She might swim, but she'd limp like a crippled duck.

The picketboat was creeping closer, the light bobbing as the crew worked the oars. Ker clenched a fist in the darkness. For a moment he'd thought they'd escaped. Now they were in deadly peril. If *Montgomery* could not free herself, her only choices were to surrender or be blown out of the water.

—All hands aft. Grab a solid shot, bear it aft, bear a hand, all hands aft.

The hands began hurrying past, each bent over a thirty-two-pound sphere of iron. Ker glanced aloft. The sails were backed, pressed against booms and masts by the southerly wind.

Then he felt it. A lurch, a grinding beneath his feet. A sliding bump, and her head began falling off to starboard. Boileaux and the other petty officers cursed the men back to their braces.

She moved ahead again, and this time no obstacle met her keel. After fifteen minutes' run Trezevant came through the wind, and dropped the quarter-boat with the pilots as they ran past the shallow South Pass. They'd have a long row, but the wind was with them and they'd be home within a day. Then the captain went below, and Ker set every scrap of canvas and raced east by south, *Montgomery*'s cutwater roaring as she tore along.

At sunup the sea was empty as it once had been for Noah. Green swells and the soaring balance of gulls the only objects that met the eye. The coast, the Delta, had dropped from sight, leaving only a bank of salmon clouds. When he climbed to the main-truck he made out only the thinnest needle against the sky, the very sky-scraper of the Federal's t'gallant pole. As he watched, it too sank slowly beneath the surging wave.

11

THEY sighted several sail over the next two days. But Trezevant held his course. Ker deduced his wish to put sea miles between himself and a possibly pursuing Porter. Also, some considerable leakage had been reported, especially when on a starboard tack. This had to be caulked, sea-gaskets made up in cheises, buntline-spans rigged, shot-boxes secured, and various other matters put to rights. But on the third morning he was in the cookroom, inspecting the Beebe patent range, when he heard the keen of the pipes, then the rattle of the tattoo.

On deck he found a sun-furnaced morning. Mast-hoops chattered in a fresh easterly. A dash of spray whipped aft as *Montgomery,* both wheels churning slow and plain sail set, ran through seas with hearts green as old bottles. The men were mustering at their stations, bareheaded, barefooted, in a motley of white duck, rusty wool undershirting, and shore-side togs. He ran up the ladder to the bridge, and took a look round. Save for the single sail, they were alone on the wide Gulf. His morning's fix had penciled a cocked-hat one hundred and seventy nautical miles south of Mobile, two hundred and ninety west of the peninsular dangle of Florida. As navigator, he oversaw the efforts of the midshipmen as well. Mr. Dulcett's observations had placed them within half a mile of Ker's; Mr. Harrison's, in the alkali flats to the west of Brownsville, Texas.

Trezevant, pulling himself up with his long arms. The captain was in shirtsleeves, a black silk cravat, a capacious pair of dark blue trowsers, and the blue glasses he affected in tropic seas. One of the Impérials with which he'd regaled the pilots dangled from his jaw. —Well, what have we?

—Sir, I just got here. Mr. MacDonnell must have sent the word down for you.

The Australian swung down from the ratlines and dropped heavily to the deck. Where it was lashed with spray, the holystoned pine had turned a rich deep brown, like oil-rubbed teak. —Good morning, Cap'n. A brig of medium size, runnin' before the wind.

—Flag?

—None I could observe.

—Quartermaster, ready the Union Jack.

Ker turned to see Grice at the mizzen, Confederate ensign tucked under his left arm, Union beneath his right, halyarding the Red Ensign with a dextrous twist. Ker uncapped the speaking-tube and passed the word to Kinkaid to stand by the engines, a chase was in the offing. MacDonnell was trimming to the new course. The crew stood waiting, swaying with the motion of the deck as gradually the speck of white grew into a visible craft.

The glass showed her running free with stuns'ls set on fore courses, yards stacked, and making the best of a fair wind, from the cream at her bow. Trezevant told MacDonnell gruffly to bring her head farther left, the stranger would pass too far off on the present course. This put the cruiser close-hauled as she'd go, the fore-topsails and t'gallants braced sharp, jibs, staysails, and gaff-topsails hauled flat as slates. The two ships neared rapidly, and finally Trezevant nodded to Grice.

Scarlet flashed as the Red Ensign streamed out in the breeze. The other came on. Then, with a tongue-flash of red fire and a cloud of cottony smoke that blew fleeting down the port side, came the flat clap of an unshotted thirty-two-pounder.

The brig seemed to sway, undecided. Then the stu'n'sails clewed up, folding like graceful wings. The t'gallants followed. She began a graceful curve to port as the foresails braced round. Then she was hove to, beam to the easterly seas, fore backed, main drawing, yards topped to parallel some imaginary horizontal that might be the level of a calm sea.

The Stars and Stripes fluttered just visible past the main.

As *Montgomery* filled away to starboard, her own sails brailing up in turn, British colors dropped and the Stars and Bars rose. The circlet of stars, Ker thought, like the old flag of the colonies; with a surge of his heart he saw how much brighter the new cloth shone than the ragged, salt-stained drabs of the Yankee's flag.

—Away the cutter, away.

The men stood to the guns as the cutter crabbed over the dipping sea. It nuzzled under the brig's lee and Dulcett threw a leg over the rail. A few minutes' time, then it pushed off and made its way back toward them.

The brig's captain's pale visage was surrounded by a fringe of stiff-looking white beard. His brown eyes were clasped in sun-wrinkles, his lips clenched. He wore a chimney-pot hat that looked as if it had been sat upon, and a knitted red-yarn polka-jacket under a hot-looking broadcloth coat. Conducted to the bridge through a gantelope of staring seamen, he handed an oilskin packet to Ker, assuming he was the commander. Trezevant slouched by the wheelhouse, observing from behind blue lenses.

Ker conned through the sheaf. The brig was *Ellen Duarte*. Out of Baltimore, owned by Montell and Company. Her captain's name was Limeburner. Her bill of lading was for flour, furniture, tin goods, potted meats, tooth-powder, pomatum, india-rubber rain-capes, medicinal bitters, and coal, all consigned for Vera Cruz.

Ker raised his voice to carry across the deck. —Baltimore, sir. With a cargo from the same port.

—I suppose you'll be taking us as prize, the old man in the polka-jacket said with sudden heat. —Or will ye be a-burning of us?

Trezevant uncoiled and made a bow. —Do not draw it quite so strong, sir. We are not your enemies.

Limeburner seemed confused. —I beg your pardon?

—A state of war does not exist between us and our brothers of Maryland. You may take your leave of us, sir. Unless you care to share our midday repast.

Captain Limeburner seemed overcome. At last he produced a tickler-flask from a pocket and extended it. —Thank ye, thank ye; I cannot stay. But will ye join me in a perpendicular refreshment, gennelmen?

—With all goodwill, the sun is not yet over our particular yardarm.

Trezevant nodded to Ker, who showed the old man the ladder down with a sweep of his arm. Not long afterward the cutter was back aboard, *Ellen Duarte*'s sails were spreading once more, and *Montgomery* too, was turning back to her original course, port wheel ahead, the starboard backing with a kick of bright foam, pulling the bow across the wind.

He went below to find Romulus and Dupin engaged in an attempt at mutual destruction. His cabin was filled with snarls, hair, and bared teeth. Feathers from a split pillow floated like snow. Ker separated them and sent Romulus aft with the slop pail. Dupin clawed onto his shoulder, explaining how shamefully he'd been treated. Ker smoothed his fur, and gave him a few walnuts. The ape set to cracking them, making the humming sound that meant he was happy.

They raised another sail during luncheon, but so far upwind the captain declined to pursue. Ker took a noon sight with Mr. Harrison, and reduced his observations with Norie's *Epitome*, trying to find his error. This time all came out right, though, and he sent the midshipman to report the noon position to Trezevant. He then made the rounds below- and abovedecks. The men had by now reaccustomed themselves to sea, though three green hands still lay face to the scuppers. The sailmaker, Jacobs, had the starboard watch busy making sword-mats and furling-cloths. The ship drove forward through the green-blue seas, driven by taut canvas and the steady revolution of the wheels. Ker stood forward of the port wheel, frowning at it. An indifferent sailer at best, the drag of the wheels made her even worse. Even under sail, Kinkaid had to burn coal to keep those great fabrications revolving.

Boileaux, pulling his forelock. —Mr. Claiborne. A word, sir.

—Yes, Boats.

—Sir, some of de men were wonderin' why we let de Yankee ship go dis morning.

Ker explained that Maryland was of the South in spirit, that only Federal occupation had prevented her from coming out of the Union with her sisters. Congress at Richmond had declined to make war upon her.

The Louisianan considered this. —Some of the men was saying dere was money changed hands.

—Foredeck chatter. I've served with Captain Trezevant for years. Have never known a man of more integrity.

—It's good to hear dat, sir. Some of de men, dey was wonderin' about de prize-money.

Ker understood suddenly. —Well, Boats, prize-money's not paid out on the barrelhead the day of the capture. There has to be a valuation, and a prize-court. They'll have to be patient. We've only been out three days, after all.

—Dat's what I tell them, me. But some of they, they right hot for dere shares.

Ker told him it was his job to moderate their enthusiasm, but to bring unrest or disaffection to his notice; or if he preferred, he could pass such warning on via the sailing-master. Boileaux squinted at that, but Ker had to admit he looked so much like the perfect melodrama villain his looks should not perhaps be held against him.

They saw nothing more the rest of the day, which he felt two ways about. They were here to take Northern trade, true. But each sail brought with it too the heart-fluttering mistrust it might be Porter, pursuing them, or Poor, or some other Yankee cruiser. Ker took the deck from White for the first dogwatch. The wind had backed to the northeast trade that pre-vailed here during the early summer, and fallen to a light air that necessi-tated carrying all sail. Yet still they encountered no one. After his watch he smoked a segar at the stern, looking pensively into a smooth, faintly braided wake, bounded by broader tracks of more disturbed water.

No trace of land remained; hundreds of miles of brine heaved between him and home. He wondered what Catherine was doing now. At one of her church meetings, perhaps, St. Cecelia's Guild or the Orientalist Mis-sion. He closed his eyes, remembering how his son's hair smelled of violet-water; how, when he'd left Norfolk, the boy had followed him to the door, crying and clinging to his sleeve. When would he see home again? Treze-vant had spoken of the South Atlantic . . . but had *Montgomery* the legs for it?

Four bells sounded, and the pipe called all hands to evening meal. He rubbed his face and pitched the half-smoked segar into the wake. The bobbing twist of tobacco receded gradually into the distance, invisibility, the gathering dusk.

The next morning they stopped a barkentine flying the flag of the king of the Belgians. Her papers attested her the *Elfrieda,* out of Antwerp, and as a neutral vessel carrying on a lawful trade Trezevant bade her captain good day with urbanity. Ker noticed the cruiser's crew gathering beneath the bridge, looking up as the two conversed. They drifted away when he stared at them.

As soon as the cutter shoved off, Ker sent a boy to carry his respects to Mr. Wescoat, and an invitation to join him by the pivot-gun.

The marine had been in the old service, but not as an officer. He'd served in the ranks in the early fifties, and fought in Panama and Nicaragua under Addison Garland and Commander Hollins of the *Cyane.* Mustered out, he'd gone back to Alabama and become a Methodist minister in Marengo County before volunteering at the outbreak of war. He supervised the crew's repel-boarders drill, bayonets and cutlasses on the main deck, but otherwise had so little to do he'd started a Bible class that met after the mess cloths had been rolled. He appeared now in the white cotton trowsers and gray coat of the CSMC, and Ker strolled him around the capstan as he discussed the attitudes he'd observed among the crew.

—Threats, sir? Or just grumbling?

—Neither, really. I just want to be forehanded. We have quite an olla podrida of a crew, after all.

Wescoat stroked a great white mustache, sad blue eyes concerned. — They do seem a medley, sir, but the boys in my Bible study are fine young men. They admit to toils with drink and the fair sex, but there are aspirations to Salvation.

—Very well, then; let us leave it at that. You will exercise at boarding-drill again tomorrow?

—Yes sir, if you wish.

Wescoat started away; then turned back, and asked if he'd like to join in their perusal of Scripture that evening. Ker said he'd like nothing better, but shipboard duties would most likely supervene.

—Sail ho-o-o, floated down from the masthead. —Two points forward of the starb-o-o-a-rd beam. Ker examined the far-off sail, white as a chip missing from the blue porcelain of sea. He made sure the captain was notified, then went below to add to his sea-letter. When he next came back on deck, some half-hour later, it was only slightly larger.

Luncheon. Ahasuerus and Romulus, who'd started hanging around the wardroom pantry, served game pie made with hung Delta duck, cherry tart, and rolls from the morning's baking. It was hot and men ate as quickly as possible, sweat beading on their foreheads, and pushed back their plates and left. Ker took Dupin on deck for an hour's play in the rigging. The ape went up the mizzen-shroud like a surf-rocket, and swung from the gaffpeak-halyard by his tail. He gamboled along the mizzen-braces, and dropped black curling turds from the main t'gallant yard to the quarterdeck. Fortunately Trezevant was not on deck, and Willie, one of the ship's boys, cleared the mess and then followed the little beast about with a broom and a frown.

The sail to starboard gradually became a bark-rigged clipper, with every line taut, all yards set and every sail, white almost as chalk, drawing. The men gathered atop the paddlehouses, watching it silently. Watching the flicker of the Stars and Stripes at her mizzen-halyards. A green house-flag streamed in the rigging too.

—Boston, White said with satisfaction, slotting the glass closed with a clap. —Henry Hallet and Company's flag. Boston built as well, and I'm not mistaken.

—Have you sent word down?

—The captain knows. You will note we're flying British colors.

A hiss, a rush of steam, a shower of soot drifting to windward. *Montgomery's* machinery thumped and clanked as it started up.

The closer they drew, the more graceful the clipper became. Her masts towered, as long as her hull. Her yards were varnished glossy and her masts sparkling white. A royal-boy looked down from needlelike spars scraping the sky. For a moment Ker wished she'd put her helm over, spurn away over the waves. So heavily sparred a craft, a sailor's wind like this, she'd quickly outstep the clumsy cruiser . . . he said harshly to MacDonnell, who'd been looking up expectantly, —Shell, ahead of her bow, should she not heave to instanter. I should say a three-second fuze.

Trezevant, formal today in a brown coat, tilted his boater against the wind and examined their quarry. Ker gave him the master's opinion and he nodded shortly, as if thinking of something else. —Let the men take their stations, he said.

A moment later he told Ker to speak her. Dulcett handed over the speaking-trumpet, and he stepped to the side and shouted across the water, —What ship?

—*Fair Seas,* of Boston. And you?

But the gunports were already dropping, the Stars and Bars breaking. Ker shouted across the water, —We are the Confederate cruiser C.S.S. *Montgomery.* You will oblige me by heaving to, and standing by for my boat.

They were close enough for Ker to catch the consternation on their faces, their astonishment at the suddenly revealed muzzles; their instinctive searching around the horizon for help. And finally, submission to the inevitable. Five minutes later *Montgomery* was clewed up and hove to, the clipper likewise, and Ker was in the quarter-boat with Midshipman Harrison, the boat crew bending and straightening as they rowed across the heaving green.

A dozen men and boys stood about the clipper's deck. As the boarding crew took their positions along the rail, carbines pointed, the captain strode forward. He was youngish and tough-looking, a head taller than Ker, with flinty-looking eyes boring out from beneath the bill of a blue workman's cap. —What the hell's this? What flag is that you fly?

—The banner of the Confederate States of America, sir.

—What goddamned humbug is this? There's no such country.

—There is now. The Southern states have seceded under the threat of coercion by the new U.S. president, Abraham Lincoln.

—This can't be. I'd have heard of it.

—Nevertheless, it is true, sir.

—It's true we've been holed up in Central America for a while, the fellow said slowly. —But why stop us? We take no part in any warlike trade.

—That will be for me to determine, sir. Your register, log, and bills of lading, if you please.

The captain's name was George Francis Caldwell, and White had been correct about the shipowner. The cargo was muscovado sugar, billet tin, and baled coca leaves, consigned to firms trading from New York City.

Ker folded the papers into his breast. —Your ship is a prize of war, Captain. You and your men have ten minutes to gather your personal effects. Then lower your boats for our cruiser.

Caldwell blustered, —I'll be damned if I will. "Confederacy" . . . there's no such animal. It's piracy, by God, and you'll be guest of honor at a hanging bee.

Ker tried to keep his expression matter-of-fact, though there was some humor in the man's bewilderment at being confronted by a war he knew nothing about. Yet there was nothing funny about losing one's ship. For a moment the Yankee seemed ready to step forward swinging. Then, glancing at the carbines, he seemed to buckle. —What are you going to do with her? he said hoarsely, glancing up at her mainmast.

—My commander will decide that question.

—And my men?

—Treated in accordance with the laws of war and of the sea. And now, sir, you have only eight minutes.

Caldwell swung away, slamming his fist down on the companionway hatch. —Get your duffels, he snarled. Presently the first boat hit the water, loaded with hastily packed seabags and sea chests, and stroked raggedly toward the cruiser.

—Another sail, sir, said the coxswain. Ker wheeled, catching it to the northward. Schooner-rigged, heading west or southwest. Caught too was the motion of *Montgomery*'s driving-wheels as she started ahead, puffing out great clouds of black smoke into the stainless sky. The clipper's boats trailing on painters, bobbing at her stern.

—It seems we must fend for ourselves for a time, he told his men. —Perhaps we'd better see what's in the cookhouse.

After cheese and bread, he took the clipper in hand. By the time the cruiser returned, hours later, he had royals doused, stunsl's taken in, and was heading northward after her. Even under plain sail, the *Fair Seas* swept through the waves with a glee that set the heart singing, and with a reassuring stiffness after *Montgomery*'s top-heavy roll. As they neared, he saw Trezevant had made another capture. A brig in the good old mold, bluff-bowed, so heavily laden her gunwales barely showed above the passing seas. Ker left the coxswain and two able seamen aboard, and shoved off to return.

On the cruiser's bridge, Trezevant informed him he'd examined *Fair Seas*'s papers and approved her seizure. The brig was *Planet*, out of Philadelphia with a hold of Pittsburgh iron: rails, spikes, fishing plates, even an engine knocked down into crates; all the necessaries to lay a narrow-gauge railway in the Costa Rican jungle. Ker nodded, looking down at a sullen knot of seamen hugging their knees by the stack, guarded by two *Montgomery*s with bayoneted muskets. Midshipman Harrison stood by, cradling the speaking-trumpet. The captain said, —I have decided to sink one, and send the other in as a prize of war.

—Aye, sir. Which to be sunk?

—I will sink *Planet* and put *Fair Seas* into Mobile.

Ker wondered how he'd made the distinction, but had no intent of questioning Trezevant, who hesitated, fingering his blue lenses.

—We can't send them both in? said the master.

—I would destroy both, Mr. White, save for the latter's cargo.

Ker asked him, —The sugar, sir? Or the coca?

The captain frowned, waved as if shooing an errant fly. —I speak of tin, sir; tin; imperative for the fabrication of percussion caps. Consult Dr. Steele for the chemistry. Also, as she is the swifter, she may stand a better chance of outrunning any blockaders and gaining port. Whom would you recommend to a prize-command, sir?

—I should recommend Passed Midshipman Harrison.

—His navigation is trustworthy?

—It should do, sir, provided he remembers to check his figures.

Trezevant raised his voice. —Mr. Harrison, take command of the clipper. Make for Mobile, or such other friendly port as you may think attainable, and report to naval authorities as to the disposition of your prize. Should you be intercepted by a federal steamer, set fire to her and take to your boats. Select ten men for your crew; you'll depart within the hour.

Harrison lifted his cap, glee dawning, and to Ker Trezevant said, —Beat to quarters for firing-practice. Load with solid shot, Mr. Claiborne, and bid the men do their duty.

From a hundred yards the thirty-two-pounders battered in the old brig's hull timbers. She sank with astonishing rapidity, dragged under by the mass of iron as if, Ker thought, by the underwater spirit that had accompanied the Ancient Mariner from the polar regions. *Montgomery*'s crew watched in ominous silence. The little ship dipped her head wearily, submitting to the sea she'd fought for so many years. Like an old mule sent to the knacker . . . Ker had seen ships burn, but he'd never seen one sink before. He imagined her settling through the fathoms with sails set . . . her former crew did not observe her end, having been sent below under guard.

Shortly after, Harrison and his prize-crew left for the *Fair Seas*. With a slow unfolding of her wings she heeled onto a starboard tack. Her sails spread one after the other, till she was a dwindling pyramid of white canvas. Then *Montgomery* was alone again.

12

Continuation of a Sea-Letter from Lieutenant Ker Custis Claiborne to
Catherine Wythe Claiborne

Aboard C.S.S. *Montgomery,*
August 3, 1861.

Dear Catherine,

Having a moment to spare I will take up the pen to continue
this missive, which may be lengthier than I had hoped, but which
on the other hand it may be possible to post in Havana, or The
Havannah, as Mr. White is pleased to style the principal city of *la
Fidelisma Isla*. Though Captain Trezevant has as yet given no order,
we may put in there for coal & provisions, & to gain some idea of
the effects of our depredations so far. Which have been considerable, amounting thus far to fourteen sail boarded & six taken, of
which one was sent into Mobile as a prize, one sunk by gunfire, &
the other four disposed of by burning at sea.

I am at liberty to write for a few minutes—it is just past five-
thirty of a Sunday morning—as it was so foggy that when I went
upon the deck just now hoping for sights I could not see our mast-
top, let alone Deneb & Altair. But from my reckoning we lie upon
this calm sea some sixty miles northwest of Havana & about the
same west and south of Key West, the which is still held by Federal

troops at last report. After dismissing the midshipmen, I stood for some time on the hurricane deck, smoking & listening to the dew pattering down from the sails. The fog moved silently past, suggesting strange shapes, some in the shape of ships, others disquieting wraiths.

We are dining well enough, in fact I might say we are dining high as Haman's gallows. I feel akin to a highwayman or brigand when I sit down to the comestibles of which we have availed ourselves from our captures. No salt junk & hardtack cruize this. We feast on the dainties of New York & Europe, sluiced down with an excellent Médoc; we took six cases off *Chryseid* before setting the torch to her. The relish though is somewhat taken off it by the gloomy faces of those captains whose ships we have destroyed. We offer them the freedom of the wardroom, but some prefer rather to mess with their men.

In fact the only thing lacking to our entire comfort is news of our loved ones at home. Not having received mail after the letter that reached me at Algiers, I can only wish for the details of your own <u>health</u> and Robert's, the which you know I always worry about during the unhealthy days of Summer. I most deeply hope all is well & that the progress of your pregnancy, if I may speak so, excepts you from the sickness which accompanied your confinement with Robert.

Although our cruize thus far has been a decided success, certain wraiths pursue in our wake as well. We are running short of coal already, not good news as we are not much more than a week out of New Orleans. We made the attempt to transfer fuel from one of our prizes before burning her, but the seas made it impossible. We must keep some sort of steam up at all times. Captain Trezevant is wary of the steam sloop-of-war U.S.S. *Wyandotte*, & also the steam-screw U.S.S. *Potomac*, both of which are rumored to be in these seas to catch just such "pirates" as we. Yet we hope such assignments only the first of many, thus diverting the Fed.l navy from the business of blockading our ports, and allowing us to draw the free breath of intercourse with Europe that may end in recognition & aid.

Reminding me, that one item in the captured newspapers we read with such avidity was passed from hand to hand & read aloud—that is, a report of our own activities under the heading "Fresh Piracies reported in Gulf of Mexican waters." The paper reported the horrors attendant on our captures of *Fair Seas, Planet, Rochefort* (originally French-built), & *Chryseid.* We had placed their crews in the latter vessel as a cartel, & apparently they making the coast of Cuba at once disburdened themselves of the most astonishing fabrications as to their abuse at our hands. Astonishing, as they seemed honest seamen, but most likely blame is due to the "journalist" who interviewed them on their return to Yankee Civilization.

It was from papers out of Rhode Island that we read of the engagement on July 21 and 22 at Manassas, which the Northern papers call Bull Run. I particularly noted that the units with which I was privileged to serve along the Rappahannock had been engaged, & of the bravery & coolness of our troops when it seemed McDowell might encircle our left flank. And of the resolution displayed by our fellow Virginian, Thomas Jonathan Jackson. And pleased to understand that the Federal retreat was accompanied by such scenes of panic and disorder as may make the invaders think long over any plan to "Anaconda" our territory again. Yet I cannot help regretting the brave men fallen on both sides, & wondering what friends found themselves in the "seat of danger." Please send my love to Aunt Sue & see which regiment Jamie is enlisted in, I should like to be able to follow any actions in which his regiment figures.

Events in Missouri & Western Virginia are somewhat worrying. I do not doubt we will win through and establish our independence. But it does seem to me that if the North should succeed in subjugating the Southland, it would be the fatal blow to liberty everywhere. Not only would we lose our freedom. The North would lose it too, in access of insolent pride & hunger for empire. Yet if we can maintain ourselves in the field, we may preserve, not only our own liberty but that of Humanity as well.

To which the convinced Abolitionist would respond: and what

of the African and *his* freedom? To which I answer: And how, sir, shall you eradicate slavery, when you can only liberate one man at the price of enslaving another?

I hold no brief for the "peculiar institution." I believe it a curse laid on us & its crueler manifestations a present from the Enemy of Mankind. Yet let us modify our own institutions in our own time, with due regard both to the owner who depends on black labor for his family's survival, & for the gradual enlightenment of those who would, if freed at one stroke, constitute only a burden & a danger on the state.

But these are vapourings on my part. Let us hope for a speedy peace with a chastened North, & mutual respect as we go our separate destinies. We must resign ourselves to the fortunes of war, and stand to our posts with fortitude.

There is really little danger on these seas unless we should have the misfortune to fall in with either a Union steamer or with a hurricane, the season of which is setting in. So that each morning & evening yours truly checks the barometer, and scans the horizon with a wholesome wariness.

I was interrupted by Dr. Steele, whom you will recall from the old *Owanee.* He is the same & desired to be recalled to your remembrance in his usual suave manner. His visit was attendant upon an altercation in the forecastle in which one of our Scottish tars was engaged with one of our native Southerners. Steele reports the Scot came off second best & required some bit of sail-making in consequence. Yet the wound not serious & both men now shackled awaiting captain's mast.

As I said do not lose a moment worrying over me, we face little danger & believe we shall have a quiet cruize. Should the worst occur I have hanging in my cabin one of the patent life-preservers I caused to be held over from the outfitting of the ship as a packet.

I have just been closeted with the captain. Considering the parlous state of our coal-bunkers, he intends to approach Havana under cover of night in case Federal cruisers are within telegraphing distance along the coast. We have altered course & the paddle wheels are thumping and swishing along outside the walls of my cabin as I write. With luck we shall sight Morro Light before dawn & I will be able to post this missive on arrival.

Good-bye my dear wife. May God bless you and Robert and the child shortly to be ours. I hope Norfolk remains secure but if any force should threaten go at once to your parents in Richmond, that city will be better defended in consequence of its being the seat of government. Unless of course your state of health should make it unwise, in which case trust yourself to the Sinclairs. I left instructions with the bank to allow you to draw up to the limit of my account. Do not trouble yourself with the furnishings or the house, I know you find pleasure in them and have devoted much time to their choice but place your own welfare and our child's above saving anything else.

4th August.

Early morning once more. We have made our passage of El Morro, and lie now safe by the famous Malecón. We will entrust our mails to the Consul, who has just now come aboard. Though it may be a matter of some weeks until you open this I feel close to you as I prepare to seal up these words knowing the next eye to scan them will be your own. The mail sack is being closed as I speak so I will now lay down my pen. I think of you always and long to press you to myself, my darling Catherine, my own. Remember me to our friends, and with love to my own dearest Wife,

Ever devotedly, your husband,
Ker.

13

MERIDIAN found them moored, in sunlight so glaring it brought tears to the eye, alongside a crumbling seawall within one of the most beautiful harbors of the world. To starboard, the levee and a waterfront promenade. To port, the soft blue of Regla Bay, ringed and threaded with shoals between verdigris and ivory. The sparkling water was so clear Ker could see conches creeping slowly over a sand bottom. The Confederate consul, a Major Charles J. Helm, had come aboard, descending from a barouche drawn by two beautifully matched bays. He'd been closeted with Trezevant for nearly two hours now.

Ker stood on the foredeck, letting the heat seep into his bones. Conscious of the gazes of dignified gentlemen in Panamas and linen suits and señoritas in mantilla and lace; more or less supervising as Boileaux finished making up greased leather rat guards for the cables that stretched to the half-buried cannon that served as bollards.

He reflected that those cannon might well have repulsed Drake. The Spanish ensign had waved beneath these azure skies for four hundred years. Yet that very morning it had dipped to the newest flag on the face of the earth.

They'd picked up the harbor pilot a mile out from territorial waters. The Castillo de los Tres Reyes del Morro was an alabastrine pile of walls and watchtowers. As *Montgomery* steamed slowly in Trezevant had engaged the pilot in rapid Spanish; and at last, ordered the men to fall into ranks.

MacDonnell was ready, and as the crimson and gold broke at *Montgomery*'s forepeak thirteen guns had boomed out one after the other in the slow count. After which a pause; and then, a puff of white from the great walls. Ker ticked them off. Eleven . . . twelve . . . *thirteen*. The first salute, so far as he knew, their new nation had yet received.

The boy, Willie, tugging at his forelock. —Sir? Captain Trezevant sends his regards, an' Major Helm's about to leave.

Ker met them at the brow. Helm was cadaverous in white linen, cool-looking straw hat, and gold-headed cane. Trezevant was in full dress, with sash, sword, and cocked hat. Gilt and polished leather flashed. A murmur ran through the spectators, and fans fluttered before sparkling eyes as he bowed in their direction. Behind them tagged Simon, in the frock coat and linen shirt he'd worn on joining in New Orleans. In one hand he carried the captain's writing case, in the other the canvas mail sack. As usual, he did not meet Ker's eye.

—Mr. Claiborne, I am departing the ship.

—And you look most uncommon fine, sir. Whither bound? If I may ask, sir?

—You certainly may, and should. I want all hands to leave word as to their destination should they go ashore. I call upon the Spanish admiral, whose flag flies on the frigate yonder. Then to the Plaza de Armas for audience with the Captain-General of Spain himself. My return I cannot predict. Perhaps before nightfall, perhaps considerably later.

—Aye aye, sir.

Trezevant took a slip of pasteboard from his cap. —Major Helm has advised us that this gentleman, Señor Jecker—I know, it does not sound Spanish to me either—will visit today to make arrangements for coaling, victualing, and such naval stores as we may require. You are cognizant of the rules of international law governing resupply in a neutral port?

—Yes sir. Sufficient for voyage repairs only; no increase of warlike potential; no arms, ammunition, or increase of crew. One question, sir. The curious of Cuba are already eyeing us.

—You may inform them we will entertain visitors tomorrow, but today must concentrate on repairs and supply. Insist the coaling proceed expeditiously. As to shore liberty, use your own judgment. Major? If you will precede me, sir?

The captain cast a last glance around and aloft; then headed down the gangplank after Helm, the purser's mate at his heels. Ker quizzled again at Simon's effeminate walk. But reaching no untoward conclusions. He'd known several men whose mannerisms could be termed exceptionable, but whose courage had been proved beyond question.

As the shore-party reached the Malecón the crush closed round them. Silk parasols dipped. Dark-bearded gentlemen bowed. Trezevant, a head taller than anyone around him, bowed left and right before disappearing into the clatter and dust of the waterfront street. Simon dogged after him, shoulders slumping under his burdens, heading for the barouche.

Just then, from the corner of his eye, Ker noticed a man slipping through the mob, intent on the party from *Montgomery.* Evidently a native, and of the lower classes, from his small stature and ragged clothing. He threw a stealthy glance at the ship, and his eyes widened as he saw Ker's attention on him. Ker snapped to Grice, who stood nearby, making up the signal lines, —Quartermaster! Take two men and protect Mr. Helm and the captain.

But even as he spoke a straw hat went flying amid a sudden recoil of parasols and Panamas. He pushed Grice aside and sprinted down the brow, shouldering Dons out of the way as he pushed toward where Trezevant had disappeared.

When he reached the barouche Helm had drawn a Deringer. Simon was lying on the pavement, hair disheveled and hands bleeding. Papers lay scattered from the upended writing desk. Trezevant was glaring round, sword drawn.

—What happened, sir? Are you hurt?

—We seem to be undamaged. But someone has snatched our mailbag.

Of course; the mailbag! Ker stared around, searching between passing carriages for the cutpurse, the thief. But he'd evaporated into the crowd, and the teeming city beyond, as seamlessly as if into air.

—I know who's behind this outrage, Helm said. His cheeks were flushed with heat and anger. —But as to obtaining a rectification of the situation, that I cannot say.

Grice panted up, leading seamen with cutlasses. Ker told them to stand down, and bent to help Simon up. The man leaned on him for a moment, and he caught a faint sweet scent that brushed across his memory. But a moment later he had forgotten it as a Guardia pushed through the crowd, demanding explanations.

The crew was topside, whiling away the time while they waited for Steele's patent preventative of Yellow Jack to work. The old surgeon had placed his smoke-pots down the midships passageway, the crew's berthing. The stench of sulphur and wormwood eddied up between the deckboards. The men complained and drifted to windward, where the breeze at least was fresh.

—Sir? Another of ours.

Mr. Dulcett, offering the deck glass and a pointing hand. Ker aligned the barrel and saw it, a mile down the quay: the same fresh flag *Montgomery* flew, streaming in the bright air from a neat little merchant-brig.

He was handing the instrument back when his gaze snagged on something moving along the open horizon between La Cabaña and the ramparts of El Morro. Refocusing, he saw the distant objects were the royal-poles of a full-rigged ship, and by the gap between them, a sizable one. It was still well out to sea to northward and would not be in the channel for some time.

If, that is, it entered at all, and he felt a sudden apprehension grip his heels to the deck. He pushed it away, not willing to compromise the relief of being safe in port with what might after all be an unfounded suspicion.

A small gentleman in the same cool white linen as the others on the promenade presented himself a little after three as Hans Jecker, the factotum Major Helm had told them would call. More alert now, after the incident with the mail, to the sense all might not be friends, Ker asked him for any evidence he might have as to his identity. He presented several personal letters in Spanish, French, and German. Confirming they were all addressed to a Monsieur, Herr, or Señor Jecker, Ker permitted him to board, and sent the quarterdeck messenger for Gibson and Kinkaid.

The belowdecks being packed with poisonous fumes at the moment, they arranged their business in the shade of the starboard wheelhouse. Jecker had no anthracite but could provide a good grade of Welsh, which Kinkaid said would be suitable for *Montgomery*'s furnaces. He pressed provisions and slop-clothing on them, but Gibson agreed with Ker that their captures had supplied them well to date.

—There is one point left to discuss, Jecker concluded. —The matter of gifts.

—What sort of gifts? And to whom?

—I must tell you there is some resistance to supplying you. It has been intimated to me by the port authorities that some, let us say memorandum, honorarium, I am not certain of the English, would go far to ensure I can deliver the articles you are requesting—most particularly of the coal.

Ker said coldly, —I'm not sure I follow you, sir. The fort returned our salute upon our entrance. Is that not recognition by the Queen of Spain? Or at least by her representatives in Cuba?

The chandler said, —Dear sir, forgive me, but your flag looks much like the United States flag at a distance. Perhaps it was a mistake?

Seeing Ker's expression, the little man hurried on. —You see, the consul general of the United States in Cuba, Mr. Shufeldt, has considerable influence with the governor-general. Above all, the Spanish understand how fragile is their grip on their last remaining possession in the New World. One might argue that the rise of another slave power might be seen with approval. But the authorities are also aware certain Southern statesman have argued for annexing this island in times past. Now those same names appear in the high counsels of President Davis.

Ker motioned Gibson aside. Heads lowered, he asked if presenting these "gifts" would be acceptable insofar as any audits of their accounts Richmond might make were concerned. The purser advising him that up to one-tenth of the total purchase would be acceptable as cost of doing business in a foreign port, Ker authorized the factor to add them to the bills. Jecker bowed, promised the coal barge would be alongside early tomorrow, and withdrew.

Two hours passed, and the sulphur stink waned. The boatswain unsealed the companionways. The men went below, holding their noses. Ker could tell from their glances toward the narrow, balcony-lined alleys what their hearts yearned for. And he had no objection to their getting it, but not before they rigged for the next morning's coaling.

At eight bells, the captain not having returned, he passed the word that the starboard watch could go on liberty after the evening mess. Boileaux was on the quarterdeck immediately, cap in hand, requesting that the petty officers be permitted to leave now. Ker said no, and told him not to come back until all the chutes were rigged. The boatswain left with a black look.

The sun was lower, but still pouring floods of light, when half the crew, in their most flamboyant shore outfits, swaggered across the brow into the old city. Ker was smoking on the fantail, having resolved to postpone his own saunter ashore until the captain returned, when Dulcett grabbed his sleeve and pointed to the channel entrance.

The flat detonations of the salute were still echoing when a black hull rounded the battlements of La Cabaña. A man-of-war, ship-rigged but with sails furled, smoke belching from twin stacks. Her sides were high and her sheer extreme, almost clipperlike. She came on steadily, parting the crystalline waters with a touch of white at her stem.

The midshipman lowered the glass. —The Stars and Stripes.

The Federal slowed further, passing inside Regla Shoal. Now Ker saw the old flag too. She passed *Montgomery* a hundred yards off, her officers looking them over. She emerged into the widening bay south of the city, then pivoted slowly, searching her sharp bow into the wind.

She steamed slowly back, as if intending to head out again. Once more glasses studied them from the spar deck. Ker stared back boldly, but in his heart did not feel so game. If only she did not pass out again. . . . Then the hollow roar of chain cable came across the water, and the black hull lay between Regla and the city, square across the path the smaller warship would have to take to reach the open sea again.

—*Potomac*, said Grice, who, with the port watch, was also taking the evening air.

Ker nodded. The steam sloop-of-war U.S.S. *Potomac* had come back to the Home Squadron from the Med as *Owanee* had returned from the

African station. She was screw-propelled. With her thin, tapering bow and fine underwater lines, drawn by the legendary clipper designer George Steers, she could make ten knots under steam and fifteen under combined sail and power. She mounted four thirty-two-pounders and twelve nine-inch shell-guns. Not quite as powerfully gunned as the Federal frigate they'd slipped past to escape the Mississippi, but far more heavily than *Montgomery,* as well as faster and much newer.

—This is not to my liking, Dulcett murmured.

—Nor mine. The Federal's menacing appearance, added to his anger at the theft of his carefully indited letter to Catherine as well as of all their official correspondence, had soured his cheerful spirits of that morning. —But her commander has made one serious error. Can you tell me, Gustavius, what it was?

—By anchoring out, you mean, sir?

—No. By entering at all. Ker pointed to where they'd first glimpsed her sticks, far out to sea. —If he'd lingered beyond the three-mile line, he could have snapped us up as we came out. Here, as the Dons have declared their neutrality in our internecine struggle, she cannot leave port until twenty-four hours after we take our departure. That is the law.

—Nor can we leave until twenty-four hours after *she* departs, Dulcett said brightly. —Or is that not right? Is it the first ship in that must depart first?

—No sir, your first statement is the correct one; if he should leave first, we would be checkmated. Ker slapped the mid's shoulder. —You are showing faint signs of thinking like a naval officer, Gus.

—Thank you, sir. I ascribe any modest progress whatsoever to your untiring and inspiriting example.

The sailmaker, knuckling his forehead in the old manner. —Captain's on the mole, sir, lighting from that hack with the yellow doors.

Trezevant strode up the brow, sword swinging at his side. He wore a thunderous look. A barefoot black boy trailed after him, carrying segar boxes in a net-sack of knitted manila. Ker lifted his hat, but the captain barely favored him with a glance. He tossed a coin to the boy. —Mr. Claiborne. When did *Potomac* arrive?

—She cast her anchor not ten minutes ago, sir.

—I have sent a runner to advise Señor Jecker we must commence coaling as soon as possible. Tonight, if he can get the barge alongside. Trezevant surveyed the deck, the few men topside; then rotated to look ashore. —You have not granted liberty, surely?

—Sir, I'm afraid so. I did it before *Potomac* entered—

—Unto, sir, unto; you have done very wrong. I only hope you have not cost us the chance to escape. Hoist the recall at once, sir, at once.

Ker felt hot burn mount to his face. But protesting or explaining would heal nothing. He managed a choked —Aye aye, sir, to Trezevant's back, descending the companionway. Awaited a summons below, but it did not come. He paced restlessly the length of the deck, frowning each time he turned at the black barrier that lay not a quarter-mile off, swinging to her anchor in the pleasant wind off the hills.

Shortly before dusk a boat put out from the Federal steamer. It made its way down the waterfront, disappearing now and then into the tangle of merchant shipping. Only after it had returned to *Potomac* did Ker realize they'd been hauling down the Confederate flags from the merchant ships.

Of course the recall brought no one back aboard. Once ashore, Jack stayed ashore, till lack of the ready or ironclad order threatened him with the cat. Trezevant sent another messenger to Jecker, but he returned with a tale of spread hands and a shrug; the Spanish could not be hurried. The only solace he had was that the Yankee did not seem in any hurryment to get under way either. In fact, a liberty barge began shuttling back and forth between *Potomac* and the mole.

Montgomery's men began coming back in scattered groups around midnight. Some few, Ker knew, would miss the expiration of liberty, and would have to be punished. What he had not expected were the tales they brought back of being set on in the bodegas.

He'd been below, hastily re-creating the letter home he'd lost in the theft of the mailbags. It was much shorter, but as he was almost out of stationery paper that was not all bad. When the officer of the deck advised that men were returning severely beaten, he went on deck to interview the returnees himself.

They were very drunk, of course. Some were insensible, dragged out of carts by their still-ambulatory mates, but all looked even worse for wear than for a typical shore liberty. The burden of their stories was that *Potomac*'s men had baited and goaded them until a fight was inevitable for any jack with a spark of pride, then fallen on them in superior numbers. Ker debated notifying the captain, then decided it could wait till morning. Dawn, and coaling, would be here all too soon. He went to his cabin, leaving word to call him the moment light showed in the sky or at the first sign of the barge.

At five-thirty he was drinking a cup of hot coffee and overseeing the adjusting of the fenders alongside. No coal barge was yet in sight, but he was worried about where and how it could be managed with the hulking paddle-boxes in the way. White and Boileaux at last agreed the best place was aft of the wheelhouse, snug under the quarter. It would mean a longer path for the coal to wend to the bunkers, and consequent delay and mess, but it was the least unsatisfactory solution. Yet another drawback to the paddle wheels, which he was starting to thoroughly dislike.

But six o'clock passed, then seven, at last eight, and the closest search of the harbor descried nothing resembling the fuel-lighter Jecker had promised. Ker sent Simon with a note to the address on the chandler's card. The purser's mate came back forty minutes later. No one had answered the bell.

Trezevant came up in undress blues and blue spectacles. He peered into the blaze of sun coming off the bay, then looked searchingly aloft. Ker locked his hands behind him and waited for the keelhauling. But the captain said with surprising mildness, —No word from our Dutch friend?

—I sent a runner to his address, sir. He doesn't seem to have opened for business as yet.

—Or has been discouraged from doing so.

—I beg your pardon, sir?

The captain took a turn around the deck, bending to look along the gunsights as he passed each carriage, and drew a segar from his breast pocket. After a moment, he offered Ker one. It was a fresh Cubana del Rey, an excellent smoke indeed, and Ker murmured his thanks.

—There is a street some hundred paces to the north lined with tobacconists and segar factors. If you should have time for a visit, it would be worth your while . . . my conversation with the admiral of the port was not completely satisfactory.

Trezevant said he had only grudgingly been received by that official, and not at all by the *Capitane Generale*. Though Major Helm seemed to be well regarded personally, the Confederate cause had not yet gained from the representatives of the Spanish crown the respect owed to them as belligerents. They also had an adversary to contend with. The U.S. consul was arguing that as coal was contraband of war, none could be provided to *Montgomery*.

—Can that be true, sir? Surely coal cannot be contraband, no more than food can be.

—I believe I argued our case well enough that we shall get some eventually. The complicating factor at the moment is the presence of our trig-looking friend in the roadstead.

Ker turned to contemplate the Union steamer toward which Trezevant had nodded. She did indeed look in every respect a well-managed man-o'-war. Every t'gallant-mast stood perfectly vertical, or "all-in-one," every yard was square, every line taut, with no Irish pennants or hang-Judases. He'd come on deck early to ensure *Montgomery* did not lack in comparison, either in appearance or the ceremonies of the morning. A ship, a crew, an exec were judged on such points, and he was satisfied by Trezevant's lack of comment that *Montgomery* looked quite as well as the other. Both warships had sounded colors at eight bells exactly, and their flags had ascended in unison. Now, judging the moment right, he told the captain about the difficulties between the crews the night before.

—Jack never starts a fight, Claiborne. He is always set upon by the other side.

—I understand that, sir; I have been boat-officer in my share of ports. But the stories from separate parties were so similar, I believe it safe to assume there was some common order or directive behind their action.

—Well, perhaps we should elucidate the matter. Again Trezevant looked across to the enemy steamer. —Go aboard and present our case, if you please.

Ker coughed into his fist, not certain he'd understood. —Go aboard *Potomac*, sir?

—Just so. Mr. White, call away the quarter-boat. I believe you will find William Brockway still her captain. If it should prove convenient, you might convey my respects. We put the old *Cyane* into commission together, many years ago. And of course keep your eye open for anything that may be of interest.

Ker said aye aye, still not certain what Trezevant had in mind, but aware too that to ask further would gain him nothing. The naval officer was expected to use his own initiative, to deal with adversity, be it wind, sea, or enemy, without detailed instructions. He went below, stripped off his undress coat, and had Rom give it a quick brushing-up as he stropped his razor and touched up his beard. He dressed his hair, and thrust his arms into the jacket as the servant held it for him. Topside again, he told MacDonnell whither he was bound, stepped into the boat, and bade the coxswain cast off.

The rowers made good time across the sheltered bay, but he had time to wonder, belatedly, if he should be proceeding under a flag of truce. No, it should not be necessary in a neutral port. Black oaken sides towered above him like a hostile fortress. Wavelets lapped against red copper bottom paint.

—Boat ahoy, sounded from above as he neared.

—Aye aye.

The "aye aye" meant a commissioned officer not the captain of a vessel was senior in the boat. He observed the resulting flurry of activity with satisfaction and apprehension. Faces appeared over the bulwarks, stared, and were hastily withdrawn. As they covered the last few yards to the accommodation ladder the coxswain glanced at Ker. —Back water and lay her five yards off the ladder, Ker told him.

—Aye, sir. Oars . . . Hold water! Back water. In, bows.

The number one men finished their stroke, tossed oars, then laid them centerline. They scrambled into the foresheets and stood with boathooks at the ready. When they drifted within convenient speech, Ker lifted his cap. —Permission to come aboard on a matter of mutual convenience.

An officer in cocked hat called down, —Identify yourself, sir.

—I am Lieutenant Ker Claiborne, Confederate States Navy, first luff of Confederate States War-Steamer *Montgomery*.

—What are you doing here?

—Request the favor of a word with your commanding officer.

—Stand by. I will determine if Captain Brockway will see you.

The day was growing warm. From here Ker could look down the

length of the channel to the open sea. He lifted his cap and wiped sweat from his forehead.

It was occurring to him, rather too late, that it might not have been wise to have given his name quite so baldly. He'd never received a reply to his letter of resignation, handed to Nicholas Duycker that fiery night in Norfolk. If he was carried as a deserter from his former service, rather than as having resigned his commission . . . images of cells, of manacles, of a yardarm noose suddenly loomed in his mind. Damn, he thought. Just what sort of shaking was he stepping into? The boat edged forward, pushed by an ebb tide, and the coxswain gave the order to back water again.

The cocked-hat reappeared. —It is not convenient for the captain to see you, sir. Can your business be conducted with the first lieutenant?

Ker considered sheering off once more, then steadied himself and called up, —Yes sir; I believe it most likely can.

—You may come aboard for five minutes only. Have your boat stand off.

Ker pulled himself up the ladder, paused at the top, and after a little hesitation took off his cap in the direction of the flag. He saluted the officer of the deck as well, but the other did not quite lift his hat, only touched the brim. Two armed marines stood with bayonets fixed behind him, askew shakos showing how rapidly they'd been called out. He was surrounded by faces, some hostile, others simply curious. They wore the same blue jackets as he. The same buttons. Only the device on his cap was different. Beyond them his attention traveled the length of the deck. Shining black guns. Damp-shining decks, just stoned. Neatly coiled line. Blacked standing rigging. And other objects; planks, piles of scrubbed canvas . . . a stocky, friendly looking fellow with side-whiskers, a pale mustache, and the sort of ruddy beef-fed moonface that would subject him to apoplexy at fifty, stepped forward. —I am *Potomac*'s executive officer. Lieutenant Reynolds.

Ker had once known a Reynolds, though without side-whiskers and thirty pounds slimmer. They'd studied trigonometry together, in the jasmine-scented Annapolis spring. —*Charles* Reynolds, is it not?

—It is. Lieutenant Charles Reynolds.

—I am Ker Claiborne.

—Ker! I remember you. You bunked above me on *Constitution* the summer of '54. I'm sorry to meet like this.

—It could not be avoided, I fear.

—Well, you aren't here to exchange reminiscences, I imagine. What is it you wished to discuss?

—It has come to my attention there were incidents between our liberty sections last night. Instances of fisticuffs and threats.

—And?

—We're in a neutral port, Charles. I'd like to keep friction at a minimum.

A voice came from the back. —Your men, at least, don't seem to steer clear of a fight.

Ker did not bother to acknowledge this, though he felt his face heat. —We're in a neutral port, he said again to Reynolds. —At the very least, we should refrain from disputing as a courtesy to our hosts.

His opposite number seemed unsure. —I don't know . . . I heard you impressed sailors, impressed Americans from your prizes. Is that right?

—You've been misinformed. We asked for volunteers. Some men stepped forward. Of Southern birth, for the most part. They were in no sense impressed.

—You want to stop the men fighting on liberty, you say. What do you propose?

Ker wished he and Charles could sit down for a moment, away from the others who pressed around. He felt sure they could come to some reasonable agreement. But Reynolds made no move to suggest they withdraw. So he said, —We could draw a line through the city. Say, the midpoint of the Malecón. Your boys stay north of that line; mine keep to the south of it.

Another murmur from the back ranks. This time Ker noted its source: a confident-looking young man with a shock of rather startlingly silvering hair and a decided sneer to his lip. He thrust himself forward, taking Reynolds's arm, but the lieutenant shook him off. The round face assumed a harder aspect. —You're not asked for, Mr. Henshaw; step back. I am quite capable of dealing with this. Then, to Ker, —You propose to re-create the Mason-Dixon in Havana? Is that your suggestion?

—No. Just to set a boundary, to avoid rows.

—I think not. My men'll go where they please. As will the United States Navy. Is that all you came to say?

—That, and to present Captain Trezevant's compliments to Captain Brockway, with whom he served on *Cyane*.

—I will convey those sentiments; and now I will wish you a good day.

Seething, yet restraining himself, Ker returned the other's curt bow. He looked aloft, taking a deep breath, then out to the bay. He lifted his cap, and the coxswain called out oars.

But as he turned to go he found the silver-haired youngster square in his path. The one who had talked in an undertone all through his conversation with Reynolds. —Y'all leavin' us so quick, suh? he said, mimicking a Dixie speech.

—I fear I must.

—A friendly question first. To satisfy my curiosity.

—I am at your service.

—I just wondered. How does it feel, forcing your attentions on a helpless slave woman?

—Mr. Henshaw! Reynolds called sharply.

But the youngster held his ground. —I was curious, sir, to hear an account from one of these sons of the chivalry himself. What about it, sir? How many nigger babies have you sired? His scornful eye dared Ker to push him aside. His fingers worked on his sword-hilt.

Ker said, as evenly as he could, —I fear the total would disappoint you, sir.

—Oh, the total would disappoint me. I see. Do your breeders submit under threat alone, sir? Or do you have to whip them first?

The quarter-boat skimmed round toward them. Ker hesitated a moment, yearning to strike the face that hovered insultingly close; yearning to give him the thrashing his words deserved, but at last obeyed his sense of military duty, and did not. Instead he stepped around him, rattled down the ladder, and stepped neatly down into the passing boat.

Or meant to. Instead his boot slipped on the wet edge of the boat platform. He was only saved from a nasty fall by the boat crew letting go the oars to cushion and receive his fall. Untangling himself from arms and oars as the boat rocked, he settled in the stern, breathing hard.

He reported himself back aboard to MacDonnell on the quarterdeck. When asked if the captain was below, the gunnery officer nodded toward the pier. Ker saw the familiar barouche, and by it a long line of ladies and gentlemen, ceilinged by the inevitable parasols, waiting, two by two, to descend the forward brow, promenade the length of the deck, marveling in Spanish, and debark abaft the wheelhouses. He also made out a shaggy form sitting on the crumbling coral-stone of the levee: a very pleased-looking C. Auguste Dupin, being plied with sweetmeats, titbits, and sips of *guarapo* by the waiting ladies.

He took off his cap to the captain and Major Helm. The consul looked disconsolate.

—What news? Trezevant asked.

—Sir, *Potomac* was compelled to enter port by lack of coal. Just as we were; and she will not now sortie until her bunkers are replenished.

—They told you that? Helm lifted an eyebrow.

—Not in so many words, sir. Rather, in the show of bottom paint above the waterline, evidencing her empty bunkers. The chutes were rigged and coal sacks laid out preparatory to coaling. Most telling was a strong smell of hickory about her stack gas. Her engineer is burning the cooking wood to keep his fans turning over, and to disguise from us the fact she cannot follow us until she fuels.

Trezevant clapped him on the back, then rubbed his mouth. —Capital detective work, Claiborne. But still we have no coal ourselves. Such is the domination of the Yankees over the Dons, it will not surprise me to see the barge that was being loaded for us alongside her before many hours have passed.

Ker said, —What do you mean, sir? Jecker still has not put in an appearance?

Helm said angrily, —A spineless boodler. Locked in his office, consoling himself with rum for his lack of backbone. I called on him to find out what the delay was. He told me, with whining apologies, that he had been informed by Mr. Shufeldt, the Yankee consul, that if he sold coal to us, he would never again sell another pound to any ship flying the United States flag. As this is a principal coaling-port for those war-steamers cruising the Caribbean, he cried bitter tears as he assured me the Confederación Norteamericana has no better friend than himself, but that the realities of business meant he could no longer supply our order.

—Could you not corrupt him back into our fold? With a "gift"?

Trezevant said dryly, —Our worthy consul attempted that expedient without success.

—There are no other dealers?

—Only three marine coal dealers do business in Havana, Helm said. —They are licensed by the crown and noteworthy by collusion; their prices are exactly the same. Where one will not sell, neither will the others. Like everyone else, it seems, these Dons should like to see the arrogant Yankee humbled, so long as it means no sacrifice of their own.

Ker looked down the line of waiting Cubans, who were chattering, smoking, flirting, and eating ices dispensed by a roving vendor. Their gaiety contrasted with the silent watcher beyond, the black sides and heavy guns of *Potomac*. He said, —Then we must buy it elsewhere.

Trezevant gave him a level gaze. —Elsewhere, sir?

—These tobacco factors, for example. Do they not employ stoves to dry their tobacco leaves?

—True, said Helm. He too was studying Ker.

—Sugar mills, which employ steam engines to drive the crushing mills. And gasworks, I note gaslights.

—Your young second is resourceful, said Helm. —Yes, our native *ingenios* and *tahonas*—the crushing mills on the coffee plantations—provide themselves with considerable supplies of coal. But loading it would be a slow process, slower than the Yankee can load from a barge. I fear she will still be able to put to sea before you; and once she is out, your fate is that of the bottled scorpion. I fear your mission, Captain, may be at an end.

A low, rather hoarse voice spoke from the front of the barouche, beside the driver. It took Ker a moment to realize it was Simon. The purser's mate said, —With your permission, Captain?

—Something to contribute, my man?

—Perhaps, sir. Major Helm, sir, you imply Jecker is sympathetic to our cause?

The consul looked annoyed at being addressed by one sitting beside the driver, but said only, —I believe he is.

—He has not been corrupted by Yankee gold, disbursed by the unseen but malevolent Mr. Shufeldt?

—I believe he is simply afraid to lose their business.

—Then let him show his good faith, and earn a sizable pourboire as well.

The three looked at the purser's mate. —Your meaning? said Trezevant at last.

—If gold cannot coax delivery, it may at least persuade delay.

Helm nodded slowly. —That's possible. And the suggestion of alternate sources . . . I can think of sympathizers who might be persuaded to help. Not marine coal, nor in barges, but good burnable fuel. In fact— here he raised his hat to an elderly gentleman on the arm of a woman so stunning Ker could not keep his gaze off her, in fact all the men in the carriage eyed her, at least all except Simon. —In fact, I see several prospects in your gawking-line at the moment. Let us see. Jecker quoted us eight dollars and fifty-five cents per ton for run of the pit bituminous steamcoal. Have I your permission to offer, say, three dollars advance on the market?

Trezevant said he would be guided by the consul's advice.

The first wagonloads arrived that afternoon, drawn by minute burros from a coffee plantation. Kinkaid inspected the load, crumbling the coal in his hands, turning chunks over, even sniffing it, while Mr. Gibson arranged the financial end with the aid of a tin box of specie. In the blazing heat four half-naked crewmen mounted the first cart and began shoveling furiously into canvas coaling-bags held by others on the ground. Everyone concerned was soon caked in sweat and black dust. Drifts of gritty powder blew across the decks. The visiting line melted away, fine ladies exclaiming at grimy smudges on their skirts, gentlemen beating coal dust from their pant legs. Two Guardias came up to remonstrate but went away satisfied with ten-dollar gold pieces.

Ker paced the hurricane deck as the men toiled like ants up the gangway, aft to the loading hatch, and discharged their burdens down chutes. He noted the time of commencement and counted the two-hundredpound sacks as they passed. At a bag every three minutes, *Montgomery* was loading two tons per hour. Not a cheering rate when one considered her bunker-capacity was a hundred and forty tons.

He glanced anxiously toward *Potomac*. As yet no barge lay alongside.

Either the Dons were exceedingly slow this week, or Simon's "gift" to Jecker had had its effect.

The loading proceeded hour after hour, the hands breaking only for a dipper of water from a scuttlebutt or a quick tot ladled out by the jack-'o-the-dust. Just before dark a boat from the Federal skimmed by. From the sternsheet, the young blade who'd blocked Ker's path, Henshaw, observed them scornfully, arms folded. Ker bowed ironically from the bridge.

At midnight proceedings were enlivened by the arrival of a gang of chained Negroes, sent by a Don Luis Tejerio, one of Mr. Helm's sympathizers. They relieved the exhausted crewmen at the shovels and bags. In the light of rush-torches and mess-lamps hung in the rigging they commenced shoveling and singing, lugubrious voices carrying far out over the harbor.

At dawn Ker was still there, fortified by a glass of cane-sweetened coffee and a segar, when Trezevant came on deck. The captain looked over the running total—thirty-five tons, the cadaverous-looking slaves had managed to outwork the crewmen—then toward *Potomac*. Then, glancing down the bay, remarked quietly that there seemed to be a barge making in their direction.

Ker went below for a bite, pastries left there by well-wishers the previous day, and another cup of coffee. When he returned the barge was making up alongside the Federal. Her yard and stay tackles were triced up and hooked, and the main-yard braced up. Lifting-spars were swinging out, men tailed on at the yards and steadying lines, and stokers scrambled down into the heaped coal with gleaming shovels. *Potomac* would load faster than *Montgomery* could from the pier. On the other hand, her bunkers were more capacious. And yet on the other hand again, the Federal did not need full bunkers. He needed only enough coal to steam out the channel and perform a short chase. Ending with *Montgomery* being overhauled, and either striking her colors or being sunk. In either case, ending her career as a corsair.

The captain stood looking down. The night-gang of cane-slaves had departed with the light, and the crew were back at their labor. He spoke without turning his head, as Ker came up. —Your estimate, sir, as to the capacity of that barge?

Ker estimated its dimensions, and applied the conversion-factor for pounds of coal per cubic foot. —I should estimate he has between four and five hundred tons there, sir.

—And his engines will consume how much per hour?

—He is rated at two thousand horsepower, which assuming an average rate of coal consumption of five pounds per horsepower-hour would be ten thousand pounds, or five tons per hour, at maximum speed.

—And he is now commencing to load, at a rate that will exceed ours by at least three to one. There are variables in the equation, but I believe the outcome is clear. Serve out a tot to all hands, put the coaling-line at double time; we will cast off as soon as we have taken fifty tons aboard.

—Sir, that will not be adequate for more than a few days' cruising.

—Then we will have to coal elsewhere. Make your preparations for getting under way. But conceal them, if you please.

Ker lifted his cap and went below. Kinkaid received the orders with a nod; MacDonnell, with a curse. —I'll fight him, but this cove'll knock the bark off us.

—That is the captain's aim, that we shall escape and not have to fight. Once we are under way first, the enemy is constrained by the law from following within twenty-four hours.

The Australian seemed about to say something, but did not. Ker left him and went forward, alerting White, Boileaux, and the others he met as to the captain's directions. Then returned to the bridge, consulting his watch again.

Now the petty officers stalked the line of running men, colts in hand. Shovelers heaved with panicky energy. Burros kicked at the traces, braying at the tumult. A seaman sprawled full length on the deck with a torn bag; a moment later the spilled coal was kicked aside by running feet. Ker cast a glance at the Yankee. The same bustle was evident about her deck as shovel-handles pistoned and coal sacks rose jerkily at the ends of whips.

A plume of black smoke shot from *Montgomery*'s stack. It hung above the harbor, an inky storm cloud, then uncoiled downwind in the sulphurous heat. They'd just given away their intentions. But perhaps everyone knew already. Boats were gathering in the channel, gaily dressed Cubans being rowed by coloreds in slouch hats.

An hour later he reported, —Sir, these last bags being carried over will make fifty tons, not including what is ready to the furnaces.

—Very well.

The quartermaster reported, —Sir, *Potomac* commencing to heave around on her anchor cable.

—Put her under way, Mr. Claiborne, Trezevant said. —As soon as it is quite convenient, if you please.

Ker cursed interiorly. The Havana pilot, for whom he'd sent a messenger some time ago, had not yet shown his face. He rushed to the side of the bridge. —Mr. White! Retire aboard at once. Mr. Gibson! Complete your payouts and come aboard. Bo's'n, cast off all spring lines, stand by to cast off bow first, then to come in on the stern.

—Ya mean to take in, sir?

—I said to *cast them off,* Boats. We are getting under way posthaste.

Another glance at *Potomac;* a brownish-gray haze shooting up from her stacks. After that first inky ejection, like the *vomito negro* of Yellow Jack, *Montgomery*'s had settled into a steadily pumping jet of darkish cloud. Ker bent to uncap the speaking-tube. —Mr. Kinkaid. Do you have enough steam to get under way?

—I have twenty pounds. Enough to get her moving.

—Stand by for bells. We *must* be first underway, or we are lost.

The purser ran aboard, tin box jangling in his hand, and the brow grated inboard behind him. Ker searched out the wind. Almost due easterly, as it had tended for the last few days. A more difficult wind to get under way into from an eastward-facing stone levee would be hard to imagine. But the lilt of a chantey came from the Federal steamer. Ker pointed to the petty officer at the bowline, and gestured: cast off. Wheeled and gave Boileaux, who stood alertly by at the stern line, the hand signal to take a strain.

He'd already run the stern line to the after capstan, and the men put their backs to the bars under a lash of Choctaw curses. Trezevant stood silently, observing. From time to time he placed his glass either on *Potomac* or the battlements of El Morro. Its gigantic guns were not of the latest pattern, but at the range the two ships would pass, they could wreak havoc from behind their ancient walls.

The bow rotated outward as the stern swung in, and a loud grinding came from the pontoon outboard of the port wheelhouse. Ker put the wheel hard aport, pivoting the rudder itself hard astarboard, and ordered half ahead on the port wheel and half astern to starboard.

The massive paddles groaned and clanked into motion, slowly at first, then gathering speed. A cheer floated over their thunder, and Trezevant stepped to the side. Sweeping off his hat, he bowed to those who'd gathered on the levee and in small boats on the Regla side. Boileaux's pipe shrilled, and the Confederate flag broke as the last line splashed into the water. Ker reached for the bell ropes again, and sent down for both wheels full ahead.

Paddles knitting the green harbor into lacy foam, *Montgomery* drove with increasing speed out from the levee. Ker put her into a graceful turn, threading among awninged day-boats. The captain stood with dignity, acknowledging the cheers and pistol-salutes with a stiff-armed doff of his cocked hat.

Potomac, directly ahead. She'd drawn close up to her anchor-buoy, the chain cable nearly up and down. Ker eyed Trezevant. Normally, one would salute a foreign warship passed in a third-country port. Another U.S. ship—he corrected himself—another Confederate would be saluted if the other commander were senior. He had no idea whether Brockway were senior to Trezevant, and even if he were . . .

—Attention to port, Mr. Claiborne.

Dulcett yelled the order to Boileaux. At the whistle the crew fell into rough ranks. Shouts and a blow or two of the colt soon brought them to a more uniform appearance. As *Montgomery*'s bow passed the Federal's the pipe keened "Attention." Ker joined the others on the hurricane deck in doffing their caps, then went quickly back to stand behind the helmsmen. Eyeing the harbor-chart, he gave them half-a-point to port, steering to conform to the channel.

Potomac passed slowly down their side. She didn't return the salute. Her men weren't in ranks. Some took off their caps; others put their fingers to their noses, cocking the well-known snook. The moment he judged their quarterdecks had passed, Boileaux piped "carry on." Ker smiled as their smoke rolled downwind, raining cinders and ash on the Federal's holystoned deck. Then he concentrated on the channel.

—Free and clear, Dulcett said. —That's right, sir, ain't it? We were under way first. They can't follow us.

—Not for twenty-four hours, Ker said. —We are quite safe now, at least for a day. He was running a line out in his mind toward the Nicholas Channel and the Archipelago de Sabana. Trezevant intended to cruise eastward along the north coast, on into the West Indies and the Leeward Islands.

—But what if they should?

—That would be violating the trust of a neutral. Ker studied the chart against his memory of the entrance, wary of the three-fathom shoal off the southern point. Three Spanish fathoms, that is; the Spanish was a fraction less than the English. The massive walls of La Cabaña crept by, the sand-colored ramparts of El Morro pushing up beyond them. He glassed the gap of sea beyond. Whitecaps. They could use a stiff breeze, with their bunkers only a third full. He passed the word to White to prepare to make all sail. Boys and men scurried out along the yards, foot ropes straining out as they cast off the harbor gasketing. The wheels drove with a steady roar, spurning white foam.

The lookout aloft, voice floating down from the sky. —*Potomac* . . . is . . . under way.

Every man on deck turned to look aft. To where the masts of the Federal showed in a single perfect line. Aligned, sighted, on them. Her black spout of coal-smoke towered up a hundred feet, then blew off over the city. They contemplated it for some seconds in silence.

—Under way? said Trezevant.

—Yes sir. She appears to be following us out.

Silence again. *Montgomery* nodded to the first swells, shrouds creaking as they took the strain.

—Not exactly *hodie mihi,* it seems, Trezevant murmured.

—No sir, it would appear not.

—Increase your speed to four bells. Hoist "request protection in your waters" to the fort. Or as close as you can get in Marryat's code.

Ker passed that task to Dulcett and Grice, and waited, gripping the hurricane rail, as the old quartermaster sent the flags whipping up. The midshipman murmured, —I thought you said they couldn't do this, sir.

—That is correct, Gustavius. According to international law, they cannot follow us to sea within the stipulated period.

—But they are?

—Evidently so.

—Now what happens?

—Now we'll see how strictly the Dons value their neutrality. Ker bent to speak to MacDonnell. —Best commence your preparations for general quarters, Mr. MacDonnell.

MacDonnell looked reluctant, glancing back at the now clearly pursuing warship, but at last lifted his hat, acknowledging the order, and hurried off.

The watchtowers of El Morro were moving past. *Montgomery*'s pennants whipped in the first gusts of clean sea air. Ker had prepared his bearing points, and took a round with his sextant. Plotting, he saw they'd clear the point on this course. When the leadsman called ten fathoms he passed the word to secure the anchors for sea and get the donkeys into the hawseholes. Their first leg would be a starboard tack, out into the Straits of Florida. Assuming, that is, the Dons fulfilled their responsibility and warned the Federals back to their anchorage. A single monitory gun from the fort would do it. They'd see it before they heard it, so he put Dulcett on the fort with the deck glass.

Trezevant paced the deck, fingers locked behind him. The sea air had dispelled the crushing heat of August noon, but the sun glare was cruel. The captain kept blinking against it, then finally sent below for his tinted spectacles. Ker took another round of bearings, trying to quell his own apprehension with navigational routine. At last he looked back again, to find the Federal abreast of El Morro.

—Anything to report, Mr. Dulcett?

—Nothing, sir. No signal from the fort.

It was then he knew, with a feeling of doom and anger, the Dons would not fulfill their obligations. No doubt letters would be sent, official protests made . . . but by then *Montgomery* would lie at the bottom of the Caribbean. Unless they could outrun the Yankee . . . which didn't seem very damned likely, a Steers-designed hull and two thousand horsepower against the converted packet's tubby hull and dragging paddle wheels.

—*Potomac*'s passed El Morro. Altering course to pursue us.

—Very well, Mr. Dulcett. Mr. White, all sail, if you please.

At his word sailors fisted braces and to the throaty chorus of "heave . . . ha," the t'gallant foreyards swung slowly around to point into the wind.

Buff canvas bellied, loosely at first, then progressively flatter as the sheets came hard home. Hoist and trim, and now the gaff-sails broke, followed in short order by jibs and stays and spanker. Boileaux was pointing at the main-rope. Ker nodded, they could use the acreage. *Montgomery* leaned to the strain, her rigging commencing to sing in the stiff trade breeze. She began plowing her way through the green seas that came one after the other down out of the east, tops blowing off, lines of spray laid windwise along the waves as if some submarine beast were running along just beneath the surface. He glanced aloft again, then cupped hands and shouted to hook and haul taut the rolling-tackle. Turned to Trezevant, who was gazing aft. —Under way on the starboard tack, sir, course north by east, all sails set and drawing, engines still at four bells.

The captain said very well, but seemed distracted. Following his gaze, Ker saw *Potomac* making sail too. He waited, then said, —Shall I clear for action, sir?

—A stern chase is a long chase, Claiborne.

—Exactly so, sir. Still she has the advantage of us.

—At what point can we come east?

Ker returned to the chart, now fluttering madly beneath its lead chart weights, and pricked off the distance. —Ten nautical miles, sir. We're clear then until that peninsula that juts up from Cardenas.

—Keep her as close to the wind as she will sail. And tell Kinkaid if he's ever made his boilers roar, to do so now. Unless he wishes to swim to shore.

Ker passed that word, keeping his eye on the fore t'gallant. He nudged her to north-northeast, then tried her at northeast by north. The leeward edge luffed and he backed off.

When he looked back again the blossomed sails of the Yankee, stacked one atop the other in a skyreaching pyramid of heartstopping beauty, were noticeably nearer. She seemed still to be gathering way, while *Montgomery* had reached top speed. Leaning over the rail, regarding the passing foam, he estimated they were making a fraction over nine knots. A cast of the log confirmed nine and a half. He was surprised she was doing that well. With the fifteen-degree heel from her press of sail, she was digging the port wheel in nearly to the housings. The blades were invisible beneath green water and froth, cupping and pushing. All very well, but that meant those to starboard were only raking the surface with their tips. He asked the helmsman what rudder he was carrying, and got two spokes to windward. That was consistent, both with drag and reduced thrust to starboard. If he reduced sail, she'd stand up, but then he'd lose the drive of the wind.

A look astern. Again their pursuer had closed. Ker made out her martingale chains and bobstay. A man clung desperately to the jib boom as she pile-drove, tossing out an immense snowy billow each time she pitched. Her commission pennant was a crimson wound on the sky. He could think of nothing to do but temporize. —Shall I come right now, sir? he asked Trezevant.

—We're not yet clear of land.

—No sir, but she'll catch us up before then.

—Then let us come right by all means.

Trezevant shouted it over the roar of the wind, the clatter of the masthoops, the crash as the paddle-boxes plowed bodily through a green sea. Ker wished he could cast them loose, blow them free with powder. *Montgomery* was an indifferent sailor, but at least he'd not have to drag them along, like a swimmer encumbered by hatboxes tied to his shoulder blades.

—Take in all sail, he shouted.

The topmen had been hanging on the ratlings. At the call "aloft all yardmen" they sprang into the rigging, were in seconds dots against the sky. The sails buffeted as the buntlines and clew-jiggers gathered them in. The main and spanker, stays and jibs slid downward, were gathered into folds and hastily gasketed by the men on deck, or working far out on the yards, swaying dizzily above the down-driving sea. When the courses came in Ker pointed her up, into the teeth of the wind. Not far ahead shoals reached out to sea. He could not keep this course long. Futile it might be, but one had to act.

Half a mile astern now, clouds of sail began coming in. He watched the Federal's topmen clawing at flogging canvas, clinging to life with one hand and fighting the sails with the other. Revealing the tall twin funnels, jetting vast clouds of brownish coal-smoke into the August sky. As her wings folded the bow wave shrank from a great handlebar to a trimmed lip-whisker, but still she came on, still she gained on the prey she pursued.

A burst of smoke on her foredeck. Ker neither saw nor heard the shell pass, but from the green sea fifty rods beyond a jet of foam shot up, succeeded by a smaller one farther off. The projectile had ricocheted. The gun-layer would be whirling the elevation screw two turns counterclockwise, dipping the muzzle an inch or two and firing on the upward pitch.

He didn't bother asking Trezevant whether they should heave to. The captain's set lips, his furrowed forehead over blue lenses gave him answer without query. The gun crews had taken their stations without orders, stood swaying as the bow lifted and crashed. He leaned on the rail and tried to make his face hard as Trezevant's. A second burst of foam leapt up to port, not fifty yards ahead. He knew there could be no more steam, but could not help uncapping the speaking-tube.

From it drummed the monstrous roar of the engines, and a stream of hot air redolent of heated metal and grease and smoke. He shouted, —We're being overtaken. Can you give us any more steam?

—We're burning resin and Kerosene oil. You have every ounce we can give you.

To their right the coast was a line of white, then brown and beyond that summer green, then the distant blue of the hills. The chase could not continue much longer. *Potomac* was ranging up on the starboard quarter, perhaps four hundred yards distant. As she drew abreast more of her guns would bear. He leaned to Trezevant. —Beat to quarters, sir? he shouted.

The captain had his watch out. At Ker's yell he glanced up. —Not just yet, he shouted back.

Past him Ker caught Grice's eye. The quartermaster was holding the hoist-line of the ensign, looking scared yet ready to do as he was bid. One word, and he'd haul down the colors. One word, and their lives could be saved. Perhaps they'd even keep the ship, when the circumstances of the Yankee's capture became public knowledge, that he'd violated the rules of war to pursue them from a neutral port. One word.

But he knew the captain wasn't going to give it.

Another puff of smoke and distant detonation, a double stroke this time, was followed by a hum through the rigging, the crack of wood being impacted by iron. Ker glanced at the towering wheelhouses. A ball through one and the churning machinery would fly apart.

—Hulled 'twixt wind and water, sir, just aft the foremast.

—Very well, Mr. Dulcett. Ker took Trezevant's arm. —Sir, we must take *some* action. Alter away? Run out? Or strike?

A pause that seemed to last forever, while he watched the captain's weathered lips. At last they moved. —Beat to quarters.

The roar of the drums and the skirl of whistles sent the last men to their posts. Ker nodded to MacDonnell. Their duties now were clear, their roles crystallized. The Australian would keep the guns in action as long as possible. Ker would maneuver so as to minimize damage, and inflict it on the opponent. The captain would stand aloof, stepping in if he thought his orders necessary. Each man aboard had his duty. It only remained now to fulfill it until death.

The port lanyards came up and the gun-bulwarks dropped away, revealing the green and running sea. Spray blew up through them in graceful arcs, glittering like broken crystal thrown tumbling through the sunlight.

—Cast loose and provide, MacDonnell shouted, and gun-captains bent to side- and train-tackles, cast off breeching, whipped off lock covers. Shellmen mustered at the hatchway. Topmen climbed skyward, muskets slung. Powder-boys, handspikemen, train-tacklemen gazed pale as death toward the approaching Federal.

—Run out, MacDonnell bawled, and the guns rolled forward into battery, black muzzles jutting outboard, over the rushing sea.

Trezevant grunted something. Glancing at him, Ker saw the captain was snapping closed the cover of his watch. He looked where his senior smiled, and for a moment was puzzled. What had given his lips this grim curve?

Then he noticed something about the Yankee. The distance between the racing ships had not changed. They pitched and rolled, swayed and yawed. *Montgomery*'s paddles churned, and smoke drove from the stacks. All was motion and chaos, but their relative positions did not alter.

The men stood to their guns, swaying with the pitch of the deck. The muzzles pointed now at the sky, now at the sea. Ker watched the Federal steamer, memorizing how its sprit poked upward between *Montgomery*'s mizzen-shrouds. Then looked away. Aloft, at the hastily gasketed sails; forward, at the whitecapped swells driving down on them; at the blue line of land pushing over the horizon, the archipelagic northward thrust of Cuba. He counted to himself, till a full fifteen seconds had ticked away. Then looked back.

Potomac had drifted aft. She was falling astern. A last gun boomed out. He saw the shell coming. The black blur hovered at the level of his eye, then dropped. It hit the water under the stern, emerged at a glancing angle, and buried itself in the next wave. A second later blew it into foam, hearted with curling tendrils of white smoke.

Over the next hour their pursuer fell progressively farther astern, losing speed, but doggedly hanging on. Only when she was miles astern did her t'gallants suddenly drop, followed by her tops. Then the rest of her sails swelled out as she fell off onto a starboard tack, still trailing them, but forced to follow on the oblique by the wind.

They'd escaped. In the hours of darkness, they could shake their pursuer. They had coal yet, and the Union vessel had exhausted hers. Though Brockway had observed their eastward heading. *Potomac,* or another warsteamer, would follow close on that trail.

But for now they were free. Ker shivered, watching as the distant sail shrank, and at last disappeared beneath the heaving sea.

14

TREZEVANT altered course to the north as soon as dark fell, falling off toward the Marquesas Keys. Ker thought it a risky move. The Federals held a base there. But as a tactical decision, he couldn't fault it. Both their initial course out of Havana, and their mail—the gist of which had presumably found its way aboard the Federal steamer—would lead their pursuers to anticipate an eastward track. Since the eight-hundred-mile length of Cuba prevented their turning south, they had only three possible courses. Westward, back into the Gulf of Mexico, might elude the steamer or steamers that would be sent after them among the islands and passes of the West Indies. But anyone who knew Parker Trezevant would know he could not consider retreat. Therefore, to the northward was the only remaining course.

Thus Ker was taken aback when, dawn showing an empty sea in all directions, the captain ordered the fires doused and the helm put to windward, altering course to run away from the rising sun. He nearly asked why, then understood.

If no one who knew Parker Cyrus Trezevant would expect him to go west, and if Captain Brockway, of the *Potomac,* had once been a ship-mate—why then, west was the only possible course to take.

The day passed in normal routine at sea. Muster at nine o'clock, then ship's work till noon. The port watch had never gotten ashore, and a crew deprived of what they considered their right to a romp had to be kept busy. He told Boileaux to overhaul the chain cables, which had so far not been attended to due to the press of getting to sea.

Before long the rusty lengths of iron lay stretched out amidships, doubled and redoubled. The ship resounded with the rasp of wire-brushes, the ringing clangs of pins being driven out of shackles and connecting links, the musical clinking as the armorer sounded each link with his hammer. The carpenter was whittling hickory shackle pins, and pots of white lead and paint were being industriously employed to lubricate and mark the shots of chain, which had been swapped end for end to equalize wear. *Montgomery* carrying three hundred fathoms of chain, Ker felt it would provide employment for the day. He left the noon sun line to the midshipmen, charging them to agree on a latitude and bring it to him for checking.

Trezevant ate alone in his cabin while Ker presided over a luncheon of fresh Cuban bread, spicy meat pastries, and fruit, using up what had been given them in Havana. Then took the deck through a glorious afternoon of wind and sun and following seas. The log gave him seven knots, but worry nibbled his mind like a rat at hardtack. Whither were they bound? Would Trezevant double back, or did he intend to reenter the Gulf? The captain neither appeared on deck nor sent word up. And when Ker sent a boy below with word of small sail to the south, he ordered no alteration of course. Which meant he was intent on making westing, so Ker set himself to doing just that.

For ten days *Montgomery* sailed west and then south. She rounded Cabo San Antonio and transited the Yucatán Channel, between Mexico and the western tip of Cuba. In all that time the lookouts reported only small sail, most likely traders running between Cuban ports. Ker found the emptiness of the Gulf most unusual. On reaching twenty-one degrees latitude

Trezevant turned east again, only this time south of the Fidelisma Isla rather than north of it.

In all that time they overhauled one small steamer that, when they made up on her, flying the British flag, hoisted in response the French; then, when they broke the Confederate flag in preparation for boarding, replied, to their astonishment, with the ensign of the United States. When boarded, the mate handed over British commission papers. Insisting on interviewing the master as to these antics, Ker found a funk of rum surrounding his bunk. He delivered a lecture about not toying with men-of-war, and took his leave with as straight a face as he could muster, considering the snickers and rolled eyes of the boat crew.

South of the Isle of Pines they ran into days of airs so faint and variable the heavy-sailing ex-packet barely made headway. The sargasso-dotted sea was as deserted as it must have been before Columbus made his landfall. Ker took advantage of the fine, still weather to replace the topsail braces, scrape and grease the masts, and at last, when the wind died away entirely, to put a boat over the side and scour the bottom with a spar rigged with holystones, keeling the ship by running the guns out on one side and in on the other.

After two days of such drifting Trezevant ordered the fires lit. Ton by ton the remaining coal disappeared into the furnaces. Kinkaid's stokers were scraping the duckboards when one morning a lofty sail lifted over the eastern horizon. Engines at quarter-speed, Trezevant altered course to intercept. A little after four bells of the morning watch *Montgomery* fired a gun to heave her to.

The *Wild-Fire* was a lovely bark, 1,286 tons, built out of Bath, Maine, owned by Titcomb & Coffin of Newburyport. She had no recent newspapers, bound northward as she was, but carried a cargo of four hundred tons of molasses and muscovado sugar for Hamburg.

When Ker boarded, her master, a Captain Stoddard, argued that the cargo was German-owned and hence neutral. Trezevant, in a sort of drumhead prize-court in his cabin, pointed out that though the cargo was bound for the Continent, and been certificated as recently as the sixth of August as Prussian property by the consul of that nation in Cartagena, the receipts themselves were consigned "to market." In legal fact, then, the certificates were nothing more than a ruse to disguise the belligerent ownership of the cargo. It remained the property of the shipper, and thus could be condemned and the ship that carried it destroyed. To this Stoddard had nothing to say. Trezevant thanked him ironically for defending the interests of his owners, and invited him to share the courtesies of the wardroom. He then told Ker to burn the *Wild-Fire.*

Ker was getting ready to lower away when he remembered the bark's holdful of bulging jute sacks. He could not say just why, but the juxtaposition of that memory, and the fumes of the last Cuban coal curling out of *Montgomery*'s stack, snapped together in his mind into something unlikely but perhaps not impossible. He sent Dulcett below with his compliments to Mr. Kinkaid.

When the engineer appeared, blinking like a mole in the sunlight reflected off the motionless sea, Ker was still studying the bark. —Yes sir? You asked for me?

—Mr. Kinkaid. I was about to return to our prize and burn her when a thought ventured into my normally empty cranium.

—I am at your disposal.

—Does sugar burn, Mr. Kinkaid? From our experience with our previous captures, I am inclined to think so.

—Sugar, sir? Yes, with a bluish yellow flame, and little smoke. It is rich both in carbon, for an enduring fire, and in hydrogen, which contributes heat. Why do you ask?

—That bark yonder contains nigh onto a hundred tons of prime muscovado. And it so happens the sea is very calm today.

Kinkaid turned the idea over. —It would be an interesting experiment. How much did you have in mind bringing aboard?

—Shall we say, fifty tons?

—*Fifty tons,* Mr. Claiborne?

—If your trial is successful. Shall we start with a boatload? Then, if you judge it satisfactory, we will bring the matter to the attention of our commander.

A furnace-charge of the bagged commodity was sailor-heaved aboard, and the trial made. Kinkaid reported that though he still preferred a choice Welsh, when spread with shovels on a bed of already heated coals bagged sugar did indeed produce a useful heat. He estimated it as equivalent in steam-generating power to a soft brown coal. Heavy use might leave a caramelous residue, but chipping-hammers on the clinker-bars and a run of the scrapers through the flues could take care of that.

—There might also be some change in our smoke, he said. Ker, standing on the bridge with him, had already whiffed it; a sweetish, pleasant odor, reminiscent of a taffy-pull, hung in the unmoving air. Ker thanked him and told White to rig thrum-mats, fenders, and whips, and ready *Montgomery* to take the bark alongside. After which he went below and tapped on the captain's door.

Ahasuerus let him in. The Negro lowered his single lighted eye, and gestured behind him with a jerk of his grizzled head. Ker noted he was wearing one of Trezevant's shirts.

The captain was seated at the drawing table, the quarter-windows open; the air was intensely hot. The hot-brandy odor had penetrated here as well. A glass of what looked like whiskey, only darker, stood before him, with an open commonplace book and a brass inkwell.

—It is a decoction of quassia, sir. If, as your face tells me, you were wondering.

Quassia was what Steele prescribed for dyspepsia. Ker nodded politely. Trezevant sipped, staring out the quarter-window at the bark.

—I understand you have solved our fuel problem.

—Not solved, sir, but perhaps ameliorated it for the time being.

—This calm will not last. Not in these latitudes. I should very much like to be steaming east while there is no headwind to retard us. I too knew the cargo of *Wild-Fire,* but did not make the connection between her contents and our present needs. You are to be congratulated on your quickness of mind.

—Thank you, sir, but it remains to be seen whether it will actually raise steam.

—Kinkaid assures me it will, and I have every confidence in his judgment.

—I have ordered preparations to take the *Wild-Fire* alongside, and to sway fifty tons aboard; trusting to obtain coal at our next port of call.

Trezevant nodded, waving to the chair opposite. —Be seated. Azu, whiskey for the lieutenant.

The black glided away. Staring after him, Ker wondered, as he often had, why the man had stayed with Trezevant after the capture of the slaver that had carried him. Its other wretched passengers had elected to be landed in Liberia; Ahasuerus alone had remained. He jerked his attention back as Trezevant said, —Yes, an uncommon resourceful young man. Competent, I should say, for any command at sea; an opinion I have passed to Richmond, by the way.

—Thank you, sir.

—You need not thank me. You have earned such an encomium, but what I have to add may not please you as much. Do you feel you were courteously treated, aboard *Potomac*?

Ker considered. —I cannot say so, sir. The captain had no time for me, and I was subject to some degree of rudeness.

—To some extent, Claiborne, I sent you there not only as an observer, but also to observe the effect on you. Do you feel the Yankees dealt with us fairly in Havana?

—Fairly, sir? I am sure they were behind the theft of our mail. Or at least the consul was.

—Encouraging their men to set on ours?

—That may not have been officially countenanced.

—Very well, you may be right in that regard. But the obstructions, the pressure put on the coal factors, to prevent their selling us fuel?

—I should call that somewhere between shrewd and ungentlemanly.

—It does seem low, does it not? To use the dollar as a bludgeon. And finally, Captain Brockway's subsequent chase of us?

—That, sir, was a clear violation of the neutral status of the port. If I had been commander of El Morro, he would not have passed my guns.

The shuffle of felt slippers, and a gnarled hand slid a bottle and glass in front of him. Ker tipped a finger of whiskey. —You will join me, sir?

—Not in whiskey, sir; but I will lift my glass, sir. Trezevant gravely saluted him with the medicine and resumed. —The point I am making addresses your sentiments on reporting aboard. I think you yet cherish some illusion as to the nature of the contest in which we are engaged.

—I don't follow you, sir.

—I fear I have not yet impressed on you the seriousness of the threat facing our people.

As soon as he swallowed the whiskey Ker felt drunk. The heat of the cabin, the motionlessness of air and deck, the smell of the burning sugar induced a strange lassitude. He struggled to sit up. —I confess I do not follow you, sir. Our opponents wish only to restore the Union as it was. Though a more pacific approach would have had a better chance of success.

—Unto, sir, unto; do you truly believe that is their only goal? To reimpose the Union?

Ker felt confused. Their conversation in New Orleans had left him with the impression Trezevant ascribed the war to the fact duty on the South's imports formed the larger part of the income of the federal government. He said cautiously, —It is their *declared* goal. They have given assurances, if I credit what I read in the better class of journals.

—A smudge, and nothing more.

—You refer to abolition, sir?

—In part. Yet I doubt even that will suffice for those who manipulate, with patient malevolence, the strings of such petty popelings as Lincoln and Seward. No, they will not stop with reducing us to penury, and those who depend on us for guidance, care, and Christian teaching, to starvation and despair.

—Then what is it, sir?

Trezevant turned sunken eyes to his. —It is their design not only to "liberate" our servile population, but so to incite them that the bloodshed of Hayti will be visited on our fair land.

—Really, sir—

—Unto, sir; let me finish. Do you remember the Congo, Claiborne?

Ker swallowed, returned by the mere name of the great river to scenes and horrors such as he'd never conceived human creatures capable of. —Sir, I do.

—Left to his own will, the Negro is no better than a bloody ape. The welter of killing in Africa proves he cannot be civilized in his own country. While a higher type teaches him to rule his brutal passions, Cuffee is a tractable child. Set him free, put arms in his hands, and he will reduce the South to the condition of Dahomey or Ashantee. That, after all, was Brown's intent in '58. And even worse is to come.

—What could be worse than that, sir?

—So to reverse the order of nature as ordained by Almighty God, as to permit the black to mingle his seed with our own. My God! Trezevant's face had suffused with blood; he hammered the arm of his chair. —I have read their ravings; this devil's gospel of race equality. It is sprung from the brain of the Fiend himself.

Ker considered the captain's excitement. He asked hesitantly, —But what possible motive could they have for such a . . . a bastardization?

—What motive? It is the nature of the Yankee to make money. Are we agreed on that? To reduce family, land, learning, art, all that makes life worth living, to the single standard of how much gold can be coined from each human interaction?

—So it would seem from many I have observed.

—That is your answer, sir. If they destroy us, then they will own all.

Ker said, —Yet I have known honorable men from the far side of Mason and Dixon's line.

The captain studied the light through liquid the color of violets. —You believe I rave, do you not?

Ker cleared his throat. —No, sir. But it does seem you ascribe too much influence to the Locofocos like Douglass and Garrison. The mass of Northerners want nothing to do with abolition. It seems to me our disagreement is simply whether the federal government is the creature of the contracting states, or their master.

The captain seemed about to reply. But at last he sank back. —Unto, sir, unto. Load your sugar and set us under steam eastward. You are too honorable a man to imagine what gulfs open beneath us. God grant we may not see the day they can do with us as they will.

He flicked his fingers in dismissal. Ker drained the heel-tap, feeling stung, and took his leave with only the barest bow.

The sugar burned well enough to make half steam in search of better fuel. On the twenty-fourth *Montgomery* put into George Town, in the Cayman Isles, but was able to procure only thirty tons of steam-coal, that being all the one dealer there had remaining. He told them a U.S.S. *Accomac,* a name unfamiliar to anyone aboard *Montgomery,* had called there four days before to fill its bunkers. Moreover, the price was $17.75 a ton, three times what Ker was used to. They remained only long enough for a stroll through the old town. The shore was of a rough, dark, sharp-looking limestone called ironstone. Homes were of wattle and daub, the roads bright crushed coral. The natives followed them, pressing turtles, home-made rope, and dried crocodile heads on the visitors. Everything seemed neat and orderly, but the mosquitoes were so bad that night Trezevant got them under way the next morning.

They quartered about south of Cuba through the end of August and on into September, using coal only when a chase required it. Though the sail were few, half of those they fell in with turned out to be lawful prey.

They stopped the *Carolinea,* out of New York, bound south with flour, cheap furniture, ready-made clothes, and other notions, and burned her, transferring her twelve-man crew to *Montgomery.* Her newspapers told them of the destruction of Hampton, Virginia, the battle of Wilson's Creek, in Missouri, and that General Frémont was suppressing "disloyal" newspapers in St. Louis. Two days later, under overcast skies, they fell in with the *Senhor Pinto,* which despite her name was registered in Philadel-phia, laden with barrel staves, baled counterpanes, ladies' boots, and casked pickles. The seasoned oak made a capital bonfire.

The next morning dawn light revealed a smudge of smoke, a steamer hull down. Trezevant speculated aloud that it might be the California steamer, a regular fast packet that carried Western bullion, mail, and pas-sengers between Panama and New York. But since it might also be a Fed-eral war-steamer, it was left to fade gradually over the horizon. Later that day they overtook *Astrophel,* laden with nitre guano from Chile. Five hun-dred tons of bird shit carried her flaming top-hamper under with the haste of a shameful burial.

By now *Montgomery* was growing crowded with the crews of the cap-tures. Meanwhile Ker had been following the barometer with increasing concern. It had been dropping since the capture of *Carolinea,* and stood now at 29.5 inches of mercury; a low figure for such fine weather. As it was now hurricane season in the Caribbean, he set the crew to work preparing chafe mats for the sail-bunts and the lee quarters of the yards, where they'd brace up against the rigging; making sure lifts and trusses were well up and taut, hatches overhauled and battened down, and an-chors and guns secured against heavy weather.

The day after *Astrophel* went down a fresh breeze met him as he went on deck in the morning. Boatswain Boileaux was there too. He knuckled his forehead and asked if he might speak freely. Ker said he could, wondering what the Cajun was taking so seriously.

—Sir, I been asked by de men to make a representation to de captain. We thought we could ask you to intercede with him, you, if you would be so kind.

—You will have to share with me what is in your mind before I can undertake such a commitment.

—Yes sir. Well, here it is. The men see us sink and burn de ships. Don't seem right to dem. Dey don't see it as like good luck.

—I beg your pardon?

—*Akaniohmi achukma* . . . don't have a word for dis in English. Somet'ing like somet'ing dat you earn, only not money.

—You seem to be groping for what Mr. Emerson called Karma. Boileaux squinted. Ker quickly added, —But are you certain this is the true basis for their misgivings?

—Sir?

—Do you feel the men would have their objections satisfied if the ships were sent into port as prizes, rather than destroyed?

—Yes sir. Boileaux nodded eagerly. —Dat is exactly how dey feel. Dat we make de prize, not burn dem up all de time.

Ker suspected that was the real point at issue. Though, pirate or not, sometimes he felt like one when some taut-rigged clipper, timbers curved to the same line of beauty as a woman's limb, sagged toward watery night or trembled to the raging fire within. At such times he gripped the hurricane rail till his fingers went dead.

The mad logic of war! Its waste and unreason ranked with the time he'd had to let a slaver go off the Ashantee coast. Walking her deck, he'd choked on the reek. The slave-fetor that the unlearned thought was the native smell of the Negro, but was in reality the universal human stench of terror-sweat, vomitus, spoiled food, and feces. He'd itched to seize the greasy smiling men who held out their registry and chain them below in place of those they carried. But slaving was legal in Brazil. He'd had to make do with cursing them, then go back to *Owanee* to bathe. The stink of the slaver had clung to him for days. Or had that only been in his imagination?

He realized Boileaux was still waiting for an answer, and cleared his throat behind his fist. —I cannot pretend I like to hear such things from the crew, but you did well to bring them to my attention. Are the men aware they are building up prize-money in proportion to these captures? That we will be paid even for those ships and cargos we burn?

—Yes sir, I told dem dat. Dey know about prize-money, dem. But dey only get dat when de war is over, *oui*?

—That I cannot say for certain; it depends upon the prize-courts, and of course what legislation Congress may have passed while we are out here. I know they were debating the issue when we left New Orleans.

—But dey will get paid, is dat right for sure?

—The full faith of the Confederate government is behind that promise, Bo's'n.

Boileaux seemed about to ask something else; then, on reflection, decided not to. He tugged his hair and backed away.

On the eighth of September Trezevant ordered a course for the Danish and Dutch possessions east of Puerto Rico, placing them in position to enter Saint Thomas or Saint Eustatius. They could get coal there, and possibly news of federal ship movements. Aside from coal, however, their most pressing problem lay in the eighty-four captives below.

In the last few days the wind had steadily increased, and the seas with it, until *Montgomery* rocked and staggered through ten-foot seas. When they hove to a small fore-and-aft-rigger named *City of Silver,* Ker nearly capsized the quarter-boat getting to her.

The schooner presented the dilemma of a Yankee cargo in a bottom that according to her register had just been transferred from Maine to Canadian ownership. Trezevant puzzled over this for an hour before reluctantly ordering her release; remarking to Ker that dependent as he was on the kindness of neutrals for coal and supplies, he must make every effort to avoid provoking them. Her master agreed to take the prisoners off their hands. They made the transfer in a rising wind, scourged by squalls depending from the low-hanging gray. By the time *City of Silver* faded astern, the seas were kicking up swelling crests off which the wind tore long streaks of foam like hide raked from the backs of oncoming bulls.

That evening Ker's dead reckoning showed *Montgomery* thirty miles south of the Morant Keys. The sun had been invisible all day, but the gloom testified it must be near setting. The wind had increased to a gale. The rigging screamed like the overture to some dark Teutonic opera. Yet the cruiser plunged on, under reefed topsails and forestaysail. Her hatches were battened down and the cook-fires put out, but her head was still pointed stubbornly east.

Ker was in Trezevant's cabin going over their course of action should the weather deteriorate further when Simon brought the word down. The purser's mate hung on the jamb, freckles dark against chalk-white cheeks as the ship reeled. —Captain, sir, Mr. MacDonnell's respects, and the lookout cries a full-rigged ship two points on the port bow, headed north.

Ker asked, —Shall we let her go, sir? It is growing quite rough topside.

—Unto, First; that is not what we are here for. Let us at least see her flag. If it is too rough to board, we will order her to heave to until this weather passes over.

Ker pushed by the purser's mate and followed Trezevant topside in the gathering gloom, conscious already of a misgiving that the wall of wind and spray that met him at the top of the companionway did nothing to dispel.

15

T HE clipper was already nearly hove to when they made up to her, slogging and crashing across seas from the east crossed by winds from the southeast—a bad combination. The steamer rolled with a long, swaying lean that set Ker's teeth on edge. He'd never felt her to show much disposition to recover from a roll. Now, with her bunkers nearly empty again, she took even longer to recover. He fought uphill to the horse block and shielded his eyes from spray as he studied the craft they were approaching.

She had the Yankee's fine spars and taut lines, the sweep of hull and sprightly sheer. Modern-looking, yet not so new streaks of salt and rust did not mark her sides. A reef-knot of oilskinned humanity regarded them from near the wheel. Her sails were nailed down with studding-sail tacks and gaskets. Her t'gallant-masts had been struck down, and as they neared he made out the black threads of lifelines stitched along her decks.

Grice asked which flag he should run up. Ker glanced at Trezevant, who made no reply. —The Yankee flag, he told the quartermaster. A moment later it snapped out in the gusts with cracks and flashes of red and white like a hoisted string of firecrackers. Ker turned his attention back to their prey. A minute or two passed before red and white and blue lurched uncertainly on a mizzen halyard.

He nodded to MacDonnell. A moment later an unshotted thirty-two-pounder bellowed out a wet-sounding thud and a compact doughnut of smoke that shot into the wind, folded inward on itself, then was flayed apart so swiftly that if he had blinked he would have missed it all.

—*Craigdallie,* Dulcett said from behind him, snapping the glass open and then closed rapidly. It was a nervous habit he had, to fiddle with things in his hands.

Ker nodded, having made out the same legend on her quarter. —Sir Walter Scott, I believe.

—*Midlothian?*

—At any rate one of the Waverleys. He was a sheriff?

—A baillie, I think, the midshipman said. —Although I could not tell you the difference.

A great gray sea came out of the gathering darkness and smashed into the starboard wheelhouse, shaking the wooden sheathing. Spray slapped him in the face like warm spittle.

She was turning now, bringing her bow gracefully into the wind. As her foreyards braced round Ker caught the smooth planes of reefed canvas set flat aback. The wind peeled her way off almost at once, and she rolled, immobile yet every part of her in motion, on the wind-lashed breast of the darkling sea.

Aft the boat crew struggled to drop the quarter-boat into the water. Against the background of foam the paddle wheel was digging out of the sea, it seemed a mere cockleshell. He fought his way against the surging deck to MacDonnell, and yelled that if the boat turned turtle he'd best have the launch ready to go in after them.

The Australian's great black beard had fought free of its usual tuck under his tunic, and stood out stiffly to leeward. MacDonnell nodded toward where Trezevant gazed out over the sea. —Can't the silly bugger leave it till morning?

—He says that's not what we're here for.

The Australian nodded grimly and said he'd ready the launch. Ker watched Dulcett hang on the Jacob's ladder, waiting as the boat rose and fell sickeningly and violently, gauging his moment to drop onto a thwart.

—Hold up, Ker shouted. The midshipman glanced upward, swinging through the air as *Montgomery* rolled.

Trezevant listened silently as Ker put forth his position. That night was almost on them. That in these seas each trip increased the risk of a capsized boat and drowned men. He raised his hand and Ker stopped.

—Unto, sir, unto. I have already told you, we will carry out our orders.

—I'm not proposing we don't, sir. Only that you permit me to carry out the examination.

—How will that reduce the risk?

—I will examine the books and papers, and make the determination whether or not she is a lawful prize. If not, I will return; if she is, I'll put her crew off in her boats, and burn her before I return.

The captain agreed that examining papers on the boarded ship would save time. The determination of contraband status was the captain's prerogative, but in the circumstances, he felt justified in delegating this authority. Shortly thereafter Ker was clutching the gunwales, being borne up and down in dizzying sweeps as the coxswain swore and the men pulled grimly at the oars.

The cabin overhead was so low he had to take off his cap. The air was thick with smoke and the smells of cider and boiled meat, no doubt from the last meal served under the oaken beams. The master was a swarthy, beetlebrowed German with a narrow face and retiring chin. His language was unfettered as he swayed clawing through the pigeonholes of a rolltop desk. Ker waited patiently, though sweat broke on his forehead from the motion. One became used to one's ship, to her rhythms, however awkward or occasionally alarming.

The papers slapped down on the fiddleboarded sea-table. Ker turned the lamp up. Register, log, shipping orders, manifest. The cargo was West Florida cedar, bound for the mills of Rio de Janeiro. The case was clear, and he looked up. —Captain Mueller, before we proceed, I must ask you one question.

—And that is?

—Your ship's name: *Midlothian*? Or *Lammermoor*?

Looking angry, the man said neither, but *Fair Maid of Perth;* it had been named by the daughter of the original shipowner.

—Thank you, sir. Well, sir, I fear the fortunes of war are against you.

—You cannot bond us? I shall be glad to sign.

—You are part owner?

—To the degree of one-third, and she is not insured. Also my wife and daughter are aboard.

—I regret inconveniencing your family, Captain, but I fear the realities of the case give me no choice.

The Yankee doubled his fists. —Damn your eyes. You're nothing but pirates. Grits-eating, mush-mouthed, secesh pirates. They say you're chivalrous. How's this, then: if you can whip me, you can have her. But if I whip you, she stays mine.

—Contain yourself, sir. This is serious business we are about.

—I'm serious as hell, you mud-sill; I'll fight you for her, how's that?

—You must submit to fate, as many good man have had to do before you. Dark is on us; we must proceed quickly. Tell your wife to assemble her personal effects. Get your men into the boats. We'll touch fire to her in fifteen minutes.

He turned from Mueller's curses, sick at more destruction, yet knowing it must be carried out. To put a face of business on it was all he could do. He signaled to the petty officer at the door and went topside, holding his sword-hilt to keep it from denting woodwork that would soon be only floating ash.

Topside the wind had increased even more. The seas, crashing in nearly broadside, threw torrents of stinging spray at face level. Ker stood watching as the cruiser-men helped lower away the crew and passengers. Then, when they were on their way to *Montgomery,* started about their work of destruction.

After months at the business, the firing party moved with practiced art. They lowered such valuables as were wanted, the chronometers, cabin stores, medicine chest, and firearms, into the boat, then scouted the hold and paint locker for combustibles. Others axed down paneling and furniture, and piled the straw-ticked mattresses in the cabins and crew's berthing forward. They poured turpentine, pitch, tar, lard, and butter on the heaps and through the passageways, then went topside. After chopping the hatches free and kicking them down into the holds, they cast halyards and braces loose. Then retired to the lee as two men carried fire from the galley stove. Before long the crackle and dancing light from companionway and deadlight signaled it was time to depart.

The row back was one of the most hair-raising experiences of Ker's life. The boat swamped twice in the hundred yards or so running down to leeward from *Craigdallie* to *Montgomery.* Only the presence of mind of all eight seamen acting in concert saved them from overturning and foundering. When the sea-painter hurled down in the cruiser's lee, the shivering blow of their gunwale against the black heavy planks of the side made clear the danger wasn't past. Boileaux's face glowed above them, illuminated by a lantern, then Trezevant's. Ker swung his arm, urging the oarsmen and then the coxswain out of the pitching boat.

Belatedly, he realized the men lining the bulwark above him weren't looking at him. Nor did their faces' ruddy glow come from any lantern.

He turned, to a blood-chilling sight. In the minutes it had taken them to row a hundred yards, *Craigdallie* had turned into a torch. Sucked into life by the draught of the gale, yellow-white flames so bright they hurt his eyes leapt forty feet high from her hatchholes. The gasketed sails streamed rippling bands of smoke. Stays, shrouds, ratlings, swifters, and cat-harpins were black bars aureoled in red smoky fire. The mizzen-stay snapped outward, spraying sparks across the dark like meteors. The mizzenmast jarred, dropping flakes of fire; then toppled, gathering speed in a fiery arc.

A shout from above: Master White, recalling him to his own precarious situation. Blinking dazzle from his eyes, Ker judged the surge and kick of the boat and stepped off. His boot only just missed the lowest rung of the Jacob's ladder. His feet plunged, the boat fell away in a trough, and he dangled by straining arms alone above an angry tumult lit by glints of red fire.

The boat came back up, lunging in to crush him against the hull. The heavy oak and iron block of the boat-fall whipped in tight circles past his head. He'd burned one ship too many, and inanimate creation was bent on his annihilation as revenge. He got a hand on the next rung, then the next. Wheezing with exertion, as the boat stove its gunwales in below him with a crunch audible even above the shriek of the storm. A desperate strength he'd never known he possessed clawed him up the ladder hand over hand to the top.

—She's burnin' through, someone shouted in his ear. Arms stunned, ears filled with the wind, he reeled from the bulwark and looked back.

Into a black storm-night, yet lit with searching rays that outlined each wave and kindled incandescence in low-scudding cloud. He thought numbly that it would be visible a long way off.

The burning ship was drawn in fire. Yellow and white at her heart, tinted with blood-color along her masts. Her bundled canvases were outlined in flame. The incredible heat of the burning cedar, stoked by a hurricane draught, was eating through her planking. As a burning mass fell away he looked through futtocks and top-timbers and iron beam-knees into an incandescent mass that shone more terrible than the sun. Waves rolled through it and vanished in clouds of instantaneous steam that only dulled the glow before it returned to cherry-hot radiance. He watched for some seconds, awed, before he noticed that her angle had altered. He seemed to be looking at her stern—no. He rubbed his eyes, which were streaming with smoke-tears.

Suddenly he realized she was swinging downwind. Unbalanced by the missing mizzen, the wind pressure was pivoting her. He started aft. They'd have to steer to avoid. But they could do so easily. The burning clipper's dying turn was stately, her progress deliberate.

But before he could reach the wheel her fiery sails, gaskets gnawed through by hungry flame, suddenly bellied in the storm wind. The yards wheeled, jerking braces apart in clouds of tornadoing sparks. Ker shouted to the helmsmen. They stood rooted, transfixed by the spectacle that was now rapidly bearing down on them.

The captain reached them before he did. Trezevant's open hand slapped openmouthed faces. Wheel spokes blurred in the fiery light, blazing and inexorable as the foredetermined orbit of Halley. Through the flying spray the rays and shadows played like magic lanterns in a fantastic theater, full of sound and fury, signifying doom.

The cold tones of the captain. —All bells, Mr. Kinkaid. Full speed ahead, and even more to starboard if you can.

Ker swayed at a sudden inclination of the deck. Then bethought himself suddenly of the spanker aft, double-reefed for the gale, but still carrying its press of wind. He swung, bellowing, and men ran.

Driven off the wind by steam and rudder alike, the naked lines of *Montgomery*'s forestays began wheeling to the left. But her fiery pursuer, lighting the bowl of night with a dazzle so blinding nothing else could be seen, still gained. Her topsails were now mere sheets and traceries of fire. Her stern reared on an oncoming sea like a huge and predaceous cat intent on her too slowly reacting prey. The chunking thud of the engines shook the deck.

But instead of thrusting ahead *Montgomery* rolled, so endlessly far he had to grab the pinrail to keep his boots on the spray-slick deck. The wheels and shafts groaned as she dug her port wheelhouse into the sea. With horror Ker saw the naked blades of the starboard paddles thrashing free. They jetted thin parings of foam astern to shred and dash against the revealed bottom paint.

Like two wrestlers moving into embrace *Craigdallie*'s blazing bowsprit, crawling with live flame from root to tip, inserted itself slowly over Ker's head. It passed between main and foremast, in among the guy-wires bracing the black iron mass of the smoke-pipe, and carried the top two-thirds of it off its castings. A blazing gout of sparks welled up from its amputated stump, blowing downwind in a fiery tornado. Yet still the sprit passed forward, searching like a vengeful fiery finger, *mene, mene, teken, upharsin,* over the foredeck, snagging and snapping braces and stays.

He suddenly became aware of a heat like the opening of a giant's furnace. Turning his head, he looked into its heart. *Craigdallie*'s deckhouse, shining with flame, was not fifty feet off, and swinging inward as the fouled rigging forward scissored the hulls together. He threw his arms over his face, staggered at another violent roll, and reeled backward into the heat-shadow of the wheelhouse.

With a sound like granite being ground to powder, the merchant's hull crashed slowly but with tremendous force into *Montgomery*'s paddlehouse. As the seas came down on the two ships it rose, then fell, the motion gnashing and crushing the two together like colliding icebergs in an Arctic storm.

Ker looked aft to see that the helmsmen had deserted their post. The lurid glare fell full around binnacles and wheel-grate, and steam rose off the cable on the tiller drum.

When he came out on the open deck the heat was so great he could not breathe nor see. Arm shielding his eyes, he groped for the wheel. Found the king-spoke, its brass cap hot to the touch. The wheel fought him, dragging to leeward; it took all his strength to force it amidships. With quick glimpses that scorched the delicate membranes of his eyeballs, he tried to judge the tilt and tendency of the two ships, interlocked and grinding like battling wasps.

He was staring forward when *Craigdallie's* still-moving bowsprit, on fire all along its length, overtook one of the seamen from behind. With the majestic imperturbability of nightmare it brushed him lightly off his feet. The next moment it had plucked him up into the air, the spiked-out bowsprit-shrouds caging him in as it carried him out over the sea. Looking down at his death, the doomed seaman clung to the burning boom for a second, two seconds, three. Then that clinging arm caught fire. His jacket took flame. And still the tapered mass of shaped and braced brilliance advanced, bearing him remorselessly out over the black water. Ker watched him struggle in helpless horror. Watched till he let go at last to drop pinwheeling into the dark. A patch of scarlet-shining foam glowed on a creaming swell. Both ships, grinding together with the fearful sound of a great mill wheel, passed over it, and he rose no more.

Seized by a sudden sense of threat from behind, Ker jerked his head round.

To stare without feeling at a sea towering over their stern. He sucked a breath and tucked his head, pressing into the wheel, wrapping his arms into the spoking. Then it was on him, tons of tumbling black water that swept his feet out from under him. He kicked at the grating while the twisting wheel he gripped like death itself wrestled him over in a complete revolution, head downward, then upward again, an Ixion in the bubbling dark, before he could brace his legs again. The breaking wave hammered forward along pinrails, hatch coamings, bridge stanchions, engine room ventilators, the legs of men hacking with axes, pushing detached and smoking shatterings overboard.

Then from nowhere the helmsmen were back, one on either side of him, and without reproach or comment he relinquished the spokes, pointing off to port. They nodded, and he took another step back, glancing from under a shielding hand at the millraces of the great wheels.

They were driving at full speed now. Foam shot steadily out along the port side. But duck low as he could, Ker could make out no thrust from starboard. He ran a few paces and bent again. Now the paddles were visible, between iron bracing and plank sheathing; yet he saw no motion in the starboard cage. At last, understanding suddenly, his sight traced mechanism. Eccentric, drag-link, inner rim were lifeless iron amid the boil of firelit sea, while the inner axis of the driveshaft spun in a blur. Smoke and steam sprayed out from the motionless sleeve clamp.

—She's broken. At last.

MacDonnell was shouting into his ear. Ker nodded, still eyeing the differential motion of the locked-together hulls. Trying to make out through fire and darkness what had to be done if they were to live through the night. They were riding together with sterns to the swell, the veered wind coming over their port quarters. That was why *Montgomery* struggled continually to turn to starboard, crowding herself into the fatal embrace.

Another swell roared behind him, then broke in a bubbling welter high as his chest. The roaring glow to starboard smeared golden-hot light over whirling foam. Ker saw with horror that the wind was forcing gouts of spray and spume into the open mouths of the ventilators. If the furnaces flooded, *Montgomery* would be helpless.

He realized the moment he bent to the speaking-tube that no word topside could be audible below. Not with the whistle the wind made in the open tube, the roar of storm and flames. He capped it and grabbed MacDonnell around the neck. Mouth to ear, he shouted, —Below, to Mr. Kinkaid. Secure power to starboard shaft. Port, all back full. The Australian nodded, ducked from under his arm, and ran staggering across the heaving deck.

Trezevant staggered aft, hatless, hair streaming water and blood from what looked like a scalp wound. Ker explained in single loud words how he hoped to extricate them. The captain nodded, eyes hard, and in them Ker saw tiny images of the flames that were now climbing over the starboard wheelhouse. At some point the inferno next to them must break apart, sink, go down, but so far the tough oaken knees and iron strappings, though he could glimpse them glowing forge-red within the flames, pinned the burning hulk together.

With a groan and a clanging ring audible even through the shriek of the wind, the port wheel braked to a halt. It hesitated for some seconds, then began revolving again, in the opposite direction now, slowly at first, then more vigorously. The paddles bit off chunks of the black water and rammed it bodily forward. *Montgomery* was stern to the sea now, her fantail rising as each swell moved in from the darkness, but not far enough to escape being swept. Ker got another dousing but this time barely noticed it. The water was warm as blood.

He watched through two more baptisms, arms locked around a stanchion, before the two ships broke apart, *Montgomery* swinging slowly left, the clipper, stern pushed around more and more rapidly by the wind, wheeling away to drift downsea. She rode lower now. The sea was gaining against the fire. Yet heeled by the pressure of the storm, her upturned hull still opened livid gaps to the molten hell within. When the swells pawed into them, like black claws thrust into the entrails of a dying beast, sparks shot up through the hatchways and flew downwind in whirling streamers. Her upperworks were mere outlines of red fire, pieces of which now and then gave way to tumble downward and outward in the storm, trailing ruddy lines of embered cables the color of cigar-coals in the darkness.

Freed of her ardent embrace, the cruiser lurched with awkward sluggishness in the trough. Her port wheel dug desperately at the sea, but the enormous accumulated pressure of the wind along her length stopped her head from coming back into the wind.

—This's a bloody bad place, mate. MacDonnell, back beside him. The Australian's voice was strained, as if he'd had to yell in the engine room too.

—You'll have to go below again. Tell Kinkaid, port wheel ahead, full steam, and keep her going as long as he wants to live.

As he reeled away, Trezevant beckoned brusquely from beside the bulwark. Ker unclamped himself and half-staggered, half-skated across the deck to fetch up next the captain. —We must keep her head to the sea, Trezevant shouted.

—I sent MacDonnell to put the port wheel ahead full.

—Well enough, but it will not suffice. We cannot stay on this course all night. Nor have we enough coal left to pin her here till the storm abates.

Ker's thoughts leapt out over the dark sea, taking instantly the import of the captain's words. The reefs and low islands of the Morants lifted to the north, at a distance, now, impossible to guess after days without a sight of sun or stars. They had to come about before those reefs tore her apart. Yet how could they bring her round without power? One wheel would keep her head close to the sea. It could not bring her through it, through the wind's eye and about on the opposite tack.

She was coming right now, though, head swinging slowly, then more rapidly as a wave seized her stern and pushed. Ker gripped the bulwark as she squared up to the wind. Beside him he felt the captain watching as intently. Once more or less head to the wind, they were safe, at least so long as sea room and coal held out. But they had to pass through the trough to get there. In the few moment's wait until they reached it, he let go his hold, worked cramped, painful hands, noticing only now he'd somehow stripped the skin from his palms. The burning clipper, he saw, was still falling away astern, rolling with sluggish acquiescence, as if surrendering at last.

The next wave hit broadside, slamming into the starboard wheelhouse so hard men dropped to their knees. She'd already been heeled to port when it hit, and at its impact the old packet reeled farther than Ker had ever seen her go, farther than he'd ever seen any ship go and live. From her gear and rigging came the splintering cracks of a dying machine. Solid slabs of black water, illuminated both by the ruddy bed-of-coals glow of the wreck, and the weird green swaying flash of a dangling side-lantern, rolled across the foredeck and broke over the coamings and guns as if over submerged reefs. Her masts groaned in their sockets, bending far out over the boiling surf as it passed out of their sight into black again.

He clung to the stanchion, feet dangling free of the nearly vertical deck. She could not live through this. No ship could.

He wrenched his attention away from oncoming doom. The helmsmen stood frozen, staring into the dark for the next one. Waiting for her end, and their own.

By sheer force of will he thrust away from the stanchion, and scrabbled across the slick, slanting boards to the helm. Rallying the frozen men, adding his own weight, he got it over once more. But heeled as she was, her only powered wheel was submerged from tip to tip. She struggled, but she did not recover. The remorseless wind pressed her down.

The next comber would sweep off the helpless human insects who clung to her.

If the wheels were useless, perhaps the spanker could help turn her head into the wind. He was turning to shout orders when he saw Trezevant and White had anticipated him. Men climbed about on the wildly whipping spanker-boom, casting loose the gasketings. But in the blink of an eye the wind snatched it from the half-loosed furlings and set it iron-rigid for one moment before a blackness showed along the mizzen. Then, quick as the flash of a blade in the dark, the sail ripped clear of its mast-hoops.

With the feeling of unreality that attended dream, Ker watched a seaman tumble head over heels in the air. He jackknifed like a diver, then plunged into the sea. Then the boom was empty, the mizzen-sail only a violently twisting kite of shredded cloth flogging itself apart at the end of its halliard.

From the darkness, crawling over the slanting deck, an unfamiliar shape, in oilskins lighter than those of the *Montgomery* men: Mueller, the clipper's captain. He shouted, —She's gonna go.

—She'll fight through.

—She's too crank. You're fuckin' fools to carry such deck-weight and no ballast. And my family's going with her, thanks to you.

—Go below, sir. You have no authority here, Trezevant shouted.

As the cruiser pounded to another assault of the sea the Yankee returned some quite sulphurous language, to the effect both ships would have made it through the storm if the Confederates had taken his offer of bond. Trezevant replied in the same vein. Ker was letting them go to it, too occupied with his own terror to care, when a movement on deck caught his eye. And a moment later, his full attention.

One of the thirty-two pounders was stirring. Then, as the deck slanted again, its shadowy bulk parted from the bulwark.

For a moment he could not believe his eyes. During *Montgomery's* conversion he'd supervised the driving of four heavy bolts, train-tackle and fighting bolts, through the bulwarks for each gun. During heavy weather the guns were secured to all four with stout cable, the whole two-blocked tight and double-checked to make sure just such an accident could not happen.

A loose cannon was proverbial in its hazard, and for good reason. It would wreck everything in its path, smash through skylights and hatch covers, kill men, and worst of all, set free the other Jaganaths chained about the deck. He could not imagine how it had happened. But no matter how, it had to be made right, and at once. He started forward, seizing men on the way by the scruffs of their mackinaws.

By then, though, the last fragment of bolt and strap had shorn and snapped, and the heavy oaken carriage had taken flight across the slick deck. *Montgomery* lay still cradled in its frightening heel, hammered down and kept there by sea after sea, and the loosed behemoth began rolling with gathering speed and a hollow rumble that lay like granite blocks under the shrilling of the storm.

Men saw it coming and scattered. The trucks grated over wood and line, but did not jam, as Ker hoped they might. Instead the black shadow skated onward, until the deck's slant lessened; then rolled partially back as the port wheel, straining at full speed, rose far enough above the submerging fluid to shove the bow into the next swell. At which point the monster slowed, hesitated, then reversed direction, gathering speed anew down what had a moment before been uphill.

A lantern flashed from the forecastle. In its light four figures stood shoulder to shoulder. So must antediluvian Man have huddled to garner courage, Ker thought, as he gathered with sticks and spears to bait the fearsome Mammoth. He took a few more steps forward, and was startled to see the others start back, pointing at him. One waved his arms in warning. He halted, glancing about as the deck hesitated in its starboard lean. Then, with the hollow boom of another impacting sea, it rolled again. Far more violently this time, with every apparent intention of continuing on over into a capsize. Far, far over she went, till the painted iron caps at the tips of her mainyards gored streaks of foam into the black sea.

Just in time, Ker scrambled from its path as the second gun left its moorings with a shriek of iron pried by main force from oak. It clamored over the snarled ruins of its restraining-tackle and headed with steadily gathering velocity for the lee side. On the way it smashed into the mainmast pinrail, sending a man spinning who'd been sheltering behind it.

Trezevant, howled into his ear, —They've got to go by the board.

—Yes sir.

—See to it. But do not place yourself in danger.

Ker didn't answer. The caution was useless. No one could venture on this deck, this night, without offering his life to Fortune with both hands.

Shaking herself, the ship was rolling back upright, though he could tell by her sluggishness she was tiring. The water was rising belowdecks, pouring down hatch and ventilator. She had only one chance to live. The guns had to go. Clinging there between the rolling masses, fitfully illuminated in their gigantic and irresistible courses, he did not see how. But it had to be done, or *Montgomery* and all those in her, servant and master, crew and captive, were doomed alike.

The lantern illuminated the men forward once again. They were advancing, gripping lines and broken billets of charred wood. It was the drill for a loose gun. Choke the trucks with dunnage, then get enough line to some solid anchor point to bridle its career. But it wasn't the answer this time. He gestured frantically, warning them back. They hesitated, and a curtain of spray blotted them from sight.

Meanwhile others had joined him. MacDonnell, hulking, the lower part of his face a mass of bearded shadow; Boileaux, with the squat shambling grace of the gorilla; the weak-chinned, outspoken Yankee captain, Mueller. And others . . . Ker pitched his voice to a throat-stripping howl, pointing to the hinged bulwarks on the lee side, explaining what had to be done. Then they parted, cowled and dripping faces turned toward the beasts they stalked. Ker watched his chance and when the deck rolled back a bit from its slant he half-knuckled his way forward, like some creeping Orang-Outan, to shout to the men forward.

He saw only one way to get the guns overboard. With time and light they might have dismounted the tubes, and pitched them overboard through the gunports; or lifted them with slings and cast them into the sea. Both impossible now, and in any case they needed the weight of the carriages no more than they did that of the burdening iron. But the carriages were too wide to run through the gunports. The only place he could get them overside was up forward, by the pivot. The bulwarks there had been hinged to drop away for twenty feet.

But first they had to coax the guns out of the waist. He didn't know if they could do even that, but they had to try. So that in the flickering dark, growing steadily dimmer as the glowing bulk of the sinking clipper receded in the storm, he urged the others on as the gunwale drove down and the sea flooded up. First to their waists, then boiling waves closed over their heads. They gasped and floundered, blinking with salt-scorched sight into lightning-pierced blackness.

At last the port bulwark slammed down, a sagging ramp into the sea. MacDonnell lost his footing and slid toward it, mouth gaped in a soundless shout, till Dulcett flung a line into his hands and they dragged him back aboard, flopping and splashing like a gaffed dorado.

The next half-hour stretched out into the timelessness that Ker had experienced only in storm or battle. Slipping and falling, in imminent peril of being run down and crushed, they pursued the rolling guns with lines and pry-bars. First one, then the other violently careering weapon was tripped up, its truckles jammed; then, gripped fast by struggling men waist-deep in black water, it was hauled bodily round by barrel and pomelion to point muzzle-forward. When he was satisfied both were under control he pointed to the one farthest forward. Signaling its keepers to hold it fast, he stood back, concentrating all his weary mind to judge ship, and roll, and oncoming sea.

Then suddenly splaying his fingers to command release. Hands lifted, lashings flew free. The black beast shot precipitously forward, jumping and rumbling as it gathered speed. Approaching in its curving orbit the opening through which it must depart this tortured present for the quiescent eternity of the mighty depths.

But as it gathered speed Ker saw by the flicker-flash of lightning that it wouldn't clear. He'd misjudged its course. Instead of going overboard, it would strike the corner of the remaining bulwark.

A moment later, an oilskinned figure leapt toward it, a baulk of what looked like firewood extended in his hand.

Ker saw his intent at once. If the truck-wheel could be braked, the whole moving mass would pivot, perhaps just enough to clear the opening and continue on into the sea.

The running man bent, and thrust what he carried beneath the obliterating mass of the moving gun.

But the accelerating shadow did not swerve. It continued on without check, and the man who had tried to stop it hesitated in its path, blinded, perhaps, by the darkness that fell as the gleam of the heavens flickered out. The next image in Ker's horrified eyes was that of the same long figure being brushed aside lightly as a child by a dray-wagon. In the next instant it was caught on some ringbolt or projection and carried on before it to be pinned, smashed, crushed against the solid oaken bulwark by a ton and a half of dense-cast metal and heavy wood.

A flash of lantern light. The man was Trezevant, mouth slack in surprise and agony. With another rise of the deck, another savage, lingering roll, the gun recoiled away again. Leaving the captain standing where the gun had smashed him, but only for a moment. He extended his arms, as if to fly, but instead crumpled.

The next sea boarded, tumbling and foaming as it swept the forecastle, and hid him from sight.

Ker started forward, but hands grabbed his jacket. —You cain't help him, someone shouted against the wind. —Any man jack steps in there now's a dead 'un.

Montgomery rolled again, with a groan of wrenching timber and straining iron louder even than the storm. The rolling gun reached its apex, paused, then recommenced its downward track. Fallen to the deck, Trezevant awaited it, propping his upper body with his arms. Frowning, into the oncoming face of Death.

But someone in a frock coat materialized between Trezevant and the oncoming mass. In the gleam of firelight Ker caught the savage grin of filed teeth. The flash of one live eye, and the silver glisten of another that looked not into the world of the living but that of the dark demons of an African past.

The gun rolled over Ahasuerus, replacing him with iron darkness. Remorselessly on across the deck, but altered slightly by that momentary resistance. So that this time it met not the oaken ramparts that had barred it from the sea but space; weapon and carriage projected itself onward, into the darkness, vanishing into the whirling maelstrom.

Even as Ker started forward, hands outstretched, knowing already, sickeningly, that help or commutation was beyond any human power.

The captain's legs were crushed, the long bones milled into jelly. The gun had smashed the old Kroo's skull before carrying him overboard. His brains were a long smear on the planking. But of the rest, there was no trace.

When Trezevant had been carried below, Ker stayed topside. He rubbed his face with horrified fatigue. With the captain disabled, the adamant duty of command devolved on him. Whether or not the ship could still be saved, he must endeavor to do so. And without further reflection he urged the wearying men back to the second gun. It followed the first overboard desperate minutes later, leaving the deck at least inhabitable without mortal danger, if still strewn with debris and intermittently swept by the sea.

Clinging to the wheelhousing in the rain, he felt her renewed buoyancy. She staggered upright now under the blows. They had some chance to survive the night, if all hands turned to. One by one he called master and boatswain and petty officers to him, and gave terse orders. He asked Mueller to take charge of the captives, and set *Craigdallie*'s crew at the hand pumps.

Controlled by stout tackles rigged before they were axed from their lashings, one after the other the remaining thirty-twos vaulted into the sea. He kept only the pivot. Kinkaid got the thrum-boxes of the steam pumps cleared. They got the bulwarks hinged up again, and the freeing ports cleared of rubbish and wreckage.

The turning point came at two in the morning, when despite the utmost fury of the wind the topmen succeeded in setting a storm-trysail in place of the vanished spanker. Its vane-effect slowly levered *Montgomery*'s waveswept bow around into the oncoming seas. An hour later, almost against his ability to believe, he fought her through the eye of the wind onto a port tack. Granting relief from the fear that any moment might run them on the submarine reefs of the night-hidden Morants, and some orison of hope they might still be afloat when dawn came.

When it did its gray cold light glowed on littered, scarred decks, strewn and shoaled with soggy embers, clawed-up oakum, fallen rigging, and hacked-apart hemp. Over it all, like strange flowers, lay scattered the pale, spiky sprigs of sargasso weed left there by the waves.

PART III

England,

September 17–November 10, 1861.

16

Nassau, the Bahamas ♦ Reflections on a Crippling and a Death ♦
Report to Mr. Whiting ♦ Enforced Idleness ♦ Instructions from Richmond ♦
Farewell to Monsieur C. Auguste Dupin

S OME days later, Dulcett sent word down that land was in sight. The passage north had been long and nerve-racking, made under sail, the cruiser's useless paddles dismounted to reduce drag. With only one gun remaining, any Union war-steamer guarding the approaches would find her easy meat. To reduce the risk, Ker had determined to address his goal from an unusual quarter. A course for the capital from the interior passage lay through an eighty-mile stretch of the shallow Bahama Banks. Their chart showed twelve feet of water there. *Montgomery* drew not much less than that, and in addition the chart showed hundreds of small coral heads, barely awash at low tide.

At seven in the morning he'd given the order to commence dismantling cabin paneling, bunk frames, furniture, and the hurricane decks. They would provide the fuel for the passage. He climbed to the masthead and conned looking down on water so transparent it was almost invisible. Cobalt-green coral-heads speckled across a sand bottom white as sugar. Though the reflection of the sky glared them out nearer the horizon, they became plainly visible two to three hundred yards ahead. Far enough away to avoid, creeping in at five knots, if one did not glance away even for a moment. They made it across just before nightfall. Another day's passage along the bottomless well called Tongue of the Ocean, the coast of Eleuthera low and everlasting green to port, and a long tack starboard and then south again.

And now, as he lit his first segar of the day, the harbor of Britain's premier port in the West Indies opened ahead. He exhaled luxuriously, tucking his thumbs into his vest. The skies were clear save for a faint wiping of cloud far above, chalk smeared on a blue slate sky. The trade breeze was steady from the east. It was a beautiful day and he felt almost exultant. Until he remembered how he'd come to be here.

He paced the length of a deck stoned nearly to the whiteness of paper, yet still inscribed with the scars and scorch-marks of its fiery trial. As usual, he thought, the sailing rig had come through better than the machinery. The topmen and carpenters had been able to replace or jury-rig most of the damage aloft, bending on new shrouds and fishing the shattered fore-topsail yard. The sailmaker's needles had flown, patching storm-damaged canvas. But as for their steamworks, Kinkaid was pessimistic. The starboard wheel was useless until the casting could be replaced. And once again of course they had no coal.

In clearing up about the deck, MacDonnell had discovered why the guns had gone adrift. The heavy iron bolts securing them had pulled loose. Not through any fault of the bolts, nor of the gunners, but because the prolonged slamming and grinding of the burning *Craigdallie* had stove in the bulwark. Thirty-two hundred pounds of cast iron and oak had done the rest, pulling and then pushing against their restraints during the cruiser's violent rolls until one after the other all four had sheared or stripped free.

Ker locked his hands behind his back and perambulated down the port side. He was remembering the scene in the surgeon's cockpit that dreadful night.

At four A.M. Willie had come on deck with a request from Dr. Steele for his attention. By then they were clawing away from the reefs, and he'd descended into the noisome, swinging, clanging darkness below. Not wanting to go, dreading what he'd see, but forcing himself to place one boot before the other.

Steele had set up shop in the wardroom, spreading sheets across the table where they'd dined and drunk and played cards. Parker Trezevant lay strapped down, staring glassily at the swaying betty-lamp that seesawed shadows across the room. Others injured in the blow lay on pallets on the deck. Groans passed from man to man at each roll, the wounded sliding into each other. Ker touched the captain's arm, gazed down at the unsee-ing eyes. —How is he? he asked the doctor.

Steele wore a blood-smeared apron over an embroidered waistcoat. Face-to-face with him the fumes of brandy were stronger than those of chloroform. They mixed with the coppery smell of blood, sweat, and bilge water, hot lamp oil and sweaty, unwashed clothes. —His legs must go by the board, the surgeon murmured. —At once, before he loses more blood. I am afraid I shall have to take them off above the knee.

—*Both* legs? Are you certain?

For answer Steele simply lifted the red-soaked sheet covering Treze-vant's lower body.

Ker turned away, clamping his teeth on his hand. He tried to steady his voice. —What if you don't amputate?

—Blood poisoning, gangrene, a painful decline, death.

—And if you do?

The old man smiled grimly. —Why, my dear boy, most likely precisely the same thing. There is merely a trifling additional chance of his survival. *Ubi turpus est medicina, sanari piget.*

Ker took a breath, looking at the bluish, attenuated visage. Trezevant's lids had sunk closed. A lock of wet black hair lay over the sheet. —His wishes?

—He has expressed unwillingness to subject himself to the operation.

—Then it would seem the case is clear.

Steele, cheeks running with sweat, explained that was not precisely so. A man's body belonged not to him but to the Service. The surgeon could not withhold treatment without the consent of the commanding officer. —And you, sir, are now in command. It is your decision, not his.

Ker looked at the closed eyes again, the craggy, sunworn visage whose every expression he knew. At last he said, —Do what best promises to save his life.

Steele had bent his head. And as Ker had made his way back up the passageway, he'd heard the nasal repetitive whine of the bone saw, and the screams that burst out with horrible force. He'd stopped there, and hammered his fist again and again into the unyielding wood. But it didn't block out the sound of a man's life being slowly carved to nothing.

In his cabin, Ker petted Dupin and fed him, instructed Romulus to lay out a fresh uniform, then went down the passageway to notify the captives they'd be debarking in a few hours, as soon as they were anchored in Nassau harbor.

He'd moved the Muellers and their daughter into the captain's cabin as soon as the conditions belowdecks made it possible. Trezevant had been moved into Steele's cabin, where the surgeon could tend him during the critical days after the double amputation. But first Ker had removed the commanding officer's correspondence to his own cabin, along with his commonplace book and the coppered padlock chest with the ship's register, funds, and sailing orders. Perusing a letter from Mr. Stephen Mallory, Secretary of the Navy, Ker learned that in the event of misfortune *Montgomery* was to report to a Mr. Samuel Whiting in Nassau for assistance and orders. The chest also contained a mass of bills of exchange, sight-drafts, bank notes, silver specie, and gold. Richmond had issued some to Trezevant as operating funds; the rest he had taken from their captures. Ker was careful to have the purser and his mate present for this review, and had them sign an entry in the log as to the total found.

Back topside in full dress and sword, he found the harbor pilot at the conn, Bob-Stay MacDonnell beside him, and a small steam-tug making up to their port side. Ker settled with the pilot for the fee and then stood watching as they negotiated the approach to a floating dock opposite the town. The waterfront itself was solid with merchant ships and the jute-brown ramparts of stacked cotton bales. Raw lumber was being assiduously knitted into more piers, and over the water came the thud of steam-hammers and the clatter of the hand-wielded article.

The pilot seemed impressed at finding himself aboard what he called "the celebrated raider" *Montgomery*. —Is it true you captured and burned over sixty vessels?

—Where on earth did you hear that?

—Read it in the New York *Herald.*

Ker said they'd done what came to their hand to do, but that it was far short of that figure. The pilot told him the war news. Lincoln had rebuked General Frémont and rescinded his proclamation of emancipation; the war had spread to Kentucky, which had so far remained neutral; the Federals had captured Paducah under a general named Grant. Asked about repair facilities, he said there was a small marine railway, but for machinery overhauls one had to send to England. Asked about Samuel Whiting, the pilot said the Confederate consul was a man of great influence with the governor. The entire port was feeling the effects of quickening trade with the Southland, Nassau being in an ideal position for quick runs in and out of Hatteras Inlet, Wilmington, and Charleston.

Montgomery was soon tied up and her unwilling guests released ashore. Ker had intended sending a messenger after Whiting, but this turned out to be unnecessary. A gentleman in white hailed them from a small boat, introducing himself as the consul. Ker invited him aboard. A glass of wine, the offer of a segar, and a leisurely exploration of their birthplaces and antecedents soon confirmed several mutual acquaintances.

Bona fides thus corroborated, Ker set to business. He began with *Montgomery*'s damage in the storm and the near-mortal injury of her captain. He'd looked in that morning to find Trezevant fevered and delirious, his condition grave; Steele had only shaken his head ominously when asked for a prognosis. —Our orders state that in case of emergency we are to rely on you. I therefore altered course for Nassau.

—Quite properly so far as I can see. Whiting had a languid air about him. His dress was of the finest, white tie and kid gloves spotless. A Masonic square dangled at his watch-fob. —I most sincerely regret Captain Trezevant's injury. He was by all accounts an ornament to our sacred Cause. But without his legs . . . I will arrange to have him transferred to a well-equipped private sanatorium. Tomorrow morning, if he is in condition to be moved. As well as any other wounded you may have to put ashore.

—Thank you, sir. Thanks to our captures, we can afford the best doctoring available. Can you arrange that for them?

—Your sentiments do you credit; of course I shall help you care for our brave boys. Well, well, you must know your fame has preceded you. We have heard much of *Montgomery*'s depredations to the southward.

Ker fitted his fingers together, wondering if he should add that the captain's servant had given his life to save him; wondering again what bond, what debt, what understanding had existed between two so different beings. But at last he said only, —So I have been given to understand.

—You do our flag proud, sir.

—If there be encomia due, sir, they belong to my commander, and to the officers and men.

—Can you proceed with your cruise?

—Not without major repairs. And even so, I have formed doubts as to the suitability of this craft for the raiding mission.

—She does not seem an unattractive vessel. At any rate, she strikes the eye as well kept.

—I take that as a compliment, sir, and will pass it to my bo's'n. But she is at best a mediocre sailer, and under steam her appetite for coal combined with her limited bunker capacity has been a continual drag on our operations. We had two near-misses with Federal war-steamers. We might as well try to rob trains mounted on a recalcitrant ass. Ker glanced round the cabin, feeling strangely disloyal, as if traducing a friend. —Will the governor limit our stay here?

—I will undertake to guarantee he will not, especially in view of your damage. I will convey your respects to him. You may wish to hold yourself in readiness should he desire an interview with our own Terror of the Sea-lanes. Whiting smiled to signal this was a pleasantry.

—How rapid are your communications with home?

—These days vessels run in to the coast at very short intervals. Normally I can place a message on an inbound ship and have an answer in rather more than a week.

—Would you do me the favor of forwarding correspondence?

—Most happy to do so. I cannot offer the security of a diplomatic pouch, but Mr. Lincoln's so-called blockade is of the flimsiest tissue. The Federals catch nothing but fishing schooners. I have from the most highly placed sources that their few seaworthy steamers are wearing out too fast to maintain at sea; the pretense cannot last out the winter. A packet for Wilmington is slipping her cables this afternoon. Have your mail at my office by two.

Ker said he would, and proposed another glass. Thinking of putting Trezevant ashore, he needed it. But the consul declined, citing press of business. Topside, MacDonnell, who'd taken on the duties of executive officer, waited beside him as he waved Whiting off. Then asked quietly for orders. Ker gave the crew evening liberty, and the notice that any mail destined for home must be turned in to the purser before one P.M. Then he went below, calling for Simon to take dictation of several letters.

Confederate States Steamer *Montgomery,*
At Nassau, Bahamas, September 15, 1861.

Hon. Stephen R. Mallory,
Secretary of the Navy, Richmond, Va.

Sir:

I have the honor to inform you we are lying in Nassau, New Providence Island, as a consequence of damage incurred during a hurricane south of the island of Cuba on the night of the 9th instant. Our starboard wheel-shaft was broken during a collision with a burning prize that same night. Considerations of survival dictated the jettisoning of all four thirty-two-pounders, leaving us with the pivot gun alone.

It is my sad duty to report that two men and a servant were lost during the storm, and that Captain Parker Trezevant was gravely injured in the line of duty while striving to save the ship. Both legs had to be amputated above the knee. The ship's surgeon does not venture to say whether he will live. As the next ranking, I have taken command pending receipt of direction from you.

During the period of our sailing from New Orleans to date we have captured and sent in as prize to Mobile one ship, the *Fair Seas,* under direction of a prize-crew headed by Passed Midshipman Cameron Harrison. We took and destroyed the following ships of the enemy: *Planet, Rochefort, Chryseid, Leonora, Wild-Fire, Carolinea, Senhor Pinto, Astrophel,* and *Craigdallie.* The combined value of hulls and cargo destroyed estimated at between one and two hundred and fifty thousand dollars. Bills and specie on hand totals eleven thousand nine hundred and forty-four dollars.

It is my professional judgment that although the above figures account her activities to date a success in terms of damage to enemy trade, this ship is not suited for further war-cruizing, both on account of mechanical damage, which cannot be repaired in this port, and her inherent unsuitability for long-range operations. She is slow under sail and short-legged under steam. The ideal raider would be a swift sailer with a small auxiliary engine only, coupled to a screw that could be hoisted or otherwise triced up to reduce drag when not in use.

Nevertheless, the crew, officers, and myself hold ourselves ready for such further orders as you may return care of Mr. Whiting.

Very respectfully, your obedient servant,
KER CLAIBORNE
Lieutenant, C.S.Navy.

Aboard C.S.S. *Montgomery,*
September 15, 1861.

Dearest Catherine,
Having the opportunity to indite a brief note for the afternoon mail I will take up my pen to assure you I am well, & to enquire with anxiety about your confinement. I have had no news or letter from you since New Orleans & knowing how difficult a time you had with Robert wish with all my heart I could be with you. I hope you decided to join your parents for the event or that at least you have engaged a capable doctor if you stay in Norfolk. My prayers are with you and I trust in Almighty God to preserve you as he has me through the last months.

We have put unexpectedly into the harbor of Nassau, in the Bahamas, after a cruize of no little interest and accomplishment but ending with a tragedy. Captain Trezevant lost both lower limbs from an injury during a storm south of Cuba. We sustained such heavy damage I do not believe this ship can continue in naval service. The captain always had doubts as to her suitability for commerce-cruizing but did his duty to the end in a most noble &

heroic fashion. He received his injury while personally endeavoring to recover the ship's stability by casting our ordnance overboard. He survived the amputation but is very weak, feverish, and off his head. I fear for his life, & if he survives, for his mind; it is fearful to think of such an active and courageous man bedridden and helpless for the rest of his life. He would actually have been killed by the loose cannon if not for old Ahasuerus. You recall the servant who gave you such a fright when you turned round at luncheon & discovered him behind your chair. He was no Christian: but truly was it said, Greater love hath no man, than he who giveth his life for his friend.

I continue well and think of you and Robert most tenderly, wishing fervently I could be close to you during your impending delivery. I have written to the Secretary for orders. It is not impossible that he will direct us to return to the . . . I almost said "to the United States," so heedlessly do the words occur to my mind! It is my fondest wish to obtain duty in Norfolk, & if that is at all possible rest assured I will make the utmost endeavor to be posted there or as close as possible.

It is very hard to be absent from you, my dear wife and child. I grow weary of these long separations. One can content oneself for a time but then something recalls you to me, & it seems then a long kiss from my love's lips would be very acceptable.

As you know, our side of the family are not large landholders. The Navy has been my livelihood as well as my calling. But when peace comes between the warring sections, it may be time for us to make new plans. It may well be that the Navy of our new nation will have no place for me. Our first duty is toward each other, to strengthen the sympathies & raise our family; beyond that we must seek what Providence has for us to do. It may be that some position associated with the port or harbor may become open, port captain or harbor pilot. If a modest amount of prize-money falls to our lot, as seems likely at present, it may be that we can buy some land, perhaps on the Eastern Shore. It is pleasant to dwell on such thoughts; but grim War may insist on dictating otherwise.

I will now lay down my pen. Good-bye my dear wife. May God bless you & keep you. Remember me to our friends. Write to me here via Mr. Richard Whiting, Consul of the Confederate States, Nassau. With love to my own dearest Wife and Child,

Devotedly, your husband,
K. Claiborne.

The next day the decks were quiet as the first contingent ashore slept off wooden heads. Trezevant was carried ashore, unconscious. Ker saw him and the others injured that hellish night settled at the hospital, a pleasant house above the harbor. Then went on to call at various chandleries. He was uncertain whether to reprovision, but purchased fresh vegetables and meat for immediate delivery. Wherever he went he was received with compliments, and residents pressed cards and invitations on him.

He turned them down, courteously, of course, but somehow he couldn't see chatting over tea while the captain lay between life and death. Whiting, however, insisted that he dine with The Right Honorable Sir George Bayley at Government House. Ker judged his reception there a success. The older men seemed envious, the younger respectful, the ladies excited by his presence. There might have been conquests, had he felt any desire for them.

A week went by in the same fashion: purchasing trips ashore, dinners with the local nabobs, a pic-nic for the crew on the hillside above the town. It was a pleasant change from sea duty, but the pleasure was tempered by his daily visits to the wounded. Also, an unpleasant sense of marking time began to grow on him, exacerbated by the discovery at muster that nine men had deserted to a blockade-runner.

Spurred by this, he rented a shear-barge and set Kinkaid's men to dismounting the wheel-shaft. An engineer from the Royal Navy and the proprietor of a local machine shop looked it over at his request. They agreed no jury-rig would stand up to full steam and heavy seas. The crankshaft itself, a forty-foot cylinder of solid cast iron machined to fit, had to be replaced.

Shortly thereafter a messenger summoned him to Whiting's office.

Without comment, the consul handed him a letter and retired.

> Confederate States of America, Navy Department,
> Richmond, Virginia, September 23, 1861.

Lt. Commanding Ker Claiborne
C.S.S. *Montgomery.*

Sir—

It is with sadness I received your dispatch conveying the news of Captain Trezevant's misfortune. Our acquaintanceship extended to when I was a member of the Naval Committee and I always respected his seamanship and skill. Not only that, but he exhibited the spirit of humanity which ever characterizes the conduct of our naval officers.

Your work and that of our other brave cruisers and privateers are driving Northern merchantmen from the high seas. The tripling of insurance rates between New York and points to the southward have resulted in immense losses in chartering, the flight of commerce to English bottoms, and agitation among Yankee shipowners for an early end to the conflict.

This destruction of private property must inevitably be painful both to those directing and those who must inflict it. Yet it is our most effectual means of striking back in the great struggle now under way for our new nation. Our Navy must act with two goals: to destroy Northern merchant shipping on the high seas and to force the blockade of our own coast. Our successes on both scores, combined with building programs now in hand, justify me in expecting that in the near future we shall restore unrestricted commerce with our friends and suppliers in Europe, with immense consequences for the maintenance of our armies in the field. If we can feed ourselves from our own fields, arm ourselves from overseas, rely on the obedience of our servants, and continually oppose a force at any point the enemy sees fit to threaten, it is plain the North's preponderance in wealth and population appear to no advantage, and our independence must soon be admitted.

I have considered your report together with previous letters sent me from the ports of New Orleans, Havana, and George Town by Commander Trezevant, and Mr. Kinkaid's reports to the Chief Engineer. With regard to the vessel now in your command, you will transfer her to the agent of the Treasury Department now in Nassau, to be repaired, renamed, and employed by that Department to carry freight inward to Charleston or elsewhere as they may judge necessary.

Discharging your crew, you will with such officers as you deem desirable to retain proceed to London by first available packet and report to Commander James D. Bulloch in that city or Liverpool as you may find him. You will also carry with you to London for delivery such quantity of specie as will be entrusted to you by Mr. Whiting, first turning over to him your funds and accounts from *Montgomery*.

So soon as any of the vessels now being contracted for in that country shall be delivered, you will in concert with Cdr Bulloch and our financial agent, the firm of Fraser, Trenholm & Co., adopt such measures as you deem best to arm and equip her as a vessel of war, rendering your ship as formidable as possible, without infringing the laws of Great Britain or giving that Government cause of offense; and having obtained a crew and all things necessary for an extended cruize, you will leave England in command of her, and proceed against the enemy. This Department will issue orders at that time for the locality and duration of your raids best calculated to be made so damaging that our opponents will be forced to withdraw their naval forces from the blockading squadrons to pursue you.

Carry out these instructions with intelligence and energy. Keep us advised of your movements and prevent their unauthorized advertizement. In all your conduct seize every opportunity to place the character of the war and Southern principles in the proper light.

I am, etc.,
    S. R. Mallory,
    Secretary of the Navy.

He sat for some time thinking after reading this, twirling out the ends of his mustache, which had grown quite long. Considering. Wondering. He'd hoped for Norfolk, but gotten London instead.

Catherine? Robert? Home? He could indeed write back to Mallory, and ask for other orders. But this was no small matter his country was asking him to undertake. A command at sea in wartime . . . no Navy man could ask for more than that. It might mean another year before he saw home again. But this war could not last another year. The Union army had turned tail at Manassas. The blockade was crumbling. The New England shippers were suing for peace. It might very well be ratified by the time he even got to England.

London. In winter. He'd need a good overcoat, shawl, heavy gloves. And he must, at last, do something about finding Dupin a permanent home. He could not possibly take the ape to London. The animals were notoriously susceptible to disorders of the lungs. For a moment he wavered. He'd miss the beast, despite all its shortcomings and foolery. Then he admitted to himself that yes, he'd miss him, but that not having him on his back, often literally, would be a vast and overwhelming relief.

When his thoughts were in order, he went in search of Whiting, to ask how he'd feel about adding a monkey to his household.

17

THE Channel at last, after a voyage beset by storm. The packet had
rolled till the tiny cabin he shared with two other gentlemen
grew close. Till the reeks of chewing tobacco and stale food and
the hoarse bark of his bunkmates retching forced him topside to avoid
joining them. They'd turned at the North Foreland light at midnight,
and run along off a coast twinkling with distant lights. Dawn revealed
green slopes dotted with country houses and stands of trees, the hillsides
stippled with moving cloud-shadows and cloud-colored dots he guessed
were sheep.

He went below for kippered salmon, bread and butter, and a mug of
hot sweet hyson. When he returned land lay close to port, dun-colored
houses heaped around a steeple. Gravesend, he guessed.

The passengers came up. The gentlemen were freshly shaven, some for
the first time since Nassau. They wore black frock coats, gold watch
chains, and top hats; the ladies dull-hued traveling dresses and bonnets.
Two aged Frenchwomen conversed animatedly, showing yellowed teeth.
They were arguing, in their native tongue, over which hotel was the better value, Mivart's or Morley's, and how poorly English hotels compared

to the article in Rouen. Ker raised his eyes to a darkness in the bright sky, an ocher aura, like the dust storms along the coast of North Africa.

With each passing hour the river narrowed. Colliers, luggers, black-sided steamers churned past, outbound to Melbourne or Canton or Capetown. And threading among them tiny sail-craft, cockleshells bobbing in the wakes like kindling chips. The river too changed as they steamed past Greenwich, from slate blue to a grayish cast.

The sky ahead had grown steadily darker, and as they entered that zone of sombered light the clear sea air gave way to a roseate and impalpable fog that had no beginning and seemingly no end. Through it gradually loomed up a wilderness of masts, rigging, smokestacks, cranes, steeples, coal-tipples. The lurid yellow-scarlet of gasometer-flares guttered deep within it. The river writhed as if tormented, and from every quarter a growling roar supplemented their engines. The air grew denser, the sunlight a golden violet, as if one looked up from underwater at its shivering rays. Warehouses and factory buildings lined the riverbanks, some close to tumbling down, others new, shining in the sun. The muddy stream now stank so horribly the Frenchwomen moaned through cologne-soaked handkerchiefs. On the waves rocked a blackened rimy powder. The water gleamed a sickening pink and green, with streaks of piss-colored foam. A sailing-barge lumbered past. Its brick-colored mainsail was lettered in incongruous gilt *Farmer & Rogers's. The Great Shawl and Cloak Emporium, 171 Regent Street.*

Their party numbered six—seven if Ker counted Romulus—himself, Dulcett, MacDonnell, Kinkaid, Dr. Steele, and the purser's assistant and captain's writer, Simon. The other officers, warrants, and senior seamen had been left with the former *Montgomery,* now *Blackhaw,* to accompany her into her new career as a blockade-runner. Dulcett, MacDonnell, and Kinkaid shared a cabin with a padlocked iron box. It contained two hundred thousand dollars in bar and coin gold, the specie shipment being forwarded to the Confederacy's financial agents. Ker had made clear he never wanted to see all three topside at once. One must always remain in the cabin, with the gold.

Steele cleared his throat portentously at the rail beside him. —The Queen of the World. Each time, she appears more inhuman, more unnatural, and more oppressive.

—You are not impressed, Doctor?

The surgeon harrumphed. —Impressed, sir? I'm appalled. Pray God our nascent nation never submits to the smutted glories of industrialization. Steele waved at the nearing pier, at the grimy throng already visible behind it. —Almost four millions of persons! Cholera morbus, typhus, the most fearful plagues of overcrowded humanity, exacerbated by a misguided burrowing that flings up the buried effluvia of ages. The most fearful agglomeration of ill-gotten capital, ignorant Irish, and misguided industry in human history. Individually I find much to admire about our English cousins. Yet alliance with them will be like standing beside a roaring machine hoping not to be caught by the sleeve.

—Better them than the Yankees. At least we'll have the Atlantic between us.

Steele regarded him soberly. —That is the first note from your organ, sir, which I have heard expressive of enmity to our former compatriots.

Taken aback, Ker was still reflecting on this when Steele went on, —Take care about your pockets, then, and beware handsome women and hansom cabs. There, sir, is the Tower; there, London Bridge; on your right hand, look up, the great dome of St. Paul's rises above the fog. We have arrived, gentlemen. We have arrived.

Jostled into place among dozens of other craft at the London Docks, their packet turned from a floating universe into a matchbox. The captain refused Ker's request to remain in their cabins overnight. He had to coal, refit, and board return passengers at once. A night's lodging thus became the first order of business. Steele vetoed Claridge's as too expensive, and anything near Leicester Square, but said Morley's was a good choice if rooms were available. Recalling the critical ladies from Rouen, Ker approved Morley's, and sent MacDonnell, as the closest article to an Englishman among them, ahead to make arrangements.

Then intervened some delay in the arrival of the customs agent. After an hour's wait Ker left the ship to stretch his legs. Remembering the theft of their mail in Havana, however, he left Gus Dulcett sitting on the trunk of specie, a loaded revolver concealed beneath his coat.

The stone quay was thick with luggage and passengers. As the wind had dropped the fog closed in. Smoke hung from boilers and furnaces. Drays and wagons streamed by. Confined by the stone canyon walls of warehouses, the rumble of wheels and the shouting of drovers were deafening. Nets of tea-chests swayed up out of holds. The herbal scents of tea and coffee, the citric tang of lemons and oranges, the smoky heaviness of hemp freighted the air. He strolled, honing his eye on specimens of the shipbuilder's art. They were either moderate-sized sailing vessels, or more modern steamers of iron. Belgian, French, Russian, Neapolitan—the world had come to trade, here in the heart of Empire.

He'd walked nearly to the end of the docks, was about to turn back when a finely turned form loomed from the fog. He groped his way over a wilderness of excavated stone, hundreds of navvies burrowing and carting great blocks of granite about.

She was a clipper-style craft of pleasing proportions. Her bows were thin and arched. Her masts were lofty, her lines slinky, her slim tapering yards squared by lifts and braces to the exactitude of a calipers. As he made his way toward her the fog parted around the figurehead of an immense raptor, wings outspread. Eight or nine hundred tons, he guessed, and with the grace of a flier.

A boy sat on the quay, face smeared with some black substance. Ker addressed him a few words, and was told in a barely penetrable Cockney that the ship was a tea-clipper. He strolled her length, admiring tarred shroud lines, her fine, strong-looking quarter-boats. From a dropped section of the bulwark aft protruded the muzzle of a small gun. Her stern was elegantly turned and her run, as he looked along her, perfectly clean from stem to stern. She reminded him of their first capture in *Montgomery,* the sleek clipper they'd sent running into Mobile with Midshipman Harrison. And never heard back a word of her . . . The more closely he looked at this craft the more interested he became. Such a ship could show her heels to any lumbering Federal steamer, given the wind, and could stretch into any sea on the globe.

When he looked up once more a breath of smoky air stirred the Stars and Stripes. A fellow in a top hat was regarding him from the deck. Ker tipped his own, and his salute was returned.

—What'll ye give for ah?

Ker frowned. —Excuse me?

The mate laughed. —Said, what'll ye give for ah? The way ye're cah-stin' your ah.

Ker smiled; what he'd taken for an uncanny guess at his private thoughts was only a crude greeting. —A prime-looking craft, sir. And well kept to rights, from what I can see.

—Thank ye, sir. We do our best.

—Maine-built, I should guess?

—What! Indeed not. Greenman and Company, Mystic, and a soundah hull they nevah laid.

—What trade are you in? Tea?

—Not exactly, the mate said.

—Not exactly?

—Spices, yah might say, said the mate, looking aloft. —Running from Foo Chow via the Strait of Sunda. Ninety-eight days from anchor to dock, against the monsoon.

Ker whistled. That explained both her fineness, and the guns. Cinnamon, cloves, nutmeg; light, high-value cargos that lost their freshness over long passages. The spice-clippers ran the China Sea, the pirate-plagued Moluccas, the Celebes. He'd known of the trade and the great ships that ran it, *Oriental, Sea Witch, Flying Cloud,* but he had not realized the Yankee captains ran the English end of the route as well. Ninety-eight days from China to London! Yet it did not surprise him. With those long spars and lofty masts she'd carry a world of canvas.

—A moneymakah, right enough, and tight as a tea-chest, the mate said.

—Her name, sir?

—*Sea Eagle.* Ya see our figahhead.

—Spices from the Indies; what freight do you carry back?

—Manchester goods, and suchlike; sundries and rail-iron, the odd patent slip, but the Chinks don't buy much English goods. Carry ah back in coal ballast, most paht.

—You have an engine stack, I see.

The mate glanced over his shoulder. —Yah, the owner hahd the stink-paht put ahn to push ah through the cahms.

—What is the name of your owner?

But that trespassed some invisible boundary. His interlocutor narrowed his eyes, clapped his mouth shut, and disappeared. Ker paced her length once more, then turned back for the landing.

By the time he got there the customs agent was finished and they were free to go. Ker sent Simon out to secure the transportation. With considerable argument and shouting, he obtained three cabs, all in the greatest disrepair: windowsashes broken, checklines missing, starved-looking horses limping with blood-spavin. The drivers were the loudest variety of Irish, caked black with dirt and quite drunken. When Ker climbed in the first hack his boot went through the floor, and the torn seat was as wet with some noisome fluid as if . . . he did not care to speculate further.

They found Morley's on Trafalgar Square, a huge neoclassical block of soot-blackened stone. Behind it rose the steeple of St. Martin-in-the-Fields. Looking at it, Ker remembered David Copperfield meeting Peggotty on its steps, during the latter's search for Little Em'ly. And around it lay Dickens's London, an enormous expanse of stone pavement thronged with omnibuses, dray-carts, dogcarts, railway buses, Guinness beer-wagons. One huge conveyance resembled a Gothic cathedral, complete with niches for the saints, except that in this case they were occupied by headless mannequins in fashionable dresses. Advertising was everywhere, on the hoardings of crumbling buildings, handbills thrust into their hands as they stepped down from the cabs, posters glued on the very pavement. And everywhere, people, top-hatted, black-coated, dun-frocked, and becrinolined, more than he'd ever seen before; he felt exhilarated and suffocated all at once.

They engaged a flat of rooms and trooped down to a late luncheon. The gentleman at the desk did not find the name Fraser, Trenholm in any of the several business directories in which he looked, though he thought he'd heard of the firm. Then he looked at Ker's civilian frock coat. —Beg pardon, sir, but are you connected in any way with the Confederate army?

—I beg your pardon? Ker didn't like to equivocate, but he wasn't sure advertising their identity within an hour of landing was wise.

—Forgive me, sir, if I intrude; but if such were the case, there are two commissioners or envoys, I am not certain of their correct title, of that government in the city at present. A Mr. Yancey and a Mr. Mann, with a Major Huse associated with them in some wise. I can give you their address, if that will be of any help.

Ker called on the commissioners that afternoon, but found no one in. He left his card wedged in the door, and returned to the hotel to wait.

He was in his room reading the *Times* when a tap announced one of the hotel staff, bearing a card on a silver tray. Ker examined it curiously. It bore the name Alonzo M. Herter, and nothing else. He turned it over, but the obverse was blank.

—The gentleman is waiting for you at the bar, sir. He wondered if you would find it convenient to give him a moment of your time.

The "bar" at Morley's was unlike that room in an American establishment. In place of floors littered with straw, peanut shells, and tobacco spittle, they were of clean waxed oak. The guests occupied separate booths, rather as in English railcars. Ker walked the length of the room, nearly staggering as the floor seemed to roll slowly beneath his feet.

A quizzical lift of eyebrows announced what must be his man. He rose as Ker reached his booth. —Mr. Claiborne, I presume?

—You have the advantage of me.

—Beg pardon; allow me to present myself. I am Mr. Alonzo Herter, Esquire. I believe we have a mutual acquaintance in Commander Parker Trezevant.

Herter was of Ker's age, slightly above his height, with red-brown muttonchops and the broadest forehead Ker had ever seen on a human being. His hair was oiled back, his rather swarthy skin rough. He wore a good suit of English cut, a pearl-gray vest, a coral stickpin in a black cravat. A mackintosh and bowler rested beside him. His speech sounded more British than American. Ker said guardedly, —You know Captain Trezevant?

—I served with him in the Levant. How is he?

—Unfortunately not at all well. When last I saw him he was still clinging to life, however.

Herter gestured to his booth. —I'm sorry to hear that. Might we have a word in private?

—That would depend on your business with me, sir. May I enquire as to what it is?

—I will not disguise from you that I represent the United States Government.

Ker had been about to sit; now he hesitated. —Why should I speak with you?

—It could be helpful to your mission here should you and I become acquainted.

—What do you mean?

Herter waved at the seat again. —A moment of your time, and you shall know. We are on neutral ground, sir; relax your suspicions. I will not stab you, neither will I shoot. He crooked a finger at a passing waiter.

Ker glanced the length of the room, but no one was looking their way. It seemed innocuous enough; two gentlemen conversing over a drink. Yet some instinct set his pulse ticking over, warned him this man's words must be closely listened to, and his responses weighed. He sat warily as Herter asked for brandy and soda, glancing questioningly at him; Ker shook his head. The Federal asked quietly for service for them both. When the servant left Ker said, —Who precisely are you, and what do you want of me?

—I'm from Albany, originally, though I've spent the last seven years overseas. As a government employee—as I said. Your activities in England will be under my scrutiny. Therefore, I wondered if there might not be some mutually convenient way we can work together, the better to accomplish both our tasks.

Ker frowned, began to speak, but Herter went on. —We know more about you than you might think, Lieutenant Ker Custis Claiborne. I understand you continued in the United States Navy even after Sumter. One might infer from such that you had some misgivings about the course the so-called Confederate states were taking.

—I had them at the time, as did others. But my views have . . . hardened since. My service aboard *Montgomery* should suffice to back that up.

—Yes, *Montgomery*. The British press covers the depredations of the rebel raiders in great detail. You follow your state, then, sir?

—I do.

—And if Virginia should return to the Union, will you follow her back?

Ker hadn't expected this question, but found himself playing it out, like a gambit in chess. If he said yes, he'd be confessing a lack of personal conviction. If he said no, he'd be saying he owed loyalty to no government at all; and Herter could proceed from there. So he parried. —I judge that most unlikely.

—But if it should, you would resume your previous allegiance to the flag you previously served with such courage. Yes? You need not answer. I understand. But may I point out that one does not find such flexibility of mind among the majority of your compatriots?

The waiter returned with glasses and a black bottle. Herter smiled at him and paid with a gold sovereign. —My own view is that the present conflict is a tremendous and tragic misunderstanding. Someone must put it right. We share the same goal, you and I.

—What goal is that?

—The speedy termination of this war. The earlier, and with the less bloodshed on both sides, we can bring it to a conclusion, the better.

He pushed the brandy forward, but Ker did not touch it. He was on the point of getting up. Yet he did not. Somehow his presence had been detected the day of their arrival in London. He could not quite see how, unless word had been sent in advance of their arrival. He sensed a vast and shadowy web, whose strands he had somehow vibrated. Bringing a creature like Herter into the light. And face-to-face with the man, he couldn't help trying to find out more about the enemy he would now have to confront—not with cold steel and powder but in some mode of warfare unknown to him.

Suddenly he felt naked and unarmed, in this warm room buzzing with talk and smelling of malt and hops and good tobacco. Herter smiled faintly, toying with his drink.

—I am a Confederate naval officer, sir. My loyalty may be of recent date, but it is nonetheless real. What precisely do you know of my "mission," as you term it?

—At this point probably more than you do. Which I will be happy to share should we come to an understanding. Commander Bulloch's activities are well known to us. As are those of Major Caleb Huse, Mr. Yancey, Lieutenant North, and others.

With this Ker knew for certain what the man wanted. Although the details of a concrete offer might prove interesting, his duty was clear. He stood, not having touched the drink. —I am not the scoundrel you take me for, Mr. Herter.

—I take you for a man who thinks matters through, Lieutenant. Your identity will be concealed. You'll have a place after the war, no matter which side prevails. You'll also benefit in a fiduciary sense—

For a moment Ker considered laying hands on him. At home such a proposal, from such a man, would have demanded a horsewhipping. But here he was unsure of his ground. It did not seem politic to attract attention with violence. So he only said, coldly as he could, —I will make no arrangements with you, sir. Nor will I hear your proposals. Do not contact me again.

—You reject our friendly overture, Lieutenant?

—You may tell your masters I do.

Herter smiled gently. —I'm sorry to hear that, Ker. Because now we'll have to destroy you.

That evening he convened the shrunken wardroom at dinner, and explained they were to stay close to the hotel until he could obtain orders. That did not mean house arrest, simply that forays would be limited to a few hours and the men must travel in pairs. He debated telling them about Herter, but some protective instinct warned him to keep this to himself. He compromised by warning them that Morley's had always been a favorite hotel for Americans; they might expect to be thrown into association with Northerners. Hostile demonstrations would not make them welcome in law-abiding England. They should simply go their separate ways. Any efforts to make their acquaintance, however, should be reported to him.

Following which, he and MacDonnell and Steele went for a short walk to shake the sea out of their legs. They paced along the narrow streets in the dusk to the Admiralty. Then, with the common impulse of sailormen, turned for the river. But rubble and pits barred their way. The Gothic towers of the new Parliament rose to the south, but the failing light made them cautious. They recrossed to Whitehall, skirted St. James's Park, then walked back up Pall Mall to the beckoning finger of Nelson again.

———

The next morning a message awaited on rising. Commander James Bulloch was in London. He wished to see their senior officer as soon as possible. He could be found at the Great Northern Railway Hotel, King's Cross, registered under the name of Mr. Grigson. Ker went there on foot, a long walk up Gray's Inn Road through a chill rain laden with the choking vapors of smokestacks and chimney pots. He tapped at the door of the third-floor room.

James Dunwoody Bulloch was of middle age and middle height, balding, with a long brown beard worn in the style of a merchant-captain. The cadences of Georgia softened his voice. He wore the double-breasted black frock coat and white tie of a London gentleman. Ker's hand was gripped with a wrestler's force, his arm shaken to the shoulder. Ushered to a seat, he accepted an inch of Jameson's, offering one of his Havanas in return. They clipped and lit, and Bulloch asked about his passage.

Ker cleared his throat and asked the question that most desperately interested him: —Sir, first of all I must ask if you have received any letters for me—any personal mail or official letters.

—Mail? No sir, I have none. It would most likely be waiting in our Liverpool office. The principal seat of our navy in England, such as we have. Bulloch eyed him carefully. —There is a personal concern here?

—It is personal, sir.

—Might I be of any assistance?

—Thank you for offering, sir, but I doubt there is any recourse but to wait. My wife was to be brought to bed a month ago, and I've not had word from her since before then. Also, I left a good friend close to death in Nassau. So you see I am rather . . . on tiptoe for the post.

Bulloch ran a hand down his beard. —Yes, that would make a man uneasy. I'll telegraph to Mr. Prioleau and see if anything has arrived. Where shall I contact you?

At the name of their hotel the sun-crinkles about his eyes deepened, and he examined the ash on his segar. Ker tried to set aside his worries about Catherine and Trezevant for more professional matters. —You suggest a more suitable place, sir?

—Morley's is comfortable. However, I must caution you that there are numerous agents of the United States in this country, well provided with gold and bank credits, who are alert for opportunities to frustrate us. Depending on where we can find use for you, I may suggest removal to a more secure location.

Ker considered this the time to tell him about Herter. The older officer listened intently, studying his face, head leaning against two fingers. When Ker had done he said, —I'm aware of this scrub. How did he represent himself to you?

—As an agent of the government.

—He's only a private detective, but unfortunately the more unscrupulous and ruthless for it. He is employed by Mr. Moran, the first secretary of the embassy here. What exactly did he propose you do for him? To shorten the war, as he put it?

—I left before listening to any specifics.

—I understand, though it would have been interesting to know the details. On the whole you chose the wisest course; it will take some time for you to become knowledgeable enough to risk matching wits with such vermin. The diplomatic representatives of the United States are well provided with a large contingent fund. As they also represent a recognized government, with high positions and means of official contacts, we operate at something of a disadvantage here. Expect to be watched at all times. Advise your men to be cautious about new acquaintances, and about their own safety.

—I rest on your advice, sir. Ker considered a moment, then went on. —Speaking of funds, I have been entrusted with a delivery. Perhaps you can assist me in making it.

—You mean cash? Ker nodded. —Excellent; we have been perplexed by lack of the ready. May I ask how much?

—Two hundred thousand dollars in specie.

—Not so much as I had hoped for, but enough to materially advance our prospects. It is under guard, of course?

—At all times, by an armed man.

—You have the right to carry private arms in England, but as a matter of diplomacy I should advise you to keep your weapons out of sight. I will make arrangements and inform you where to deliver it.

Ker agreed, and handed over the letter from Mallory. Bulloch read it, folded it, handed it back. —I had expected a rather more senior officer . . .

but that is not to say I am displeased. In fact, quite the contrary. We have been following your career here.

—*My* career, sir?

—I should perhaps rather have said that of the *Montgomery.* The London shipping journals have afforded extensive coverage of your depredations in the Caribbean, and those of Commander Semmes in the South Atlantic. They have been the subject of comment on the part of the naval authorities as well. A Captain Tremayne has written an interesting study on the vulnerability of the British Empire to such cruisers.

—Pleased to have been of service, sir, but any successes we enjoyed were due to Captain Trezevant.

—Unto, unto, sir. Bulloch smiled and lifted his glass. —Is that not what he would have said? I knew him years ago. It says much of you, sir, that he employed you as his executive, not only once, as I understand it, but twice. Or am I misinformed?

Ker said that was correct, he'd served under Trezevant both in the United States Navy, in *Owanee,* as well as during the more recent cruise. Bulloch tapped his lips, reflecting. —Yes, yes; *Owanee.* Refresh my memory, sir; were you not continued in command of her after he left? By the Lincoln administration, by Mr. Welles?

Ker wondered glumly what he'd have to do to live down this particular memory. Others had postponed their decisions till the split was inevitable. Colonel Robert Lee, for one. He said as casually as possible, —I was, sir, briefly. I was loyal to the old flag until my own state left the Union.

To his surprise Bulloch leaned to slap his knee. —Say no more, sir. I struggled with the same quandary aboard the United States mail-steamer *Bienville,* of which I had the command. But was there not some haste or precipitancy about your leaving the former ship—

Ker said, rather more shortly than he had intended: —No sir, there was not. I left her in charge of her exec, and clear of danger. It is true she was attacked afterward by a privateer, but without my foreknowledge. There is *gossip* in circulation as to my conduct on that occasion—

Bulloch stopped him with an upraised hand. —Not in these quarters, sir. As I said, my own loyalties wavered at first. Mr. Lincoln's precipitate calling out of the militia against us settled the matter in a great many minds. Unfortunately, it has left the South rather grabbling to catch up for a struggle that must inevitably be decided at sea. We have no machine shops, no yards, no shipwrights. It therefore follows . . . he turned his hands outward, waiting.

Ker supplied the finish to his sentence. —That such things must be purchased abroad.

—Precisely so. And it would be a straightforward enough matter but for two constraints, funds and permissions.

Ker was beginning to relax, to see how Bulloch operated. He did not issue fiats; the commander was drawing him out, inviting him to make observations. So he said, —So far as the latter goes, I had understood the situation as follows. We have not as yet been recognized by Her Majesty's government. But the powers have admitted that we form a de facto government at Richmond strong enough to raise armies and levy war. As such, we should be permitted to raise and forward supplies in England upon the same conditions as the—government at Washington.

Bulloch leaned back, tented his fingers, a man preparing himself for a lengthy disquisition on a complex subject. —Unfortunately, sir, international law is not a science. The most learned judges variously interpret its provisions. It is a code that has never received the unanimous consent of nations, but rather the usage of the strong in relation to the weak.

—Like all law?

—You take my meaning. Well, international law expects that those nations which declare neutrality in a struggle must back it up by prohibiting acts of war by either combatant on their territory, as well as measures tending to increase their power to make war—such as repair of ships in neutral ports.

—I have had some experience with this in *Montgomery*.

—I daresay. The point being, to prevent one belligerent from making war on the other using the neutral's soil as a base. The English law which addresses this is the Foreign Enlistment Act of 1819. The relevant provisions prohibit the building, equipping, fitting out, and arming of belligerent vessels. Which of course— Bulloch tilted smoke toward the ceiling —is our entire reason for being here.

Ker waited, and after a moment the commander continued. —I have

looked into the in'ards of this Act with the assistance of a very able solicitor, Mr. Hull of Liverpool. Unfortunately, its provisions are open to interpretation, and no case has yet been decided under it. Mr. Hull solicited
the opinions of two eminent barristers. Their conclusions are, first, that it
is no offense for any person to build a ship within Her Majesty's domin-
ions, including all proper tackle, apparel, and appurtenances, so long as
said craft is not "equipped, furnished, fitted out, or armed" for war; and
second, that it is the armament itself, that and ammunition, which alone
fit her for war.

—But are we *not* purchasing such arms? I had understood we were.

—You are correct, sir, both Major Hume and myself are in constant
negotiation for war material, both light and heavy, and ammunition for
same; and the purchase and shipping of such is completely legal under
British law. Last month we dispatched a shipful of goods for the War and
Navy Departments direct from West Hartlepool for Savannah. I hope to
have another with eleven thousand rifles under way next month; with
which I intend to return to the home country myself. The point I am
straining for, however, is that we are engaged in an activity which skirts
the intent if not the letter of British law. Lord Palmerston and Lord Russell are not adverse to our cause, but neither are they particularly favor-
able. Important elements of the country favor us, others the North. We
will have to conduct ourselves with the utmost wisdom and self-control.

Ker turned this over. —You speak of building, sir, but it seems to me a
more expeditious way to put ships to sea might be purchase. I presume
you have explored this avenue.

Bulloch turned from the window. —Thoroughly, sir; assisted by my
lieutenant, who I believe is mounting the stairs just now.

The grate of a key in the door. The next moment Ker found himself
face-to-face with a familiar visage. The hair was longer than five months
before, the upper lip newly adorned with a ragged mustache. But indis-
putably the same hard green eyes of Lieutenant Henry Lomax Minter. He
seemed to hear again the denial of ravens in the Richmond dawn. The
two stared at each other as Bulloch, oblivious, introduced them.

—Mr. Claiborne and I are . . . acquainted, sir, Minter remarked.

—Is that so? Excellent. Shipmates?

—At one time, Ker said. Neither added anything, and silence ensued.

Bulloch glanced from one to the other, then cleared his throat. —Well, then. Minter was sent out from home to assist me in the procurement process. Henry, Richmond has now added to our effectives Lieutenant Claiborne from the *Montgomery,* which he left in Nassau—

—He *left* it, sir?

Bulloch frowned. —That is what I said. Did you not understand me?

—Oh, I understood you quite well, sir. It is only that Mr. Claiborne has rather a habit of . . . *leaving* his posts.

Minter spoke coldly, with deliberate meaning. Ker stood instantly, and they measured each other across the room. But Bulloch did not see this, or pretended not to. He said only, —Mr. Minter has been engaged in exploring just such purchases as you mention. He has closed on one already, and has located three more likely prospects. The specie you brought will suffice to acquire at least one of them. I propose you add your experience to his and advise us on which purchase will best fulfill our requirements.

Minter said hotly, —Sir, I've already advised you on that matter.

—And I am modifying your instructions, Mr. Minter. Are they clear now?

Minter looked wrathfully between them as Ker turned away to observe the gray air outside Bulloch's window.

18

A SWARMING of wool-clad humanity, hissing steam, a confusion of
hansoms and portmanteaus. Grim-looking women in travel suits
with shoulders bowed under showers of cinders. A local puffed
past beneath the arched cast-iron-and-glass shed, new but already coated
with a black jacket of soot and grease. Ker swung the coach door open, relieved to have arrived at last after nearly a full day locked into a compartment with the silent glowering Minter.

He'd attempted a reconciliation by trying to draw out his compartment-
mate about the ship he'd bought, but Minter had replied very shortly indeed. He'd next tried an appeal to pride.

—Come now, sir. We are gentlemen, and professional naval officers.
We have our orders. Let us put aside our personal differences long enough
to execute them.

But the lieutenant had simply said, —I have nothing to say to you, sir.
Then turned his head, scowling out at the passing Chiltern countryside.

So they'd rolled through the hills and towns of southern England and
the smoky hell of Birmingham, and come at last to the North and the
Mersey. The speech and the very look of the people had changed. And in
the jolting, intimate compartment their manner to each other had jelled

to a steely politesse. They spoke only on matters of business, and then as briefly and to the point as possible.

Very well. He could stand it. Ker looked to his baggage. He'd brought only one trunk, leaving the rest at Morley's with the others. He followed Minter's stiff back through the station and out onto Lime Street. From its elevation he could look down the street toward the river. Or at any rate, where the river must lie. For between rose a gray cliff of impenetrable smoke. The gas-standards above the street were burning in full day. A bellowing, metallic clangor, the endless ringing of thousands of hammers battering iron into shape, came from the rising smoke. This was the greatest forge on earth. The shipbuilder of Victoria's seagoing empire. No city in the world had more shipways or launched more bottoms than this sprawling metropolis of dirty air and dirtier faces.

Minter took them to the Adelphi. Ker checked in and sent up his trunk. They then called at Fraser, Trenholm & Co. at 10 Rumford Street, a warehouse office that Ker thought not very impressive for the financial foothold of the Confederacy in Europe. The front office was a simple whitewashed room with a gasolier burning in the smoky noonlight over an age-darkened wooden counter. A clerk led them past letterpresses and cabinets, bookcases of legal tomes and account ledgers, down a hall to another, unmarked door.

This opened onto a modest suite of rooms with small high windows and an eclectic decor. Cabinets held leather-bound books and lumps of mineralized rock. The walls were pinned with Royal Hydrographic Office charts of the Atlantic and the Bahamas, and in the corners rifles and carbines of various lengths and types of actions, many with bayonets fixed, leaned among the yellowing fronds of potted ferns. A large Confederate flag stretched above three aged copy-clerks with green eyeshades. They were scratching away with steel pens at high desks that made Ker think of the office of Scrooge and Marley.

An Englishman in his mid-forties rose and came forward, bowing politely. As Minter made no move to introduce them, Ker at last introduced himself. But Mr. Charles Prioleau, the resident agent, was gracious in his welcome, saying Commander Bulloch had telegraphed ahead about the valuable addition to their ranks in England. (Minter snorted softly at this.) As soon as Ker heard the soft *r*s and lingering cadences, he recognized the sandy-haired gentleman with the friendly eyes and long, slightly bulbous nose as no Briton but a native of the pluff-mud Low Country. Prioleau ushered Ker into his personal office and called for Scotch, water, matches, and segars. Ker accepted the drink, but declined tobacco; he'd smoked so much during the train ride his mouth tasted like a spittoon.

Prioleau picked up a long-nozzled brass can and began watering the ferns. —The commander telegraphed me about your mail. I'm sorry, but nothing as yet has come into my hands. I hope the news from Norfolk, when it arrives, will be cause for celebration.

Ker said his thanks with a feeling of dread. He tried to tell himself it meant nothing; only that his own movements had been so rapid any letters were still finding their way to him. He knew he had a tendency to expect the worst, no doubt because of the death of his parents so early in his childhood.

Like everyone else in England, it seemed, Prioleau had read of the activities of *Montgomery*, and plied him with questions about her captures, her captain's loss, her transfer to the Treasury, the strength of the Union navy in the West Indies, the efficiency of the blockade, and his personal opinion on whether the North could long continue the war. He smiled when Ker passed on Whiting's remark about the blockaders catching only the fishing schooners. At one point he wondered if he was being sounded out as to his own availability as captain of a blockade-runner, but perhaps this was his imagination; Prioleau did not recur to the point.

The agent explained that Bulloch had three ships in progress in Liverpool: *Oreto*, at William Miller & Sons; her engines building at Fawcett, Preston and Company. An as-yet-unnamed hull number 209, under construction by the Laird Brothers at the great Birkenhead Ironworks across the river. Lieutenant Minter's purchase, *Astacian*, was outfitting at the Toxteth Dock. All were contracted for through various private parties and companies to mask the identity of the final purchaser, more from the prying agents of Secretary Seward than from the British government; as long as a private buyer was dealing with private sellers, and ships were not actually being armed in British ports, the Liberal government had neither power nor desire to interfere. Finally, Bulloch and himself had already purchased and sent forward to Bermuda two ships that seemed suited as blockade-runners.

—And your own assignment, sir? Prioleau smiling, bending forward.

Ker looked at the open door, wondering where Minter had gotten to. But Prioleau must have thought it an expression of doubt, because he said —You can speak freely here, sir. All our staff are devoted to the Confederacy. Your interests are Liverpool's interests, after all.

—I am to assist Commander Bulloch in his work. He has asked me to begin by taking a look at the . . . *Astarte?*

—*Astacian,* sir. I understand it is a species of lobster. Prioleau tapped ash from his segar and smiled. —It is not my business to enquire as to how the Confederate navy names its ships or assigns its personnel. But I believe you may be in Commander Bulloch's mind for her commander.

—I don't think so, sir. Lieutenant Minter's already assigned to that position.

Prioleau cocked his head, like a parrot considering which of his stock of words he might produce next. But he came forth with only, —I have the utmost faith in Commander Bulloch, and in the rightness of the Southern cause. Once again, sir, welcome to Liverpool. I should be delighted if you'd dine at my home. Several prominent local gentlemen would consider themselves most honored to meet you. Will you be available tomorrow night?

Ker said he would be, and that he'd be delighted to dine. Seeing the agent was now consulting his watch, he rose. The Carolinian accompanied him to the door, parting with a warm press of the hand and a request that if he required anything to be done, anything whatsoever, he remained his most respectful servant.

The Toxteth was a short jaunt by hackney through a chill mist mixed with smoke and river-fog. During the ride Ker pondered over what Prioleau had said: that Bulloch was considering him for command in place of Minter.

Now the stubborn animosity of the man riding opposite was explained. No hunger was so strong as that of the lieutenant for command. In the United States Navy only the dreary accumulation of seniority lifted men from that catchall rank. Many remained lieutenants into their forties, grew gray, grew old, wearing the double stripe. Any chance to rise—

and command in wartime was that chance above all—would be grasped with both hands and all ten nails. Ker too felt its attraction. But he didn't want it enough to connive, or politic, to snatch it from the other. No matter what the suspicious brain of the man who glowered opposite might conceive.

While he pondered they clop-clopped through rutted streets loud with the clatter of machine shops. Street railways ran over it on arches of hand-laid stone. Dray horses strained at immense flatbed wagons laden with iron ship-furniture, oaken beams, spar timber. They descended at last outside a paling fence. They walked a quarter mile past boilerworks and warehouses, ship houses shouldering up the gray sky, and at last came out along a stone quay where fully two dozen nulls were rafted out. Still stubbornly wordless, Minter crossed the deck of a grimy collier and down a gangway to the deck of what Ker realized after a moment must be the ship he'd acquired.

He paced the deck slowly, careful to avoid gaping holes beneath which men could be seen working, sitting, and some even lying on their backs looking up through the open deck at the sky. When they met his eye theirs slid aside. He noted that the deck was of pitch-pine, Royal Navy practice, and that the timbers, where they were exposed, were quite heavy. He judged her about two hundred feet long and about thirty beam, with three stump masts (not yet rigged with topmasts or gear aloft) and two funnels. She was screw-driven, which was to the good, but was very little larger than *Montgomery*. He strolled back toward the poop, where Minter was discussing something with a workman in denims.

—This is *Astacian,* Lieutenant?

—It is.

—What is the rated tonnage of this lobster-boat?

He'd intended it as a joke, a pun, but from Minter's flush he saw he'd succeeded only in offending the man more. —Her gross tonnage is nine hundred and seventy, the Mississippian said coldly.

One question at a time, Ker established she'd been built at Blackwall in 1849 as a Royal Navy gunboat and had served in the Russian War carrying dispatches. She drew eleven feet six inches and retained her original Maudslay and Field three-hundred-horsepower horizontal double piston-rod return connecting-rod engines. Her screw was fixed and could not be hoisted, and she had a bunker capacity of only a hundred and sixty tons.

He fingered his Vandyke, disturbed. —Do you know why the Royal Navy surveyed her?

—They want iron ships now. Commander Bulloch prefers wooden.

—Why is that?

—They can be repaired more easily at sea.

—I see. Have you ordered guns?

Minter elaborated grudgingly. He'd bought two seventy-pounder rifles from the Whitworth Ordnance and Rifle Company of Manchester, together with carriages, shell, mounting tackle, and outfits. He'd also purchased four used but serviceable forty-two-hundredweight thirty-two-pounders from the East India Company. The guns and ammunition had been shipped to Hartlepool, where a merchant ship had been contracted for.

Ker paced the quarterdeck, looking up at the stump-masts. Then caged his top hat in the pinrail, ducked beneath a safety line, and lowered himself hand over hand down a grease-slick ladder into the engine space.

An hour later his misgivings had taken on concrete form. The old gunboat had her good points. Her coal-bunkers were arranged to either side of the engine room, and she had a condenser and fairly powerful, though antiquated and probably inefficient, engines for her size and lines. But she was rotten. At some point she'd been laid up ashore, and rainwater or fresh water had penetrated to her vitals. In the depths of the bilge his knife sank into crumbling, friable wood. The frame timbers were sound, and the deck planking in reasonable shape, but decay had riddled the bedding-beams beneath engines and boilers and probably the deadwood through which the screw-shaft passed.

He sat back on his heels in the dim aftermost compartment, remembering with a shiver the way *Craigdallie* had loomed over him, afire, inbound, vengeful, and malignant as the prodigious charger of Frederick Metzengerstein. Only *Montgomery*'s toughness of hull had brought her through collision and storm south of the Morants. Hundreds of miles at sea was not the time to discover your shaft vibrating, engine warping out of alignment, seams opening. *Astacian*'s small bunker capacity meant she'd also suffer from the same shortness of gait that had hobbled Trezevant in the Gulf and West Indies.

The true raider, he thought, had to be free of the necessity of wheedling fuel out of reluctant neutrals. Which meant a wind ship. Free as an albatross to cruise the ocean expanses, appearing only at widely separated points and long intervals to pounce upon unready commerce. Attracting after her, by inexorable logic, many times her own displacement in enemy steamers, each of which meant one less maintaining the blockade.

But Trezevant too, Ker remembered, had had his misgivings. He'd had to accept his commission nonetheless.

He emerged to find Minter gone and the workmen vanished. A shower had begun, laying a glaze of silver fog along every topside plank and spar. The rain was cold, reminding him winter was nearly on them. It dripped from the blocks of a shear and ran pouring through the gaps into the darkness below. Adding, no doubt, to the process of disintegration. If he had to take over, his first act would be to get into drydock, find out how far the rot had progressed and what could be done about it. But *Astacian,* or whatever she might be renamed, could never cut the blazing swathe through the enemy the South required. He knew that as surely as he knew he was soaked and cold, his kid gloves dirtied beyond redemption, his top hat lying flattened by the pinrails. It looked as if someone had stepped on it. He could imagine whom.

Looking out toward the smoke-shrouded city, he felt inexpressibly alone. He could not shake off the fear. Catherine had come so close to death with their first child. Not only had there been difficulties with the birth, but she'd contracted the terrible fever that so often followed. Only gradually had she regained her strength. He'd written from Nassau telling her of his posting to London, and had expected to find a letter waiting. Yet Bulloch had nothing, Prioleau nothing. He turned his collar up, staring into the steaming surface of the dock. Trying not to let himself imagine what it might mean.

The next night he paused on the landing of Prioleau's town house. A pale gentleman in dress blues looked back from the mirror, Vandyke neatly trimmed, hair brushed back with macassar oil. He had no desire to join the gathering he heard in festive mood below. It was part of his duty, like setting fire to a fine clipper. He sighed, heading down the stairs, toward the music.

The host made the introductions as he rounded the room, shaking hands with the men, bowing over the gloves of the ladies. A Mr. Frederick Richard Leyland, a languid young gentleman with an air of great wealth, was dressed in neck-frills, knee breeches, and buckled shoes, for all the world as if it were 1812. Ker met heavyset bearded gentlemen in evening dress and shining linen: owners of the great yards along the river, their names Curry, Preston, Laird, Butcher, Kellock. A Mr. Hull, whom Ker recognized as the solicitor Commander Bulloch had mentioned. Mr. William C. Miller, shipbuilder, and his wife, Margaret, who spoke a Welsh accent so thick Ker could not understand a word and was reduced to smiling and nodding. Mr. W. J. Fernie, introduced as a Liverpool shipowner and merchant. Captain James Duguid, with his wife, whom Ker was given to understand was Mr. Miller's daughter. A Mr. Whitworth from Manchester, who Ker realized only afterward must be the inventor of the famous Whitworth gun. Mrs. Mary Prioleau, a beautiful woman indeed, a native of Liverpool. The ladies spoke little but smiled constantly. They wore more elaborate dresses of heavier cloth than would be seen at such a gathering in Richmond or Charleston. All murmured congratulations on Confederate victories. Forcing something he hoped resembled a smile, Ker allowed himself to be drawn into a discussion of Liverpool weather as compared to that of Virginia. A bit later Whitworth asked in a confidential tone about the steam-frigate being rebuilt into an armored battery in Norfolk. Ker said that aside from the doubtful honor of helping burn *Merrimack* at her moorings, he knew nothing more about her than what he read in the *Times*.

As the hall clock struck eight the butler threw the doors open. The table was set for fourteen, each piece of silver and china aligned with a precision that would, Ker thought, have doubly pleased old Professor Chauvenet; the Academy's mathematics instructor was not only a demanding geometrician but a notorious stickler for neatness. The room glowed with dozens of beeswax tapers, each with its paper shade to prevent glare annoying the guests. The centerpiece was verbena, heliotrope, roses, and calceolarias, arranged tightly as a lady's tussy-mussy.

Ker was called on for grace, which he rendered briefly, in the Episcopal style. The party sat, and the first course was announced as a macaroni consommé. The food began: haddock in anchovy sauce, partridges in pastry. Roast mutton. Celery and peas, mince pies, and to finish, a frothy omelette. His servant recharged his wineglass each time the barometer dropped. After months of shipboard food Ker had to ration himself. The lady to his left was an earnest member of the Manchester Ecclesiological Society, and he was treated to a lengthy disquisition on piscinas and encaustic tile.

At ten Mrs. Prioleau rose. The gentlemen scraped back their chairs, and the ladies passed out with many a rustle and laugh. The men loosened cravats and unbuttoned vests. They lit segars at the candle flames. Glasses of port flashed out ruby gleams upon the tablecloth. Ker had expected to be called on for a toast, but none were proposed and the conversation immediately turned to what were obviously the subjects of consuming interest to everyone, politics.

The gist was that several of the guests were trying to form a combination through which purchases for the Confederate government could be consolidated. Miller said one reason prices had advanced on certain materials was heavy buying by officials of the United States, but another was the risk involved in losses to the blockade. Merchants as a class were friendly to the South, were looking forward to what someone had estimated as five hundred million dollars of annual trade between England and the Confederacy. He proposed a fund to which the largest companies and landowners in the kingdom could contribute in proportion to their shares. The fund then to purchase and make up cargos for the Confederate government, distributing the exposure of any individual across many ship-bottoms. Ker listened with interest but declined with thanks when Miller asked him if he could make such representation to Secretary Mallory. He'd only just arrived in the country, he said, and was a naval officer, not a financier. They had best apply to Commander Bulloch, or better still, to the commissioners in London.

Rising late the next morning, brandy fumes lingering in his head, he called at Prioleau's office at a little after ten o'clock to find the ferns being watered again, steel pens still scratching away, and Commander Bulloch in. Sitting with him beneath the Confederate flag was a stranger. A heavy-set, blue-eyed, brown-haired gentleman who eyed Ker from a round, childlike face. Bullock introduced him as James North, entrusted by Secretary Mallory with purchasing ironclad vessels in England and France. Both men seemed uneasy, glancing at each other. Ker was wondering if he should excuse himself when Bulloch cleared his throat and reached into his desk.

He looked at the small stack of paper squares, tied with a red ribbon, that Bulloch had placed on his desktop. The commander rose, nodded to North, and they left, easing the door closed behind them.

Ker sat for a moment looking at the letters. They lay so innocently on the polished wood. He forced himself to reach out. His fingers did not seem to work very well, but he got the ribbon off. There were several official-looking missives bearing the Navy Department seal, but the one he wanted was at the bottom. His heart sank as he saw that it was addressed, not in his wife's familiar handwriting, but in her mother's. And that it was bordered in somber black. He fumbled for a letter-opener, conscious as at a far distance of the trembling of his hands.

Richmond, Virginia,
September 16, 1861.

My Dearest Ker,

I pray God this finds you well and safe in England, where Father was told by Mr. Mallory's office you have been ordered. My previous letters, directed elsewhere, I believe, will reach you later perhaps.

I am sorry to tell you our little girl did not live beyond two days. She was no doubt weakened by her long and difficult passage into this life. Before she died, Reverend Butler baptized her, with her grandmother looking on. We will meet again in a happier land where we all will be together with my Mamma and the others we love and miss. Her name was Elfair, after Mother.

Although I am quite weak just now there is every hope I will recover my strength. Do not be angry but I did not engage a doctor for this confinement. At the suggestion of my sister we engaged a well-respected local midwife. I thought her very good but now that all has turned out as it has I torment myself that perhaps I did wrong after all. I do not know. Perhaps no one could have saved her—it was God's will she return to Him who justifies all suffering. I should so have liked to have you here when we had to bury my littlest darling. She lies now in the churchyard by St. John's.

It was quite the hardest thing I have ever done—to let them take her from me and lay her away in the ground—I am afraid I behaved in a way not suitable or reasonable. I was not myself, and for this I have apologized to those who tried to help me at that most bitter time. I pray God He will forgive me for my feelings of despair. I do not cherish them in my bosom but they seem to steal on me whatever I find to do.

I am slowly regaining my health & hope with all my heart you will be sent back to Norfolk or Richmond soon. We have much to talk about and I want above all to visit her little grave with you. I do not blame your absence or anyone else, only myself that I was not strong enough to give her life.

Truly thine, your loving wife,
Catherine.

He sat without moving for a long time, staring at the nodding leaves of the fern. He wanted to destroy things. He wanted to love someone. He didn't want to be here, alone, in this cold land. Even the goddamned monkey would have been some kind of company.

At last a tap recalled him. He rose quickly, pressing a handkerchief to his eyes. —Come in, he called.

—Bad news?

—The baby. My daughter. I'm afraid we lost her.

Bulloch pressed his arm and asked North quietly to bring whiskey. Ker said, trying angrily to stop his tears, —It's not necessary. Thank you. There is no anodyne for this.

—Perhaps we'd best leave this for tomorrow—

—No sir. I would rather proceed to business, if you don't mind.

—If you'd prefer, Bulloch said, carefully not looking at him as he re-blotted his cheeks and eyes and blew his nose. The commander closed the door again, and hesitated. —Well . . . well then. You have viewed the ships under construction?

—I have, sir. He cleared his throat. —I viewed . . . I viewed *Oreto* at William Miller and Sons. I inspected the engines building at Fawcett, Preston. I was received by Laird Brothers and inspected the progress of Hull 209.

—And *Astacian*?

—I have inspected her with especial care, sir, as she was represented as closest to being ready for sea.

Opening his notebook, still fighting the thickness in his throat, he summarized his observations. *Astacian* was both unseaworthy and un-suited to the mission for which she had been purchased. —In presenting this opinion, I do not wish to be understood as detracting upon those who contracted for her. I understand the selection is limited and the need great. She should make a reasonably well-suited blockade-runner, if coal's available at both ends of her run—say Bermuda and Wilmington. Con-sidering her shallow draft, she might also serve to patrol the Carolina sounds, or on the Mississippi. But she is not suited for a cruiser or raider on the high seas.

North spoke first, heatedly, as if he'd been attacked personally. —They send us here without ready money, and expect us to purchase ships. You can't deal with the British that way. One must have gold.

Bulloch waved him to silence. —Thank you for your counsel, Lieu-tenant Claiborne. But I must confess I did not find Mr. Minter's purchase quite so hopeless as you seem to view her.

—Not hopeless, sir. Only unsuited to raiding. She'll spend her time limping from coaling-port to coaling-port, and be swept up by the first average-fast Union steamer she meets.

—Yet those craft that are suited are already employed in profitable trade. And building them to order, as you must have observed, takes time.

—I reckon you're getting good value from Laird and Miller, sir. Those will be excellent ships. If the British permit them to leave the country, that is.

Bulloch grimaced, and Ker realized this was his constant anxiety. —I think so too; but you're right, conditions could change. The Yankees are beginning to suspect what we are about. I should not be surprised to hear of a fire one morning on the stocks. *Astacian* may be the best we can do at present. If so, the question becomes, will you take her to sea.

—I had understood Mr. Minter to have the command of her. Was he not sent here for that purpose?

—Your concern for another's career is praiseworthy, Lieutenant, but there are clear reasons for placing you in command instead. You have experience raiding. The secretary's letter directs me to place you in charge of a raider. The defense of our new nation requires me to man our ships with the best I find to hand. Should I judge it necessary to place you in command aboard *Astacian,* with Lieutenant Minter as your exec, I will do so. Bulloch paused, then added in a gentler tone, —Unless, of course, you should desire to return to Virginia for personal reasons.

Ker pondered this. —I need time to puzzle this out, sir.

North grunted, —Certainly, an instant decision is not required.

—But I would point out two things, Ker added. —First, that Mr. Minter would probably make as good a lieutenant-commanding as I. He's a good seaman and a daring officer. Second, that if I accepted the appointment, I should prefer not to have him as my second. Personal differences between us would not be conducive to the smooth administration of a man-of-war.

Bulloch said briskly, —Let us leave matters so for now. Meanwhile, I've been invited to several social engagements in London. But most like, they'd find a young hero more to their taste than an aging administrator. I will assemble the details, and make a list as to certain purchasing matters you can look into in the City for me. Call again this afternoon.

Ker took that as dismissal, rose, and bowed. Bulloch and North both stood, both shook his hand. But he noticed they did not speak again until the door was shut between him and them.

19

ULLOCH'S list was long and detailed. Ker studied it in the train. At
the twenty-minute stop in Coventry he bought a tongue sandwich
and bottled ale at the station bar, and a yellow-backed trade direc-
tory and Reynolds's Map of Modern London from a bookstall. On the
rails again, alone in his rocking compartment with rain rattling against
the window, he began jotting down possibilities.

The list seemed to encompass everything a nation at war might require in the way of marine supplies, but Ker knew it was only a small fraction of the embattled Confederacy's needs. Still, he had to locate and
contract for lignum vitae, quicksilver, glue, canvas and rubber hoses,
bunting, belting, bolt canvas, sole-leather, marling, proof alcohol, varnish, sperm oil, screws, wire cloth, vises, files, billet zinc, marine com-
passes, telegraph wire, stationery supplies, and two patent india-rubber
lifeboats. Letters of introduction to bank directors and packets of blank
bankdraughts were tucked into his overcoat, along with a commercial
cipher-book should he have to telegraph for instructions. His directions
had been to the point: purchase on the best terms possible for delivery in
Liverpool within the fortnight.

That night he stayed with MacDonnell at Morley's. The company had diverted itself while he was gone with visits to Cremorne Gardens and the Crystal Palace at Sydenham, and were ready to go to work. He settled their bills and instructed them to pack for a removal to the East End. He briefed them on the purchasing mission and split them up into teams, each assigned a class of associated wares; an arrangement Steele jocularly referred to as the Claiborne Purchasing Agency.

The next day was taken up with business. They found temporary lodgings, a suite of cheap rooms in the East End between Whitechapel and Commercial Road. The landlady, a tiny, blinking, stuffed-looking curiosity named Mrs. Turleady, eyed Romulus doubtfully. She touched his hand, as if suspecting his hue might rub off, but when it was explained he was Ker's body-servant seemed satisfied. They left Simon and Romulus engaged in unpacking and airing out the rooms. Following which, the "Agency" split up about its tasks.

Ker's first call was on a ship-broker in Leadenhall Street. Another office smelling of coal-smoke and gaslight, another counter walling off the hat-in-hand customer from the privileged within. After a wait of nearly an hour he was shown in to a Mr. Fickling, who seemed to have little time for him. He listened to Ker's specifications with averted eyes, sniffing through a reddened long nose, then said there were few articles on the market just now that would suit. A Mr. Soderbaum had been in earlier to see him on what sounded like very much the same errand, did he know Mr. Soderbaum? Ker said he did not, but sat up; a Union agent, perhaps, seeking to forestall Southern purchase?

He told the ship-agent his requirements were somewhat different perhaps; what was available? Fickling sighed, leafing through a packet of plans. There were numerous sailing-craft on the market but Ker's requirement for auxiliary steam power ruled them out. Newer, iron-built craft were available, but Ker knew their main decks would be too lightly constructed to bear the weight of ordnance. He excluded others for being too small. He asked about tea- or spice-clippers, remembering the one he'd seen at the Docks, but Soderbaum said they were heavily engaged, the business just now being brisk.

At the end of the interview he was left with only two possibilities: a rather elderly Russian screw-brig and a Scotch-built paddle wheeler. One was in Hull, the other in Southampton. The prices were reasonable, less than nine thousand pounds, which most likely meant their condition was not all that could be hoped. He took down names and telegraphic addresses, but doubted they'd be any better than what Minter had already looked at.

He was on his way out when Fickling called him back. —Yes sir?

—I wondered if one point had occurred to you, sir. The agent sniffed. —How badly do you want this ship of yours?

—What do you mean?

—You have looked over our ship list. But mark you, it contains, after all, only those craft which are for sale. D'ye take my point, sir? Perhaps not, you look fuddled. The agent spoke slowly, as if enlightening an idiot. —First find a ship you fancy. Then make the owners an offer. We should be happy to handle the formalities. You have my card, of course.

Ker wished he had more experience in the commercial end of things. The patronizing air with which the advice had been given rankled. It also sounded like an expensive way of proceeding. But he thanked the broker nonetheless and left for his next call, a caoutchouc manufacturer in Houndsditch.

He kept himself occupied all day. But that night, as Romulus dressed him for dinner in the little bare whitewashed room, a handful of Mrs. Turleady's coal on the grate dimly illuminating a threadbare carpet, a glazed crockeryware Prince Albert, and a speckled looking-glass, a black despond rose in his throat thick as the Thames tide. The rain streaked the glass like tears. In the street consumptive-looking men in stovepipe hats lit the gaslights one by one.

He could not rid himself of the images Catherine's letter had brought to his inner vision. He wished there were some way he could speak to her, share her grief, other than through the creeping medium of letters. If only the transatlantic telegraph had not failed.

But then he remembered Bulloch's offer.

He could go home if he wished.

———

The dinner that night was grander than Prioleau's, as much grander as London was than Liverpool. The house was larger, the women's jewels more resplendent, the titles resounding. The host of the evening was a Sir Henry de Houghton, a baronet. Ker knew this was not a high rank in English nobility, but to judge by the size and landscaping of his town home, the opulence of its furnishings, the age of its paintings, and the liveried servants who hurried to carriages as they drew up, he was a wealthy man indeed. The male guests were in dinner jackets, save himself and a few regimental officers in mess dress, while the ladies were elegantly gowned. Ker was shown to de Houghton as he stood talking with Mr. Yancey and Mr. Mann. He bowed past them to a tall colonel in the uniform of the Hussars; the officer returned the inclination with the most amazingly precise degree of condescension due their difference in ranks. De Houghton recognized Ker's name, and conveyed with lazy politesse how honored he was to have one of the heroes of the embattled Southern Confederacy in his home. Others nodded, including an elderly gentleman whose high cheekbones and faint half-smile struck Ker as somehow familiar.

—Lord Russell, let us present Lieutenant Ker Claiborne of Virginia. Claiborne: The Right Honorable Earl Russell.

The foreign minister's handshake was strong despite his age. —Sir, I feel distinctly honored to meet you, Ker said.

—The honor is mine, young man. Claiborne . . . you would be the young gentleman from the celebrated privateer. The great champion of Reform, former prime minister, and current foreign minister of the British Empire examined him with more interest.

—With the greatest respect, my Lord, not a privateer. A commissioned officer of the Confederate Navy, and *Montgomery* a regularly commissioned warship.

Russell did not seem put out at being contradicted, but already his eye was roving beyond Ker. —Of course; the distinction is evident. However, our public will insist upon confusing the two. Nothing entertains our newly literate public more than tales of . . . pluck. I should like nothing more than to sit down with you for an hour and hear all your tales of rapine and plunder on the high seas. It does sound as if you are making the Atlantic unwholesome for the American commerce. Although I had rather hoped the civilized nations had progressed beyond such methods.

—It is a legitimate form of waging war, sir.

—Was it not your own Benjamin Franklin who said that he had never heard of a good war, or a bad peace? Or was he a Northerner? I do not at this moment recall.

—I believe all mankind may properly claim Doctor Franklin, my Lord.

—Just so; well said, clever boy. Russell cuffed him gently. —Well, sir, though as a government minister I must observe the most scrupulous neutrality in the contest, may I extend my personal wishes your new nation may secure its independence at no distant date.

The others said gruffly "hear, hear." Russell proceeded smoothly, —Perhaps you can enlighten me on an issue which has us of a puzzlement in this country, Lieutenant.

—I should be most happy to try, sir.

—I have noted with interest the recent slowing of the war news from your side of the Atlantic. The quiescence since the great battle in July. Can we take this to mean the active phase of hostilities is over?

—I am sure you have more trustworthy sources of counsel on such matters than myself, my Lord. I am a naval, not an army officer. Moreover, I have spent the entire summer and fall at sea. I have however encountered the Union army upon one occasion.

—With what result, pray tell? The minister's eyes were roving beyond him again.

Ker said, —They seemed inclined to fight.

—And you too, no doubt. But do you not fight rather at a disadvantage?

—They shall find us not wanting in courage, at any rate.

The next moment Russell had put his hand on his shoulder. Ker at first took it as a gesture of encouragement; then realized he'd been deftly moved aside, that Russell, that arcane smile still playing about his lips, was now advancing through dinner jackets and elegant coiffures toward another old gentleman whose back was to him, but who turned, face wreathed in smiles, as they met.

Ker managed a smile at Yancey, unsure whether he'd just been complimented, insulted, or both. At any rate he had not committed any faux pas when so suddenly confronted with the man whose single word could decide the issue of the war. He felt sweat prickling under his jacket.

Yancey and de Houghton moved on to discuss a recent editorial in the London *Post,* coming out for British recognition of the Confederate and the resumption of free commercial relations, backed if necessary by the Royal Navy; cotton must be had and right speedily if English industry were not to slow to a near-halt. De Houghton asked why the victorious army of Bethel and Manassas was not being put to better use. Yancey replied smoothly that theirs was not a war of conquest but a state of present defense. Once the Union recognized the futility of further aggression, the field would be clear to a peacemaking initiative from abroad. To that end, new diplomatic commissioners were en route, a Mr. Mason, of Virginia, the new commissioner to England, and a Mr. Slidell, of Louisiana, who would go to Paris.

Ker was glad enough to stand quietly on the fringes nursing glass and segar for a while. Major Huse was announced, and bowed to him. —What news?

—I just had a word with Lord Russell.

—Anything of interest from the great man?

—He thought we were laboring at a disadvantage in opposing the North, but wished us well on a personal basis.

Huse nodded, looking concerned. —It recalls to my mind a conversation I had last April, on the train from Philadelphia. Caleb Cushing was in the seat behind me. The congressman from Massachusetts. He was kind enough to introduce himself—there is some slight connection between our families—and I asked him what he thought of our chances should events proceed to war. I believe I can quote his words. "The money is all in the North; the ships are all in the North; the arms and arsenals are all in the North; the arsenals of Europe are within ten days of New York and they will be open to the United States government while the South will be blockaded. What possible chance can you people have?"

—Yet you are with us, and not them.

—I told you his words; I did not say I believed them. I myself feel the issue was decided at Manassas. If we can hold our border peace will be ours by spring.

—With British help?

—If they recognize us, our cause is as good as won. Huse inclined his head, indicating the well-dressed crowd around them. —These people think decades ahead. They realize how much to the Empire's advantage a weakened Union would be. It remains only to convince them we're in earnest.

Ker nodded. Despite the affected-sounding, lisping tones of the florid-faced men and imperious women around him, he could not help reflecting that this, indeed, was the *gros jeu,* these bright perfume-laden rooms the ultimate battlefield. If the British navy intervened in favor of the South, not even the industrial might of the Union could stand against her.

Drifting through the crowd, he was suddenly confronted by a middle-aged gentleman of middle height and rotund build, whose white curls and ready smile took on a chill as he looked Ker up and down.

—Young man, I understand you are quite the talk of the town just now.

—I doubt that, sir. Allow me to present myself. I am Lieutenant Ker Claiborne, Confederate States Navy.

Behind the gentleman, a furious head-shaking from Huse. Ker blinked at him, then returned his attention to the man who was now saying, —Mr. Claiborne, is it? I am Charles Francis Adams, the United States ambassador.

Ker ducked his head. —I beg your pardon, sir—

—Pardon for poor judgment is readily granted, sir. But rebellion and treason are more fearful crimes.

—We are not rebels, sir. Only Americans defending our rights. Resistance to tyranny is no treason.

—I refer to your crimes against the human race.

Ker bowed respectfully, seeing they had no common language. He was turning away when it occurred to him that Adams might at least answer the conundrum that had baffled him for months. The one he'd posed to the bedraggled, beaten troopers at Smith Point. He turned back, and said, quietly, as if as a commonplace of conversation: —What is it after all that you people want of us, sir? Why can you not simply let us go?

—Democracy has a destiny in the world, young man. Your self-anointed aristocrats and their hoodwinked myrmidons will not deny us that destiny.

—To subordinate men against their will is not democracy, sir. I believe the word you mean is empire.

Adams smiled again, the same Bostonian frost on his lips as in his eyes. —Whatever you like, young man, he said. —Whatever you like. In plain words, then. Empire? Well then, you shall be our first colony.

Ker was staring at him still, barely comprehending their exchange, when the gong sounded for dinner.

When the meal was cleared and port served out de Houghton made a long speech in honor of the newly minted Earl Russell, to which the latter replied with a few well-chosen words. In the course of the evening Ker was called upon for a toast, and acquitted himself reasonably well, speaking simply about the friendship of the South for a mother country whose traditions and spirit she'd always tried to emulate. He caught Yancey's narrow-eyed approval. He was left with invitations to their clubs by several gentlemen, and to a weekend of shooting, which he regretfully declined, citing press of business.

He got back to the boardinghouse tired from too much rich food and wine. I need exercise, he thought. There had to be a rental-stables near St. James's Park. Romulus was unlacing his shoes when there was a tap on the door. —Sir? We're going out for something warming. Will you join us?

He almost declined, then remembered he'd spent very little time with them of late. —Just one moment, he called. Ensure your doors are locked when you leave. Rom, just give me the civilian greatcoat, I will put that on over my shirt. And the top hat, if you please.

—You wants your pristol-gun too, sir?

—I do not think that will be called for.

He watched the servant move about. In Richmond, Rom had been part of the house. A figure he'd felt the need to contemplate no more than the hangings on the walls. In this bare chill room he took on a new aspect.

And in fact in London he was not what he was at home. Under Victoria Regina's sway the black man was forever free.

He watched the boy hunt through the clothespress with patient slowness, moving with the loose-limbed grace he'd observed in many of his race. As if life were a dance, lived to some internal tune only they heard. Humming, the boy brushed the top hat, then laid out a white linen scarf with exaggerated gestures.

Propping his chin on two fingers, Ker wondered what went on inside that nappy skull.

As a boy he'd trapped muskrats in the Machipongo marshes with black Hanny, a crippled elder whose cunning and even wisdom were legendary. On the Eastern Shore white and black worked and dwelt side by side in the monotonous rhythms of the land, intertwined in a closeness that could only be compared to the ties of family. What could the emancipationists offer better? Hatred? Separation by force? The freedom to starve, like the miserable Irish in the North?

—There you is, sir, you is all set.

Ker said slowly, —Rom, do you know that at this moment you could be considered a free man?

—Yassuh, I knows dat. So's they told me, Massuh.

—Who's "they"? Who has been speaking to you? Suspicions of Herter, of Yankee agents leapt to Ker's mind.

The boy did not look at him, just went on folding linen. —Jus' folks. When I goes to take your shirts to de laundry and such. Soon's they hear where I from they say, Dey no slaves in England. You is free as de birds.

—And yet you are still here with me. Why is that?

—Where else I belong, Massa Ker? The boy glanced up, surprise plain on his face. Then looked out the window into the night. —I been with Massa Wythe's fambly since I crawling roun' shitty assed on de floor. Don't think I be needing to go anywheres else than right here with you. And you needs Rom, you do for sho'. My mama, she tell me to stick by you. You ain't been raised to take care o' yo'self, no how.

Ker blinked at him, taken aback at this turnabout. At last he said, —Thank you, Rom. For your service. For your loyalty.

—Aw, thass all right, massa. The boy ducked his head, looked embarrassed.

—We should be back in an hour or so. You needn't wait up for me.

The little band numbered four: Ker, Dulcett, Steele, and MacDonnell. Simon had declined the invitation and Kinkaid, who was having difficulty breathing, was drinking beef-tea in his room.

Outside the street was flickering into dimness. The fog glowed a disquieting deep red from numberless jets of gas. A cold wind lined with rain buttoned itself about their necks. Women in worn-out coats, shawls pulled over thin cotton housedresses, hurried by, pale-visaged, shivering. The Southerners ambled eastward, past Cannon Street Road and into a warren of narrower and wretcheder streets beyond. As they crossed each street ragged boys shouted "four toffs" and madly swept the curb and cobbles; then put their brooms on the ground and tumbled in cartwheels, faces and naked feet black with dirt, then came forward with hands outstretched. —Ha-penny for Jack, sir, their thin voices piped in the cold air. Steele tossed them a penny each and they whooped off, repeating the process at the next crossing.

The ground floors of all the houses were shops. But what shops, and what goods. Ker gazed at misshapen shoes, castoff dresses, at windows filled with lewd engravings. Dulcett stared, face to dirty glass, until MacDonnell yanked at his sleeve. From Commercial Road came a rumble of omnibus-wheels, dray-wheels, a murmur of humanity and the shriek of a whistle from out on the river.

The wind dropped, the rain lessened, the fog deepened as the night advanced. A diminutive gentleman with tired eyes and a red geranium in his lapel lifted his hat as he hiked past. Brightly dressed women accosted them, offering vices they were only too willing to specify. One lampreyed herself to Dulcett, hanging on his coat and murmuring into his ear as his eyes got wider and wider. Till MacDonnell told them —Begone now, ye donahs.

The painted lips twisted. —Wot yer bleedin' toffs come to Lunnun for then? Bum-tags! Ponces! Fookin' omipalones!

—Barrack me, will ye? Kiss me wild colonial arse, ye shickered poons!

The conversation descended from there. Between the Australian and the whores Ker could not have judged the clear winner.

When their voices faded at last Dr. Steele said condescendingly, —Really, Bob-Stay, what harm were they doing? The fair mercenary ones have been a godsend to each of us, I daresay, when circumstances left no other resort. They are only what society has made them, and I for one shall not cast the first stone.

—That little one had her hand down Dulcett's trowsers.

—And what of it? A young man must sacrifice to Venus. To curb his natural desires at his age will only force him to the solitary vice.

—He can find better goods than that. For his first time.

Dulcett, sounding strangled, —Can't we for God's sake talk about something else?

Ahead a mass of light burned diffusely through the deepening mist. They pushed past yellow-cheeked women, children weeping or staring vacant-eyed at the brightly illuminated doors through which men and women were continually passing and repassing. THE CELEBRATED HONEY-MEDICATED GIN, a sign announced. RENOWNED THROUGHOUT THE EMPIRE. Steele declared they had not seen London until they witnessed the depths. They followed him through one of the many doors that opened and closed endlessly beneath a huge inverted tree of gaslights, burning with an audible roar and roiling the fog as it rolled in ever-denser waves down the narrow streets.

The smell of the place was like a breath in the face from a dying potard. An exhalation of rotting teeth, urine, and cheap spirits. But at least it was warm. A high ceiling soared to darkness, but the regions below were lit by ribboning flames of gas fully two feet high. They lit half a score of barmen drawing and dealing glasses across the greasy counter. The bar was so close to the narrow doors, swinging open and clapping shut again, Ker was whacked in the back repeatedly. Ragged men and women darted in, clapped their pence down, drained their glasses, and reeled out. In its essence, he thought, not so different from the whiskey-bars of New York and Philadelphia. But the rags, the smell, the pallid, hungry, hopeless faces were a world beneath.

A barman demanded their orders. Steele requested a brandy. He sniffed at the brown liquid set before him, raised his eyebrows, and lowered it untasted. Ker attempted the "celebrated medicinal honey gin," but the stuff made him gag. He passed the glass to a trembling bony hand that appeared from behind him.

Outside the fog was more impenetrable, the cold more intense, the passing faces more desperate. The four men lit segars as one. —I for one have had enough, MacDonnell said. —Cremorne at least were gay. This is the very dunny-pail of Hell.

—What's wrong with that woman's face? whispered Dulcett fearfully.

Steele: —That is called pemphigus, my boy. A chronic affection of the skin characterized by watery vesicles or bullæ on various parts of the body.

—Did she get it from . . . ah, sexual congress?

The men looked at the midshipman. But Steele took the question seriously, expatiating at length on the venereal disorders and differential diagnosis by means of their characteristic and various lesions; hard and soft chancres, gummata, pustules, and rashes. Ker was sick of the subject by the time he realized they were lost.

—Do you recall the way back?

Steele said, —I believe it lies somewhere to our right. At worst we can strike downward toward the Thames, making our way back along Back Road, or Cable Street, wherever we chance to strike it.

They were feeling their way along a narrow lane when the gaslights vanished, leaving only the sickly yellow glow that phosphored it seemed from the fog itself. They drew together and pressed onward, boots clattering and sucking in alternate pavement and pools of semiliquid mud underlaid with battens of thin flexible deal-board, remnant of some street repair never completed. Ker wished now he'd brought one of the dueling pistols, as Romulus had suggested, heavy and awkward as they were. He peered back over his shoulder, into the seething darkness behind. Wondering at the thickness and peculiar smell of this London fog, a texture and presence he'd never observed in a sea-fog.

It was then he caught the outline of two black figures behind them. They wore battered plug hats, black mackintoshes, and carried heavy canes or shillelaghs. They passed beneath a faint light from an upper window, and he saw them more clearly for one fleeting moment: gaunt, intent, shoulders hunched, invisible faces seemingly fixed on the four companions.

Ker touched MacDonnell's arm and jerked a thumb back. The Australian nodded grimly and reached to halt the others within the beams of a guttering lamp. When their shadowers saw they'd halted they faltered a step, then came on, staying to the far side so the light touched them only glancingly. At Ker's inspection they screwed their heads deeper into upturned collars, averting their faces. He was fairly certain neither was Herter.

—Shall we knock the bark off these kangaroo dogs? MacDonnell, voice low.

—No. But we shouldn't be out here. We'd best return to our lodgings.

—But which way do they lie?

—I should judge, uphill from here.

It was not to be that simple. They groped deeper into a maze of fog-filled alleys only occasionally lit by ancient wick-lamps. The shops were shuttered, some obviously long abandoned. An exhalation of petrified shit, wet clay, unutterable age and rottenness breathed up from the mud. From the leaning tenements echoed screams, curses, weeping. Ker found himself shivering, whether from the sound of human despair or the raw cut of the wind he was not certain. The sense of danger grew, hastening his breathing, clenching his fists in the dark. The fog hurried past them. Until all at once it opened to reveal man-shapes only a few paces behind. He whirled, shouting —Stay back!

—Ye theer, said a voice from ahead. —Your purses and weepons, gin'lemen, and we'll be a-lettin of ye to gae free.

He couldn't be sure, but he suspected they were the plug-hats. They knew this labyrinth, and had circled back to trap them.

—I have only a few pounds, Steele said. —I am dropping them to the ground now. Do you hear the jingle? But I have a pistol. Be wary, my friends.

—Our purses, but not our weapons.

—Yeer weapons too, gentlemen, or 'tis your bodies they'll be findin' wi' the rays of morning.

Ker called, —Don't give them up. To the wall! Backs to the wall, with me!

Now other shapes coalesced from the whirling smoke-fog, dark as that fog, all with the same crumpled hats. Forced back, the Confederates found the rough stone of an ancient wall pressed against their backs. Their shouts brought only an ominous, waiting silence.

—Buggers, MacDonnell muttered. —Back to back, then, mates.

The blackness suddenly split with the spit-flash of a small revolver. One of their assailants cursed. A thud announced the impact of club or cane on flesh. The groups collided with threats and obscenities, the muffled grunts of effort and blind blows hurled in darkness.

Ker grappled with a broader, more muscular man than himself, whose breath stank sweet with uisquebaugh. His hand brushed a sharpness. He grabbed for the man's coat, pulled him close, and drove his knee into his stones. His opponent grunted with pain and thrust at him. Ker felt the slicing impact of a blade. He struck at the man's face, felt teeth crack. But a blow from a heavy stick telegraphed pain up his arm. Another blow smashed white sparks through his brain. He reeled away and collapsed into the mud. Someone kicked him. He doubled, cradling his skull, waiting for more blows. Then heard a close, snuffling snort, and the pounding of heavy feet.

The darkness came suddenly apart, pierced by lanterns and the batter-slam of heavy bodies into walls and doorposts. Hoarse hot breath passed over him, accompanied by the sucking of hooves in mud.

By the lantern-light he struggled to his feet, surrounded by the rushing bucking backs of hundreds of enormous hogs, mad with panic and the lash, rushing through the street as if down some immense slaughterer's chute toward their doom. A swaying beam of light showed him one of their assailants, glaring toward them from the other side of the river of flesh. Then the spit-flash shot again from the outstretched arm of the old doctor and the face turned about and sank beneath the rushing, bobbing backs.

Ker's boots found a slippery footing. His searching fingers found one of the shillelaghs. He swung hard as another figure loomed up suddenly in the dark, to the hollow thwock as oak hit bone and a strangled cry.

—To me, to me, *Montgomery.*

Dulcett's voice, high and exultant. Ker made for it, hearing as he did so the high distant shrilling of a bobby's whistle. Then they were together again, panting, under the overhang of a second-story shop, a candle suddenly glaring down as someone looked out, peering down into what must have been an impenetrable darkness.

20

The East End Docks ♦ A Mystic-Built Clipper ♦ Purchasing and
Ship-Brokering ♦ Advice from Liverpool

T HE next day he sat over the cipher-book Bulloch had given him;
then walked with MacDonnell to a station of the Electric and International Telegraph Company and sent a telegram describing
the attack on them the night before. It was essential to warn the naval
commissioner the struggle had moved beyond bidding for the same lots of
goods. He and Prioleau might wish to take precautions, both as to the security of their office and that of their persons.

On Dover Street, at Manton & Son's, he bought the largest-caliber
Tranter revolver he could fit into his coat pocket.

Toward afternoon Ker found himself on High Street. The great Docks
of London began south of there, in the crowded shambles of Shadwell,
and stretched westward, a watery honeycomb of basins, docks, warehouses, lift-bridges, and piers, to the grim walls of the Tower. Ships lay
rafted at anchor in The Pool until it was their turn in the queue to load or
unload, then entered through chasms in the city of stone to the great enclosed docks. He had remembered Fickling's condescending advice to find
a ship he liked and make an offer for her.

That was how he encountered *Sea Eagle* once again. Her lines caught
his eye as they had the first time, and then he saw the great gilded eagle
shining out in the murk. She had shifted her berth, and lay now

along the north face of the long central pier. Her sides gleamed glossy black, freshly painted, and her brass fittings glowed in the shifting light. Her houses were a light oyster, and her waterways were touched out in bright yellow. Her masts were finished bright and her yards and sprit black, and he saw chain aloft and iron where it was most necessary. He eyed her as he worked his way round the basin, and at last turned to MacDonnell. —See that clipper? Where the tug just put a knuckle in the water?

—I've been watching of her all the way from the other end of the dock. Flash jack, she is.

—She's Mystic-built, very fast, with an auxiliary and deck guns.

The Australian didn't seem curious how he knew these details. He only studied her again. —American flagged?

—Unfortunately, yes.

—She'll not be available, then.

—Perhaps not; perhaps not. But I wonder, Bob-Stay, if you would do me the favor of participating in a subterfuge of war.

When MacDonnell left him Ker walked the length of the docks, but no other ship caught his eye as the lovely Yankee had. He left the river behind and paced north toward their lodgings, through the poverty-stricken streets and back lanes of the East End. But instead of continuing, stopped at an eighteenth-century pub not far off Cable Street. He spread directories, maps, and buying-lists out in a booth that, he thought, Samuel Pepys might well have drunk at, and worked as he waited. MacDonnell ambled in an hour later. Ker ordered another porter, and the two huddled over their mugs like conspirators.

—She sails Thursday next, MacDonnell began. —For Canton, in ballast of a hundred and eighty-five tons of coal. But first she will call at Benares for the government opium sale; thence through the Palawan Passage to the Chinese Ladrones.

—Opium, Ker repeated. Not spices?

—Spices? MacDonnell smiled. —Not hardly. You thought her a spice-trader?

—That's what her mate told me.

—He was having you on. She's an opium-clipper, and fitted for the trade in the most thorough manner.

Ker sat back, absorbing this as his assistant went on. —I presented myself as a deck-officer in search of a berth. They said they'd just hired a new third mate, but as I seemed keen they were kind enough to show me around.

MacDonnell described a well-built craft with heavy scantlings. The frame was of the best New Hampshire oak, banded and riveted together with iron. She'd been begun in '54, held over during the Panic, then completed in '58. She was two hundred and twenty feet between perpendiculars and thirty-six feet at her beam. Her draft was eighteen feet loaded. With her flat bottom, that gave her more displacement than one might expect, something over a thousand tons. Full-rigged, with a suit of twenty-one sails, East India outfitted and classed 7A1 by Lloyds. The guns were smoothbore British twelve-pounders on the good old Nelson-style carriages. The engine had been installed in Scotland; not overpowerful, fifty horsepower at most, but essential when becalmed in the Philippine narrows or off the treacherous Hokkeen Coast. The screw hoisted into a slot and her stack telescoped down to avoid interference with the mainsail. The bunkers held one hundred tons of coal, not counting that shipped as cargo. Her speed under engine alone was about seven knots, but she had run three hundred and two miles from midnight to midnight under sail.

—Twelve and a half knots, Ker said approvingly. —She'd show her heels to anything.

—These coves want a swift horse under them, and not only for the pirates. The Manchus hate them as bring the yen-pock. I say nawt of the morality of the trade . . . but they sail fine ships, and make a fine profit.

—She'd make a capital cruiser.

—That she would; she'll swim like a duck and steer like a fish. But she's still bloody Yankee owned. Unless we could persuade them to sell?

Ker said such things were known; in Richmond he'd been invited to skipper a privateer sold by a Northerner to Southern interests. But a well-found clipper would cost at least thirty thousand pounds, not to mention the premium the seller would ask once he realized who the buyers were.

MacDonnell said that was a great deal of money. Ker agreed. —But the sum is not at issue here. What is in my mind is due to something that happened yesterday.

—Them street boyos?

—Disturbing, I grant you. But actually it was at Lord de Houghton's dinner party. I was called a pirate, to my face, and by a person I could not call to account.

MacDonnell drank porter, then scratched his head. —All the Yankee rags call us pirates. Are we to give a tinker's fart?

—If we are to be denominated buccaneers anyway, it seems to me we might as well deserve the appellation.

MacDonnell puzzled over this before comprehension lit his eyes, like a lucifer struck in a side-lantern. —By God! You mean to cut her out?

—The possibility had crossed my mind.

—And wouldn't it be a tale. But . . . you mean, cut her out and bond her? Or burn her, like the others?

—Neither, Mr. MacDonnell. Ker glanced about them, then went on. —We were sent here to put a cruiser to sea under the Stars and Bars. We were told there were only two ways to secure a hull. Buy, or build. I would propose a third way exists: to take one from the enemy.

—Capture it ourselves, MacDonnell murmured. —I should have to think about that, sir. I should have to think about that very thoroughly.

Ker stretched back and lit a segar, for some reason enjoying himself hugely. Perhaps it was the thought of the expression on Charles Francis Adams's face when he got the news.

—Do you recall the name of the mate they hired?

—The new third? As a matter of fact, they did let that drop. He were off a collier, just now laid up in the Grand Surrey.

They smiled together.

The next morning Ker left for Liverpool, having carefully instructed Mac-Donnell and Dr. Steele on what to do in his absence. He judged it best not to inform the others yet; the fewer in the know, the fewer could peach. They were given the bulk of the purchasing duties and kept clear of St. Katherine's Dock.

In Liverpool he held several conferences with Prioleau and Bulloch, arguing his case. They had their doubts, but from the first mention Bulloch's bushy eyebrows had gone up in delight and envy. He thought such a coup would be risky. It could end with the assaulting party arrested, or shot down. On the other hand, it might unsettle Yankee trade even more than the raiders had to date. The essential questions were, where would an attack most likely succeed, and how could it be carried out?

A China Sea merchant would be well-armed against boarding, although her guard would be down in the Thames and Channel. They might approach by small-boat once she was under way, but they'd have to make her heave to in order to board. Prioleau warned that any attempt must be well outside the three-mile limit. Taking her from shore would be a clear violation of English law. Bulloch agreed, nodding vigorously. They must do nothing that would infringe upon Empire neutrality. To do otherwise would imperil the purchasing effort on which the Confederacy's armies depended. They had to attack in international waters, in uniform, and under a clearly displayed flag. Under those conditions the British could not object, and they would receive the treatment due prisoners of war should the attempt misfire.

—Should we succeed, sir, of course, we will turn her over to you to command.

Bulloch wavered for a fraction of a second before inclining his head. —I could not take from you the spoils of such a daring coup, my boy.

—And if we succeed? Armament and ammunition?

—We have thirty-two-pounders, not of the newest class but perfectly suitable, and two fine Whitworths from the Manchester factory.

Ker was about to go on when he remembered. —But those are Mr. Minter's guns.

—He will not object, if it puts another raider to sea.

—Sir, Mr. Minter *will* object, and vigorously.

—*Lieutenant* Minter will obey orders or I will know the reason why. Mr. Whitworth will simply have to provide other guns for him. I daresay he will not object too much, at seven hundred pounds apiece . . . with the repairs now in hand it will not slip *Astacian*'s commissioning to any significant extent. Bulloch placed his hands on his chair and shoved himself up. —It is a capital enterprise, Claiborne, and William and myself will move heaven and earth to back you. But we must move swiftly with so few days left to her sailing. We will equip you; we will supply you; we will begin immediately to recruit a crew of stout Liverpudlians. It remains to you to determine on the mode of attack that will gain your prize without subjecting you to be hung by the neck until dead, dead, dead, as they say in the Old Bailey.

Ker nodded, dourly conscious that it might end precisely that way, not just for him but for all his men, if a Union cruiser happened by at the wrong time.

But war entailed risk. He could have died at Smith's Point, if the minié had struck a few inches higher; or been blown apart crossing the Mississippi bar; or been crushed or carried overboard in the shambles with *Craigdallie*. When duty pointed the way, no naval officer could do otherwise than face the enemy with boldness. No matter what trepidation lurked in his inmost heart. —Then I will leave you, sirs, with the caution that the two of you only will know the identity of our prey.

—Exactly what I was to propose myself. Good luck, Lieutenant, and Godspeed to you.

Ker shook their hands firmly, and bowed himself out. Realizing only when he was out on the street, with mingled guilt and astonishment and regret, that like one of Poe's dream-walkers, or madmen, those who looked a moment after on what they had done with sudden horror, that he had made a choice without even noticing an irrevocable and fatal decision had been made. That with those few words, in the room he had just quitted, he had closed off any possibility whatsoever of returning home.

21

S HE seems indeed a capitally appointed craft, Steele observed, pouring himself another dose of Calvados from an already crippled bottle. —Sturdily built, so far as I can judge, and most meticulously kept. Mr. MacDonnell is right about her accustomed cargo. The inspissated juice of *Papaver somniferum* has a smell that once nosed is not lost to memory; it lingers about her still. Under pretense of considering a cabin-passage to India, I was permitted to wander over her quite freely, though they did not care to have me touring the engine room unescorted. I may have inadvertently given some impression of unsteadiness on my feet.

Dulcett coughed into his sleeve. The surgeon spared him a censorious glance before returning to his topic. —There remain some uncertainties, however, Captain. Serious questions about your plan. Oliver, m'lad, will you do me the favor of reaching me that candle.

The purser's mate silently brought him the flame, and Steele bent it into his pipe with faint sucking noises. They were foregathered in Mrs. Turleady's so-styled "dining hall," cleared for the occasion and the landlady herself sent in search of a roast for the evening. A small, mean, and dirty enough room, but it offered the privacy for a lengthy discussion with all the former *Montgomery*s around the table.

On the train back from Liverpool a melancholy and self-questioning Ker had developed doubts about his own idea, to the point of considering setting it aside. He had resolved to present it to those who would have to execute it, and decide whether or no to proceed based on their reaction.

—She's an American clipper, you say? Kinkaid asked, looking up from the patent pocket revolver he was oiling. Since the assault by Herter's men, Ker had insisted they go armed at all times. The engineer held the pin-fire to the light, inspecting the bore. —The one on which Bob-Stay has been, ah, employed?

—Precisely. Ker nodded to MacDonnell, who had not been seen much about the rooming-house since being taken on in place of *Sea Eagle*'s third mate, who had suddenly been offered a second mate's position on a Bermuda-bound trader by a Liverpool firm.

MacDonnell repeated much the same information as he'd gleaned on his first visit aboard, though in more depth. The clipper carried a two-bladed Griffiths screw that hoisted into a trunk notched into her stern. She had a hundred tons of iron kentledge in her hold to steady her under press of sail and a bottom coppered with Muntz metal to defend her from fouling. There was a chicken-coop aft, a small pigpen, and sheep in the cutter. The Australian said the coal-ballast had been loaded and her sailing date noticed in the *Times* as the first day of November. Her trade was opium from Patna and Benares exchanged for silver specie and Chinese luxury goods, with a run back to England every other year for overhaul.

Being more or less on a schedule, she retained the most of her crew from voyage to voyage, rather than discharging them in home port to save wages. She carried a double crew, making an even sixty hands, thirty per watch. They were of all nationalities and MacDonnell suspected some were Royal Navy deserters. He added the interesting information that several of the crew were North Americans, and had expressed in his hearing sentiments that did not argue their adherence to the Union cause. He had not explored this further, however, deeming it wiser to maintain his masquerade as an Australian subject uninterested in the American struggle.

Dulcett asked, —Should we succeed in gaining control, what do we do for guns and powder? And men? Some might come over, as Mr. Mac says, but what about the rest?

Ker assured him he'd addressed these questions with Bulloch and Prioleau. They'd engaged a merchant-steamer to carry guns, gun-tackle, salt beef, hardtack, powder, and shells to an offshore rendezvous. A crew would be thrown aboard at the same time, and the clipper then commissioned as a man-of-war.

—You mentioned an auxiliary engine. Are you sure she can actually steam? Kinkaid wanted to know. —A purely sailing raider will take few prizes.

Ker wasn't sure he agreed with this statement. So far as he could judge, three-quarters of *Montgomery*'s prizes could have been taken as readily by a swift sailer as under steam. But as commander, he intended to let his junior officers speak before he made the final decision. That was how Parker Trezevant had run his wardroom, and Ker had seen how it developed those resources of expedient and initiative one wanted in one's seconds. So he only listened, drawing out his mustaches, as MacDonnell explained the engines had been tested before he came aboard, but he'd find out more. What he did have— he unfolded it —was a pencil-sketch of main deck, second deck, holds, and sail-plan. He'd prepared it with the boatswain's help, under pretense of familiarizing himself with the ship.

—He's a foreigner, German, but a right sort of cove. I believe he thinks me dense, to have to draw pictures, but I don't think there were any suspicion. All their talk's of India.

Steele put in, looking over the sketch, that he'd neglected to state that as to belowdecks arrangements, she had a dining saloon, a small ladies' saloon, captain's and officers' quarters, and cabins and staterooms for fourteen passengers, though the purser said they were seldom fully occupied. An enclosed toilet opened off the ladies' saloon.

—What about their deck armament? Ker broke in. —Will we be able to board, once they're under way? I had envisioned running a spreetie alongside, perhaps off Sheerness, where the Thames widens.

MacDonnell said he'd asked about that. *Sea Eagle*'s quarter-guns were loaded only during transits of those narrow straits known to be infested by native pirates. Twelve-pound charges of grapeshot sufficed to drive off "lorchas" and "vintas," lateen-rigged sailing-canoes, but the clipper also carried solid shot in case of pursuit by the empress's war-junks. He doubted they'd keep watch for boarders in the Channel.

—So it would be possible there?

—No sir, I don't think so. Captain Peabody prides himself on swift passages. He claps on all she'll carry as soon as he casts off the tug. If the wind's there, he'll be tearing past Sheerness too fast to think of boarding. Unless, of course, you can make him heave to.

—Can you find some way of doing so?

MacDonnell sat silent, honest face troubled beneath the massive beard. —You mean cripple her? Cut the mainbrace or something like that?

—A lot could go wrong there, Dulcett observed. —If they catch you, you'd be better off in Hell pumping thunder at three cents a clap.

Kinkaid said dryly, —Then they're on their way to India with you in irons, and we're left eating wake.

Ker was sitting back, letting them have it out, when he noticed Simon had withdrawn. The enlisted man's seat was empty. He thought no more of it as Steele groped for the brandy again. —I confess, gentlemen, I do not quite see why you do not overpower her where she lies. Perhaps at night when the crew is ashore, seeking those anodynes to human cares they will be denied once their Celestial voyage begins.

Ker explained nothing must be done to violate neutrality. Huse's buyers were supplying the armies in the field with British powder, rifles, caps, everything down to the buttons on their uniforms. Equipment the South could not make herself, yet without which she could not hope to stop the army the Young Napoleon was training at her gates. That trade could not be jeopardized. The capture had to take place at sea.

—If we could stow away, Dulcett mused. Capture her from within, once we're outside the limit?

—One man might stow away successfully. Not seven.

Steele pointed out he'd be a cabin passenger. Romulus might attend as his man-servant without exciting suspicion. MacDonnell would already be aboard as the third mate. That left only Ker, Dulcett, Kinkaid, and Simon. If they and their personal arms could be smuggled aboard, and hidden until London lay behind, the conditions for a capture might be fulfilled.

Ker said, —It's worth thinking about. We should have to find a place to hide. The boats?

—Most merchants fossick them for stowaways afore they casts off, MacDonnell said.

They fell to arguing how a small party might conceal themselves until the time was right for a coup de main. As Greeks had once, concealed within a wooden horse—offering to the gods. The tobacco haze grew thick.

Until a tap came at the door. They fell quiet. After a moment Dulcett got up and, at a nod from Ker, lifted the latch.

—I beg your pardon, is this Mrs. Turleady's?

As one, the men rose to their feet. The lady was young and well-shaped; the gaslight from behind, as she stood framed by the door, showed that. But they could not yet make out her face. Steele recovered first. Bowing gracefully for a rotund old man, he said, —It is, my dear. May I offer you some service?

—Perhaps a seat for a moment. I have quite exhausted myself mounting the stairs.

Kinkaid, Dulcett, and MacDonnell immediately offered their chairs. The young gentlewoman, who was tall and of a pleasing outline, though rather slim for the fashion, smiled demurely as she came into the circle of light.

She wore a dark green traveling dress with a shawl in the Chinese pattern. Her hair was a rich gold under a black snood and small black velvet hat. Dulcett held her chair; Steele offered a brandy. MacDonnell apologized for the tobacco smoke, offering to open a window. She refused in a pleasant voice, flicking a blue glance up at Ker as he stood rooted, unable to move, unable to believe his eyes.

Cool and condescending, Miss Olivia Simpson of Petersburg, Virginia, folded gloved hands over a reticule. She held his gaze for a moment, during which he tried to speak, but found he could not. Then she turned to the others. —Don't you recognize me, boys?

—I beg your pardon? said Dulcett. He had been looking at her hands, then at her shoe, the toe of which peeped out. Glancing up to see her watching, he blushed furiously, turned away, drank from Steele's glass, and knocked it over as he set it down.

—Do you not recognize me? she said again, this time in the hoarse lowered voice of Oliver Simon.

—Great God, said Kinkaid.

—I confess, you quite deceived these old eyes, Steele said gaily. —You make a better-looking woman than half the cotqueans of London, my lad.

—It seemed to me a tenable disguise. If we were willing to consider it, Simon said, in his male voice. —Dr. Steele has said there are ladies' accommodations apart from the main saloon. Certainly five ladies might travel together, say, to India.

—Wives of army officers? Dulcett mused. —Of Indian Service offi-cials?

—We don't sound English, Kinkaid objected. —As soon as we open our mouths, they'll know where we're from.

—You need not be English, Steele said pontifically. There are French colonies in the East. Pondicherry. Chandernagore. You could be French-women on their way to their husbands in Saigon. In my chirurgical ca-pacity, I might be a credible escort for such a seraglio.

—No, no, you must travel separately. Why ask them to swallow more than they have to?

—Just a moment, said Kinkaid. —You may do as you like, but I at any rate am not impersonating any woman. That wasn't in the articles I signed.

Ker was trying to recover, if not his sangfroid, at least his ability to speak. The shock of being confronted again by Miss Simpson, then of re-alizing she'd played him, played them all, for fools throughout *Mont-gomery*'s cruise, left him both astonished and then, almost instantly succeeding, very angry indeed. Even angrier as he realized that of course he could not admit to having been tricked. The others still took her for a young man posing *en travesti*.

—Impossible, he said coldly.

—Oh, Lieutenant, why so quick to say nay? It seems to me a capital lark.

—Capital it may be, Doctor, but we should hardly convince in the role of ladies.

Dulcett: —But look at Simon here; isn't he it for all the world? Wouldn't you ask him for a gavotte?

MacDonnell: —Ay, he's a right sheila. Wouldn't you fancy him for a little horizontal refreshment?

As they broached suggestions of increasing bawdiness Ker grew un-comfortable. Then thought: it was nothing more than she must have heard a thousand times before, in the blunt sailorly speech of a man-of-war. Almost as bad was the steady grin with which she bore it, though not contributing. He realized now she never had. He'd set that down to shy-ness in the slim young man who'd reported aboard as just another sailor, enlisted to serve the Cause.

—Until you got those crinolines off. What do you say, Simon?

Simpson grinned as they pelted her with good-natured billingsgate, still eyeing Ker with a dare-you smile. Who said, trying again for control, —The laws of war are clear. We must be in uniform, under the national flag—

—We have *Montgomery's* flag.

—And we can wear our uniforms underneath our dresses.

—Until it's time to strike.

Ker slammed down his hand. —That will do, gentlemen. We will discuss it no further.

When he rose they stood as well, to attention, by their chairs. Only Alphaeus Steele remained seated, rolling the snifter absently in his palms. Did he know? Had he known all along? Ker nodded coldly to them, then turned back. —Purser's mate.

—Sir?

—A word with you in private, if you will be so kind.

The hallway was deserted, cold, and dim, lit only by the hissing gaslight at the top of the stairs. Olivia closed the door behind her and leaned against it. Ker shook his head, pointing to the landing below. When they were concealed by the shadows he did not look directly at her. His voice shook as he said —You followed me from Virginia.

—I admit it.

—This is a gross violation of my trust.

—I admit that as well. Yes, I followed you. Yes, I disguised myself. A false mustache. Tincture of iodine for the freckles. I confess, I was surprised. No one even suspected. But you are shouting, sir.

She kept her voice low, and he moderated his own, though it took an effort. —How could I conceive of such a thing? You had no right aboard, Miss Simpson. I could not protect you if your identity became known.

—When I nursed you, you did not call me that.

—What?

—You called me Olivia.

She spoke without defiance, almost submissively. But her very presence was a defiance. Her bosom rose and fell. His vision seemed to tunnel to her parted lips, to the breath that in the soft light puffed out warm and visible. —Will you not admit that degree of friendship between us, at least?

He could not resist. Bending to her even as he told himself it was wrong. What he'd dreamed of had returned, somehow, from the past; that a doorway he'd thought closed forever had opened again. As roads untaken beckon again in dreams. And obeying the rush of blood rather than the discipline he'd thought cored his marrow, for one blind breathless moment he pressed his lips against hers.

The embrace did not last long. But while it endured he lost himself in it, in the fresh-wheat smell of her flesh, the rustling caress of her hem against his boots.

Then she drew back, leaning away against the door, and he drew his sleeve across a ragged breath.

—I should not have done that. You must pardon me.

—I shall never pardon you, Ker Claiborne. But that kiss was not your offense.

—I am no Theseus, to penetrate your riddles. I will arrange with Commander Bulloch for your transportation home.

—I will not. I have taken the oath of enlistment; to leave would be desertion.

—It hardly obtains, considering you took it under false pretense.

She whispered coolly, her voice a mist in the darkness: —I choose where I go. *You* will not reveal me, Ker. No one would believe you had not known about me all along. You're perfectly aware what sort of relation all would assume exists between us.

—I have no idea what you're talking about.

But of course he did, with a sickening clarity that the disorientation of his senses did not help. They'd call her his mistress, his kept woman, his whore. It would run through the Navy, then the sewing circles of Virginia like a brushfire in a drought August.

And yet he wanted her, now, spread-eagled against the stairs. He trembled, aghast, unsure, compassless with passion.

—Would you wish that on me? On your family, and mine? For all involved, you must keep silent. I am a good sailor, after all. No less of service than any other.

Ker passed his hand over his hair as if to compress his own lust and bewilderment and rage. And yes, his admiration. She'd taken a tremendous risk. What if she'd been discovered, and insulted by one of the crew? —Unto; unto, Miss Simpson . . . Olivia. This is madness. We could not keep such a secret long.

—I've kept it so long now I forget at times there's any secret at all.

—Enough. You'll leave at once. Tonight.

She touched her hair, the same gesture he'd seen in Simon as well; yet so essentially feminine did it seem now he could not take his eyes from her hand. She said, —That I will not do.

—You refer to the oath of enlistment, but you won't take orders?

—We're fighting for a country of our own, Ker. I told you once: I would do anything to support our glorious cause. I have proven, have I not, that I can render service? On this at least, you will agree?

He said reluctantly, —I must admit you have. On land . . . in the sickroom, and . . . at sea as well.

She pressed his hands in hers, leaning back to look into his eyes. —Then admit you err. Is that so difficult? If you wish to take the Yankee clipper, you'll need help in this matter of disguise. But now, just now, we are alone. Let us tell each other the truth. You know I love you. I have loved you since the day we met. Will you kiss me again? Or no?

For one moment, holding her gloved hands in the darkness, he was ready to throw it all away. He told himself that it was madness, but in vain. Here was the woman he wanted. Family, name, honor, vows, all counted at this moment less than dust.

He struggled not to pull her to him, and stop her whispering with kisses. To slide his hands beneath the cloth that separated their bodies in the chill night, and let the rest of his life and his eternal soul go to blazes.

She waited, looking at him levelly in the dim. When he could find no further words, no more arguments or orders; when all he could do was stare at her lips, gaze into her mysterious, phosphorescent eyes, she reached out, brushed his cheek with her fingertips. Then turned and rustled up the stairs, leaving him pressing his fingers dumbly to the spot where her glove had touched him, so lightly it seemed he would feel it there forever.

22

Report of the Honorable Charles Francis Adams, United States Minister to
Great Britain, to the Secretary of State; with Enclosure of a Copy of a Letter
from Captain Malachi Peabody, Esq., Master, Steamer *Sea Eagle*,
to His Owners in Boston

London, England,
November 13, 1861.

The Honorable William Seward
Washington.

Sir:

It is with shock and outrage that I forward the below account of
an infamous atrocity committed upon our commerce, in violation
of the hospitality of Great Britain and of all the laws of civilized
war. A nest of pertinacious traitors have seized a United States tea-
clipper, the *Sea Eagle,* owned by the respected traders Mssrs. Ed-
ward Sloan and Samuel Kitchell of Boston, on the high seas.

The actions of these pirates, headed by a young Virginian
upstart named Claiborne, were not unanticipated in these quarters. We had warned the present government here that the
Queen's proclamation of neutrality, with its according of belligerent status to the Southern insurgents, would be taken by them as
an invitation to make war from British territory. We received

much information as to the activities of the rebels in London and elsewhere, and undertook the most strenuous efforts to bring them to the attention of the proper authorities. Where the home authorities would not act, we took measures ourselves, though they were less than successful due to unforeseen circumstances.

It now seems our anticipation that they were bending their efforts toward the purchase of a vessel blinded our agents as to their actual intention. I had in fact through accident encountered the chief of this desperate party in person some days previous. I found him a cool and arrogant young sprig with the typical bearing of the Southern cottonocracy, that is of self-congratulating pride, cutting a dash, etc. This "son of the chivalry" carried his enterprize forward in great secrecy, so much so that even though our agents had reported a scheme of some sort being in hand, no particulars were available through which we might forestall the event.

I have most strongly remonstrated against the presence of the rebel "representatives" in England from the moment they set foot on these shores, but to date Her Majesty's Government wants to back both sides of this horse for reasons of their own *haute politique*. I have repeatedly sought to impress upon the Foreign Minister and the Prime Minister that such plucking of the Eagle's feathers will not redound to good relations when this insurrection is behind us and the other questions which lie between our two nations—that of the status of Canada, for example—return to the forefront of our attention. I have this day drawn Lord Palmerston's attention to the gross outrage upon the sovereignty and peace of the people of these Islands when such an outrage is planned on their soil and committed in their waters. I have pointed out the gross disregard shown by the rebels of the laws and usages of war, the contempt shown to the Crown, and the consequences to Her Majesty's trade if such outrages are permitted; those including not only the disfavor of our Government and the eternal enmity of our reunited people, but the strangulation of trade in all ports of the Empire if every disgruntled and rebellious faction is accorded the privilege of acting as highwaymen on the high seas. How if we permitted Fenians to engineer the theft and destruction of British merchant vessels calling in New York? Though his response was not all I had hoped, I have been assured by Lord Russell that an investigation will be commenced pursuant to determining which of the provisions of the Foreign Enlistment Act and other statutes of this realm have been violated by the act of the pirate Claiborne and his accomplices.

As to the particulars of this matter, I can do no better than to enclose a fair copy of the letter of the captain of the *Sea Eagle,* lately returned to this city from the Madeira Islands. His missive outlines the particulars of the piratical act. When last seen his ship was headed north, presumably for a passage into the Mediterranean, which information I hope you will pass to Secretary Welles for the dispatch of a cruiser in search of her. I may particularly draw your attention to the gross disregard for the status of females exhibited by the rebel pirates, and the contempt exhibited by them for the usage of all civilized nations. They have with this act openly declared themselves the enemies of all humanity and I trust they will when caught by our Navy or by that of any other Power pay the price of their crimes with a spirited jig at the end of a hempen cord.

I will meanwhile do my best to turn this outrage to our mutual purposes.

> I remain,
> Your most humble and obedient servant,
> C. F. Adams.

> Funchal, Madeira,
> November 6, 1861.

Mr. E. H. Sloan
Sloan & Kitchell
102 Beacon Street
Boston, Massachusetts.

Sir:

I have the unfortunate duty to communicate to you the v. sad news as to the loss of the bark *Sea Eagle,* which you entrusted to me under your hand. The particulars of the event I have also relayed to the Portuguese authorities in this port, the British consul, and to the U.S. consul. My officers and I and the most of the crew, exceptions as set forth below, are safe here in Funchal after the most harrowing circumstances. The ship's log and commission, and other official documents and correspondence are also in my possession. All else unhappily is lost.

The facts of the matter are these. I completed our overhaul and refitting and we were lying to the St. Katherine's Dock. I loaded outbound cargo and ballast consisting of one hundred and eighty tons of Welsh coal. I had shipped two new crewmen and a new third officer, an Australian by the name of MacPhee. All preparations were complete for sea and I had advertised our departure for the first of November in the *Times*. My purser had already signed one passenger, a medical gentleman with his colored servant, when a reservation for our remaining passenger cabins was received by letter, accompanied by a cheque which I immediately sent to cash and found to be sound.

Early on the morning of November 1st, four ladies in heavy veils boarded before dawn. I did not observe them personally although their arrival was reported to me by the mate. He reported that although most seemed "uncommon homely" one was young and v. stylishly dressed. The ladies indicated by signs they spoke no English. They were helped below to their cabins with the assistance of the men who carried down their personal baggage and eight heavy trunks, such as milliners use, leaving them in the ladies lounge. On one seaman's asking what was in the trunks, he was told they were the latest Paris fashions, having been ordered by the French colony in Indo-China.

The remainder of the morning passed in the routine of casting off, steaming up the Pool, etc. Off Southend, with a t'gallant breeze from the north and the tide not adverse, I cast off the tug and pilot and made sail for the Channel. The sky was but slightly overcast and the temperature not far above freezing.

During this time we had seen nothing of the ladies. The only passenger we saw was the medical person, a Dr. Milliron, who came on deck from time to time, standing quietly on the poop and observing our activities, then retiring below. I did not find this suspicious at the time, but exchanged courteous words with the old gentleman. Wishing him a pleasant time with us, and so forth, to which he returned the most urbane response, giving promise of interesting conversation, so much so that I extended him an invitation to dine at my table, which he did over the next few days.

At about two o'clock in the afternoon we were clear in the Channel. For the next five days our courses and distance made good are per the log. Finding the wind fair for the passage, though the seas rough, I proceeded south apace, making over two hundred miles good each day and on the fourth two hundred fifty miles by observation between dusk and dusk. During all this time the ladies came on deck only twice, and only at night. They remained veiled, took meals v. quietly in their rooms, sent chamberpots out, etc., and did not hold intercourse with me or the crew, except for the young woman previously remarked. Mademoiselle Eugenie Sarron, as she styled herself, made remarks to some of my hands which I fear may have turned their heads to some extent. They being young men and susceptible to the influence of the fair sex. She professed herself interested in how the ship steered and on one occasion was given the wheel for several minutes. Coming on deck, I immediately caused her to be removed from that post and reprimanded the helmsman and the mate. She however persisted in her attempts to ingratiate herself. Indeed, this man was so believable in his role as to strain credibility that he was not what he represented himself to be—that is, the English-educated daughter of a high French official in Saigon.

This pleasant passage came to an end the dawn of the fifth of November. At that time our position was fifty miles off Ilha da Madeira, which I had intended to sight that morning to confirm our navigation. The morning was clear and the wind brisk, as it had generally continued since our departure from the Thames. At a little after seven o'clock, I was in my cabin working out our course from Funchal when I was interrupted by a knock. I requested to know who it was, when I was informed my attention was invited to a matter concerning the French passengers. I did not recognize the voice, but apprehending no danger, at once opened the door.

I was instantly taken in hand by two men in blue uniforms of the naval pattern. They were armed with pistols and swords, and informed me that my ship and my person were now prizes of the navy of the confederate states of America. Being unarmed I judged it best to submit, though promising them they would be dealt with most harshly by the law.

There was by now considerable commotion belowdecks and shouting from the forecastle. Apparently the uprising or takeover had been in train for some minutes before I was taken in hand. At one point some of my officers offered resistance. Arms were instantly produced and they were treated with the utmost roughness and discourtesy, being threatened with bodily harm if they did not immediately follow in all respects the orders that would be given. The ringleader of this band of ruffians was of small stature and clean-shaven. He was addressed by his men as Captain Clayborn. I was relieved of the key to the arms-chest and marched topside.

There I found both watches assembled by the mainmast with both twelve-pounders loaded with grape and trained on them. The pirates had obviously caught the weasel asleep, and this threat rendered the men obedient and whatever opportunity I might have had to organize resistance was gone. The outcome of a rush was obvious and I restrained those of my young men who offered to do so. I was disappointed to find that the best of them, the Australian whom we had signed on in London, was now in the raider's uniform and obviously in their company. On the whole they had us on the hip and I determined to submit with as good grace as possible, while looking out for a chance to turn the tables should one present itself.

I was then addressed by the leader, who introduced himself as Lieutenant Commanding Ker Custis Clayborn, of Virginia and the "confederate states navy." He also referred to the privateer cruiser *Montgomery,* of whose lawless depredations I had read in the En-

glish journals. He informed me that I and my ship were now prize
of the confederate states. On my inquiry as to his intentions, he
stated we would be politely treated and set ashore, most likely at
Funchal. When I inquired as to his intentions toward the lady passengers my reward was loud guffaws, catcalls, and knee-slapping,
to such effect I understood at once that here were those self-same
ladies. I was even brazenly pinched on the cheek by the young man
whom I had removed from the helm. These manifestations of
ridicule I sustained with a dignity as befitted the master of a Sloan
& Kitchell liner. The medical man, Milliron, also ranged himself
on the side of the highbinders, though I did not see arms in his
hands.

Upon acknowledging that they had captured the ship by force
of arms, they at once released me and the ship's officers on our parole not to attempt to recapture her, and directed me to set my
course for Madeira. This I did and rose Pico Ruivo about sunset.
We stood on and off that night without incident, the pirates keeping the deck under arms and allowing only deckhands up to work
the sails.

At sunrise on the sixth Clayborn assembled the crew on deck
after breakfast, mounted the horse block, and informed them they
would shortly be put adrift in the longboats, to make their way to
land and safety as best they might. Unless, he went on, they decided to stay with the ship. He then announced the mainbrace to
be spliced with a double ration of my best cabin-whiskey, and
hoisted a rag which he made out to be the flag of the rebels and
traitors under which he sailed. At this time a string trio played a v.
lively rendition of the tune called Dixie.

Following the conclusion of this musical interlude, during
which my whiskey made its impression, Clayborn made a v. senti-
mental and misleading address in which he called on those boys
who loved "freedom and adventure" to join the "rebel standard,"
promising many advantages including high pay, a generous daily
ration of spirits, and liberal shares of prize-money from the Yankee
merchants with which they would fall in, their course being laid

for the eastern Mediterranean. He played on the love of adventure and romance so strongly pronounced in the unlettered tar, and painted those who did not respond to his call as the craven creatures of Northern aggression and tyranny, bent on riveting chains upon free men whose only crime was that they desired to separate peaceably from a "voluntary union" of the states.

I regret to report that fully fourteen of the hands signed articles with the enemy upon the conclusion of this pretty oration, v. many of them, however, of foreign or British birth. Neither I nor any of my other officers were suffered to recall them to their duty, or to warn them of the fate that would befall those who turned their backs on their country, else certainly they would have bethought themselves more soberly of the consequences of turning pirate.

The remainder of our ordeal is briefly told. Those officers and men remaining loyal were placed in the longboats and swayed overboard. We were streamed astern for three hours, during which the pirates steered close enough inshore that we would have an easy time pulling in to the land. They also lowered to us bread, salt meat, and water enough to sustain us in case fluke of wind or sea should drive us off the land. I estimate we were not more than six miles off the western coast of Ilha da Madeira before the painters were cast off and we were bid to make our way to safety. On our last sight of her she was standing out to the northward under plain sail.

Taking charge in the boats, I pulled round the island and before dark gained the land at Porto Moniz. Traveling to Funchal by donkey, I reported to the United States consul who invited me to indite this report, which I am now concluding in the study of his home. All concerned here have been most helpful to us.

In closing may I once again express my regret for the loss of such a fine ship; the one ray of light being as you know she was v. well insured through an agency of Lloyds against all dangers of the sea, including piracy. It was not within my power to retain her; but with the timely collapse of the Southern insurrection, it is not unlikely that we may regain possession. In which case I will hope again to command her, unless sooner employed as master of one of your other liners, in which condition I will endeavor to give as faithful service as I have to this date.

Your most humble and obedient Servant,
M. W. Peabody.

P.S. We will proceed from Funchal back to London by the next available vessel. Please direct any reply to me care of the Company office there. I have sold the longboats to a local merchant, to provide for our passage, I hope that meets with approval as otherwise we should be stranded here until another ship of the Company should call.—M.W.P.

PART IV

C.S.S. Maryland,
November 6, 1861–January 10, 1862.

23

KER spent several anxious days after dropping the Yankee captain
and his remaining crew off Madeira. While still in sight of their
boats he'd hauled around ostentatiously to northward, using a
fresh westerly to push the clipper along under easy sail. Plain sail, for
with only fourteen hands he dared set no more. Fortunately *Sea Eagle*'s
boatswain had come over to them, a slow-moving but powerful Dutchman named Kaiser. The kind of man, Ker judged, who could horse a sail
or a fractious seaman, who kept order with his fists if need be; who might
be able to turn a forecastle full of Liverpool *maquereaux* into man-of-
war's men. With his help, MacDonnell organized the hands into
watches. Double-reefed, the yet-unchristened cruiser kept on till they
were over the horizon even from the highest point of the island, then
came round to eastward.

Dawn broke over the rugged outline of Porto Santo, crowned with a
volcano so lofty clouds trailed from it as if it were still active. The land-
scape was subtle tones of ocher and lavender, with vegetation tinting
the slopes above a golden beach. Still reefed, and keeping a sharp lookout
aloft, he passed it well to the east, then doubled back to nose into the

cupping channel between Santo and the coast of Madeira proper. Here, sheltered from north and west, he ran without haste into the wide bay beneath the volcano and set the bower in eight fathoms.

Then waited through the next day, then the next. No sail appeared, save coasters or fishermen who stayed close under the larger island. The wind continued westerly, and squalls swept over them as the changeling pitched at her tether of sixty fathoms of heavy chain.

Meanwhile the former opium-runner wanted bracing under the foredecks. She needed more gunports, ammunition-scuttles to be cut through the deck, boxed, and lidded, and expansion of the shot-lockers and the magazine. Ker directed more portholes for ventilation, and her foredeckhouse cut down and decked flush. The passenger-quarters fell under the axe. Choice walnut paneling, furniture, and false bulkheads disappeared into the cookstove, replaced with open bays where a raider's crew could swing their hammocks. In a separate compartment forward, he directed the setting of iron staples ratchet-notched with files—an old slaver's trick—and sledged down burying-deep into the deck-beams. He did not want to have to worry about any prisoners they might take.

The transformation under way, he retired to the master's cabin. He'd bought a bundle of *Lloyd's Register* and other shipping journals in London. Now, with the lamp-flame reeling and swaying above him, he began comparing them with Maury's *Wind and Current Chart of the North Atlantic* and *The Physical Geography of the Sea.* He worked late each night, the clipper pitching and groaning around him. A sound he anticipated hearing more of; he planned to range into latitudes that would test every spar and man aboard.

The fourth dawn disclosed a sail to the northward. It made slowly around the east cape, in bright sunlight and falling winds. Brigantine-rigged, but of a heavy, oldish-looking style of hull. Ker ordered the twelve-pounders loaded as a precaution. But when she ranged alongside he made out a familiar flash of red-blond hair, a hard, scowling face. Across the green waves, Minter lifted his cap reluctantly.

Ker cupped his hands and shouted across, —I trust you had a pleasant passage.

Minter looked away and Ker sighed. Why did Fate keep throwing them together? They were like two magnets which pole to pole repel, like two chemicals which inevitably ignited when brought into contact.

—I am ordered to report to you, the other called at last.

—Very well, consider yourself reported. Did you bring my guns?

For answer he got a sour nod. Ker shouted he was short on boats, he'd thank him to come aboard in one of his own.

Half an hour later they were seated in his cabin-saloon. Ker considered offering the Mississippian a drink, but knowing the gesture would be rebuffed, did not. Minter, whose taut lips and stiff posture conveyed his contempt and resentment more effectively than words, handed over a letter from Bulloch. Ker broke the seal to find his sailing instructions and a signed commission. The instructions contained no surprises. He and the commander had discussed his operations, should the takeover succeed, in detail. They'd have to be confirmed by Secretary Mallory, but for the time being these would suffice.

Minter said the merchant, a tramp Prioleau had rented under the name of one of his clerks, had loaded in Liverpool, evading notice among dozens of other vessels competing for the Manchester to London carrying trade. Her master was a Captain Duguid. Ker recognized the name from Prioleau's dinner in Liverpool.

The next question Ker asked was, had he brought a crew? Minter said he had, but not as many as Bulloch had hoped to supply. Scouring docks, pubs, and alehouses, Fraser, Trenholm had found twenty-five men willing to engage for a cruise of indeterminate destination and length. For officers, he had an assistant engineer, a Mr. Shepperd, and another midshipman, Mr. Bertram. Also with them, recommended to Ker's consideration as ship's boy, was Mr. Prioleau's eleven-year-old Sam, whose endless pleading to join a ship of war had at last been granted by his reluctant parents.

Ker stroked his newly stubbling chin. Twenty-five more hands made barely half those he needed for a full-rigged ship with a reasonable suit of guns. Officers he could shift about to some extent, make do with or without as he must. But without hands he could neither sail nor fight.

Questioned as to the guns, Minter said the two Whitworths and four thirty-two-pounders were in the brig's hold, along with iron pivot-rail circles for the larger guns, and diagrams showing how to mount and secure them to the deck. Also ammunition, Royal Navy–pattern cutlasses, two cases of short Enfield rifles, provisions, and engine room consumables.

—Those are the weapons you had intended to install in *Astacian,* are they not? But I suppose you have time to secure replacements.

Minter did not look at him. He muttered, —It hardly matters, as I've lost her.

—Lost her?

—Bulloch will give her to the next lieutenant who arrives. You've convinced him she's too rotten to go to sea without major repairs.

—I don't understand. I thought her to be yours—

—He ordered me here. As your exec.

Ker rubbed his chin again, taken flat aback. His first thought was, This wasn't good. Then he tried to see the matter objectively. True, he desperately needed more watch-officers. It was also true Minter was a well-qualified, competent seaman, passionate about things being done right. But he simply did not see how they could work together, unless the man could master his fixed idea that Ker had wronged him and was his enemy. The captain of a warship was closer to God personified than the Autocrat of All the Russias. If Ker packed him back to London no one could object.

But as that captain, he had to think not of his own preferences, but of his ship and mission. And striving to do that, to be evenhanded, he said, —Come, come, Mr. Minter. Is it not time at last to declare a truce between us?

For reply he got one of the hardest glances he'd ever encountered. —I do not forget an injury, sir. Nor overlook an insult.

—Precisely what do you mean by that?

—I am a patriot. A man like you will not benefit from having me aboard. You'd better send me back to London—

Ker broke in, angry at last, —I am perfectly aware of my rights, sir, and do not require to be advised of them. Nor do I consider myself deficient to you in honor or patriotism. My God, man, you speak as if you had a monopoly on being a Southerner.

—I am a son of Mississippi and proud of it.

—That does not matter a damn. What I need are sea-officers, and I don't care where they hail from. My first is from Australia. My engineer's from Pennsylvania. If you can take orders, I can put you to some service to that flag you rever. Unless of course this is not patriotism but bombast.

The lieutenant had flushed, had risen to his feet, was gripping the table. The two stared at each other across the green baize, exhausted of words, of all but their mutual hatred. For the first time, Ker grasped the meaning of the phrase "sworn enemies." Minter hissed, —You dare impugn my patriotism? *You?*

—I'm challenging you to prove it. By deeds rather than hot words.

—Then I shall do so. Minter came to attention. —I report myself for duty, sir.

Ker cleared his throat, so angry he could hardly speak. At last he got out, —Sit down, then, damn it. Let's proceed to business.

—Aye aye, sir. Minter had moderated his tone, but he remained standing. —We shall need smoother water than this to transfer.

Ker cleared his throat again, and turned to his chart-table. —I agree, a snug harbor would make things much more convenient. However, I want to stay outside Portuguese waters.

—The Desertas are within half a day's sail.

—I have studied the chart, and see no advantage there. This bay is quite unfrequented. Yours is the first sail aside from fishermen. The wind is from the west; we shall find a lee in that direction. We shall simply have to run in as close as we can.

Minter mulled this and at last nodded reluctantly. —And we shall have to do it quickly, Ker added. —Before a Union cruiser happens on us. Are we in agreement?

—We are.

The lieutenant turned to leave, but Ker riveted him in place. —I have not dismissed you yet. Stand fast, sir.

Minter came slowly to attention once more. Now the threat that blazed from those lucent eyes was beyond mistake.

Ker was past caring. He'd tried to make peace, and failed. From here on he'd use Minter's hatred. Unpleasant, and dangerous. Mutinies had stemmed from less. But until a better solution offered, it was a hand he'd have to play out. Ker kept him braced up for several seconds before flicking his fingers. —Very good, Mister Minter. Now you can go.

A last look, a pale thin line of compressed lips. A moment later Ker was alone again, alone with the faint rattle of light chain as the betty-lamp oscillated above him.

Swaying heavy weights from ship to ship was ticklish at best, and in any sort of swell could result in casualties, damage, and losing the guns overboard. The brigantine followed as they felt their way inshore, keeping the leadsman busy, till they came to anchor again inside a deserted island-spit.

Here, though the seas thundered to either side, they lay in comparative shelter. Seabirds wove through the windy sunlight as the two hulls drew closer, banded by hawsers to the capstan drums. The boatswain, Kaiser, growled at the men, who were quickly rigging fenders from timbers and old hawsers. At last the strakes met with the shrieking creak of heavy baulks of oak wearing against each other.

Ker, MacDonnell, and Kaiser had discussed how to get the guns and carriages aboard. Now the mainsail was furled and its lower running-gear unrove to clear the hoisting tackle.

The thirty-twos came up fairly easily, the Whitworths less so. One of the seventy-pounders snapped a stay and crashed to the deck, narrowly missing the line-party on the forward guy and splintering a three-foot hole. But after a day of backbreaking work, skinned hands, and raw voices, the merchant floated higher and the clipper's lighthearted bounding had stiffened. She creaked as she settled, her very shape changing, the flexible wooden hull folding gradually in like a closing envelope. Ker made sure carriages and tubes were lashed down securely. He wanted no more rogue guns should the weather turn.

Dulcett reported two and a half tons of English gunpowder, a hundred and twenty flathead shells for the Whitworths, and a corresponding number of solid shot and shells for the thirty-twos safely stowed below, though the magazine had not yet been completely framed in. Duguid had not brought as much in the way of comestibles, ship-bread and so forth, as expected, but Ker felt he could eke the foodstuffs out from captures; and the clipper after all had been provisioned for a voyage to India. There was also a strongbox containing ten thousand dollars in gold and a large quantity of sterling bills with which to purchase stores during the cruise.

With this counted, signed for, and locked in the cabin safe, he bowed Prioleau's captain-confidant out. As Romulus laid out a fresh shirt, Ker felt his cheeks before the mirror. The stubbled skin felt strange. He missed his mustaches; restoring them to their former glory would take months. He checked the barometer, then went topside again.

A *tour d'horizon* satisfied him that they would not be interrupted before the transfer was completed. He ran his gaze up the rigging, and reminded a subdued Minter to set up the shrouds now that they were loaded. Then told him quietly to muster all hands on deck.

They ranged before him, officers and men, among boxes and barrels, a litter of broken fardage and tallow-paper from the hastily unwrapped ordnance. The hands native to *Sea Eagle* looking at home, but so few, so very few of them. The new men from Liverpool looked intimidated, a ragged, unhealthy-looking lot who stood squinting and shading their eyes as if they'd never seen sunlight before. He reminded himself to issue them new woolen clothes from the slop-chest. Kaiser stood at the forefront, massive arms crossed. The Dutchman ruled by fist rather than eloquence, his orders a jumble of German and English. Minter and the former *Montgomery*s stood to the side—MacDonnell, Kinkaid, Steele, Dulcett, and Simon.

No, not "Simon." He studied Olivia's profile as she stood with hands locked behind her. How could he have missed it? Without the fake mustache it was so clear. She could not continue her masquerade indefinitely. It had already gone on far too long. He shuddered to think what could happen. A woman simply did not belong aboard a warship.

He pushed it from his mind and nodded to Minter. He had to begin depending on the man. But he already missed the free and easy relationship with MacDonnell. As the exec passed down the ranks Ker examined one of the thirty-two-pounders, newly set on its carriage. Glanced down at the crew from the merchant, still alongside, who'd gathered to smoke and skylark after their labors of the morning. Captain Duguid lifted his cap in salute; Ker returned it gravely.

When Minter called the men to attention Ker strolled amidships, hands behind his back, and looked from one end of the line of expectant faces to the other.

—Gentlemen, I am Captain Claiborne. You have signed aboard a warship of the Confederate States Navy, and I welcome you as shipmates. How many have served in a man-o'-war before?

Hands rose, a few; a leavening. With luck, he could recruit gunners and perhaps a petty officer or two from among them.

—I understand most of you are green men, so far as the Navy is concerned, and will require some little drilling and instruction to make proper gun crews. I will take that into account, but I must rely as well on your application. You will find me disposed to deal lightly with men who do their duty, but severely with offenders against shipboard discipline. Mr. Minter and the bo's'n will make clear what sort of conduct we expect. Make no mistake. If differences of opinion should arise, mine is the interpretation that will prevail.

He caught the attentive regard of the brig's crew, and raised his voice to reach them as well. —As you all no doubt know, the government I represent is made up of states which have voluntarily dissociated themselves from a union they had voluntarily joined. Against our wishes, we now find ourselves at war with those once our countrymen. They proclaim a higher law than the Constitution: that of conquest. Intent on reducing us to vassals, they invaded our country at Manassas, and were thrown back by the resistance of free men. But, not taking from this the lesson they might, they are even now preparing a new army against us.

—The object of our present cruise is therefore to destroy the commence of that government, to drive their flag from the seas and bring the hardships of war home to the money interests who began this internecine struggle.

—We will now commission this vessel into the service of the Southern Confederacy, under a new name commemorating a state that in heart and soul is with us but which groans under the heel of the tyrant. You are entitled to a bounty, to be paid now and in gold, of ten pounds. You will also receive wages of between four and seven pounds per month, depending on your capabilities and deportment; along with clothing allowances, a generous daily ration of spirits, and wholesome and plentiful ship's rations supplemented, I venture to hope, from those ships which we will capture. Not only will you receive bonus and pay, but also prize-money, at the rate of one-half the assessed value of the ships and cargo we destroy, divided according to the usage of the sea.

This brought heads up and made eyes burn brighter. But then, he thought, few were native Southerners; the most were English, but judging by their accents also Italians, Greeks, Irish, Germans, the sweepings of Europe. The Confederacy, State's Rights, the Constitution meant nothing to these hungry bellies. Welded into a crew, they'd fight for shipmates and flag; but that would come. He raised his voice for the peroration.

—I cannot *promise* you fortune. That lies in the lap of Fate. But I can promise adventure. Our instructions are to burn, sink, and destroy, and that I promise you we shall do. We will knock seven bells out of Yankee commerce. Should we encounter United States warships, we will run from them; fighting them is not our mission; if cornered, however, we will stand and fight. We are not a privateer or a pirate. We are a man-of-war, and I emphasize again I will insist on the observance of all the accepted laws of war on the high seas. I ask the blessing of Almighty God; and as to the outcome of the contest, we will put our trust in Providence and the armies of the Southern Confederacy.

—Have any of you questions?

He waited them out, and was about to speak again when a commotion came from alongside. Then suddenly heads appeared above the bulwark, and four men leaped down onto the deck. Kaiser wheeled, bellowing a Teutonic bull-roar, but Ker silenced him with a wave. —Stand easy, Boats. What is it that you fellows want?

—We wants to join yer, Cap'n, that's what it is we wants. If ye'll have us.

—All four?

They nodded vigorously. Ker looked across to Duguid. The latter nodded cheerfully and gestured them on. Ker bowed and turned back to them. —You are welcome; welcome indeed. If you will fall into ranks with the rest, I will ask all to uncover. Our Surgeon, Dr. Alphaeus Steele, Esquire, will now read our official commission.

Steele looked surprised, but came forward readily enough. Ker passed him the document and stood back. The surgeon cleared his throat, glancing down the page. Then up at Ker, mouth curving in a gratified smile.

—To all unto these presents shall come, send greetings, Steele began hoarsely. Then cleared his throat, and his speech gathered force and carried out over the silent men.

—Know ye, that we have granted, and by these presents do grant, license and authority to Ker Claiborne, captain of the steam barque called the *Maryland*—

Here Steele lowered the paper and bowed gratefully toward Ker. Who smiled back, and with a gesture invited him to go on.

—Called the *Maryland,* of the burden of one thousand tons or thereabouts, and mounting eight guns, to fit out and send forth the said barque in a warlike manner, and by and with the said barque and the crew thereof, by force of arms, to attack, subdue, scuttle, and take all ships belonging to the United States of America or any vessel carrying soldiers, arms, gunpowder, ammunition, provisions, or any other goods of a military nature to any of the army of the United States or ships of war employed against the Confederate States of America in a hostile manner. And to take by force if necessary any vessel, barge, or floating transporter belonging to said United States or persons loyal to the same, including tackle, apparel, ladings, cargos, and furniture on the high seas or between high- and low-water mark, rivers and inlets accepted. (The ships and vessels belonging to inhabitants of Bermuda, the Bahamas Islands, and Great Britain and other persons with intent to settle or serve the cause of the Confederate States of America you shall suffer to pass unmolested, the commanders thereof permitting a peaceable search and after giving satisfactory account of ladings and destination.) And that such ships or vessels apprehended as aforesaid, and the prize taken, to carry to a port or harbor within the domains of any neutral state willing to admit the same or any port of the Confederate States, in order that the courts therein instituted to hear such claims may judge in such cases at the port or in the state where the same shall be impounded. The sufficient securities, bonds, and sureties having been given by the owners that they nor any person in command of this vessel shall not accede or transfer the powers and authorities contained in this commission. And we will and require all officers whatsoever in the service of the Confederate States to give assistance to the said captain in the premises. This commission shall remain active and in force until this government of the United Confederated States of America shall issue orders to the contrary.

—Given under my hand this fifteenth day of October 1861 in Richmond, President Jefferson Davis.

Steele paused, holding the paper, and Ker stood at attention, conscious of the mysterious transformation that had taken place to the iron and oak and hemp around him. He said quietly to Minter, —First Lieutenant, hoist the ensign.

Caps came off in ragged unison, and with the shrill of a pipe the Stars and Bars fluttered aloft. A twelve-pounder banged out with a flat thunderclap. Ker waited as the flag rose, unfurling, the wind playing with it, then as it reached its peak, streaming it out full length into the sunlight. New as a flag could be, unstained and brave, it seemed made of stars and the sunlight. He vowed to himself that come what might it should not descend in infamy.

He next read the Articles of War; the same articles his own captain or exec had read every Sunday since he had gone to sea. The Confederate Navy had adopted them as written. Then nodded to Minter. —First, post the watch and make your preparations to get under way. He stepped to the windward side of the quarterdeck, the sacred quarter, now consecrated to his own use as the commander.

Kinkaid, lean and anxious-looking—the exec would not grant him any men exclusively assigned to engineering. Ker explained patiently that he planned to spend little time under power, that *Maryland* would be a sailing-cruiser; under their shorthanded circumstances there could be no such thing as a dedicated black gang. —I will have Mr. Minter designate men on the battle bill to be yours during combat or auxiliary steaming. And of course you shall have them for training; only, I cannot let you have them exclusive of other duties. I really have not the hands, sir.

—Running an engine's not a part-time job, Captain.

—You will have to accommodate your requirements as best you can, Mr. Kinkaid. I really cannot do anything more for you just now.

Duguid, stepping aboard, took off his cap to the ensign, then shook Ker's hand warmly. —I wish you the best of luck, sir, the best of luck. I only wish I could sail with you.

—You are serving in your own way, sir, perhaps better than I.

—You are a modest young fellow; I like that. Well, I have one thing more to leave with you. May I present my sailing-master, Mr. Zdzislaw Osowinski.

Osowinski was slight and erect, with a pointed black beard, high cheekbones, and the faintest tinge of foreignness in his very precise pronunciation. He clicked the heels of brightly polished boots and bowed. —Captain Claiborne. I too know what it is to yearn for national freedom.

Confused, Ker looked to Duguid. —You say he's your sailing-master?

—Monsieur Osowinski speaks at least four languages, and is a capable mate indeed. I let him go with regret, but he's his own man.

Ker shook the Pole's limp hand; told him to see the purser about a place to put his traps; then shook Duguid's. The latter said jovially, —Well, I expect you will want to be about your burning and slaughtering.

—Yes sir, but one or two matters remain. Ker felt inside his coat, then looked about the deck. Feeling torn, but knowing that what he was about to do had to be done.

Olivia stood by the companionway, looking as if she was heading below. He beckoned to her, and said to Duguid, —I have important communications for Secretary Mallory in Richmond. My muster roll, request for confirmation of my cruising orders, and where the answer can meet me. Commander Bulloch has the means to forward mail, but I should like it to be personally couriered. May I introduce Oliver Simon, my purser's mate.

He handed her the package. She took it, though her brow folded with uncertainty. Duguid examined her curiously, but said only, —I most assuredly will, sir.

—And this letter, to my wife?

—With the greatest pleasure.

—My servant is bringing up Simon's duffel. He can go with you now.

She understood then, and started to protest. He frowned, and cut his eyes at those close around them. Smiled gravely, and shook his head. —I am afraid that is an order, my man. It is time for you to leave us.

—I had anticipated—

Ker shook her hand heartily. —I understand, believe me. I and all your shipmates will miss you. But I wish you to take this important letter to Richmond. I deeply appreciate your services, and hope we meet again under . . . circumstances of more freedom. I thank you for your service to our country. Farewell. Captain Duguid, if you please.

He accompanied them to the side. Then had a moment of misgiving, facing them both. Facing Olivia Simpson, lids reddening with tears of fury as she realized she'd been tricked.

—You will do very well, Captain. Duguid's big soft hand cramped his. Leaning close, he murmured, —We all have moments of misgiving. They look to you now. You must not fail them.

Ker stood looking after them. Looking after her, as she stood on the far deck. Her head lifted proudly. Her slim figure balanced surely as a dancer's on the rolling deck. For a moment he felt guilty, almost panicky. He yearned to call her back: lifted his hand; controlled himself only at the final moment.

He felt the cold edge of a lonely terror pass across the back of his neck as he realized her departure was only the latest abandonment. First Trezevant. Then his pet ape, both resented and loved. His wife, and his unknown child. Now Olivia. One by one, fate and duty and time were taking them from him. No one was lonelier than a commander at sea.

Or was he renouncing them? Walling himself off, trowel in his own hand, Montresor and Fortunato at the same time? Let us be gone. For the love of God. Yes, for the love of God.

But let us first taste the Amontillado.

In a harsh, crackling voice he barely recognized, he called to Minter to cast off.

24

HIS most persistent fear in those first weeks was of a spy. Not aboard; the possibility of a turncoat aboard *Maryland* cost him no sleep. His dread was of someone in a snug office in Liverpool or London. Some money-hungry copyist who unbeknownst to them had betrayed their true destination to Herter, and through him to the U.S. Navy. So that his first attention had been to trim, then to clawing every sail aloft he could. Setting the newly christened hunter plunging down the latitudes on a tack that set his heart in his mouth when he clung to the pinrail and watched her plunge.

In those days, as they tore south across oncoming combers, MacDonnell would stand beside him in total silence. Watching the still awkward crew inching out on a yardarm to fist in the flogging remnants of a torn t'gallant. Watching the long sprit dip and sway in nodding lean above the oncoming seas, green as old ice.

They struck the trades north of the Cape Verdes, on a day the wind veered around the compass thirty degrees in an hour and then fell off till the sea rolled strangely violent under the merest zephyr. Working from that dawn's four-star fix, Ker reckoned their distance made good, divided it by the hours she'd run.

Then blinked at the result. Even against the seas, they'd made nearly nine knots since Porto Santo. Her speed on a reach, the best point of sail for a square-rigger, he felt like dancing to think of.

They were driving toward the goal Parker Trezevant had dreamed of.

The theory of the *guerre de course* was clear. Destruction of the enemy's commerce was only a means to an ultimate end: to convince the enemy the game was not worth the candle. That the sacrifice of its merchant fleet, and all the commercial and financial interest bound up with it, was not worth the aims for which the state had gone to war.

Maryland had to deal a hammer-blow to the consciousness of the Union. To sever a jugular, rather than inflict a hundred tiny cuts.

So that when during the remainder of the passage south the lookout cried a sail, he did not deviate from his course. The odds were against these being Yankee ships, and hailing and stopping neutrals would spread word of their presence. They were scarce at first, *Maryland* being to the southward of the routes from Liverpool to the South Atlantic. But as she made westing the sails became more plentiful. He was hard put to pass up a long-sparred beauty with New England written all over her. But he did, though he felt the eyes of the crew on him as the stranger gradually dropped astern.

On the twenty-fifth of November he came on deck at noon to feel a balmy warmth out of step with his idea of the month at home. He set the sextant to his eye and brought the sun down in a smooth turn of the graduated drum. Steadied it there, rocking it back and forth until its lower limb skimmed the flat horizon of the South Atlantic. —Mark, he said, and beside him the Prioleau boy, Sam, face solemn as an acolyte's, made note of the time from the chronometer he cradled in its wooden box. Ker turned the sextant over and read the elevation, knowing already, even before applying the corrections, that they'd arrived. Then reached for paper and began his calculations.

A step on the quarterdeck; Minter, still snug in a reefer-jacket and un-dress cap despite the equatorial warmth. Behind him the Pole, Osowinski, was reducing his own observation on a sheet of foolscap. As he did when-ever they encountered each other, Minter lifted his cap, assuming an air of cold-blooded officiality only a thousandth of an inch short of studied con-tempt. —Sir, I believe it is time to retard the ship's clock another hour.

—I agree, First. How goes the forenoon watch?

—The wind still falling. Light from the northwest at the moment. Morning watch reported a light dew. It may disappear entirely later today.

—And Mr. Osowinski?

—I believe he is ready to stand deck-watch alone.

—Make it so. Well, we are still to the northward of where we may ex-pect the trades. I hope the doldrums do not extend north of the equator. But I must say it is indeed most salubrious weather.

Minter did not respond. Sam handed Ker the chart, and he unrolled it on a convenient area of the companion-house. Prioleau held two corners down; Minter condescended to lean on the others. Ker worked for several minutes with pencil and notebook, then shut his patent rules with a click. —I hold us some four hundred miles off the coast of Brazil.

—At the crossroads?

Ker nodded. The crossroads. It was as good a description as any.

For this momentarily empty circle of sea around them was one of the great meeting places of the earth. Just north of the equator, off the north-eastern jut of Brazil; a hundred miles west of the barren islet of St. Paul and some hundreds north of Fernando de Noronha, six great tracks con-verged in the unfurrowed sea. Natural pathways of trade, here ships bound from Australia and the Far East to Europe and North America met others bound from England to Cape Horn, New York to Capetown, China and India to the New World. This was the hunting ground toward which he'd driven as the patent-log whirred on the taffrail and sea swal-lows darted along the crests and the chickens, spray-soaked and mutinous in their wicker coops, cackled and threatened.

Clearing his throat, he gave the exec his instructions. To quarter about four degrees, zero minutes north, thirty-two degrees zero minutes west, the point of intersection for Maury's recommended sailing directions for the various passages; to maintain the most vigilant lookout aloft, and report sail at the first moment, whether or not their identity could be guessed; also to remain alert for smoke, especially at dawn or sunset; and to continue to drive her along under full sail. Minter raised his eyebrows at this last, as if to object. Ker said, —I understand we have no proper destination at the moment, but we must drive her nonetheless, as any merchant skipper in these waters would in these light airs. I wish to resemble a trader until the moment we drop our mask.

—And if the wind dies completely, as it may . . . this is a changeable quarter of the ocean.

—Set the men to overhauling the studding-sails and stud-booms.

—Should you not prefer to steam?

—No. In these latitudes, steam is an unmistakable sign of a man-of-war. Also, have a target-cask or two made up. We want practice at the guns.

Steele pulled himself grunting up out of the companionway, returning a distant half-bow to Ker's lifted hat. The surgeon had pressed to break the passage at St. Paul's Rocks, where he wanted to search for signs of a pre-Achaean civilization. The doctor had explained that a single great ridge beneath the ocean, of which the Azores, the Madeiras, the Canaries, the Cape Verdes, St. Paul's, Ascension, and St. Helena's were all outcroppings, was the remnant of Plato's sunken continent of Atlantis, and that the man who confirmed this supposition would win undying fame in the annals of science. Ker had been brusque in his third refusal to alter course, and Steele had been short with him since.

He turned back to hear Minter murmur, —We should be exercising them on worthier targets than empty beef-casks.

Ker felt like throwing him overboard. He was sick of the lifted eyebrow, the curled lip Minter invariably presented. Suppressing his anger once again, as he had to a dozen times a day, he said, —I have explained to you, if we encounter a ship of war, it is my policy to escape rather than to risk battle. Our mission is to destroy commerce, not attack warships.

—Running's not in my blood, Captain.

—Nor in mine, Mr. Minter, Ker observed with matching coolness. —I agree, it is a difficult assignment for a fighting man. We will both, however, obey the orders given us by our superiors.

The Prioleau boy was looking from one to the other when a cry drifted down from aloft. —Sail ho. Broad on the port bow.

They followed the pointing arm of the t'gallant lookout out across the blue to a speck so distant even its color could not yet be made out with certainty. Ker nodded to Osowinski. The Pole sprang into the ratlings, glass tucked into his blouse, making for the crosstrees. Ker swung to place the breeze either side of his cheek, then told Minter to alter course toward. Steering ropes creaked on the drum as the helmsmen brought her head round. Another nod from Minter, and Kaiser braced in the yards as the wind hauled aft.

Two hours later they rode alongside *Vandeline,* a bluff-bowed old whaling-barque that by the looks of her had been riding the seas for many a long year. On *Maryland*'s hoisting the Stars and Stripes she'd answered with the same ensign. When both ships were hove to Ker ran up the Stars and Bars. A longboat slid smoothly down.

Her master brought the smell of a whaling-vessel aboard buttoned into his black coat, a heavy stink of oil and rancid fishy meat. Ker gave him half an hour to gather his dunnage. He sent the whaler's mates to cool their heels in the wardroom and herded the crew below. Then told Minter coldly to cast the guns loose.

In the next week they came up with sixteen sail, of which four proved to be English, one French, two Portuguese, one Neapolitan, and one privately owned by an Indian company but sailed under the Red Ensign. In most cases they did not board, only ran alongside and spoke the deck; it was evident from the slack cuts of their jibs, these were not Yankee ships. During these interceptions he kept the British flag hoisted, or sometimes the French. The remainder seven were Americans. The first was a clipper out of New Bedford, *Clerisa Scott.* She put her helm up the moment Ker broke the Confederate ensign, and was duly put to the torch, Dulcett passing on to Bertram and Osowinski the techniques of setting a ship afire he'd mastered and refined aboard *Montgomery.*

The New Yorker put them to more trouble.

The winds had stayed light and changeable. When the lookout cried her she had all sail set on a port tack, running nearly due south and very fine to a southeast breeze. *Maryland* had been running east when her poles poked over the horizon, and Ker came right to parallel the chase's course as the wind rose and then fell away to barely enough to caress their cheeks.

At the first observation he'd taken bearings with the azimuth compass. Observing the set of the chase's sails, he steadied as close to her tack as he could guess it, whilst sending the watch aloft to shake out t'gallants and royals, stays, and jibs; having adopted the practice of cruising without the loftiest kites, that he might observe others without being glimmed himself. This let him judge his quarry's sailing qualities, and adjust tactics accordingly. They ran parallel for half an hour, during which he had the satisfaction of noting she drew half a point aft. Very gradually, he eased the helm over. MacDonnell, who had the deck, proposed setting the studding sails. Ker told him they could do so later if the other did, but that they'd overhaul slowly with the present suit.

The clipper, a black-hulled beauty with raked masts and all sail towering like distant lighthouses, drew slowly closer over the calm sea. Not a cloud or a patch of haze marred all the broad ocean. Only the smallest cat's-paws ruffled the flashing surface. The only sounds were the chuckle of water under the forefoot and the faint chug of luffing canvas. The chase did not touch a line until her pursuer was a mile distant. Then she luffed up, fell slowly off, and filled away, showing them a tastefully gilded stern-gallery off the windowpanes of which the sun flashed like a heliograph.

—She suspects, Dulcett said. —And if we don't hold this board, she'll know.

Over the last hour most of the off watch had come topside, and stood now along the port bulwark or perched on the overturned keels of the boats. The hesitant notes of an apprentice fiddler came from aft, along with the outraged cries of the cock, which went mad whenever anyone except the cook approached the coop. Which Ker had always thought strange, that he was wary of everyone except him by whose hand death would one day come.

—A long shot, said Minter. —Into her stern-ports. But we might make it, with the Whitworth.

—Not yet, Ker said. —A shot striking there would range her length, and quite possibly cause loss of life. I believe we have a slight superiority of sail.

—She's a fine-looking craft. She may show us her heels.

—If so she'll have earned her escape. Cast the log, if you please, and record our speed as we come through the wind. Mr. MacDonnell.

—Sir.

—Let her fall off a bit to gain speed, then put your rudder over gradually. Remember to hold the foresheets till well after the helm is over.

The chase was still turning, leaving a curving crease upon the water as if a ball had been rolled over tinfoil. As her stern came abeam Ker ordered MacDonnell to bring the bow round after her. He was not completely certain that *Maryland* would go in stays properly in this light an air. Yet it was worth the trial. The alternative was to wear round to starboard in a great loop, which he'd do if this failed, but that would leave him well astern of the now receding prey.

MacDonnell glanced aloft and to windward, then began the evolution by putting the wheel gradually astarboard. He hauled the spanker amidships, held the foresheets by giving no order in their respect, and hauled up the mainsail.

Aloft, the topsmen gathered in the upper staysails as she began to curve into the wind. With a heave and a ho the line-parties brought the main-yards bracing around. Ker observed critically that it was done too soon, if MacDonnell had waited a few seconds more the wind would have helped bring them round without strain on the gear. He glanced at the Australian, and saw him grimace behind his regenerating beard. He'd grasped his error and would not repeat it, but was already shouting to the boatswain to make haste on rounding in the port main braces before they fouled.

The wind had set the square sails aback, retarding her progress even as she lost their driving force. The cruiser came head to wind and coasted nearly to a stop, rolling sleepily, like a child comforting itself in bed. Ker said "very well," judging the card could fall either way. The sails rustled. The chain-rigging jingled like sleigh bells. But to his pleasure she carried slowly on around. Her sails luffed and then bellied. MacDonnell hauled the head yards around to the new tack, sheeted the spanker, and boarded the fore and main tacks. The deck heeled and she steadied, gathering speed.

But during *Maryland*'s slow tack around the chase had not steadied on the opposite board, as Ker had expected. She'd continued around to seven or eight points off the wind, and steadied up northeast by north. Now she was half a mile away and her stern was slightly squatted.

—Fore stu'n'sl-booms going aloft, said Dulcett, from behind the leveled deck glass. —She's raised us, and wants to make it a race.

MacDonnell asked if he should set their own studding-sails. Ker said he might begin getting the spars ready to socket, but not to set them yet; their quarry was most likely losing speed by carrying them. He had no sooner said this than the lower studding-sail on the chase's windward side crumpled and was hauled in, followed by the port.

Minter, looking more interested in the game. —We might could reach her with the forward pivot.

Ker studied the fleeing clipper. At last he said, —Across her bow, no closer than a hundred yards. One of the solid shots, if you please. We have not overmuch shell to waste.

—Our flag, sir?

—Hoist our own; it makes no difference now.

The white and blue and red snapped to the breeze, but Ker was unsure the chase could even see it, masked by their sails. They were closing, slowly, but they were closing. He saw men watching them from the poop.

The pursuit ended as soon as the ball sent white spray tossing up half a point ahead of the clipper. She turned head to wind and her foresails began to drop, one by one, like chemises and petticoats shed one by one by a graceful woman. Unbidden to his mind came the image of Olivia Simpson dressed as a man dressing as a woman. Then a memory of his wife. He was dismayed at how hard it was even to remember what Catherine looked like. What kind of monster was he? He shook his head. Turned aside and lit another segar, sucking the smoke angrily.

The clipper's captain boarded with her papers and her log. He wore a resigned expression beneath his beard. The *Good Shepherd* was two weeks out of South Street. Her cargo was a steam pressing-mill, complete with engines and rollers. Her hold was packed deep in long boxes of iron parts. Ker sent Bertram and a boat's crew for the New York papers, charts, navigation books, chronometer, and the cabin stores. He single-manacled the crew in *Maryland*'s hold, and remanded the captain and officers to the growing company in the wardroom. By then it was night, and they lay to by the doomed ship through the hours of darkness.

His entry into the wardroom that evening interrupted a buzz of conversation. As Romulus and the cook, a shaky, sherry-smelling old Cockney called Uffins, served out meat pie and potatoes fresh from New York, he was shown the reason: the two-week-old *Herald* Dulcett had brought back from the *Good Shepherd*. Ker read through it quickly as the others debated what it would mean.

The news stunned him. He'd carried Captain Charles Wilkes, U.S.N., to Norfolk the night the navy yard burned. The only American to discover a new continent had a reputation for self-regard, high-handedness, fearsome discipline, and hasty action. Yet if the newsprint could be believed, this time Bruin Wilkes had outdone himself. The notice was headlined SEIZURE OF MESSR. MASON AND SLIDELL FROM BRITISH STEAMER TRENT. Followed by "Particulars of their Capture. The Traitor Envoys to Go Direct to Prison."

The *Herald* declared breathlessly that Wilkes, in command of the screw-steamer *San Jacinto,* had overhauled a British mail-steamer bound from Havana to England. Ignoring the protests of the steamer's captain, and senior Royal Navy officers aboard as passengers, Wilkes had arrested the Confederate commissioners and their secretaries and taken them aboard *San Jacinto* by main force, landing them in Hampton Roads for disposition by a military court.

—The import is clear, Minter said. —They have dishonored and violated the British flag by stopping a British vessel. To regain their honor the British must declare war.

—No one can tell what the Lion will do, Steele observed, setting an old-fashioned flint and steel lighting-kit to a new English pipe. Bertram watched the plates vanish with obvious regret; he had not yet finished, the midshipmen being served last, but when his seniors lit up his meal was over. —As I understand the law, their course is far from clear. Captain, perhaps you can throw light on the matter. Is there not some consideration relating to the carrying of dispatches for the enemy?

Ker leaned back and deliberated, fingering a beard that was now recovering nicely. The military law course at Annapolis had been thorough on blockade and neutral rights. —Correct, Doctor. A warship may stop and search any vessel suspected of carrying dispatches for the enemy. If *Trent* had been carrying contraband of war, Wilkes would be perfectly right in seizing not only the contraband, but the ship as well. It is widely understood that dispatches are contraband of war as surely as weapons and ammunition. If our commissioners carried instructions, letters, official papers of any kind, *Trent* is liable to condemnation by a prize-court.

He took a breath, rather enjoying the attention of all; even Rom and Uffins were staring at him in riveted concentration. —On the other hand, such interpretation is contrary to our own practice, that is, American practice, during the Revolution and in 1812; and it will be quite hazardous to the relations of the two countries if Whitehall should take offense—as they probably will.

Remembering the spare visage of Lord Russell, a man whom he doubted anyone could overawe or intimidate, he tapped his fingers together, realizing only after he'd done so that it was exactly the gesture with which Trezevant had always closed his ex cathedra pronunciamentos. He gloomily reflected that his old skipper was most likely long dead by now.

Osowinski turned his wineglass round and round. —But as to the persons of ambassadors, sir? I had always understood those to be inviolable. As in ancient times.

—There one might encounter differing interpretations. You are correct in that ambassadors are not subject to hindrance in their movements. But as the United States do not recognize us as a country of our own, they may not extend to our envoys the immunity accorded to foreign diplomats.

Dulcett, rather timidly, —The question hinges on that distinction, sir?

Minter said hotly, —Not at all, this is legalistic cheeseparing. Our envoys were under the protection of the British flag. The British will countenance no interference with their commerce; *they* will not let the Yankees insult their flag; and certainly they have the naval power to redress such an outrage. Gentlemen, we may by now be allied with the British Empire in war.

—*Nemo me impune lacessit,* Ker murmured.

—I do not believe I have heard the sweet sound of Latin upon your lips before, Captain. Is it Horace? Steele asked him, with a charming smile.

—No one may insult me with impunity, said Osowinski, in his too-precise accent, each consonant clearly sounded. —Is it not, Captain Claiborne?

—Actually it is from Edgar Allen Poe. Mr. MacDonnell, how would that suit you, the English coming in? Being a subject of the Empire yourself?

—So long as I can stay with my mates here, sir.

Kinkaid said, breaking the silence he usually maintained at table, —Ten or eleven British men-of-war would break Lincoln's pretense at a blockade. Their new ironclad alone could face down the whole Yankee fleet.

The company discussed the new British steam-frigate, and what she'd do in an encounter with *Wabash* or *Minnesota,* the most powerful ships in the United States Navy. *Warrior* had been lying at Chatham while Ker was with Bulloch in Liverpool, and Dulcett and the engineer had made time for a professional visit. The great steamer was plated with iron four and a half inches thick, and powered by ten boilers that pushed her to a speed in excess of any other warship in the world. Her armament was hundred-pounder Armstrong rifled breech-loaders firing shells filled with molten iron. She could bombard New York or Philadelphia with impunity; could steam up the Potomac to Washington, and end the war without firing a shot.

Ker studied the engineer's face. He was from Philadelphia, and at the mention of putting it to flames a shadow came over his eyes and he did not speak again.

—It seems events call for a toast, Steele said. Ker thought he'd had more than his share of the salubrious already, but stood dutifully as the old man proposed "the bonny blue flag." All murmured assent and drained their glasses, and after a time a songfest was proposed.

The next day the wind blew harder and Steele did not appear on deck until four bells of the afternoon watch. By then they'd made a fresh capture. When breakfast had been piped down Ker sent the carpenter over to the *Good Shepherd* with his augur. As she settled, a small schooner, barely more than a coaster, had danced over the horizon to offer assistance. From miles off he'd interpreted the scene, one clipper lying near another, as a merchant skipper standing by a sinking vessel. He was not only the owner, but his family was with him, his frightened wife and two resolute boys. Ker wavered for some time. The craft was negligible in terms of war-value, and he disliked the idea of penalizing a good Samaritan. Liners and packets carried insurance, but this family would lose everything. At last he came down reluctantly on the side of duty. The family silently watched home and livelihood burning from *Maryland*'s poop.

Over the next few days the wind fell away again, this time to a faint hot breath over a glassy smoothness in which *Maryland* was reflected like a towering ghost. Drifting, she took *Cressida, Tackahominy, Hawker,* and *Erasmus C. Woolcott,* burning them all after taking off the crews. Of especial pleasure was the discovery two were laden with Chilean nitre, which would be denied to the Northern powder factories. The towering pillars of smoke by day and fire by night brought ships over the horizon, most European, but some few Yankees. He did not linger about near the burning ships, having no taste for vulturing on good seamen, but when *Tornado,* out of New Hampshire, happened to pass near on her way to render assistance, he did not let her go.

The cruiser's hold and cabins were by now crowded with captives, not all of whom were sailors or even male. Whaler captains often carried their wives, and some ships carried cabin passengers. Now the spar deck was continually crowded with ladies, who after their initial shock often became quite gay. The wardroom held a second seating for females, and a third for the captains and mates of the captured vessels. Ker gave them the run of the ship, not least because a few tars volunteered from each capture. But the sheer numbers were becoming overwhelming. He hailed three neutral merchantmen before a Hamburger consented to board ninety passengers for the few days it would take to reach her next port of call, which was Pernambuco.

He'd been running slowly south all this time, and at last struck the southeast trades, though their strength was less than he'd expected and there were lulls when the clipper nodded airless in a long swell. He quartered east and west across the trade routes along the line of two degrees north. Reflecting as he sat in the little enclosed closet cut into the overhanging stern, listening to the rush of the wake, that two or three more sea-wolves lined out across this belt could cut off the North from the intercourse of half the world. The sea-raider building at Laird's, if only she were here! They'd scissor apart the sea-lanes. With such richness of trade converging, how could the Yankees not have stationed a steam-kettle here? Surely they could read Maury's charts as well as he.

He reached for a copy of the *Herald,* not the issue concerned with the *Trent,* which they'd pinned up in the wardroom, but another, reserved for more practical purposes. And smiled, remembering that news. If England came in, independence was won. He would not have to burn ships, would not have to kill men whose only crime was that they insisted upon a union whose time had passed.

Would God all would come right, and soon. He dropped the scrap through the hole, watched it hit the passing wake and drag along after the clipper's sternpost, whirling in the eddies, till it was sucked from sight.

The next day put all they'd done till then in the shade. Between dawn and dark they ran down four New Englanders: *Mars, Rigadoon, Sugarbird,* and *Ocean Nymph.* Pillars of smoke ascended from all the quarters of the horizon, and the waist and wardroom filled again with the faces of strangers.

But not all the smoke came from burning ships. As dark purpled the west the lookout reported a steamer to northward. Ker eyed it for some time, then at last came about and ran south, away, till the smoke was obscured by the horizon and then by the night. The next day he hailed a Portuguese bound for Rio, and offered gold to take his passengers off his hands.

By now they were a hundred and twenty miles north of the equator. He was considering a run to the south anyway, thinking that even in so rich a grounds, it might not be the best of tactics to linger overlong.

Midway through the first dogwatch, they'd sighted only two sail, one of which was too far off to catch, the other French, out of Nantes bound for India. Ker was smoking a segar topside when the lookout reported something in the water ahead.

—Bring her to, Mr. Dulcett, Ker said, —And lay her to under a maintopsail.

Maryland rounded into the wind, and the on watch went to their stations. Some smiling, others with puzzled looks.

A gigantic figure levered itself over the bow, clambering up footropes, apparently rising from the water itself. It wore a huge oilskin and a painted crown of wood and canvas, from which hair yellow and coarse as Manila yarn cascaded over broad shoulders. It carried a speaking-trumpet under its arm, and a wooden trident painted black. With this apparition was another, in a sacklike Mother Hubbard of canvas daubed over with painted flowers. As this pair advanced down the foredeck a third appeared, cursing as he clambered over the bulwark and staggered past the forward pivot-gun. He carried a razor a yard long, made from iron scrap and a wooden handle. As the leading figure gained the quarterdeck it stopped, footed the trident with a resounding blow, and roared out, —Vat schipp ist dis?

Ker stepped forward and touched his cap. —You are aboard the Confederate cruiser *Maryland,* sir, and may I enquire your identity?

—You know me, zor, you met me when you crossed my line off der Cameroons.

—Quartermaster, it is my good friend King Neptune. Pipe him aboard properly, and fire a gun in salute.

The twelve-pounder banged out a charge, and the pipes keened. Neptune surveyed the crowd with an imperious frown. —Und are dere any apoard, who haff neffer crossed der Line pefore?

—I believe there may be some among us.

—Pring dem pefore me! he commanded, and suddenly the deck was a roughhouse of scuffle and interrupted flight. Men leaped atop the boats, and Sam went up a backstay with astonishing agility, but the shellbacks swiftly collared them and hauled them down.

Ker confined himself to a benevolent neutrality, making sure the traditional solemnities were observed but that the frolic did not get out of hand. To his amusement he observed both Minter and Osowinski standing naked, the former livid, the slightly built Pole with a melancholy expression. Then a half-stripped man broke from a struggling knot at the afterhatch. Ker started back. It was Kinkaid.

—Captain, these men are assaulting me.

—It is immemorial usage, upon crossing the Equator, Frank. I fear you must submit with as good a grace as you can muster. He winked at the crew, and in a moment the engineer was naked and being hosed down with saltwater by yelling men at the hand pumps. The polliwogs scrambled through a chute filled with mess-garbage and chicken dung, then were "lathered" with Stockholm tar and roughly "shaved" by the Royal Barber, behind whose painted features and reeling gait Ker descried a thoroughly levitated Steele.

At that moment MacDonnell, who had the deck, drew Ker aside. —I have smoke to the southward, sir.

Ker accepted the long glass. Thin and transparent brown, the smoke was most definitely that of a steamer. He clapped the glass shut. —She does not seem to be heading in our direction.

—Sir, I believe she is. You're judging by the direction of the smoke, and thus of the wind.

Ker shook his head to clear it; he might have had too much Jamaica himself. —Thank you, Bob-Stay, you are quite correct.

—That boyo's headed right for us.

Kaiser had noticed them in confabulation, and was ready when Ker told him to secure the festivities. He quickly declared all polliwogs "eg-cepted Shellbacks und members of my Royal Realm of der Sea" and that *Maryland* had permission to proceed. The royal party clambered back over the bow as the initiates were reunited with such scraps of their clothing, and self-respect, as they had managed to retain.

The pipe keened All Hands on Deck, and the holiday mood suddenly vanished. Ker passed the word that men unsteady on their pins were not to go aloft, and in rather more time than usual had all sail set away from the oncoming smoke. At the base of which, the masthead announced, a good-sized steamer was coming on under plain sail and engine-power with a decided bone in her teeth.

—Does she show a flag? Bertram called aloft.

—She . . . flies . . . the . . . Yankee . . . rag, came back from aloft.

He was standing by one of the twelve-pounders when Minter touched his cap. —Sir.

—Mr. Minter, what is it?

—Surely you are not going to run again.

Ker's rush of rage was so overwhelming he barely restrained himself from a blow. It must have showed, for Minter took a step backward.

—Another word like that and I'll relieve you of duty.

—You wouldn't dare.

—Wouldn't I? We are no longer two lieutenants dealing privately with each other. I will court-martial you, strip you of your commission, and set you ashore on Fernando de Noronha. Now repeat what you have just said.

Minter's cheeks reddened, but he managed the apology. —I did not intend my remarks in a personal aspect, sir, and I regret they were misinterpreted. What I wished to ask was, How much longer will we run before every shadow?

—An armed steamer is not a shadow, Mr. Minter.

—We are heavily armed and with nearly a full complement. There is no reason for us to flee.

—I owe you no explanations. But our orders direct us to evade pursuit where possible. Though our crew may be sufficient in numbers, they're not yet fully trained to the guns.

—I did not take this uniform to burn unarmed merchants.

—Nor did I Mr. Minter, nor did I. Ker held the man's gaze, hating the bitter heart even as he admired the hot blood that animated it. —I am not free to divulge my intent for the future. But I promise those who sail in *Maryland* will not be spared the crash of guns and the cries of the wounded.

—You will commit us to battle?

—Take the men in hand, Mr. Minter. Drill them like dogs, and practice daily at the guns. I promise you, we'll have as much danger as you can stand.

A moment more, then the exec nodded shortly. Ker studied his retreating back, visualizing just where he'd love to place a pistol-ball. Then turned back to find the steamer's sails a white dot on the dimming bowl of the sea, her smoke a stain on the dimming blue-black of the enormous sky. He had no doubt they could slip away during the hours of darkness.

But now his suspicions were answered, his doubts at an end. They were known. Sooner or later, if *Maryland* lingered in these waters, one or another of their pursuers would fall on them. In a region of such light airs, the odds of escape would be slight. Bringing their depredations to a close, and all aboard to imprisonment. Or a more ignominious end . . . The

New York papers had carried Seward's thunderings against the raiders, his threats that officers of "rebel pirates" would be hung on capture. He had to give the man that, there was no equivocation in him.

Bulloch's orders had been clear. *Maryland*'s movements, though broadly laid out as to geographic areas of operation, were to be determined by Ker's judgment. They'd had good hunting here. It was time to move on.

Darkness came, black velvet drawn across the deep. Their pursuer faded, visible at last only as an occasional flare of red from the top of her stack. An hour into darkness Ker brought *Maryland*'s head north. The distant red-orange ember slowly sank, to be lost to sight at last. He stayed on deck very late, looking to where Polaris lay. Still beneath the horizon now, invisible at this latitude, but it would rise. The purser served out double tots of whiskey, and the men played music, danced, and spun twisters far into the tropical night.

25

FROM the equator to their destination measured three thousand three hundred and sixty sea miles, ruled in a pencil line across Mercator's chart; such a course as a crow might fly, could crows cross oceans without rest or food; such as a steamer might set, were there steamers with unlimited coal and infinite power.

Instead *Maryland*'s track was that of a reversed *S*, first tending in toward the coast of Brazil, then northward in a great looping sweep past the Lesser Antilles. As the prevailing wind veered east of the Bahamas she swung to leeward, into the gigantic northward current Maury called the River in the Sea. The sky grew overcast and the sea roughened, then eased almost to glass; then built again until winter storms hammered at her bow timbers, and the water changed from green translucent warmth to the steep combers of a New England winter, hard and black and cold as Vermont slate.

But Ker did not see all this. For most of the two weeks of that lonely run he lay unconscious of the world. Shivering, with vacant eyes, the spectres of delirium haunting his brain.

DAVID POYER

He'd felt the onset as they cruised the equatorial regions. As if the heat had awakened some malignity deep-dwelling in his bones. Steele's brandied breath washed over him, and he blinked up into watery eyes behind steel-rimmed spectacles. Words drifted through his brain, rounded and pulsating like bladders of blood. "A capital article of intermittent fever . . . cathartics and disphoretics, *antimonii et potassae tartras,* I believe." Hands pried his jaws apart. He gagged on noxious potions. He drooled, sweated, shat, and vomited. His back was stripped and rubbed with something that burned like fire. Till he screamed aloud, struggling against leather straps that held him helpless to move.

Once again he rides the whip, upward and then down again with tremendous speed. Strapped to a hellish seesaw that whirls him from heaven to hell. Only this time the ship plunges with him. He holds to the bunkboards with desperate hands.

The shadow of a monkey looms, aiming the shadow of a cocked pistol. Worms coated with sharkskin writhe and crawl in his throat. Catherine bends close, passing a cold hand across his brow. Her painted mouth writhes with London billingsgate. Fever. Fever. The door opens and he pants and then screams. The doctor is here once more.

Alone in his freezing cabin, he wakes to a presence conjoint with him. Faintly he makes out the whine of rigging in a northwest gale. The thunder of the widowmaker battering against hollow oak. The clatter and slide of unwilling forced men stumbling dead tired about the deck. He lies frozen with dread, suppurating back so painful he cannot lie on it, yet so weak he cannot turn. At last he opens his eyes.

It sits upon the congou-chest in the corner, regarding him with steady, thoughtful gaze. Its hood shadows its features. He cannot see its face. Yet he needs no introduction.

Mr. Poe has taught him what this presence is. What it has come for.

When next he looks, sweating, its interested regard has turned his way.

The mouth is a bloody absence. The upper teeth are visible to the back. Air gapes and sucks through a scarlet horror.

He looks on its grim visage with neither yearning nor terror. Only

326

gazes into that grinning vacancy, the empty sockets above it. Then turns his face to the bulkhead, and listens in a bath of icy sweat to the crash of the waves.

The next morning he woke very watery but with the same crystal clarity of mind he'd felt in a farmer's house in Heathsville, with Olivia nursing him. He lay listening to the wind. The ship protested in every hanging knee and stringer as she plunged. He lay recalling the dream, or vision, or experience of blackness, marked only by a tiny, unimaginably distant red star toward which he plunged at terrific velocity; yet without rush of air nor any sense of motion other than the sense of helpless and interminable motion itself. He could no longer recall how that dream had ended. The blood tided from his feet to his head as the iron and wooden fabric enclosing him rose, hesitated, then plunged downward again.

The door creaked and Romulus poked his head in. Yellowed eyes studied him in the gray light that filtered through a dogged port. Then a smile broke across the boy's dusky face. Ker felt his eyes burn to see it, it was suddenly dear and in some way even sacred. Every object seemed to glow in the gray light, familiar and precious and holy.

—Is you awake, Massuh?

—I am.

—Wassum soup an' coffee? Got it hot from de galley.

—I should be very glad of something hot, thank you, Rom.

—You sounds better, Massuh. I is glad of dat.

—Come over here, boy.

The lad approached with a questioning gaze. Ker felt for his hand. It felt rough and warm, padded, like a glove. He squeezed it, feeling how impotent was his own grip, and blinked rapidly. Here at least was something resembling companionship.

—Will you undo these straps now?

—Guess I can do that, if you can keep y'self in durin' the rolls.

—I am very grateful to you for attending to me during my illness.

—Thass all right, suh. You feelin better now, I best git the doctor.

—I should be very glad if you did not. Would you ask Mr. Minter to stop by, if it is convenient for him. And then get me that coffee, and put in it, if you please, a drop of that Demerara in my cupboard.

Minter pulled off his cap, drew the chair with a scrape, and sat hunched, not meeting his eyes. Water dripped off his oilskins. A powerful smell of wet wool, mildew, and unwashed man came off him. Ker was wolfing the last mouthfuls of hardtack crumbled into steaming bean soup from a heavy china mug. He had never tasted a meal so satisfying.

—Merry Christmas, sir.

Ker blinked. Confused recollections surged in his brain. So this was Christmas. This dank room, smelling of mold. This mug of soup, welcome, but not what they'd be sitting down to at home. Where had he been a year ago? Off the Guinea coast, running sweat in a hundred and twenty degrees while the pitch bubbled in the deck seams. Perhaps someday he'd make it home on this blessed day of Our Lord's birth.

His first question was, where were they. The exec told him calmly they were in latitude 41 and a fraction, as best he could dead reckon, having gone without a glimpse of a star for days.

—Where will that put us on the coast?

Minter said he held them about sixty miles off Cape Cod, according to the patent log, compass, and clock. Their eyes met, and for a moment neither spoke. Then the exec added, —I took the liberty, since you were indisposed, to read the letter of instruction Commander Bulloch furnished you with. As we were at sea, nearing enemy waters, and I had to determine what to do.

—You did properly. Ker struggled up on one elbow. —Have you soundings yet?

Minter told him with that official voice that he'd essayed a cast of the lead at dawn, two hours before. They were still off soundings. The wind was westerly varying from a strong breeze to a moderate gale. *Maryland* was close-hauled north by northwest under single reefs and t'gallants. They'd spoken only one ship since Ker had gone under, a steam-packet from Liverpool bound for Halifax. Minter had asked whether England and the United States were at war. The packet had answered not yet, but British troops were being ordered to Canada against that eventuality.

—The officers and men?

—Sprains and scrapes, and one of the landsmen fell from the spanker-gaff. He fell into the belly of the sail and caught at a vang-rope. He was lucky.

Steele, at the door. —I understand our patient has recovered himself. You must not exhaust him, Minter. This was a narrow escape. He needs rest and restoratives. I will prepare—

—No! I will have no more of your treatments!

—There, he attests our success himself. There is no more infallible sign of recovery than resistance to further medication. The surgeon peeled back Ker's crusted eyelids, checked his pulse. Ker demanded another dose of rum, and after a moment Steele nodded indulgently.

When he had gone Minter made as if to leave too. Ker restrained him with a gesture. —So you read our orders. Your opinion?

—It's long overdue. Enter the port, sink or burn any warships at anchor or alongside, and shell all military facilities we can reach. Minter's green eyes seemed to shine in the dim. —The Boston abolitionists started this war. The long-haired men and short-haired women. Now we'll visit it on their heads. Revenge their invasion of North Carolina.

Ker recalled his conversation with Bulloch. —Revenge is not a strategical move, Mr. Minter. This plan is coolly drawn. A raid on New England will send every merchant and shipowner to the telegraph office. Their screams for protection will force Washington to withdraw the blockade, permitting us to export cotton and import the materials of war.

—As you will. As to myself, I will have victory, sir, or will have death.

—Mr. Minter. I desire victory as much as you, but I repeat, revenge is not our goal.

The exec smiled tightly. —You're a sick man. The surgeon certifies you so.

Ker caught the words he'd been about to hurl. Minter had brought *Maryland* safe through to Cape Cod, while he could not yet muster the strength to roll out from his bunk. Perhaps it would be best to give him the benefit of the doubt, at least until he could regain the deck. So he only said, —I am still weak, true. Please carry on. I shall note your acting as commander during my incapacitation.

—Do me no favors. Minter stood, looking hard as he ever had.

—I do it for the flag, not for you. In fact do it in spite of you.

Damn the man, forbearance was wasted on him. —I should not have it any other way, Ker said coldly. —You are dismissed.

A moment later the candle guttered beside an empty chair.

He made it topside the next day, feeling stronger until he actually reached the top step of the companion. Then his legs weakened and Romulus had to steady him as he made his way to the quarterdeck, and sagged down on the cap-square of the twelve-pounder.

The sea ran rough. A low scud blew close over the waves. The cold air bit past the upturned lapels of his reefer-jacket. The bow crashed through the seas, which came from starboard, the cruiser having tacked during the night in toward Cape Cod, the lighthouse of which Minter said he'd hoped to sight but had not. Ker looked anxiously southward, then west, where the danger lay. From here on things would become progressively tighter. This fog didn't help. Supposedly there was a fog-bell at Race Point, but he heard nothing. They'd not sighted land at all. They could be anywhere, inside the Cape or out.

Lighting his first segar since the fever, he drew in the harsh smoke with mingled relish and nausea. He'd never entered Boston Harbor. It did not look like easy navigation. The first barrier was Stellwagen Bank, and after that the charts showed dozens of rocky banks and shoals, any of which would tear her bottom out in these seas. Nor could they expect mercy should a Federal man-of-war loom out of this grainy gray.

Kinkaid, Shepperd, and several others, smeared with soot, grease, and coal dust, clustered at the stern, pointing down. Ker ambled toward them, stumbling as the deck rolled, and leaned to see what they were looking at. Kinkaid was explaining the procedure for lowering the screw. It housed in an enclosed box beneath the steering gear, another reason they'd been unable to mount one of the Whitworths as a stern-chaser.

When he straightened he nearly fell. His head swam in the afterweakness of fever. As MacDonnell came up, asking how he felt, Ker told him he'd want all officers at luncheon for some important word.

Nodding to Uffins, he shoved back from the table, and flattened the harbor chart on the dining cloth as the betty-lamp reeled shadows around the cabin.

As he explained their courses, the locations of the forts and their armament, the likely currents in the Narrows, their eyes lingered on his. He felt a sudden rush of that same emotion, that same, yes, *love,* he'd felt with Romulus. These men had come so far with him. He might be taking them to their deaths. Yet they smiled and joked as he asked each for the readiness of his division. Only Minter remained withdrawn, eyes narrowed, intent as a wolf contemplating its wounded leader.

He stayed on deck the rest of the night, peering into the storm for some sign of where they were as they seesawed slowly northward on a port tack. It came at midnight, a tossing star Osowinski identified from the light-list as Minot's Ledge, a light vessel to the south of Nantasket Beach. According to the signal book for the harbor, booty from a Yankee they'd burnt off Brazil, a magnetic telegraph line ran from the Outer Station there into the city. Incoming merchant vessels could run up signals identifying themselves for transmission to factors and owners waiting ashore. Ker considered doing this, using the *Good Shepherd*'s four-digit code, but decided against over complicating things. He could be wrong—events would tell—but he suspected bad weather, surprise, and swiftness would take them into the harbor better than an overrefined cunning.

As for getting out again, that would be the test of both captain and crew.

Snow, falling since dusk, cut his cheeks like the tips of uncovered épées. The wind was from the northwest, blustery and as intensely cold, he thought, as Dante's tenth circle of hell. Even with the limited fetch, no more than ten or twelve miles, it kicked up a steep chop through which the clipper labored under tops and foresails. Ker had decided to enter under sail, with the stack folded down. A clipper returning from sea was no object of curiosity. Once their identity was revealed, the equation would take a different form, its terms being time and speed and how rapidly the Yankees reacted.

—Captain? A black outline, sou'westered into shapelessness.

—Bob-Stay, is that you?

—I hold us to the north of Minot's Ledge. Aloft reports Boston Light bearing west northwest. According to the chart we can run in on its bearing. So I sh'd like to come about.

Ker did not see the light, nor, apparently, did MacDonnell, by the way he'd phrased it. The only man who could was the t'gallant lookout, perched and rolling high above in the utter dark. Ker felt rocks around him like sharp objects in a darkened room. The first he'd know of them would be the crunch of their timbers being stove in.

—And who's up there?

—Purcell. A Galwayman. Shows the rogue's-thread ashore, but he's a right cobber sober.

—I hope he is sober now, we shall be betting our lives on him tonight. Soundings?

—Twenty fathoms, sir.

—Make it so, then. Only wear around, if you please, no point straining our braces in this wind.

Shadows moved about the deck. A distant cry of "On the fore: shift your heads'l-sheets," and shortly thereafter, taking her time, she lurched round in the dark and stood inward toward what Ker now made out as the distant yellowish spark of the first lighthouse in America. The snow blew over her decks, lit for a moment green, then red, then whirled back again into outer darkness of a North Atlantic winter night. Ker's hands were wooden blocks despite his mittens; he could only imagine how cold it was aloft.

Below, consulting the chart, he ran a line in toward the land and checked the tide tables. High at five forty-one; presumably that was at the inner harbor; they'd have the advantage of a making tide. . . . Their success, and even more their escape, would depend on split-second obedience. Once in the harbor, his attention would be divided too many ways to attend to each detail. He could issue all the orders he liked once the shot began flying, but the men would do what they'd been drilled to do. Like Voltaire's God, he could set the machine running, but after that it would tick to its own clockwork.

Topside again, pulling his scarf up to fend off the slicing wind. He paced, leaned, paced again. Slowly the yellow spark drew nearer. Slowly the black to seaward turned to the dirty gray of an overcast, storm-shrouded morn. Masses of snow-choked baggywrinkle became visible on the shrouds, growing there like Spanish moss.

The quartermaster, hand to cap. —Flag shall I hoist, sir?

—United States flag, Epping. Have our own made up and ready to break at my command.

As the Stars and Stripes cracked out in the wind, individuals emerged from shadow. Osowinski, taking a bearing with his sextant. Kaiser, pointing out a slack leeward shroud to a landsman as the coast emerged from night. Far to starboard hovered a dazzle of snow and formless light among which faint shadows loomed: low whale-humps of islands scattered across the slaty sea. The larger were topped with gray scrub. The smaller were just masses of bare granite, shining dully in the growing dawn.

Closer in, rounded rock emerged black and abrupt off the starboard bow, vertical stones frosted with guano like powdered sugar. The sea was beating itself to foam against their northern faces. The chart called them the Eggs. The oyster-white shaft of the lighthouse towered above them on its pedestal of naked rock. To port two hilly lumps above a slate-gray bay, Point Allerton and Hull, spiky with winter-nude trees and here and there a lone-looking house. The whole scene was wild, desolate, and cold, an impression strengthened as flurries of snow eddied across it. In all the sweep of land and sea they were the only sail, the lighthouse's yellow glinting the only evidence of life.

—This is the pilot-station, I believe, Minter said. Ker lowered his glass; he'd been studying the channel past the Brewsters, and a squared-off mass deep in the snow and inchoate light. —Are we to stop for a pilot? The fine is fifty dollars, if we do not.

Could the man be making a jest? An overture, at long last? Ker cleared his throat. —Well . . . a pilot might be of material assistance, First. D'you think we should invest in one?

—A Yankee'd as soon run us aground as take us in.

—I fear you are correct. We shall have to grope our own way, and pay our fine in iron coin if we are caught.

He looked aloft. The exec had t'gallants, spanker, jibs, and staysails flat to the wind. *Maryland* was moving fast, clipping off eight or nine knots as she left the swells of the open sea for the more sheltered waters of Boston

Harbor. Unease stirred in his belly. He fought it in silence. He had a stout ship, a fast ship. He had confidence in his crew, and in his senior ratings, men like Kaiser and Eppings and Jacobs. Above all else they must keep moving. As long as she could fly, she could live.

Then the snow parted, and Minter said, —There's the beginning of our gantelope.

Ker put the glass on the mass of masonry. The fort's walls were vertical masses of solid Quincy granite. A row of square, irregularly spaced gun-embrasures ran low above the ground. But he knew from the New York papers its fierce-face was sham. The fort had mounted no guns when war began. It had been hastily occupied the summer previous to burn off the overgrown parade ground and throw up hasty barracks. The Bay State's militia had gone south; he himself had carried part of the Third Regiment to Gosport aboard *Owanee,* and other regiments had reinforced Washington. He was fairly certain those frowning embrasures were still empty. As to the fortifications deeper in the harbor, he'd conned out all the captured newspapers and still did not know. The *Courier* said they were fortified; the *Post* and the *Commercial Bulletin* called for their reinforcement, implying they were still unarmed, or occupied only by light garrisons.

Maryland pressed on, steadily running down the distance between herself and the fort. Ker glanced along the wet-shining deck. The light showed him all guns run in, all gunports closed, the smokestack lowered. The port-watch were huddled under the bulwark, sheltered both from the wind and from eyes ashore, which would find such a mass of men out of the ordinary for a peaceful merchant returning from sea. The U.S. flag streamed overhead. He could see nothing to alarm a freezing lookout, drowsy from hours pacing icy ramparts.

MacDonnell, Minter, Dulcett, Osowinski, and Bertram stood alertly on deck. They wore civilian headgear, sea-hats or duffel-caps, knitted wool pulled down over their ears. Ker himself had left uniform cap below for a red wool scarf bound Turkish-fashion about ears and head. He could imagine how he looked, but it was warm. Beside him the helmsmen fed spokes to the wheel as Minter brought their head around, aiming down the Narrows. He rubbed his mouth uneasily as he saw how truly narrow they were. An easy pistol-shot from the granite embrasures to the low stony beach of Lovell's Island. He shaded his eyes ahead, but with the snow and the inchoate gray light he could not see what lay at its end. At any moment a steam-frigate could loom from that formless luminosity.

—Signal from the fort, sir.

Ker swung instantly. The quartermaster was pointing, heads were swinging. Some men got up to look. He called angrily to Kaiser to keep them under cover.

High on the ramparts a greatcoated figure metronomed a flag. Ker hesitated, balanced between acknowledging and ignoring it. Did the fort have telegraphic communication with the city? Then, suddenly, he understood. A commercial vessel would have her number hoisted. He nodded to the quartermaster.

The flags ran up, dithered about the halyard, then snapped out. A solid red; red, with a white cross; white next the lanyard, outboard edge red; and another solid red. One, five, three, one, according to the Boston merchant code; *Good Shepherd*'s number. She too had been three-masted and ship-rigged.

—Slacken speed, sir?

—Steady as she goes, Mr. MacDonnell. We will carry on like the innocent visitor we are.

Perhaps the hoist satisfied their querier; perhaps it didn't matter. At any rate he lowered the flag and disappeared. Moving steadily through thickening snow, they left the fort behind, pressing toward whatever lay beyond. Gallop's Island passed to port, a nondescript curved heaping of earth. Then a rock-jut the chart called Nix's Mate. Out of the milling cloud of gray light the swells came toward them as if created out of nothingness, and passed beyond them into uncreation once again; like the passing of events and lives, no more to be predicted or foreshaped than the height or conformation of the next swell.

Then the channel opened, broadened, and through a fray in the curtaining snow Ker glimpsed hills and the distant spikiness not of trees but of masts. Spires rose at the crests of hills, and for a moment, trembling through the glass, the vertical thrust of a granite needle at the end of their watery road.

He slid the circle of vision to reveal a second barrier of stone, and the most potent guardian yet. Fort Independence was more compact than the first fortification they'd passed, but far more daunting. This granite face was dotted with low gunports between the outworks. A bare flagpole, a spindly guard tower rose above some central keep.

Here, the *Boston Post* assured him, forty-three mounted guns and magazines of ammunition awaited any enemy. The deck rolled anew under his feet, picking up a swell coming down from Broad Sound, but ahead the land closed in quickly indeed. Perhaps six miles separated them yet from their goal. His hands still shook with weakness as he cupped a lucifer to a fresh breva, then straightened, puffing smoke into the wind. Lord, he thought, Let me not be found wanting in the hour of trial. Let those with me pass through this valley of shadow.

The world wheeled as the helmsmen paid off. *Maryland* swung with majestic deliberation onto the beam reach that was her best point of sail. Osowinski called commands. The braces tautened, men set their backs, the yards slowly swung round. Looking over the side at tearing foam bubbling along her waterline-strake, Ker estimated her speed through the water at no less than ten knots. Bowling along, canvas-board stiff in a wind still unshadowed from the land. And a two-knot current behind her.

MacDonnell drifted down the quarterdeck, stood casually by his side. His black spade-shaped beard thrust out from under a red-and-green tartan muffler. A porkpie hat pressed down black curls. He cleared his throat. —It were the better part of gallantry to open the ball ourselves, Captain.

—A shot from the forward pivot?

—Me thoughts exactly.

Ker deliberated it—any suggestion from MacDonnell he treated with respect—but at last shook his head. —It's to our advantage to put off announcing our presence as long as possible. If we can, until we're actually off Charlestown. Surprise is our most potent weapon, Bob-Stay. Besides, I do not believe we can damage this fort with a few seventy-pound shells.

—Put through an embrasure, one could ignite a magazine.

—Possible, but unlikely. Let us hold our cards a bit longer.

The fort had crept closer over the term of their exchange. He could see guns clearly now atop the parapet. But the only human figure visible was a sentry, slowly pacing along the rampart; that and a lonely mackinawed oarsman stroking a row-boat under the seaward face, and making heavy weather of it. Wood-smoke rose, then bent to the southward. Beyond it stretched the heights of South Boston, and beyond yet ships rode at wintry anchorages scattered across Dorchester Bay. Uncorking his watch, Ker guessed the smoke from a breakfast fire, the garrison newly reveille'd for the working day. Surely from that tower a long-glass was turned their way. Surely the golden eagle at their prow would awake memory in someone's mind, some brow-furrowing recall of a news item about ships a-burning, crews set adrift.

A sudden flash, a bursting blossom of white smoke made him flinch. He tensed, waiting for the whir of shot, before he realized a banner was climbing skyward on the distant flagpole. Morning quarters, nothing more; the greeting of day with the ritual gun.

—Stand by to dip, Minter instructed the quartermaster.

Maryland coursed on, her flag curtseying. The fort returned the salute after long minutes with a reluctant lowering of the ensign. But no other evidence they'd been noticed.

Ker realized he was holding his breath. He passed his finger round his neck under the scarf, feeling sweat dewing his skin. Darkening the horizon ahead, the peopled hills of Boston. Guided by Minter's pointing he picked out the skypricking needles of the Old South Church, the lofty dome of the State House, and ahead, clear now, the vertical pillar marking Breed's Hill.

From beside him a voice spoke. —I was there in '43, Minter said.

—In Boston?

—On Bunker Hill; when they dedicated the monument. My father took me. I was only a child, of course.

—Your father had interests here?

—He was a cotton broker, buying in the Delta and shipping it here. They resold to the mills in Lawrence and Lowell. In '57 the panic hit. The mills canceled their orders. Leaving my father's Boston partner holding the contracts.

—Your father tried to help him, Ker guessed.

—He extended credit, yes. And lost his business when Mr. Eaton declared bankruptcy.

The Mississippian shaded his eyes to where the city ran down like black lava to the slaty meeting of the Charles and Mystic. —That's where our war came from. Women who think they're men. The temperance fools. And the pious apostles of abolition. We're mired in sin, and they're put on earth to bring us to the right way of thinking—at the business end of a Sharps.

—Half a point right, Ker said. —And slack the braces, if you please; we are advancing rather more quickly than is desirable.

Minter passed the order, cheeks flushed by more than the cold. *Maryland* coasted ahead, slowing as the topsails refused the wind, spilling it off their trailing edges in noisy luffings.

Ker glanced behind them, making sure his way back to sea was clear. This was the heart of Yankeedom, as Minter said. He did not want to think now about what it would be like attempting to exit, past two forts and an aroused city.

—I shall be below for a moment, he told Minter. —You may beat to quarters now, if you please.

—Aye aye, sir.

The tattoo was followed by the hammer of boots, the clatter of fire buckets, hoisting-whips, of gun-tackle being cast loose, the irregular thump of fire hose unreeling across the deck. He was reascending the companionway, buttoning his trowsers, when he heard Minter's voice raised in command. —Man the port guns. Cast loose and provide.

Panting with effort, he pulled himself into the light to see the ports dropping, the gun crews bent. With a heave and a ho and a grating rumble the guns ran out, black swelling muzzles appearing one after the other, like deadly jack-in-the-boxes, aimed at the city that sloped down from the heights to the Long Dock.

—Belay! he shouted. Faces swung to him; others, not hearing, or not wishing to hear, lowered to sights and primers. Ker raised his voice, but weak as he felt, could sense it die along the deck. He started forward, then a massive figure loomed up in front of him.

—Zilence! Kaiser bellowed, and this time, hearing the magazine-order, every gunner froze in his steps.

—Step back from those guns, Ker shouted. —Now. At once. Cease fire!

Minter wheeled, cheeks flaming. —Sir, this is the city that tolled its bells at the news of the murderer Brown's execution.

—I am aware of that, sir. What relevance has it to our orders?

—You have it under your guns. Strike back at those who strike at us! He turned back to the gunners, who looked uncertain. —Point, I tell you!

Ker saw the officers' expressions, a study in confusion and horror. A few steps only separated him from Minter. As he covered those few paces he found time for doubt. Could he be wrong, and Minter right? In Carolina the invading Yankees had committed theft and outrage, vandalized and burned helpless townships. Was this not the time to strike back, and bring the horror of war home to those who'd unleashed it?

But the British had burned cities, thinking to cow rebels against their rule, and turned an entire country against them. The civilized powers would recoil from such an act, and unctuous connivers like Adams would swell the organ of their sympathy. *Montgomery* and *Maryland* had burned ships and cargos, sent hundreds of thousands of dollars up in smoke or into the depths. But they'd not harmed one human creature.

Firing on an undefended city wasn't war. It was barbarism, and he would not descend to it.

He reached Minter at that moment, and swung him around with what felt like his last grain of strength. —What in God's name are you doing? I have not ordered the guns run out.

—That is why I have done so. Because you have not.

—Then step back, if you cannot obey. Take in your spanker, sir. Take in your spanker!

The last order was almost shouted. Minter said something unintelligible, eyes averted. But he turned away from the gun crews, and went aft.

Ker regarded him, then jerked his mind away. He must keep his attention on what mattered now . . . they were passing the Long Docks. Sheds and warehouses stretched out. Alongside, the sleek black hulls of clippers and brigs and packets. Aloft, the bristle-web of top-hamper, as if hemp-spinning spiders had bred in a stripped forest. Breed's Hill rose where the Charles left the confluence of the harbor to wander westward. Sloping down from it were streets of houses, and at its foot, the Union's wooden walls. Ships in ordinary and under repair; a tall smokestack, masting shears, great tented ship houses, and dotted among them the naked branches of winter-stripped elms.

The Boston navy yard at Charlestown. Less than a mile away, he no longer needed the glass. A receiving ship, an old ship of the line, lay close along the seawall. He believed it was *Ohio*. Behind it the enclosed shimmer of timber-docks, where white-oak knees and timber lay salt-seasoning against the day they'd be needed. To port, a tall, curiously fluted brick chimney; at the moment it was belching great volumes of inky smoke. It was echoed here and there about the yard with more coal-smoke, wood-smoke, the pure white plumes of exhausted and escaping steam. A raising of his gaze gave him the windows of the Commandant's House on the hill; then a redbrick jumble of sail-lofts, storehouses, ropewalks, timber sheds. Dropping his eye again, he examined the stern of a sloop-of-war propped in the only drydock in the North. And stretching away to the eastward, the ship houses and docks where the U.S. Navy was furiously building for blockade and war.

He turned, to MacDonnell's anxious countenance. —Sir, should we not run out.

—It is yet a trifle early, Mr. MacD.

—My colonial oath! Early? Are you shicker, sir?

—Your tongue, sir; restrain your tongue, Ker said sharply. A wave of dizziness washed over him. He had to clutch at the pinrail to keep erect. They were all staring at him. He must compose himself. He looked aloft, then at the swiftly passing shoreline. The yard half a mile ahead and closing, and *Maryland* still with most of her sail set.

—Mr. Minter, starboard your helm, bring her around into the Charles. Back your sails and prepare to wear. Mr. MacDonnell, gunners stand fast until Mr. Minter brings her around. At that time we will run out, prime, and point. Mr. Shepperd, you may erect your smokestack and prepare to engage the shaft.

Suddenly the tableau unfroze. Seamen bent to lines. The braces hauled round as Kaiser set them aback. The helmsmen paid off, hands blurring like those of loom-girls on piecework. The cruiser's head began to pay off to port. Almost imperceptibly at first, then more rapidly as she gathered turning-way. Ker hoisted himself with difficulty atop the pinrail, the better to see.

The river divided here. Boston lay to his left; Charlestown to his right, though dropping back steadily as *Maryland* pivoted, swinging with massive grace about her turning point. She was still nodding ahead, though more slowly now, through the calmer water of the inner harbor. Ahead of her, timber bridges leapt the Charles. To port he examined the North Boston docks at close range. *Very* close range, no more than a hundred yards off . . . but they were still turning, still wheeling.

Kaiser braced the foresails around with a slattering bang. The jibs came taut, sheeted home as the cruiser continued around, rocking, then slowly fell off onto a port tack. MacDonnell bawled aloft the spanker and the mizzen staysail. Ker opened his mouth to remind him of the main-yard, then remembered they had not set the main; it might foul the stack. Instead he told him to slack jibs and ease foresails. He did not desire speed just now, though he would in a very few minutes.

—Mr. MacDonnell.

—Sir.

—You will oblige me by listening closely. You will aim first at the dry-dock, firing solid shot through the floating gate, if possible; then lifting your point of aim to the vessel in the dock. Next, shift fire to that long building to the right. I suspect it contains the pumping engines and joiner's shops. Continue that as your aiming-point until we are abreast of the timber docks. Then shift to five-second shell for the machine shop.

The bushy-bearded lieutenant stared landward. —There by the chimney?

—That is correct. Destroying the engine-repair and boiler-repair facilities will materially damage the federal fleet's ability to steam. The ship houses and the coaling-piers you will also take under fire with shell. Cut your fuzes carefully. Our time will be limited. I shall make only one pass. Therefore, once we commence, reload and fire as quickly as you can.

—Aye aye, sir. MacDonnell lifted his cap, turned away smartly, shouted for his gun-captains to assemble for orders.

And now she gathered way again, having made a tightly coiled turn in the narrow Charles, nodding like a pony as she gathered speed back to-ward the yard, the stack, the bluff bow of the anchored *Ohio*. Ker scanned the waterfront one last time. At last, the shrill of whistles, the clatter of re-leased spring-alarms sounded across the water. Others had not taken the warning, not yet; they gawped out from the decks of moored ships, as-tonished at the slowly approaching vessel; considered them from the ship-ways, caulking-tools drooping in their hands.

Epping at his side, waiting wordless. Ker knew what the quartermaster wanted. —You may break it now, he said softly. And to MacDonnell, looking from where his gunners gathered, —Port battery: run out. Prime. And point.

Now the last of the bulwarks dropped away, bounding and slamming as they tensioned their lines. With a grate and squeal of wood on sand-sprinkled wood the thirty-twos rumbled out. The pivots rotated on greased iron, pointing like hungry wolves toward their prey. And with the snap of a breaking-line, a mass of fabric flung itself to the breeze from Breed's Hill, where Americans had first died for freedom.

He stared up at the broad bars of red and white, the blue square of the jack with its circlet of golden stars. It rippled proudly in the wind, and about the deck he saw other faces upturned as well.

Yet he could not woolgather. Despite weakness and sweating he must keep his mind on the business at hand. *Maryland* was all but drifting now, canvas luffing and rippling like the flag, the last cable's-length toward the yard. Ahead he glimpsed white faces at *Ohio*'s empty gunports, on the crowded spar deck. Fingers eagerly stabbing up at their just revealed flag.

The old three-decker was a receiving ship, filled with green recruits. Ploughboys and clerks, weavers and laborers, about to be laid now as living sacrifices upon the altar of Mars. He stared into their eyes, men who in a moment would be blasted into rags of bloody flesh. Many mere boys. But enemies now, and therefore doomed on this gray day to mangling and death. How strange he'd always found it, that men settled their differences in this way. He looked downriver once more, finding the harbor still empty except for a lugger coming in from seaward; a coal-schooner, perhaps, or late-season codder back from the Banks. The city lay open to the morning light, the pearly glow from the clouds given back by snow in houseyards, on roofs.

It was the day after Christmas. A day for mercy, and forgiveness.

He said, without exultation, —You may commence firing, Mr. Mac-Donnell.

Claps of thunder, a shock of air, a great screen of white smoke blowing back instantly in their faces as their first salvo swept the dock area. Solid shot tore through wood, toppled shears, sent fragments mowing along the stone flags. The report of the Whitworths was deeper than that of the thirty-two-pounders. He'd always considered the thirty-two a murderous piece of ordnance, but he could see at once the huge rifled shells did far more damage. One hit the caisson square, and hull-wood flew into the air. He had no doubt the heavy iron projectile had continued out the other side, on into the length of the ship propped helplessly beyond.

A moment of silence succeeded the first detonations. Then came shouts and clamor, both from *Maryland*'s decks, where swabbers stepped in, thrusting their staffs down the smoking bores, and from ashore. A long mingled screaming swelled. Steam whistles joined in, plumes bursting into the icy air, like a devil's calliope. The second salvo boomed out. The gunners finished loading, as the gun-captains laid their pieces with a glance along the top of the tube; then stepped back and jerked their lanyards, faces averted to avoid the bits of hot metal and primer that burst from the touch-holes.

Master, mover, initiator, Ker found himself suddenly with nothing to do but watch and marvel. Minter had his orders; MacDonnell his; every jack tar and engineer aboard his bounden duty, worn deep by now in grooves of drill. All he the commander had left to do was to stand in plain view upon the quarterdeck, hands locked behind him, a ready mark for bullet or grapeshot when fire was returned. He wished for something to occupy himself. At last he took out his watch, thumbnailed the cover open with a shaking hand, and began counting seconds between salvos for the after-pivot. It had lagged in drill, but seemed to be keeping up today. Both Whitworths were firing more slowly than the lighter guns. Two men to lift one of the great shells, two more to push it down the bore. The tiny hand oozed round with incredible slowness.

The cruiser's main chains passed the head of the drydock. Ker noted holes in the caisson, smoke rising from the dock beyond. The deck guns were loading with shell now. The midshipmen, Bertram and Dulcett, nodded as the cut fuzes were presented for their examination.

At that moment a powder flash and smoke cloud burst out ahead, where the timber-dock jutted out into the river. Raising his glass, Ker saw bluejackets wrestling with a small piece, perhaps a nine-pounder. Little more than a saluting gun. Perhaps it *was* a saluting gun. Ker weighed the danger coldly, then sent four men forward with muskets to bang away from the eyes of the ship. He could not spare a major gun for them. Not with such a limited time available, and such rich targets as swam before their sights.

A third salvo echoed back from the hills. Behind it, behind the singing in his ears the last shot from the after thirty-two, handspiked around to aim off the quarter, had triggered, he heard something else. A keening, a wailing? A crying in the streets, a murmur as from many voices? It seemed to be coming from the sky, the river. Like the hum of wasps troubled in the nest, accompanied by a dull, insistent metal clanging he recognized only belatedly as church bells.

Maryland slid over the black eddying water, sails slatting and luffing. He told Minter to ease her a point. That would clear the timber-dock and bring the forward guns onto the machine shop. The shop doors were open. Humanity showed black at their mouths. They were fleeing. But killing trained workers would set back the federal war effort as effectively as destroying machines. They were as much his lawful targets as the Dahlgrens laid in rows in the gun parks.

He nodded to MacDonnell, *shift fire,* and in a crashing sudden wall of flame and smoke the shells left their iron homes and arched in short flights into the buildings. Several landed short, striking stone, and rebounded in showers of sparks spinning end over end to crash keyholing through brick walls. Detonations flashed within, and roofs erupted in gouts of white smoke.

His watch gave him back four minutes since they'd opened fire. He'd lost track of the number of salvos—the midshipmen, telling peas from one pocket to the other, were keeping the definitive count—but now the whole sweep of the yard boiled with fleeing figures, panicked, bucking mules, flame and smoke. Fire rose from the drydock.

Yet the cruiser pressed inexorably on. The next targets were the great tented ship houses. Their dry old timber went up like fat-pine kindling; a shell or two apiece did for them. Along the piers huddled masses of shipping. The new steamers the Federals called "ninety-day gunboats." Hastily bought merchants, being rebuilt to warships. All crowded close, and none, apparently, with men bold enough to stand their ground or load a gun. For their crews too were abandoning them, vomiting a thronging struggling mass onto the piers, where they shoved and fought and pushed each other off, to flounder briefly before disappearing beneath the icy water.

Then shell swept over them too, and burst in flashes that bit gaping chunks from hulls and left fire and smoke leaping from the carnage. And *Maryland* moved on, her thirty-twos shotted now with grape and canister to mow down those who losing all cohesion now had only one thought: to escape. Though more and more often now, a flash from amid the smoke notified Ker someone was firing back. So far none had found their mark; the Confederate flag streamed above an untouched crew, and only a few rifle-balls had whacked into the bulwarks.

It could not last. Minute by minute more balls whizzed their way, like hornets buzzing from the awakened decks. Marines leveled muskets along the waterfront. So that as they came abreast of the timber-docks that marked the extremity of the yard, he gave Minter the order to withdraw. To send four bells to the engine room, for full steam ahead. Then to fall off downwind, turn from destruction, and bend their efforts to escape.

The sailing-watch scrambled to their feet. The yards swung round, bellying suddenly into taut incarnations of driving force. The deck heeled as they paid off. The engine's beat accelerated, like a heart girding itself for flight. Smoke and sparks burst from her stack.

She was a quarter-mile distant when a portion of the waterfront leapt upward in a black cloud. From it slowly tumbled pieces of timber, unidentifiable items of iron, human bodies. Ker watched something reach across the surface toward them, as an advancing squall-wind moves visibly across the calm waters of a lagoon. Then the sound hit them, a rumbling blam like the opening of the doors of Hell.

Steele had come up on deck. He was leaning on the pinrail, looking aft, segar trickling smoke into the wind, when a nearly spent rifle-ball clanged off the binnacle, leaving a scarred dent in the brass. The surgeon hastily sought the shelter of the bulwark. The projectile had come from nearly directly astern, as the cruiser, still wheeling, passed her fantail through the wind and steadied on what Minter, studying the compass, had decided would be their exiting course. Ker caught a glimpse of his expression. He was glancing from *Maryland* to the wharves of East Boston, and then to starboard, at the city itself. The waterfront streets had grown it seemed a black mold of humanity.

He suddenly realized Steele was speaking to him, and bowed to indicate his regret he'd missed the remark. The doctor said, louder, —They marvel at the sudden tangibility of insatiate War.

—Indeed, Doctor, indeed.

—How powerful is curiosity. I could not remain below myself.

—I have read all Washington turned out to view the battle at Manassas. . . . Alphaeus? I am glad of your company, but could you please dispose of that sot-weed. We have a great deal of powder exposed on deck just now.

Steele pitched the stogie hastily overboard. —You have left your mark on the Cradle of Abolition today, I should say. You shall be a marked man as well, from here on.

Ker looked ahead, to where the lugger he'd noted earlier had sheered off into some side channel; perhaps ducked under Governor's Island. The smoke from the yard, and from their own extended stack, blew before them across the waves. His eye plucked the gray gleam of granite from the blowing snow.

Steele said, —Are we clear of danger, then?

—I fear not.

—Ships in wait?

—Forts, Ker said. Thinking that leaving to the northward, they'd avoid Fort Warren, but Independence they could not avoid. It lay athwart their path to the open sea, and this second time, dread Cerberus would be awake.

He was looking aft again when he heard MacDonnell's roar, heard Minter's equally hot reply. He swung round, to hear the exec shout: — There it lies before you. Prime, I tell you! Starboard battery—you have not yet struck at the enemy. There he is!

Twenty swift steps brought him amidships, but also brought him to the verge of collapse. The world faded, turned dark, and he grasped out for support. Found a shoulder, and clutched it. For a moment fiery eyes glared into his; then the exec shook him off. He staggered back, head colliding with something hard behind him.

He was shaking his head to clear the sparkling darkness when a voice shouted, right into his ear, —Are you all right, sir?

—Good *God,* don't *shout* like that, Dulcett.

—We must take him below. Steele, close at hand, concerned.

He threw their hands off, struggled to stay on his feet though his head was swimming, the clamor of innumerable bells crashing through his skull. —No; I will stay. I have the deck. I am the captain, and I have the deck! Answer me!

But Minter was drawing himself up, fist doubled on the hilt of his sword. —Will you let him run from battle once again? The enemy lies defenseless. This is the time to strike. For hearth, for home!

—Yock ho, Mr. Minter. Yock ho!

—I will not be silenced. Don't you understand? This is *war,* my friends. War to the knife. If we don't understand that, they'll destroy us! My God! Prime, and run out!

Hands on Ker's arms, beneath his elbows. Supporting, or restraining? He shook them off again, this time with more will than strength; the world still remained tinted with night. —Go below, sir, he shouted.

—I will not! Listen to me, men. He's never been one of us. He's a traitor, and a spy!

Around him fearful faces turned from him to Minter. Ker understood now he could not have this man on deck. Nor could he trust himself to tenant consciousness much longer. He could think of only one thing to do.

Minter stared down at Ker's revolver. His hand tightened on his sword-hilt. —You would not dare.

—I'll shoot you down where you stand. Speak again, sir. Say one more word.

He did not answer. —Mr. MacDonnell, Ker said coldly, not turning his eyes from the lieutenant's. —Bo's'n. Bo's'n!

—Here, sir.

—Here.

—Take the exec below, and lock him in his cabin. He rebels against discipline; let him taste the fruits of rebellion.

The Mississippian made as if to speak. Ker stamped his boot, —No more, sir! Go below! In shackles if you must, but go you shall, this moment.

Minter hesitated, teeth bared; then spun on his heel. He turned at the companionway for a parting shot. —You boys remember this. Remember every word he said. The war he refused to wage, though we urged him.

—*We* urged nothing, said Dulcett. —We're with Captain Claiborne.

—Below, MacDonnell growled. —Captain's orders; do you hear?

When Minter's head had vanished below the coaming Ker shook off Steele's hand. He looked aloft, then ahead. Croaked, —Mr. Dulcett, take the conn, if you please. Make all sail, and send to Mr. Kinkaid for all the steam he can give us. We have a pursuer.

It had appeared from the Mystic, from some upriver yard or anchorage; a steamer, black-hulled, bare-poled, sails ashore or gotten under way without time to bend them on. It must have raised steam very quickly indeed. In which case its boilers would be under considerable strain, gone from cold to hot in minutes with a reduced charge of water. Stem on, it was hard to judge its size. He tried to steady the glass at his eye. Could not, and glanced at Dulcett, who supplied, —Side-wheeler. Twin masts. Low freeboard. A converted ferry? I see one large gun on her foredeck.

—Thank you. Bring us left, if you please; I should like to crowd the port side of the channel, leaving the fort to starboard. But mind the soundings, if we ground here we're lost.

During the altercation the city had fallen astern, the Long Wharf succeeded by Boston Wharf and the lower peninsula of South Boston. His gaze snagged on what resembled embankments ashore. Earthen ramparts. Though the glass revealed neither flags nor the mouths of cannons. But the fortress ahead grew steadily larger. No way to avoid passing it. The chart showed three and a half fathoms between Winthrop and a middle shoal south of it. But that channel was unmarked, he had no pilot, and the tide was falling now. He didn't feel like sticking his head into a noose—maybe literally. He looked astern again, to find the steamer was most definitely gaining.

—The whole nine yards, if you please, Mr. Dulcett.

—Aye aye, sir. Bo's'n! Sweat those courses up, and be damn quick about it!

Ker said mildly, —No call to curse at the men, Mr. Dulcett. They take their cues from us. We must keep our heads.

The midshipman stammered an apology, casting a scared glance over his shoulder. Ker called a boy and penciled a quick note to Kinkaid, explaining the situation. It had no sooner left his hand than MacDonnell wanted instructions on how to deal with the fort. It was now less than a

mile distant, and activity was visible atop the parapet. Ominous activity, involving puffs of smoke he suspected were from furnaces for hot shot.
—Shall we take her under fire first? the gunnery officer wanted to know.
—We can throw shell at longer range than they can; perhaps cut some of them down, those in the open—

—You make capital sense, Bob-Stay. Put your best gunner on the forward pivot. Commence firing as soon as you feel we're in hitting range.

Sam Prioleau, with an answer from below. Kinkaid had the engine full ahead, all the screw-thrust he could give. Ker looked aloft again. The snow arced down straining curves of canvas. *Maryland* was driving before the wind. Rooting her nose down into the slaty seas. He shouted, —Mind your trim, Mr. Dulcett! She's plowing potatoes. Trim-box aft at once!

A tuft of smoke from the ramparts; a leap of spray, well short but in line. Some overeager gunner, no doubt feeling the colt about his shoulders at this very moment.

Uffins, with another note. Ker opened it with his attention on the fort. It was from Minter, apologizing and asking to return to his post on deck. He ripped it in two and handed the scraps to the wind as the six biggest landsmen aboard labored aft hauling the trim-box, a heavy coffin-crate filled with scrap iron and lead. The words of an old Eastern Shore table-grace occurred to him. *For what we are about to receive, dear Lord, make us truly grateful.* A wintry smile twisted his lips. He had the feeling what they were about to receive would not make them grateful in the least. A twist of his head told him the steamer was still coming up on them. Its battle-flag emerged now and again from the volumes of smoke erupting from its stack. It did not seem quite as large as he'd first guessed. But of course a harbor-defense vessel did not have to meet the challenge of the open sea; nor did it need to displace much tonnage, to mount guns enough to make things interesting.

The crash-thud of one of the Whitworths, closely followed by the second. The double cloud of gray smoke fled toward the bleak islands to southward. Glass to eye, he awaited the fall of shot. He'd planned to exit via the northern channel. President Roads, Broad Sound Channel to Broad Sound, and thence to sea. The wind, however, seemed to have veered while they'd been occupied inside the harbor.

Shell-bursts, white against gray stone. MacDonnell was already shouting, so Ker kept his peace and swung to inspect the steamer once more. She was still closing. He looked aloft again. The trimming had helped, but he saw no further way to squeeze from her another quarter knot. Not on this point of sail. Once past the fort, though, he could haul to windward, bring her up and boardsheet everything.

If they made it past. Another double-barreled salvo; the rifled Whitworths reaching out. Both shells burst not far from the ramparts, perhaps somewhat beyond—it was hard to judge, the wind blurred tears from his eyes.

Then gunlight flashed, and a creamy smoke replaced Yankee granite. For a moment he saw them, suspended above the black sea; moving so swiftly they were gone even as the eye registered; tiny specks approaching and growing with wondrous speed.

The detonations arrived, deep bumping thuds like colliding coal carts. Plumes like those of leaping tarpon surrounded him, magically white from the black sea.

There was a savage beauty in being fired upon. Like staking one's entire estate on the turn of a card. His body wished to cringe, to cower. He braced his spine vertical, facing the fort as suddenly the sea, the distant land, seemed heartbreakingly dear, the familiar oak and pine around him precious. The very breath he drew tasted sweet.

A plunging howl overhead, a descending scream; the steamer had opened fire too. Ker could not reply. They had only light metal aft, only the twelve-pounders, and even these could not fire directly over the stern. Considering how often they'd been chased, he wondered now if that had been the right decision. He picked out a buoy opposite the fort. It marked the end of the Middle Shoal, the point he could safely turn. Another four hundred yards.

The fort settled to a drumfire, smoke rising as if from a conflagration. Balls ploughed and spun about them as in some insane shooting gallery. A projectile struck twenty yards off, glanced up, and sailed over his head with the angry hiss of a smoothbore ball. Another crashed into them forward. It sent bulwark-rail and hammock-bundles flying into the air, then plunging into the sea. *Maryland* was nearly opposite the fortification now, and from the murk in which it was hidden ravenous tongues of raw red fire licked out.

But MacDonnell was hammering back. The waist battery was coming into play now, the thirty-twos recoiling in gouts of fire and noise one after the other, their crews jumping back, then dancing in to commence the intricate minuet of loading. They swabbed and loaded, primed and fired. In such moments the mind had no realm; the only master was reflex. The boys dashed along the deck, cradling passing-boxes to their chests.

Another ball hit, aloft, a clattering deafening impact like a strike in a giant's bowling alley. Hemp and painted pine rained down on the fore-deck, laying out two men on number two pivot. The gun-captain dragged them aside and cursed his crew back to their places. So far, Ker thought, the fort was firing ball, not shell. This might be to their advantage. That had been the lesson of Sinope, eight years before, when Nakhimov had annihilated the wooden frigates of the Turkish fleet with shell-guns. Nor was their marksmanship as good as he'd feared. Militia, willing enough but hastily trained, were at the guns of Massachusetts. Such men had won at Bunker Hill, but this was 1861, not 1775.

—I believe that is our turn buoy to port, sir. Another three hundred yards and I shall starboard my helm. I have given the order for staysails and all jibs.

Dulcett's boyish good looks were smeared with grease and burnt powder; his lips were stained red where he'd bitten them. Ker said reassuringly, —Very well, Gustavius. You are doing handsomely. Do not wait for orders, brace around instantly when you judge we are clear.

It was painful to see the pleasure his compliment spread across the waxen face. The midshipman lifted his cap and turned back, shouting out orders to the sailing-watch.

Just then a shudder vibrated the deck. Ker tensed. Surely they hadn't touched! They were crowding the side of the channel, certainly, every yard of additional range from the gun-muzzles opposite robbed the projectiles of velocity; yet . . . the chart showed a tongue of shoal licking out to the west. That must be what they'd brushed. She drove smoothly now; her headlong speed had carried her over, he hoped without damage.

More leaps of spray, ahead, astern; another crashing impact forward. The fort had found the range at last. With a heavy crack a shell exploded. So had the steamer. They were bracketed. He straightened his craven spine with a jerk.

The next moments were wounding hell. As heavy iron tore through the upperworks, more pounded into the hull. Men screamed. Splinters tore through the waist. Gunners reeled and fell bleeding across their barrels.

Then Dulcett was screaming at the helmsmen, the wheel-spokes were blurring. For a moment Ker breathed in relief.

But as she came round the buoy he realized they were still in danger. Stern to the fort, a well-laid shot could rake her. Not only that, her own shellfire had been lifted from the ramparts. On the other hand she was now half a mile distant from those shoreward muzzles, and each passing minute added four hundred yards.

A tremendous explosion ahead recalled him to the pursuing steamer. It was no longer closing. They were picking up speed on this tack. But it was hanging on their heels; and the humming howl of its projectiles as they went by testified the large gun on its forecastle was rifled, like his Whitworths. But now MacDonnell's gunners were putting their shoulders to iron, slewing the carriages around to lay their sights in return. Presently they spoke, and huge columns leapt up near the chuffing monster that dogged their trail.

The drumfire from the fort redoubled. Balls flashed past, skipping from wave to wave, and sank. They crashed through the sails, opening great rents to the tearing force of the wind. Yet what Ker feared most, a mowing-machine reaping the length of the deck, did not happen. Not from minute to minute, though he waited for it to strike his unprotected back. He could not turn his head from terror. To keep his back straight and face forward, though his bowels were water, was all he could do.

Maryland tore onward. The horizon opened as Deer Island loomed through the seething snow. Dulcett at his side, animated. —The wind's veering further, sir. We may be in for a nor'easter.

Ker had noted that sky, the blacker blackness like an early night. Noted it with dread. He did not relish a storm in a ship damaged alow and aloft as *Maryland* was swiftly becoming. But aloud he only said, —That would not be inconsistent with the barometric indications.

—It may impede our progress on this point of sail.

Ker told him as calmly as he could that they'd have to hold this course for the time being. Their escape lay between Deer Island, Lovett's Island,

and the nub of Nix's Mate. Past that they'd have to come even further to windward to pass the outlying shoals, Devil's Rock, Green Island, The Graves. They'd haul as close to the wind as they could, that was all.

Another shell moaning overhead reminded him it was not just a matter of seamanship. He called angrily, —Mr. MacDonnell, can you not swat that fly for me?

He was startled at the roar that rolled along the deck, at the begrimed faces that split into grins as his jape passed from mouth to mouth. To his astonishment a ragged cheer rose. Then they swabbed and loaded, and rolled the guns out once more.

The headland of Deer Island slid past, and the open sea widened ahead. In one sense, the beckoning of escape; in another a new threat, from Nature rather than Man. She dipped her bow to a great roller, staggering as Dulcett braced her round into the oncoming storm. A t'gallant staysail split with a deafening crack, then began flogging. Men scrambled the ratlings, clinging desperate tight as the cruiser plunged.

Here, where the sea shallowed, great green billows humped toward the sky. Ker glanced over his shoulder. They were out of range of the fort. An occasional flash pursued them, but not even the sound reached them now. But the steamer plowed doggedly after, rolling to its scuppers though still intent on the pursuit. And now, on the far side of the shoals and marshes that lay between him and the city, two more sets of upperworks were moving slowly out the channel.

More pursuers, these fit for the open sea. If the lead hound could not sink her fangs, they'd take up the chase.

Osowinski joined him, melancholy features even more downcast. —Damage, Mr. Master? Ker asked him.

—Spars forward gone, and the fore topmast sprung. The Slav stared grimly to leeward. —This course, we will not escape, he added. —She's falling off.

Ker glanced too, and felt a stab of panic. There gigantic gray seas first stacked up, then burst explosively over black rocks. They surged white over those that were submerged, but that could still rip a ship's guts open and spill every soul aboard from a torn hull, shrieking as the sea pounded them into insensate jelly. He wasn't even sure which islands they were. What he searched for in the chart had no counterpart in the black ghosts that wavered beyond the driving snow, the swiftly advancing unlight of the storm.

In that sinking sickness he saw the Pole was right. Pitching violently, nearly head-on to the steadily veering wind, they could make no way on this tack. Yet to fall off meant threading a trackless welter of half-submerged rock, in falling darkness, with death as the penalty of error for all aboard. An easterly passage existed. The chart showed Hypocrite Channel, a needle's-eye among half-exposed fangs of ugly rock. The Devil's Rock to the north, Alderidge's Ledge to the south. But he didn't know one mass of foaming sea from the next.

A shell howled overhead like the fabled banshee. His weakness rose from his knees. Blackness swam behind his eyes. He raised them to see topmen struggling desperately aloft, boots slipping off ice-glazed foot-ropes, hands crimped into icy bleeding claws. He prayed for wisdom and strength. But found only weakness and fear. Or was there something there? Perhaps only a last despairing willingness to hazard all.

—Port your helm, Mr. Dulcett, he told the disbelieving eyes before him.

—Sir, we can't!

—We can and will, boy. Obey me, if you please.

—Sir . . . sir . . . The midshipman cast a despairing glance at the chaos and hell to leeward. —We'll run her to her death.

—Port your helm. Trust me, my lad, and come to east by north. Secure from general quarters. All topmen aloft to reeve damage. We are going through.

He was rewarded with a look of confidence and hope such as he'd never seen in a human face, though sometimes in that of a dog. A look that only Divinity, Ker thought in ecstasy and terror, could merit. A captain could not, could not; lofty and alone though he might seem, in the extremity he was no more than any man. Dulcett turned away and shouted, —Helmsman! East by north, handsomely! Hands secure from the guns, topmen and repair-parties aloft!

With a last puff of powder-smoke, the steamer hauled up as *Maryland* fell off the wind. A comber smashed it broadside and it rolled desperately, gunwales scooping up the sea like bailing buckets. Its paddlehouses plunged down into black foam, then soared up until the tips of its wheels churned clear of the unbroken waves. Far beyond it, past the headlands, Ker caught the streaming-up of an immense Niagara of smoke.

One glance back, like Lot's wife, at their handiwork. Then he turned his brow forward. To the seething mass of broken sea, the patches of foam glowing deep in the coming dark that marked each a broken keel and death in the icy wave. The clipper groaned within her wooden heart. All about, the cruel rock. Ahead the passage they must negotiate or die. Behind, the pursuers, eager for retaliation.

The strength he'd prayed for came at last. That, or the recklessness of despair. He lifted his face to the stinging snow, and laughed.

26

Touching at Bermuda ♦ Cargo of the *Gladiator* ♦ Call upon Major Walker
at the Globe Hotel, St. George's ♦ Gift of a Lexicon from
Mr. Secretary Mallory ♦ Double-Sealed Orders

SALT-stained, hull-patched, stays juried with rigging-stoppers, *Maryland* broke her pilot-flag on a cold rainy afternoon miles off St. George's, Bermuda. Later, threading the reefy web that had claimed so many ships, she stood in. A steam-tug lay waiting, puffing out clouds of coal-smoke that merged with a charcoal sky. Past the Point the seas gentled to a rocking gray like a cast-iron cradle.

Ker paced the quarterdeck as the pilot conned them into a sheltered bay overlooked on the north by the town. A dozen craft lay at anchor, including several of the island's famous cedar clippers. He made out British flags, United States, Dutch. A great steam two-decker flew the White Ensign. She dipped her flag as *Maryland* slowly churned past under the drive of her screw. Epping returned a curtsey of the Confederate ensign. As they passed under her stern several of those standing about on deck lifted their caps. Ker, MacDonnell, and Osowinski lifted theirs high, returning the unexpected salute.

The crew stood bundled in pea-jackets, clattering like gulls about pay, liberty, and satisfying a woman-hunger of two months' standing. Letting a crew go ashore posed its risks, but Ker had prepared as best he could. Their strongest incentive to return would be the pending prize-money.

The amounts building up opposite each man's name in the purser's book were approaching small fortunes, and deserters, of course, got none.

His own total as captain was beyond belief. If he survived this war, Catherine need never worry about stretching a pay-allotment again.

—Pilot recommends we drop the hook a hundred yards on, sir, between the two-master and the point with the oak trees.

—Do so, Mr. Bertram, and do not neglect your anchor-bearings.

Kaiser's bellow and the clank of a sledge on a pelican-hook was followed by the roar of iron chain-cable as the anchor fell through the bay's roof. Ker signed the pilot's receipt and escorted him to the side as the pilot-smack furled its gaffsail and swayed in, bobbing to the wet gusts that whirled across the wintry bay.

The smack carried two notes for him, sealed in oilskin against spume and rain. Ker retreated to the companion-hood to scan them. The first was from a Captain Bird, of the steamship *Gladiator,* to the effect that he was lying at St. George's with cargo for *Maryland.* The second was from a Major Norman S. Walker, Confederate States Army, conveying his respects. Walker regretted ill health prevented him from greeting Captain Claiborne personally, but invited him and his executive officer to dine that night at the Globe Hotel. Asking the pilot to stand off for a few minutes, Ker went below and dashed off replies to both notes, sanded them, sealed them, and handed them down with a shilling apiece for the runner-boy ashore.

Though the air was warmer than it had been off Massachusetts, sleet began to fall as the quarter-boat headed for Piggoty's Dock. The men had been promised liberty directly upon their return to the ship, and they plied the ash so hard the brine foamed in their wake. The surface of the bay dimpled about them. Each pellet disappeared as it struck the water, then returned, floating, till the whole bay through which they rowed was dotted with tiny white spheres. It reminded Ker of the sweet tapioca he'd loved above all else as a child.

Gladiator was a sizable screw steamer with three masts. Judging by the seamanlike harbor-furl on her buff canvas, they were often put to use along with her engines. Ker spent an hour with Captain Bird, whom he remembered from Liverpool; he was related to the fabled Trenholms of Charleston by marriage. Warming himself with Jamaica rum in his cabin, Ker went over the invoices, meanwhile pumping the Englishman for the latest news as to the affair of the *Trent*.

Bird said the Privy Council had demanded both an apology and that the persons of Mason and Slidell be restored. Secretary Seward was presumably cogitating his response. Meanwhile the Royal Navy was pulling ships of the line back into commission. He refused to commit himself as to the likelihood of open war, saying only that public fury in London at Cousin Jonathan's high-handedness was intense, and that war or peace depended upon Lincoln's response to the ultimatum.

Ker had become skilled at reading lading documents by now, and noted from Bird's that most of *Gladiator*'s cargo would continue to Charleston. Over a thousand cases of Enfield rifles, twenty to a case; riflepowder, cartridges, caps, and bayonets; Remington and Whitney revolvers; army shoes, blankets, lead, morphine, quinine, uniforms, canvas, and dry goods. His heart lifted. Truly, here was the lifeline, as essential to the war Jackson, Lee, and thousands of other brave men were fighting as an air-line was to a deep-sea diver.

—These revolvers, sir; were they not manufactured in the North?

—Trenholm has an affiliate in New York. He buys them on the open market and ships them to Liverpool.

—I see. Are you long in St. George's, sir?

—Only to coal and send down my topmasts before running in to the coast, Captain. And of course, to deliver that part of my cargo earmarked for you.

Bird said Ker might want to buy his wife a cedar-chest, or some handmade silver, as long as he was in town; the island crafts were highly prized. He then turned over a paper listing *Maryland*'s receipts, to be delivered where met, or, missing her, to be warehoused in Bermuda until she should call. Ker noted with satisfaction it included two hundred flat-nosed Whitworth shells, more than replacing the eighty he'd expended in Boston. Bulloch had also forwarded powder, provisions, blue wool winter togs for the crew, badly needed, and a number of comfort items, such as segars, wine, cards, books, tracts, and music.

—You look pleased, Captain.

—I am impressed. We cannot say we are not being well supplied.

—We could furnish even more, were it not for the paucity of funds made available by your government. But I'm sure they do all they can, I did not mean that as criticism . . . ahem. The port regulations prohibit transfer of ammunition alongside a pier. I propose to get under way tomorrow and anchor by you. I have already made arrangements with a local firm for a barge and laborers.

Ker asked for a delay of a day, as he was sending the starboard watch ashore tonight and the rest tomorrow. Bird said that was fine; he had several days yet until the moonless period he'd need for his run in to Charleston.

—And do you have any private letters, sir? I shall be glad to post them upon our reaching Carolina.

Ker said he did, and would be grateful for the opportunity. He would also impose on the captain to take one of his officers home. Ker was returning him to the Department in Richmond, accompanied by a letter explaining the matter. The older man said gravely that he should be glad to do so. Ker then took his leave of Bird's snug rookery, and hiked alone along the waterfront through chilly mizzling rain and dying day toward Duke of York Street.

The Globe Hotel was two stories of pink stucco, with chimneys framing the front door. Push-out shutters eyebrowed the upper windows, streaming rain. Enquiring at the public-room, he was directed to a private apartment upstairs, from behind the door of which, just before he tapped, came agonized coughing.

Walker was in bed with a coal-fire in the fireplace and flannel at his throat. A floor-shakingly large colored woman answered the door with her hands full of knitting. Ker bowed apologies for intruding. Walker's cheeks were red and swollen. The smell of camphor was heavy in the room, which was very hot after the chill rain. He said hoarsely, eyes closed, —Captain? I regret not being able to rise to greet you, sir, but I really am too weak. It is the influenza, I am afraid.

—Do not trouble, sir. I am Ker Claiborne, commanding the Confederate States Steamer *Maryland.*

—Proud to make your acquaintance, sir. Walker's hand was dry and feverish. —Your exploits off the Brazilian coast made exciting reading. I understand you also made a foray upon the bluenoses in their home quarters.

—I had the honor of paying a call on Boston.

Walker coughed miserably, wheezing as he breathed. Ker looked away in sympathy. —It will help end the war, I am sure. This spring, at the latest . . . I thought after Manassas it would be over sure . . . Mayree, a rip of rum for the captain.

Invited to sit, and bustled up a poker-heated mug of Barbadoes by the nurse-servant, Ker considered offering Dr. Steele's services; decided there was no point increasing Walker's suffering. He determined to make his visit short. —I'm here in response to your note, sir. I assume you are the Confederate consul in this port?

—Not so fast, sir. I have the honor to be the resident disbursing agent. And yes, I have official mail for you. Rather a lot of it. But before we proceed you must tell me all about Boston.

Ker did so with as little detail and thus as quickly as was consistent with courtesy. Walker listened with fever-glittering eyes, exclaiming now and then. The colored woman looked on with tranquil tolerance, knitting in a rocking chair. She was fashioning a tiny knit jacket, the size a newborn might wear. It made him suddenly pine for Robert. When he was of a size to wear that Ker had cradled him in one arm, and pressed kiss after kiss on his astonishingly warm head. . . .

A knock announced covered trays from the public-room. Roast beef and potatoes and wine. Walker waved his away. The nurse urged him to eat, but he refused with the petulance of a sick child. Ker attacked his own plate. The wine was thin but the beef excellent, juicy and still hot, albeit with an off-flavor that made him guess it had been hung rather long, then cooked over a coal-fire.

Walker said, —We heard of your raid by the New York packet. You have already been denounced in the United States Senate as a pirate and freebooter. Secretary Welles is detailing steamers to patrol the approaches to Boston, New York, and Philadelphia. The other coast cities are screaming for protection as well. I congratulate you, sir, not merely on a successful raid but a significant diminution of the blockade.

Ker said the plan was Bulloch's and Secretary Mallory's, not his. The credit was his crew's, who had performed with great courage and consummate seamanship in a demanding action. *Maryland* had been hit upwards of a dozen times; she had suffered several wounded, but fortunately, not one soul had been killed.

—You are too modest, sir, for one whose capture is being demanded by Governor Andrew and Senator Sumner. The associated merchants of Boston, indeed, have put a price on your head.

—Surely you speak figuratively.

—I assure you I do not; they're offering five thousand dollars. Mayree! Ask Mr. Haven for some rope here, we'll make our fortune. He laughed, then gasped for breath.

—Did these papers say what Lincoln's response was to the British note? About returning Mason and Slidell?

Walker said they had not, but that the militia in Bermuda had been mustered and issued new weapons. Speaking of the emissaries, did Ker know, at the time he'd raided Boston, that Mason and Slidell were being held there, at Fort Warren?

—I did not. If I had, I should have rendered honors as I passed.

—Should the Queen declare war I have no doubt this island will be invaded.

—By the United States?

—Most assuredly, it would be a decided strategic advantage. It would be useful if in such case you would be willing to serve under British naval command.

Ker considered this. *Maryland* could not stand in a line of battle, but she might serve to carry dispatches or harry the fleet train. For a moment his brain limelighted a Western Trafalgar, the midwifing of Southern independence by the Royal Navy. He cleared his throat. —Nothing would give me more pleasure. Though I'd need official instructions . . . but you're in regular communication with home from here, is that correct?

—The Federals don't even pretend to blockade between Wilmington and Beaufort. The passage to Wilmington takes seventy-two hours. Captain Bird will be leaving in a few days, if you have mail.

—I've already had the pleasure of a talk with him. We will be loading ammunition from his holds soon. I only wish I could get letters as easily as I can send them.

The woman, still rocking and knitting, —You not heard from your family?

Ker started, surprised she'd spoken. —I'm afraid our movements have been too rapid and unpredictable for the mail to catch up with us.

Walker called hoarsely for another rum-toddy. —Your plans, then? Oh. You told me. My head feels like it's stuffed with rags. To load ammunition, and then?

Ker said patiently, —You said you had orders for me?

—I'm sorry; there are several things here for you. Mayree, step downstairs, ask Haven to open the safe.

Ker said when she was gone, —Subject to any new orders, I plan to coal, arm, and make essential repairs. Then I'll start burning my way through the New England fisheries. When I see too much steamer-smoke around us, I'll go somewhere else.

The nurse came back with a leather dispatch-case. Walker coughed and coughed, his shaking hand pawing through its contents, holding each in turn to the firelight; until at last he thrust out five envelopes. —Mayree, get him the receipt-book.

Ker noted with a leap of his heart that one was addressed in Catherine's spidery hand. He wanted to rip it open, but restrained himself. Later. Nothing, apparently, concerning Trezevant. He was very much afraid that the Old Man must have died—with such grave injuries . . . The others were from the Navy Department. One was quite bulky. Walker's glittering eyes encouraged him. He arranged them in order of the dates of postmark and penknifed the first one apart.

Confederate States of America, Navy Department,
Richmond, Virginia, November 20, 1861.

Sir—

The orders given you upon the occasion of your departure from England by Commander Bulloch are officially confirmed, viz: To take command of a prize taken by yourself on the high seas, to be named C.S.S. <u>Maryland;</u> and to arm and equip her as a vessel of war, without infringing the laws of Great Britain, or giving that

Government just cause of offense; and having obtained a crew and all things necessary for an extended cruize, you will proceed against the enemy in whatever quarter of the ocean circumstances may then indicate as affording the best chances of success. You are authorized to confer acting appointments upon such officers as you may deem necessary. This Department, the speed and qualities of your vessel being unknown, is unwilling to assign any particular localities for your operations; but desires particularly to impress upon you the importance of rendering your vessel as formidable, and your cruize as destructive, as practicable, leaving to you entire freedom of action. Should your judgment at any time hesitate, it may be aided by the reflection that you are to do the enemy the greatest injury in the shortest time. A speedy recognition of our Government by the Great European Powers is anticipated. You will therefore keep yourself informed to the best of your ability as to the condition of peace or war existing between this Government and that of the United States, that warlike acts may not be accomplished after the conclusion of a truce or cease-fire. As following the winning of our independence, the neutral powers will become our close commercial relations, their rights cannot be too sedulously observed; nor should an opportunity be neglected of cultivating friendly relations with their naval and merchant services. You will avail yourself of every opportunity of communicating with me, using, when you deem it expedient, a cipher for the purpose, based upon the text which I have the honor to enclose. The Department relies with confidence upon the patriotism, ability, and conduct of yourself, officers, and men, and with my earnest wishes for the prosperity of your cruize, and your triumphant return to your country.

I am, etc.,

S. R. Mallory,
Secretary of the Navy.

The second package, which he saw now had formerly been pasted to the first with tape, contained a small red book titled *Multum in Parvus: Lyman Cobb's Reticule and Pocket Companion, or, Miniature Lexicon of the English Language.* Trezevant had shown him how such codes worked.

Each word was denoted by two numbers, the first being the page, the second, the number of the word it was desired to indicate, counting from the top. If both sender and recipient had the same edition, communication was simple; if a message thus coded was intercepted, it was opaque without the key.

The second letter was from Commodore Franklin Buchanan, now apparently head of the Bureau of Orders and Detail. Which Ker found interesting, he had not even known "Old Buck" had thrown his lot in with the South. Dated in early December, it was an exasperated request for a report of his operations. Particulars had been gleaned from various newspapers, both Northern and English, all redounding to *Maryland*'s credit so far as effective action against enemy commerce; but no official report had been received as yet. "Old Buck's" waspish tone softened in the last paragraph. It informed him that Buchanan had the honor to enclose Ker's commission as Commander, Confederate States Navy, with heartiest congratulations.

The document was folded inside the same envelope. Printed on cheap paper, it was not as impressive as one might have wished. Still, he could not help showing it to Walker. The major insisted on another toddy in honor of his promotion. Ker jerked open his collar. The good news, the heat of the room, and the alcohol combined to make him giddy.

The last envelope was double sealed. Walker said, coughing, —That arrived only last week, on a runner from Wilmington.

Inside was a column of figures. Ker blinked at it before remembering the code. He asked Mayree for a pencil, and set to work with the lexicon.

He felt even drunker when he blinked down at the result.

The message, if he was interpreting it properly, stated that Confederate privateers and raiders being known to be at large along the Atlantic seaboard, and the first Panama steamer of the year 1862 scheduled to carry home three million dollars in fresh-minted California gold, the United States Treasury Department had requested an armed escort to meet her as she passed through the zone of danger. Accordingly, the Navy Department had directed a war-steamer to rendezvous with the liner on January the sixth, at latitude thirty-eight degrees, fifteen minutes north, longitude sixty-nine degrees, ten minutes west, from which point it would escort her and her cargo to New York.

Ker sat astonished. He could only conjecture as to how the Confederacy had gained access to such well-guarded information as the track of the Panama gold-steamer. But as the rest of the instructions emerged word by word from the rows of numbers, he tensed with excitement.

Maryland was to intercept the liner south of the rendezvous point, posing as the escort, but joining a day early. Ker was to "effect interception without fail, and capture the vessel in the name of the Confederate States." He would then remove the precious cargo, and either take the screw-steamer as a prize, if he deemed her suitable for conversion into a steam-cruiser, or sink her in the open sea, taking precautions to place crew and passengers in the way of reaching safe haven. The specie safely aboard, he was to shape his course for Liverpool and turn over all monies to the account of Fraser, Trenholm. The message was signed by Commodore French Forrest, Secretary Mallory's operational aide.

He sat trying to scrape his wits together, fuddled both from the liquor and from the thought of three millions in gold. Such a sum in Huse's hands would mean all the artillery and rifles Britain could pour out would be the South's. The gray armies now training with flintlocks would meet McClellan in the spring as well armed as their enemies. He did not sell the Northerners short. But equally equipped, he'd wager on his own countrymen to repel any attack whatsoever.

—The orders you hoped for? wheezed Walker, wiping tears from his eyes.

Ker started; he'd forgotten for a moment he was not alone. —I beg your pardon? he muttered.

—I said, were those the orders you had hoped for? Commander?

—I'm sorry, Ker said. —They are secret naval orders. Significant ones, possibly.

—Maybe the Yankees'll make the price ten thousand this time.

Ker tried to smile. He folded the papers carefully and put them away within his coat, next to the revolver that had nestled there through the row ashore, through his interview with Bird, through his walk in the rain. He'd prayed it might be a short war, and that he might make a difference. Too many brave men had already fallen, on both sides.

Perhaps it might be granted him.

Shortly thereafter, he made his courtesies, and left.

27

The Hospitality of the Island ◆ Disposition of Mr. Minter ◆ Sabbath-Day at Sea ◆ Preparations for an Encounter ◆ Early at the Gate ◆ Recollection of a Scene of Melville's ◆ Surprised at the Rendezvous ◆ Old Friends and Old Enemies ◆ A Decision for Battle

MUNITIONS struck below, coaled, and watered, *Maryland* put to sea after days of stiff winds, scudding clouds, alternating warmth and a damp penetrating chill. The authorities had been generous with their facilities, and the civil population even more hospitable. Bermuda and Virginia had been connected from the very earliest times; the island had been settled by men and women bound for Jamestown, shipwrecked on what had till then been the dread Island of Devils.

Ker visited Rose Hill, and called on Governor Ord and at the Admiralty House. To the Tuckers, the Carters, and the Bournes he returned polite notes regretting press of duty prevented his attendance. He allowed himself an hour of shopping, buying a cedar-chest for Catherine, a plaited-palmetto hat for Robert, and a shark-oil barometer for himself.

Minter had left the ship, carrying a sealed letter addressed to the Bureau of Orders and Detail. In a stormy interview in the commander's cabin, he'd told Ker he understood his game. He was no convinced Confederate, but an opportunist angling for rapid advancement in a new service. The right offer and he'd follow renegades like Farragut and Samuel

Lee over to the enemy. Someday, when their military status could be set aside, Minter would even the account.

Ker had responded coldly with his own view of the matter. As the commander of a ship of war he could not overlook disobedience and disrespect, much less an inclination to precipitate action in delicate situations. He went on that regardless of their personal relationship, he still regarded Minter as a capable officer. In the letter to the Department, he had taken pains to set forth his conclusions in a manner that would not militate against his further employment. He only recommended that for safety's sake, Minter should be placed under the supervision of cooler heads.

At this the lieutenant had burst out with such wild threats Ker had ordered him from the cabin, and an hour later a silently fuming Minter had been rowed over to *Gladiator,* en route to Richmond via Wilmington.

Now Bob-Stay MacDonnell was exec once more. Ker had promoted Dulcett to acting lieutenant, Bertram to passed midshipman, appointed Osowinski a lieutenant, and advanced the other officers and petty officers in their turn.

He took a turn around the deck, regarding the clear hard varnish of the guns, the die-straight line of rolled hammocks. The crew had worked like beavers. Under Osowinski's accented but meticulous direction, they'd replaced the damaged topmast, spars, and rigging. The ship's carpenter had adzed and bent new hull-planks. Only two men had deserted; scum, Kaiser declared, whose absence would only raise the crew's spirits. Into their places stepped several volunteers from *Gladiator,* whom MacDonnell placed on the number two pivot to replace those injured and sent ashore.

So that all in all he handed the pilot down into his smack with satisfaction, and eagerness to be about his business. Their course from here he had discussed with no man. He'd burned his translation of Forrest's message and locked the original in his safe. The dictionary-key stood on his bookshelf, secreted like the Purloined Letter among *The Kedge-Anchor* and Hawthorne, Epictetus, Tupper, and J. H. Ward. He waited until Bermuda was only a smudge on the horizon, till a hearty luncheon had been set in the wardroom and consumed, before announcing a council of war.

The assembled officers responded with glee. They had no questions, and he had few for them; they'd been together long enough each knew what was expected, and Ker knew that expectation would be fulfilled.

He sipped wine as he studied them. MacDonnell's bearlike form was expansive in an oversized leather slipper-chair. He'd discovered it in the hold of a burning barque, and scorched the seat of his trowsers getting it into the quarter-boat. Dulcett was slim and elegant in the fitted frock coat he'd had tailored in London. His callow tentativeness had given way to a self-assured competence on deck and off. Bertram sat square-set, imperturbable, masking youth and uncertainty with a grim expression. Osowinski, a touch of Central European culture amid the Anglo-Saxons; he knew what it meant to pine for one's country. Steele, elevated as usual, gripping the brandy bottle as a servant-girl would the neck of a chicken. Kinkaid was reserved, faintly disapproving, as if revelry were some offense against dignity. And behind them Romulus, his good-natured phiz wreathed in a shining smile.

He took back their attention with a rap on the table. —Very well, then. Everyone knows his duty . . . we will make our rendezvous five days from now. Mr. MacDonnell, I should like you to oversee an hour of boarding-drill each day. Exercise the men at both boarding and repelling boarders, as well as sharpening our gunnery and sail-handling. Make certain all our boats are ready. I shall want to send over a force large enough to make certain she is ours.

The next day was Sunday, for which Ker had set their first general muster. As four bells sounded he smoothed his hair, regarded himself in the mirror. He'd shaved his cheeks, trimmed his beard, and waxed his mustache, which was attaining a respectable length again. Rom had brushed his coat and dubbined his boots. On deck he found an overcast sky, a fairly heavy sea running, and the crew turned out in the new blues and soft hats. Toeing the oakumed seams, their shadows swayed to and fro.

He read the Articles of War deliberately, letting the dread repetition of the penalties sink in. For mutiny, death; for disobedience, death; for intercourse with the enemy, death; for sleeping on watch, death; for cowardice in battle, death; for failing to seek an encounter, death.

After MacDonnell had called the muster, the boatswain piped "divine services" and Quartermaster Epping broke the church flag. Ker removed his cap as Seaman O'Meara bent his hoary head. Kaiser had reported grumbling at permitting a Catholic to read the prayer, but in Ker's mind the message of the Savior, no matter in what form it came, could not but dispose men to a more elevated frame of mind.

They reached the interception point, a day earlier than the appointed time, which was in itself twenty-four hours earlier than the Yankee man-o'-war would be at its station a hundred and eighty miles farther north. Ker ran easy that night under single-reefed topsails, and in the morning chill, in those magical minutes when the impending sun limned the horizon, took the most painstaking fix of his naval career, nearly freezing his bare hands in the process—one could not adjust the vernier-drum of a sextant with gloves on. After which he bolted a hasty breakfast of biscuit, jam, and black coffee, eager as a groom on his wedding day.

A few fleecy clouds hung about the points of the compass. Save for that the sky was unencumbered. The morning light gilded every line and sail, and the decks glistened with a treacherous ice-glaze. Aloft no shroud or brace needed the slightest touch. The whole broad sea heaved empty as if new made.

Dulcett, buried in a melton reefer, touching his wool stocking-cap. His new stripes gleamed golden. He'd been attempting a mustache, and for the first time, seeing its fuzzy trace above his lips, Ker thought it might succeed. —Good morning, Captain; hope you slept well. Wind's from the nor'west at a moderate breeze. I have t'gallants and spanker shaken out and we're making four knots. Sounded the bilges and she's dry. I have doubled the lookouts aloft and instructed them to watch particular sharp to the south'ard this morning.

—Very well, Mr. Dulcett. But what is that upon your lip? Have you been sniffing the buttercups?

Dulcett lifted an eyebrow. —There are no buttercups at sea, sir.

Ker wondered what had happened to the old rule that every pleasantry a captain attempted was to be greeted with uproarious laughter. But he didn't care. He'd wanted *Maryland* to be a band of brothers, not the canvas-topped tyrannies he'd suffered. Save for a landsman caught forcing himself on one of the boys, he'd not needed the cat once. Seamen served willingly enough if treated like free men, and not as prisoners.

He went forward and down and then aft again, fetching up in the cramped auxiliary room. Shepperd showed him the fires ready laid, the greased shining rods and valves ready to flail into life. The Panama steamers were fast and well-found. But he planned to close bow on, with the United States ensign flying. The natural assumption would be that *Maryland* was the escort, joining a day early. That should bring them close enough to place her under the Whitworths. A bull from those dictators should bring her to heel.

When he emerged again MacDonnell was waiting. Ker went over the plan once more with him, emphasizing the necessity to approach in such a way the steamer could not get a beam view. —Our lines are finer than a typical sloop-of-war. The moment she catches sight of our sheer, the game will be afoot. I should like that not to happen until she is well within range of our guns.

—Should we not erect the stack?

—A capital point, Bob-Stay. Get it up without delay. Lower the screw, and light off as well; they'll expect their escort to be steaming her engines. But remember, do not run out the guns until we are so close she cannot turn away.

He had no specific time of rendezvous, and in reality one could not time a meeting at sea with any expectation of exactitude. So later that cold glittering day MacDonnell conducted sail-drill and boarding-drill; and after evening meal the men took their ease about the deck, huddling from the wind under the bulwarks, the music of a mouth-harp and the murmur of a hand of cards over a mess-tarpaulin a somnolent accompaniment to the rush of the sea along the strakes. The raider was running east and west, wearing at each watch so as to remain within ten miles of the meeting-point. The day eased toward night in a lemon-yellow glow that lingered about the western bowl of sea, lighting the clouds vermilion below and silver-gilt above, while a deepening violet stole slowly up from the east.

Ker sat smoking on the cap-square of a twelve-pounder, lapels turned against the chill that had deepened with each degree of northing. He'd found an angle of bracket and barrel that fit his back. This had become his corner of the quarterdeck. No one approached but to speak him, and he noted with amusement that they avoided it even when he was forward. It had become taboo, like the Polynesian groves he recalled from an obscure writer named Melville, who'd apparently spent some time at sea in his youth.

He remembered a scene. The marooned sailor had watched a native woman unselfconsciously loosing her dress and holding it to the wind as a sail. She'd stood naked and erect in the bow of the canoe, a graceful mast nude and unashamed as Eve. Yes, that could seize in a man's memory. . . . Like a kiss in a darkened stairwell, and a choice he even now wasn't sure had been the right one.

He sat there till the constellations glowed overhead, a wilderness of darkness and light through which the masts circled, ever moving, yet never moving, fixed as the pole of the universe amid the revolving of the eternal stars.

At a little past ten bells, another bright day of steely cold and a scattering of cloud, the lookout reported smoke to southward.

Ker ordered general quarters and the Yankee flag broken. *Maryland* was quickly put in order, boats rigged out, and all other preparations made for hailing and boarding. Meanwhile Osowinski, who had the deck, altered course two points off the smoke, to gradually close while gaining the weather-gage in a wind that had stayed northeast, but dropped considerably during the night.

Ker stood chewing on an unlit Cubano, looking first overboard and then at the faintly outlined cloud ahead. The sea through which they slipped was a translucent green, the color of the frosted sea glass he'd searched the beaches of Chincoteague for as a boy. Pale sprigs of sargasso weed tossed on two-foot waves. The Stream was still warm, though the air was chilling winter. The great river in the sea bore all its creatures onward, mother and executioner, cradling them in its warmth, to ultimate death. After some time he swung to the ratlings and pulled himself aloft, first to the maintop, then farther, the shrouds narrowing as they apexed, into the slanting eyrie of the t'gallants.

Here the sea was far, the horizon close, the sky most intimate of all, surrounding him with light and wind. As close, the saying went, as sailors ever got to Heaven. The air was fresher than down on deck, and he put his face close to a shroud and inhaled the pungent smokiness of hemp, the pine-reek of tar. The slow creak and thud of stay and chain-tie about him spoke of somnolent calm. He remained there, as the distant stain gradually became more solid, until he made out a white pinpoint beneath it: the royals or t'gallants of a craft under both sail and steam.

The beard-truncated oval of the Pole's face below. Ker dangled his cap, to signal slacking the sheets; pointed out a course change, putting them head and head to the oncoming steamer. He mimed extending a glass, and a little later the ratlings swayed as the Prioleau boy swarmed it up to him.

The lenses jumped her close across miles of sea. She was bow on; he could make out very little of her hull. Not overmuch canvas aloft; perhaps t'gallants and tops. Nonetheless all her jibs were set. No view of her stack, but the blackish jetting of coal-smoke rolled off across the heaving sea. No paddlehouses. He'd thought the Panama steamers were all paddle wheelers. *Central America* had foundered in a storm four years before, the paddles being one cause of her loss; she'd gone down with the Pacific mails, twenty tons of gold, and four hundred and fifty lives, a disaster headlined throughout the land. A granite obelisk had been erected at Annapolis in memory of the heroic Captain Herndon.

He clapped the glass closed, thrust it into his coat, and descended. Standing on the bulwark, he looked searchingly along the deck. The men looked silently back from the gun-carriages.

Kaiser touched his head, coming up. —Sir, about der midday meal.

—We shall be coming up with the gold-steamer shortly, Boats. The men must stand fast.

On the quarterdeck Osowinski and Dulcett acknowledged his return with a lifting of caps. MacDonnell leaned against the pinrail, arms folded, boots crossed at the ankles. There was nothing to be done at the moment. All the topmen had to do was cast off gaskets and they'd be set for the chase.

Their quarry was visible from the deck now. Three glasses tracked it, and Ker pulled himself back from that scrutiny and turned deliberately to scan the rest of the horizon. Yet the whole blue circle lay empty.

Once the gold was aboard, he'd have to decide what to do with the steamer. Under no circumstances could *Maryland* accommodate four to five hundred passengers. Therefore, despite the letter of his instructions, he had no intention of burning his prize. He was leaning toward taking her to Liverpool with him. Perhaps Bulloch could work out some way of arming her. Especially if by then Britain and the United States were at war. He entertained for a few minutes the prospect of not one but a squadron of raiders, of closing down Yankee sea-trade altogether. And surely a man who'd added three million dollars to the coffers of the cause might hope for preferment. Commodore Claiborne . . . he recalled his wandering mind, disturbed at his imaginings. Perhaps he was not as free of the fiend Ambition as he'd conceived.

The steamer was perhaps two miles away now, bow on to them as they were head on to her. Her jibs prevented a clear view of her, but she seemed to be coming on rather more rapidly than he'd judged from aloft. White glimmered at her stem. In minutes they'd be beam to beam, and the raider's identity revealed. Thanks to the newspapers, the telegraph, and the mails, the trim clipper with the figurehead of a great golden eagle must be known now throughout the seagoing world. First, a shot across her quarry's path, with more to follow should her captain try to show his heels. His glance crossed MacDonnell's blue steady gaze. A hand moved over and over the black pirate's beard.

—Sir, Mr. Kinkaid reports steam pressure at twenty pounds.

—Very well, Mr. Dulcett, two bells ahead, if you please. Mr. Osowinski! Prepare to wear about. Quartermaster! Stand by with the battle flag. Mr. MacDonnell! On the forward pivot, prime; on all guns, cast loose and provide. He held out his hand and the deck-boy seated the brass hollowness of the speaking-trumpet in his palm.

A thousand yards now, and the steamer forged toward them still. The closing rate was terrific. The beat of the screw now added to the press of *Maryland*'s canvas. Ker picked out the point where he'd wheel into his prey's wake, positioning MacDonnell to rake from astern. In this light breeze the steamer might outrun him, but she could not outrun a shell.

At eight hundred yards, both ships still onrushing, sprit to stem, a huge jet of black smoke ballooned into the stainless air above the other's sails. Ker frowned, then nodded to Dulcett. —Port your helm, a point to starboard.

The wheel groaned. Slowly, deliberately, *Maryland* paid off to leeward.

Her sprit, aimed like a couched lance at the oncoming steamer, slowly swung off, then steadied again. Ker judged the two would pass port to port and seventy to eighty yards apart. His eye returned to the oncoming stranger. Ran past the jibs, to the sheer-line just now being revealed behind the shielding canvas. Strange; the Panama packets sported a red line running their length; this hull had none. It was totally black, studded with bosslike protuberances. . . .

His eyes widened. —Hard aport your rudder! he screamed, as it all fused together in his astonished brain, as he cursed himself for a simpleton, a credulous, green, lubberly fool.

Why the other, a steamer forging into the teeth of the prevailing wind, yet carried her useless jibs.

Why she'd come about to point directly at the approaching cruiser.

Why the men on her forecastle were even now pulling canvas aside, and the hull, now coming into view as *Maryland*'s turn began to carry her around, was studded with the crowned muzzles of run-out Dahlgrens. While a swollen pod aloft suddenly rippled out into blue and white and scarlet, unfolding into the gauzy flaunting of an immense Union battle-flag.

—It's *Potomac,* MacDonnell said beside his ear. The great chest rose and fell, the black beard bristled toward the oncoming enemy. —The same daggy buggers as come after us in Havana, as cruised for us off Brazil. We been sold, Captain. Only question is, by who?

Ker didn't answer, clinging to the rail as moment by moment the long brawny hull was uncovered by the turn. It was indeed *Potomac.* Instead of the gold-ship at the fated rendezvous, a powerfully gunned, heavily engined Union screw-sloop. They'd been betrayed, and baited, and trapped, and sold, as surely as a hayseed guessing which walnut shell concealed the pea. Dizzying suppositions spun through his mind, but he thrust them away like gaudy vain pinwheels. How it had happened mattered not a whit. Not face-to-face with a nightmare. All that mattered were the orders he'd utter next. Orders that would either save them, or consign them to ruin and defeat and death.

—It'll be close, sir, but we can break once we're past. Break to the east, and run for all we're worth.

—I fear that will be futile, Mr. Dulcett. Under full steam as she is, this warship will outrun us at any point of sail.

MacDonnell growled, —We've a bloody engine too. Shall I ring up full ahead?

Ker did not answer. His mind was too busy. The auxiliary might add a few knots, but he could not outrun a battle-steamer.

Then too he was becoming conscious of a curious indisposition to flee. For months now he'd run at the sight of that flag. Only once, on the shores of a mighty river, had he stood against it, and helped fling back its claim to dictate to him and those he loved. How queer, that human affections could change so! Once that flag had meant home, country, freedom, honor. Now he gazed across the fleeting water at it and those who served it, ranged behind the rows of waiting guns, with loathing and with hatred.

—What flag shall we break, sir? I have the British and French ready as well as ours.

He was only half-listening. He was studying the enemy. Gauging the narrowing variables of wind, and distance, the distribution of metal about the other's deck and his own.

He spoke without realizing he was doing so. —Break our own banner, Quartermaster, if you please. Mr. MacDonnell, I should be glad if you would run out the guns.

28

I
N those first minutes he had much to think on. Of the foremost were
not only how to maneuver at the opening of what promised to be an
action of the greatest peril, but whether to give battle at all. Bain-
bridge had surrendered *Philadelphia* to the Tripolitanians. James Barron
had yielded *Chesapeake* to *Leopard* without firing a shot. The Navy had always recognized the right of a commander to hand over his sword if he
was at such a disadvantage no hope of victory existed. The laws of war did
not require him to sacrifice the lives of his crew. On the contrary, humanity dictated that he save them, and himself, if the contest could have but
one result.

In those frozen seconds, though, staring across at his newly revealed
enemy, he did not think such a condition existed. He *was* outgunned,
true. *Potomac* carried four thirty-two-pounders and twelve nine-inch
smooth-bored Dahlgrens. His own rifled Whitworths fired a slightly
heavier shell than the nine-inchers, and would be accurate at a longer
range. But as to aggregate weight of metal, his battery was inferior. The

Union cruiser was also far more heavily built and sparred than the converted clipper beneath his feet.

On the other hand, he had confidence in his crew and officers, *Maryland* was more maneuverable at close range, and the wind, though light, seemed to be on the increase. A cloudbank to the north promised more; if he could win time, he might venture a race with some possibility of success.

The heart-stopping thump of a heavy gun, and a spray of water burst up thirty yards off the bow. The ball caromed away, bounding and jumping like a porpoise, then sinking at last.

Along the deck men were looking to him. They shifted uneasily, nervous at the lack of orders.

Then his fingers moved, of their own will, separate from his half-dreaming mind. They moved to his vest, took out his watch, and thumbnailed the cover open.

It was the same thing he did before every gun drill. The very familiarity of the gesture restored him, returned him to command of a warship ready for battle. He nodded curtly to MacDonnell. —Run out and prime the starboard division, First.

He saw the doubt in the exec's eyes, the question all but spoken aloud: Starboard, sir, do you not mean port? But discipline won and he wheeled and shouted down the deck. While Ker grabbed a handhold, and pulled himself up onto the horse block.

Across the rushing sea another form had mounted to sight as well. Its bellow came distant-sounding across the waves. —United States Ship *Potomac.*

—Confederate States cruiser *Maryland,* sir.

—It has been a long chase. Will you strike, sir?

Ker turned his head. To Dulcett he said quietly, —Hard aport your helm. Then shouted across the water, —I will not strike, sir. Will *you* strike, sir?

A moment's pause, then, —You are outgunned and outengined. You cannot escape. Your last chance, Captain Claiborne.

For answer he lifted his hat, and jumped down. The last exchange had been barely audible as the two craft drew apart, *Maryland* heading south, the other north.

But by now the clipper's port helm was carrying her round to starboard. Ker waited tensely as her stern swung past the Federal. An accurate broadside just now might settle the matter at once. But the lightning did not strike, and looking back he saw that his adversary too had put her helm over, and was coming round into the wind some two or three hundred yards off. In less than a minute they would be running parallel to each other.

—Four bells, Mr. MacDonnell. Inform Mr. Kinkaid that we are standing into action. I must have as much power as he can give me, and instant response to my orders, both as to the engines and as to the sails. As for your gunners, remind them once more to fire low.

A single mighty roar, so close together as to be indistinguishable as individual detonations, announced the end of irresolution on the Federal's part. The salvo struck as Ker steadied his helm three points off the wind. Black smoke gushed from *Maryland*'s stack, and the deck began to tremble as the auxiliary pistoned up to full speed.

A howling hurricane seemed to sweep over them, an unholy hail-clatter from aloft, and suddenly the sails were peppered with a pox of small oblong rips. Ker blinked, hardly daring to believe his luck. The Yankee's guns had been loaded with grapeshot. If he hadn't sheered away, they'd have taken that awesome charge at close range. Not one man on deck would have survived. But now the other was wheeling to port; Ker held his own course and told MacDonnell to fire when his guns would bear. The thirty-twos ranked along the starboard side bucked back one after the other in claps of thunder and clouds of sulphurous white, followed by the Whitworths cracking out their high-velocity shot with ear-whacking violence.

—All sail, Mr. Osowinski, he shouted.

—Aloft, sail-loosers, echoed down the decks. The topmen broke from beneath the bulwarks, and the bright sky gradually became overshaded with layer upon layer of filling canvas. *Maryland* forged ahead swiftly under the double impetus of sail and screw, and along her curving sweep of open deck men bent and jerked and whirled in a feverish tarantella. Serve, sponge, load, ram, shell, run out, and prime. Followed with a snatch of the lanyard and a bellowing discharge. Tongues of lambent fire lay like horizontal pillars within clouds of smoke. Like the maw of an iron mill, where billets of white-hot metal rolled out amid flame and fume and on-going sound so great it squeezed the lungs and boxed the ears like an enraged father.

Ker dashed smoke-tears from his sight. The wind was blowing it back in their faces. The Yankee's, to windward, was drifting down on them as well. He shaded his gaze to make out through the cream-yellow murk the black length of his adversary. To her *Maryland* must be only a bank of smoke, from which perhaps her trucks emerged. *Potomac* was firing by the numbers, by command, and for as long as a minute and a half was only an inert shadow; until suddenly from stem to stern she lit in one rippling flash, like a line of mirrors reflecting the sun.

A procession of impacts marched down the starboard side, a cracking succession of blows followed by muffled but powerful detonations beneath their feet, as if deep beneath the sea. Ker felt his confidence spin away. At least four solid hits. The damage below would be terrible. But his own steady drumfire must be having some effect too. The Whitworths particularly seemed to be giving a good account of themselves. Once he glimpsed the shell in flight, a red-hot glowing arc that went so low he feared it would end short, but which bounded up from the surface in a burst of spray and slammed fairly into the enemy's stern. He saw no outward effect, neither explosion nor damage, but the iron darts were fuzed to explode, deep in a vessel's oaken heart.

A renewed salvo collided like runaway railcars, not with the hull but with the rigging aloft. The gunners opposite had lifted their aim. The heavy whistle of great smooth bolts of metal rushing through the atmosphere. They burst in the air with jagged cracks and cotton-bolls of white smoke. The sea boiled in foamy cascades as hot iron churned the surface. But others found their mark. With a tremendous cracking and splitting, like a glacier breaking up, shattered spar-ends and top-blocks, dead-eyes, line, and bodies began coming down. An impact beside him made him start back; a heavy length of leather-covered curb-chain, the parrel for the topsail-yard, rebounded from the decking. A yard to windward and it would have struck him down. At the same moment a bloody mass heaved itself up out of the companionway hatch. A second look told him it was Steele, scalp hanging loose across a bloodied visage.

—Doctor? Are you all right?

—It is a slaughterhouse below. A slaughterhouse!

—Go back down; he's shifting his attentions aloft. You're safer in the surgeon's cockpit.

He turned away, could spare no more time, could take thought neither for his men nor for the steady wrecking of all he had labored to build aboard *Maryland*.

He must reach across to divine the mind of the captain opposite. The commander who was even now studying him, seeking the same advantage.

The two war-craft were running parallel now, a rifle-shot apart, the Yankee to windward and bleeding gouts of smoke from his shot-pierced funnel. His jibs were furling back like slowly closing flowers, although only now were they drawing. He valued sight above sail area, and why should he not with his deep boilers and powerful engines. Ker found the other's intent perfectly clear: to steam alongside and hammer his opponent into submission by sheer weight of metal. To stand like bare-knuckle fighters face-to-face and slug away until one or the other fell.

Ker saw no reason to accept this interpretation of the battle. In all her scantlings and fittings, *Maryland* was less substantial. She could not stand toe-to-toe with an opponent of this caliber. Nor could she outsteam her.

But he'd wager his soul, and the bodies of his men, that she could out-dance her.

A note in his hand. Kinkaid. *Shell burst in starboard coal-bunker. Unexploded shell in galley. Leaks forward. Pumps holding water. Standing by for all bells.*

—Hands to the port braces, Mr. Osowinski, smartly.

The command ran down the deck, and forms rose like ghosts, and with a groaning protest aloft the yards braced round off the wind. Ker nodded to Dulcett. —Full astern, if you please.

—Full astern, sir?

—I shall not repeat myself again, sir.

—Aye aye, sir. Full astern, sir. The clang of the bell sounded sharp in the murky air, immediately obliterated by the slamming arrival of another salvo of nine-inch projectiles. This time one burst flashing just as it passed over, an incredible feat of fuze-estimation or luck that sprayed a cruel hail of fragments through the waist.

Horror and screaming, the butcher-shop red of freshly mangled meat and gushing of bright blood. Men reeling from the guns. The grim faces of the gun-captains, the lash of colts whipping them back. A pirouetting puppet clawing at where its eyes had been scooped away. Ker saw again, as if in nightmare, a faceless figure striding toward him. It was the dying Yankee at Smith Point. The hooded figure from his fevered dreams. He wanted to cover his own eyes with his palms. He wanted to mole down through the gritty pine beneath his boots. Instead he must stand upright though his legs were quivering. Neither flesh nor wood could take much more of this.

But now through the thick air he glimpsed the Yankee drawing ahead, edging from off *Maryland*'s beam toward her cathead, and before she could respond to her target's sudden loss of speed he rapped out, —Coming about! Helm alee, Mr. Dulcett, and give our engineers full ahead once more. Mr. Osowinski! On the main . . . the fore . . . the mizzen . . . ready about! Mr. MacDonnell! All hands to the port battery, with double charges, run out and prime. Fuzes for five seconds, quoins in to the utmost, fire on my command.

Dulcett and MacDonnell answered, hoarse with the shouting they'd already done. But the Pole did not, and glancing about Ker found him sagging by the mainmast pinrail, fists clamped to his skull. A length of shattered spar lay at his feet. Ker wheeled, pointing to the captain of the mizzen. —On the mizzen: boom amidships.

—Port your helm, Dulcett was shouting at the helmsmen, one of whom was down, coughing blood into his fist. The other stared at the compass with wild eyes, as if to look away would be to break some spell that kept him invisible to iron and lead.

—Another hand to the helm, Quartermaster Epping. Bo's'n! Kaiser! On the main: raise tacks and sheets. On the mainsail: mains'l haul! Rise staysails!

A juddering blast from the white murk, flashes, shouting. The thuds rolled away over the sea, echoless, heavy, ineluctably final, like the impact of a gigantic gavel announcing judgment. Bursts of iron-hearted foam along either side, miraculously none finding the arrowed needle of *Maryland* herself. Which was swinging rapidly past her assailant, invisible in the cloud of unseeing, the milling of powder-smoke and coal-smoke twisting like pigtails of gray and cream through the shattered air. Falling off now on a port tack. Gathering speed as her canvas, braced round, caught the breeze anew, and she leapt ahead, still swinging right to cross under her enemy's now-receding counter.

Ker could see nothing now in the smoke, though he'd expected this tack to clear their vision. He steadied the rudder at due north and watched the sea's surface on the port side instead. The wooden trucks of the thirty-twos grated on sand and blood as they ran out, and the cries of the gun-captains sounded: muzzle right; muzzle left; quoin in, you bastard, listen t' what I tell you or I'll let light through your skin.

—Steady as you go. On the fore: foresail, haul. Shift staysails!

Now that the guns were silent, an eerie screeching rose clearly from the deck, from the companionways and hatches leading below. From where he hesitated Ker heard what he thought at first to be an echo. The same sound repeated from out of the murk. No, not from their own decks alone, but from that of the Yankee. He hardened his heart against the possibility of pity. He had no way of telling how much human horror, how much damage to the material fabric of her antagonist *Maryland*'s guns had wreaked. But some measure of her indebtedness was being repaid.

A line chalked on the sea came into view beneath the roiling smoke. Ahead, off the port bow. He held his course, held his fire, as the men threw their weight against the Whitworths and they too wheeled slowly round to point into the murk. As the gun-captains stepped up to prime, then back, sighting into the inchoate fog. Then looked to him, for command . . . he drew his sword and presented, then pointed it into the tops. Held their attention with the gesture, himself looking not at them or at anything else but the narrow patch of sea in view to port.

A smoothed path perhaps twenty yards wide came into view forward of the main chains. It was littered with bits of wood, bobbing like nautiluses. Slow gyres circled foam on its deep green surface. It was the Federal's screw-wake. Ker waited till it bisected the gun deck, till half his guns were forward of it and half behind. Till his guns were pointing directly at the smoke-shrouded stern of his enemy. Then lifted his blade even higher, and slashed it down.

Six heavy charges went off in a simultaneous crash of sound, a blast of shock that reeled the clipper to starboard. The murk recoiled, then swept back, redoubled, choking and blinding as the stinkpots Steele burned to root out Yellow Jack. The crash of iron splitting wood and striking metal, ripping into bulkheads and flesh, came back clearly as if he were watching it. He stared fascinated as the smallest hand on his watch jerked forward, again, again. At which time several muffled explosions were followed instantly by a thunderous boom that struck the soles of his feet first and then, an instant later, rattled every block and timber aboard. As it bled away, leaving his ears ringing, thin screams succeeded, like the cries of sirens from the murk.

Unfortunately they gave him no clue as to which way the Yankee had turned. That, of course, would decide which player came out of this hand with the advantage of position. To port, and they'd be circling away from each other; to starboard, and they'd once more be sailing parallel, but on the opposite tack as before.

He decided to assume his opponent a man of as much determination, or stubbornness, as himself. He stepped to the helm and laid his hand on the shoulder of the man frozen there. Loudly enough for Dulcett to hear, he said, —You are bearing up well, lad. Now I want you to keep your helm over and bring us on to the right. Steady on a northwest heading if I do not give you another order, but be ready to continue on around.

—You intend to wear, sir? Dulcett asked.

Sam Prioleau came by carrying tin pannikins of liquid. Ker suddenly became aware of how dry and powder-seared his throat was. He grabbed one with both hands and thrust it to his face, then remembered they looked to him for their model in battle; he took a more decorous grip, but still gained four long swallows of what tasted like raw cane spirit and water before lowering it. The boy ran forward, leaving, Ker saw, prints of his bare soles in a river of blood that eddied back and forth, only partially absorbed by the reddened sand. Handing the cup to Dulcett, he said, —That will depend on the Yankee's actions, when next we catch a glimpse. If he has turned to port, and perhaps evidences damage to his propelling machinery, I may try to retire on the starboard tack. If he turns to starboard, we shall have to sustain another exchange.

—That explosion. Could it have been his magazine?

—No, Gustavius. We should all be deafened and the sails blown out.

A boiler, perhaps, or ammunition in ready service. There, the smoke is thinning; in a moment we shall see.

The lieutenant glanced round; his glance lingered at the stern, where two loblolly boys were dragging a body. Ker noted with chilling absence of feeling that a pile was accumulating. Blood ran from it toward the freeing-ports. He understood now the British practice of painting the scuppers of warships scarlet. One man lay propped in a sitting position, eyes wide, seemingly directing a puzzled regard upon those who fought on. A jagged splinter of oak protruded from his forehead like a horn. Steele wanted only the wounded taken below, preferring to leave those past help topside. Ker thought this hard on those who remained, but had not contradicted the overburdened surgeon's preference. —Kaiser.

—Sir.

—I should be glad if you would cover the faces of the dead.

—Aye aye, sir. You, boy, grab dot sail and drag it over der todt men.

The smoke was definitely thinning, or they were sailing out of it. To port one could see again the open sea. *Maryland* was forging ahead at speed now, having come through the wind and fallen off on the starboard tack. Ker turned where he stood to find *Potomac* visible some half-mile away, also heeling in a starboard turn. The glass clacked open and as he focused it the last haze blew free, showing him the swelling black porpoise-backs of the Dahlgrens, silent for the moment, and a pall of black smoke rising aft, where the Confederate broadside had just raked her. She didn't seem much damaged aloft, but one of her gunports was empty. He looked closely and made out the bottom of a carriage, capsized and dismounted.

MacDonnell, blue eyes shining praeternaturally through the black mask of burnt powder, seized the proffered pannikin and drank deep. When he lowered it, it was empty. —We've heavy damage below.

—Mr. Kinkaid assures me it's in hand. We're still fighting, Bob-Stay. The guns?

—Getting short-handed, but we can still work 'em.

—Go ahead and water your men. We shall have a few minute's respite before our next course of play.

Gauging the speed of the Federal's turn, Ker told Dulcett to put his helm over once more, and keep it there. His mind moved forward, running out the moves as in a game of chess. *Potomac* had missed her chance to rake in the smoke. She could not play the same trick Ker had just played on her; the clipper could turn inside the larger, less maneuverable vessel. *Maryland* was still coming right. In a few minutes both craft would be vulnerable to the broadsides of the other, this time both turning, guns playing across the diameter of an immense gyring circle perhaps eight hundred yards across. He gave the requisite orders, then stood waiting. Looking aloft once to make sure the flag was still there. She waved against the bright sky, her colors still luminous despite a tint of powder-grime. He stared up at her for long seconds, fists clenched.

Another rippling flash along the enemy's decks. Shells glanced off the water, crashing into the clipper's sides or sailing over her deck, the heavy projectiles rushing over their heads with a sound like a watermill at full flood. At the same moment *Maryland*'s guns bit back, and the powder-smoke once more blotted out sight, at least for the seconds it took the wind to accept the rolling out of the banks of smoke, bring them to a halt, then move them off to leeward, thinning and rising above the green sea.

But one of the enemy's blows had found their mainmast. With a terrific crack aloft and a prolonged groaning and snapping of shrouds and stays it leaned slowly over and then collapsed, not cleanly, like a falling tree, but sagging over, half-supported in its descent by the tangle of rigging it dragged down with it.

Ker closed his eyes. He'd tried from the moment the cruiser had appeared from behind her screening jibs to visualize how this contest might end without *Maryland*'s destruction. Escape, if he could cripple or distract his opponent, had beckoned. The loss of his mainmast closed it off, firmly and irretrievably as a chain-boom.

Once more surrender tempted. He'd taken enough casualties, inflicted enough damage on a superior enemy that the most unforgiving board could not fault him for premature surrender. Yet the smoke rising from the Federal's decks, the reduction of her broadside by the dismounting meant hope still existed. *Maryland* had taken grievous damage. The growing heap beneath the canvas attested to that, as did her laboring heaviness as she turned, the tired acquiescence with which she leaned to the breeze. But a lucky shell in the other's boiler could still turn the tables. The clipper still had engine power. He could still coax a knot or perhaps two from the fore and mizzen.

They'd simply have to hammer as hard as they could, and let the god of battles decide.

Every minute and forty seconds, the Whitworths spoke. Every minute and thirty, the thirty-twos. At intervals the heavy Dahlgrens opposite angrily replied, their black bottle shapes recoiling. The two men-of-war traded shells arching across a narrowing disc of water around which they slowly spun. As they held their rudders hard over, each striving for the advantage, Ker saw it would grow tighter, closer, in a murderous simulacrum of the dance of courtship.

A shell crashed through the quarterdeck bulwark, hissing splinters out in a mist a yard above deck. One caught Ker in the thigh, and he regarded it stupidly for a moment. It looked like a handleless carving knife protruding from his meat, and he heard his own flesh sizzle as it seared. He yanked it free with a jerk that curiously brought with it no pain, only a pump of blood that ran warm down his trowsers. Another shell crashed into the bow. He could not complain of the other's gunnery. The impact of his own was more difficult to judge. The fire on the cruiser's stern seemed to be growing. Ker could see the nodding plumes of hose-sprays, stroking the flames. Fire was a ship's mortal enemy. Once established, it could be hard to root out. The conditions under which it had to be fought in battle, amid the wreckage left by exploding shell, made it doubly difficult.

A lanky form at his side. Kinkaid, in red woolen shirtsleeves and grease to his elbows, tallow and coal dust smearing his forehead. He stared at the shambles about them. A shell howled overhead and he ducked, then checked himself as the line officers chuckled. Ker said, —Mr. Engineer. What news from the infernal regions?

—The water's gaining on our pumps.

This was unsettling. The Pennsylvanian explained that the carpenter and his mates were doing their best to patch shell holes, but much of the damage was below the waterline. Not where the shells had hit, but where they'd exited. Those which had not exploded had penetrated through and through.

With a dull, fractured-sounding crump, one of the thirty-two-pounders burst. Men staggered back, gripping their faces. One reeled forward blindly, fell through the open gunport, and vanished over the side. MacDonnell was nowhere to be seen. Ker searched frantically through the gunpowder haze and at last found him leaning against the foremast. Blood sheened his face, but he was shouting orders. The wreck of tube and carriage was quickly hacked free with axes and shouldered overboard to topple and fall. The surviving crew turned immediately to a gun on the unengaged side, unreeving its gear and trundling it round with handspikes.

A veritable hailstorm rebounded from the sea to smash through the thin side-planking. The deck exploded upward, sending pine rocketing aloft and leaving a gaping, smoking hole, through which Ker could see the top of the boiler. A shriek of steam succeeded, and white clouds of it began billowing up.

—I'm going back down, Kinkaid said. —Must I continue at a full bell? I can't keep the water back without more steam to the pumps.

—We must maintain our speed for tactical reasons. I can't let him cross the stern and rake us. Bearing this fire athwartships is hard enough.

—Give the carpenter more men, then. Get those holes stopped up.

—I have not men enough for the guns. This is not the time to slacken fire.

The engineer said, —You'd better get ready to swim then, sir. He looked as if he were about to say more, but did not. He ran lightly forward, hesitated at the engine room hatch, looking anxiously across at *Potomac;* then ducked his head and disappeared.

Ker ran his mind over his situation again, but did not see what more he could do. At last he called down the foretopmen still aloft and sent them below to the carpenter.

Shells burst overhead, alongside, the concussions making his head ring as if he'd been punched. Dulcett falling heavily beside him. Ker bending, thinking he'd been hit, finding he'd only slipped on a patch of gore. A boy with another pannikin, a swift draught, this time of fiery straight liquor. One swallow, and he sent him forward to the gun crews.

The Yankee was still smoking heavily. The deadly arena was still narrowing as the opponents circled, gradually slowing, both with helms hard over. Less than three hundred yards separated them now. The sails were forgotten, the two ships locked so tightly, spiraling so rapidly the distinction of weather or lee made no difference other than to visibility.

Ker consulted his watch to find his gun crews were getting off a shot every two minutes. Fatigue was taking its toll. Yet he could neither break away nor let up. Reversing his helm to escape the deadly circle would expose his stern to a dead-on raking. Neither could his opponent flee or falter, though now flames had burst into view, climbing mizzen and spanker in a sheet of laddering flame.

Maryland's deck tilted. She was slowly settling by the head. At the same time he sensed he was losing power. The screw-beat from below was gradually slowing, like some failing heart. The green sea, littered with foam and scraps of wood, went by more and more slowly. The helmsmen cursed, struggling with the wheel.

A folded note. *Losing steam. Lines cut by shell. Water nearing the grates. Request all hands to man pumps. Will keep steam pumps running as long as possible. Kinkaid.*

Ker secured the crew of the twelve-pounders, as contributing the least in weight of metal, and sent them to the hand pumps. The others he kept at their firing, although the intervals between shots were stretching out. The Yankee too had slowed her discharges. Her smoke swept down on *Maryland*. The smell and crackle of seasoned oak ablaze smelled cheerful as a cooking fire on a winter's day. Yet her flag still waved. Ker heard a ragged cheer from her deck, but could make out nothing to celebrate. For some minutes the two lay so, and from time to time guns still boomed out and shell cracked.

A high, rapid clatter. Ker lifted his head. The rattling of alarm-clackers. Calling the other crew to stations. But for what?

The Federal cruiser slowly pivoted. A fresh new jib rippled aloft, replacing the ragged, shot-torn one that had come down some time before. Ker looked aloft, but his top-hamper was a useless wreck. *Potomac* had the weather-gage. Apparently her captain was going to use it. Ker frowned. But to what end? What was the man doing? His sprit was still creeping round. His after guns fell silent as they were masked.

Then Ker saw the crowd gathering on her deck, the glitter of axes and bayonets, and his heart fell. The cup would not pass. He bawled out, trying to keep his voice from breaking in despair, —Prepare to repel boarders, at the waist, to port. Then reached for the stub he kept in his trowser pocket and scribbled, *Enemy preparing to board. Must have power astern on my bell.* —Run this to Mr. Kinkaid at once, he said, handing it to Prioleau. —Then fetch my sword-belt and pistols from Romulus, if you please.

Kaiser, covered in blood, harried the men from the guns. They came stumbling and weaving across the deck with slack jaws, hands still jerking, as if they could not stop the reflex motions of loading. Ker blinked disbelievingly at his timepiece. They'd been in battle for forty-five minutes. It felt more like seven hours. He'd long lost track of salvos, nor did MacDonnell know how many they'd fired. They'd exhausted the shot-lockers topside and had to slow not, as he'd thought, from exhaustion, though exhausted they were, but by the time required for the monkey-boys to run charge-bags and shell through wrecked passageways and up the fouled scuttles.

Their hands were bloody raw and their eyes holes burned through blackface makeup, but when the crew jerked waist-belts and pistol-frogs, primer-boxes and broadswords and pikes from the racks they fell into the same ranks they'd practiced time after time. How dreadfully thinner, though, those ranks were now. He counted just fifty left on deck. The rest were wounded, blown overboard, or piled whole or in parts beneath the canvas on *Maryland*'s rounded stern.

On the order "prepare to repel boarders" the swordsmen stepped up close to the bulkhead. The pikemen took position behind them, a few steps back, and swung up the sharpened steel heads of their weapons to rest on the hammock-rail. It had been badly cut about by grape and fragment. Many a man, Ker thought fleetingly, would be growling about the cost of a new length of canvas to swing his weary body. Or perhaps those lucky enough to survive would not complain. . . . On Kaiser's command they crouched below the bulwarks to await the Federal's lurching drift downwind. Quartermaster Epping fell back beside the wheel, ramming ball into his pistol as he watched the oncoming prow. His leather-frogged sword scraped its point on the deck. Four men staggered up from below with carbines, faces blackened like the chimney of a badly trimmed lamp, and ranged themselves between Ker and the waist.

Young Prioleau, with Romulus a step behind. The servant stumbled over a body the loblolly boys had not yet seen to, looking about with wild eyes. He carried a varnished wooden box in both hands. The white boy had Ker's English revolver in one hand and his regulation saber in the other. Ker belted it on and unlatched the pistol-box the servant held out. The polished octagonal barrels of the dueling set gleamed up. He loaded them with shaking hands and thrust them into his sword-belt.

Now ensued some minutes of waiting, dread and long. He occupied it in checking the caps on the Tranter, making sure none had come adrift of their nipples, and that tallow covered the mouths of the chambers. Unless it did, the first shot would flash fire from round to round, with disastrous consequences on both ends of the weapon. A look behind confirmed that the twelve-pounder crew had remanned. The gun-captain nodded at his questioning glance; held up spread fingers, the sign for canister. A gunner stood at each of the remaining thirty-twos as well, lanyard drooping in his hand.

Ker popped his head up to judge the remaining distance, and a whack-ing of rifles instantly began. The balls chopped like axes where his skull had been. But by then he'd ducked back into the shelter of the bulwark. The Federal was almost on them. He grabbed Dulcett's shoulder, shook him back from his gape-mouthed stare at the oncoming ship. —Now, Mr. Dulcett. Four bells astern! Mr. MacDonnell, on contact, sweep her decks with grape.

Beneath their feet the screw pounded again, yet with the fading, reluc-tant pulse of a dying heart. She wallowed backward in the water. Just suf-ficiently that when the final collision came, the final impact, *Potomac's* bowsprit lanced not through her waist but over her forecastle. It came in slow and remorseless, thrusting through the tangle of fallen gear, lifting and scraping along the bulwark. Then came to rest with a grinding shock that rocked the clipper to port. The canted deck pointed her loaded and shotted guns upward. So that when Ker shouted "fire" they exploded into the faces of the men who suddenly appeared atop *Maryland's* bulwarks, cutlasses and pistols raised, mouths twisted in shouting. When the smoke swept away they'd vanished as if by sorcery. But an insane screaming came from beyond, and a moment later a second wave appeared, a leaping, yelling surge of blue uniforms and beefy bodies that paused only to dis-charge pistols or carbines before leaping down into the bow. Some im-paled themselves on the pikes; others toppled, reaped by the steel arcs of broadswords. Others found their paths cleared by pistol-balls, and commenced to hew down the defenders.

Ker stood judging the flow of the battle. His concentration was interrupted by the sudden detonation of a heavy gun not twenty feet from his ear. The entire bulwark behind him disintegrated into a hail of splinter, swept away by the blast of a Yankee Dahlgren firing directly through it.

Potomac's sides were loftier than the Confederate cruiser's, and Ker looked across sudden vacancy at sweating, blackened, grimacing faces as they bent to swab and load. An officer sighted a pistol-barrel across his forearm at him. Ker drew a dueler and swept it upward, snapping off his shot, and had the immense satisfaction of seeing the other drop his weapon and stagger back. Carbines barked behind him, the gun-captain went down too, and suddenly the entire gun crew broke and deserted their piece, running for cover.

Tucking the empty pistol into the back of his sword-belt, he saw that the thin line of *Maryland*'s defenders was crumbling, faced with half again their number, and more leaping down by the moment. Square in the center of their line a huge red-faced Yankee marine in white crossed belts and handlebar mustache was laying about him with a broadsword. Drawing the second dueler, holding it out level, Ker advanced, sensing rather than seeing Dulcett, Epping, Prioleau, the helmsmen, and the carbine-party moving with him, bayonets fixed.

Fortunately their enemies had exhausted their small arms, and had not had time to reload. He halted by the stump of the mainmast, shot the marine, tucked the second dueler into the small of his back, and drew the revolver. One did not need to cock it, simply to pull the trigger, and he aimed and fired until it was empty.

Ker unsheathed his sword and advanced once more, over a barricade-tangle of blocks and cordage and writhing, begging bodies. He reached the Federal line, parried an enthusiastic but clumsy lunge, and ran the man through the stomach. From the corner of his eye he saw Dulcett go down beneath a pike-thrust, then rise again, swinging upward savagely with his saber. A sallow foreigner began a *moulinet*-and-cut with his burning eyes fixed on Ker. Ker did not hurry to forestall him. One never hastened hand-to-hand on a littered deck, the footing could too easily betray you. He waited for the cut, ducked it, and ran him through as well.

Maryland's carbinemen charged with a yell and the Federal line broke. The flanks melted and the boarders fled in a confused mass back toward the forecastle. There they found themselves trapped. It was easy to jump down from a bulwark, quite otherwise to climb it with bayonets at your back. As the *Maryland*ers closed in those left standing threw their weapons clattering to the deck.

Ker wiped his sword on a fallen sail and looked beyond the Federal's sprit, which groaned as it worked up and down like a saw on *Maryland*'s bow. Great masses of black smoke streamed up beyond it. After the exhilaration of that advance he felt as if no bullet could touch him, as if he could outfight any man with a blade. Certainly the poorly trained, stumbling oafs who'd just thrown their weapons down had made no very good impression. Boarding fodder, nothing more, untrained beyond the most basic cuts.

His thoughts seemed disordered even to himself, but *Maryland*'s slow roll and lurch beneath the down-pressing weight of her opponent penetrated to his understanding. He'd recalled the men on the pumps to repel the assault. His ship was hull-holed, shattered belowdecks. She was dying beneath him even as he stood panting. Feeling now the first penetration of pain in his pierced and cauterized thigh.

He had to choose. Either strike his colors, or gain the victory in the only way left to him.

—Boarders, he shouted, and his throat felt flayed to the bone. He breathed smoke and hot air, a tarry reek of burning. Across the Federal's luffing jib a lurid light flickered. —All hands on deck, all up from below! Form on the port gangway. Prepare to board from the starboard waist. Look to your weapons, charge your weapons, reload.

Kaiser's thick Dutch accent, bawling orders into the companionway, the engine room hatch. Hands tore up the gratings, as they'd done so many times in drill, and rushed them to the bulwarks, propping them as ready-made ramps. Shouting came from the far side, and a mist of spray wet his cheek. He looked toward the top of the ramp, at the sky and smoke beyond. Feeling, just at that moment, the most powerful sense he'd done this all before.

He remembered one sweating night off the coast of Guinea, the long chase of the raked black sloop. How the slaver had twisted and turned, till she could flee no more; then how he'd followed Parker Trezevant onto her deck with sword in hand. But not even the taking of *Arachne* had been a carnage such as this. The slavers had resisted, but their numbers were few, and the fever had sapped them. Beyond this wooden wall were healthy, beef-fed men, shotted guns, officers as skilled as he in the arts of white steel. Yet possessed by the elation of battle, he could not even conceive of accepting defeat.

He glanced upward, and caught through the smoke and sparks the blue and white and broad red stripes of the Southern banner still streaming out in the breeze. Riddled by shot and splinters, but still flying free.

Flying free! For that flag, now, he found himself perfectly willing to die. His life, his family, even wife and son, weighed against it no heavier than the fragments of a half-remembered dream.

He looked along the ragged line that had mustered with him. At Mac-Donnell, at Dulcett, limping but erect, at Shepperd, carrying a blood-stained boarding-pike. Uffins, the Cockney mess steward, brandishing a boarding-axe. Kinkaid, a cocked carbine in oil-stained gloves. Osowinski, who'd come up with bandaged head from the surgeon's cockpit at the call. A strange smile played across that high-cheekboned visage; and with the graceful presentation of a saber, effortless and elegant as if in a fencing-display, the Pole brought the sword-tip first over his left shoulder and then his right. Ker ran his eye over a growling red-cheeked Kaiser brandishing a boarding-pike, Epping with a clumsy bowl-hilted cutlass that must date back to 1812, at three dozen others. Some were the gutter-sweepings of Scotland, Wales, England, Ireland, all Europe; yet they did not look out of place among the true Southerners, shoulder to shoulder and all in the foremost rank; soft-spoken boys from Georgia and the Carolinas, Florida and Virginia, Louisiana and Tennessee and Arkansas and Mississippi and Alabama and Texas, who'd stepped forward from *Maryland*'s captures. Patriots from throughout the Southland and the border states, a few even from the North. But all with the staunch hearts and the loathing recoil from tyranny of every rebel from the dawn of time.

—*Creagan an Fhithich!*

He turned, startled, to the man taking his place on the right of the line. —What is that you say?

—The ancient cry of war of the MacDonnells of Glengarry, sir. Shall I lead then, sir? The giant Australian, head-wound staunched with a bandeau of what looked like fearnought torn from the magazine curtains. With blood and powder-smoke covering his face, his great beard shining with gore, he looked the very incarnation of Teach or Kidd.

—We shall lead together, Bob-Stay. He looked back once more at the slanting, littered field, the guns rolling backward as the deck slanted beneath them; at the huddled prisoners at the bow, cowering under the frowning guard of an eleven-year-old and a sixty-eight-year-old.—Prioleau, pointing a bayoneted musket taller than he; old Jacobs, shaking a boarding-tomahawk . . . he wished he had a flag to carry into battle. Then remembered.

It flew even now above them, and always would. A flag made of stars and liberty, the stainless banner of men who would never kneel.

He lifted his sword, and shouted, —Assail the enemy, all hands, *follow me!* And from the throats around him burst a fierce high keening cry that wavered, and rose, mingling with the rising smoke and flame.

The top of the bulwark, gained without effort, and the length of the enemy's deck opened before him. In Havana every line had been flemished. Brass and bronze and copper had glowed with polish. Now it was strewn with fallen spars and tackle, spent primers, cartridge papers, and fully as much horror and blood as his own. The dolphin shapes of the Dahlgrens were pushed back at odd angles, loading tackle abandoned, the black peanut-sized grains of corned powder sown across the sanded deck. He hesitated, then jumped down. Expecting a hot reception, but the yipping, screaming *Maryland*ers were met by only a thin screen of seamen who looked as if they'd hung back when the boarding party went over; they rose belatedly from this corner and that, parried and thrusted halfheartedly, then fled.

It was what lay beyond that appalled him, faltering his steps before he pressed unwilling legs back into motion.

The stern of the Federal was a mass of white-hot flame, a towering wall of crackling, bellowing fire. The heat sent them stumbling to a face-shielding halt before they reached the mainmast. Hoses snaked between their feet, pulsing as human forms straightened and bent like children see-sawing against the innards of Hell. Curves of water leapt, descended, vanished without apparent effect. Stringed fire dripped from aloft, the tarred burning hemp of mainstays and shrouds. *Potomac*'s crew had their backs to them. Their attention was riveted on the fiery monster that champed its jaws on the whole after quarter of the burning ship.

Then soot-smeared faces swung in their direction, distorted in rage. Seamen bent to snag up hand-weapons, or turned from one threat to face this new one with the same axes with which they'd battled the first. Ker ran faster, adding the shock of speed to the shock of their appearance. Howling as he ran, his single individual voice lost in the immense bellow of the destroying element, then in the cries of a hundred men as they crashed, recoiled, then separated into isolated and desperate combats.

Suddenly silver flashed in the air. As graceful a draw and step and present as he'd seen on or off the fencing floor. Lips drawing into a snarl of disdain, a gleaming of flowing silver hair, incongruous and startling about so young a man.

From full run Ker was halted in two steps. No, he was falling back, confronted by the slow circling of a glittering point before his suddenly concentrated eyes. By the stamp of the right foot in a classic fencing appel. And suddenly he was back in the fencing loft at Annapolis, and somewhere the spirit of Monsieur Corbesier hovered over the scene as two of his students faced each other on the deck of a burning ship. Ker remembered the master's tone of Gallic irony as he'd failed to carry off a showy *flanconade. Zet parade is rarely employed, M'sieu Claiborne, because it is so rarely successful . . . as you have done us the favor of demonstrating once again.* Ker had lowered his own point as he charged. Now he brought it up slowly, cautiously, to return the Union lieutenant's sardonic salute.

—Mister Rebel. We meet once more.

—Your servant, Mr. . . . Henshaw?

—Very good, you recall our meeting in Havana. On the quarterdeck, it was. That time you stepped around me.

—I shall not do so this time, sir.

Perhaps the courtesy was rather spoiled by his panting, no doubt also by his disheveled, bloody appearance, but that did not matter. What did was the restless searching of that glittering point. Ker went *en garde*, then immediately lunged to *tierce*, the sharp of his blade held outward.

The silver-haired officer brushed his *faible* aside with his own blade with contemptuous ease, nearly twisting it from Ker's hand, then immediately lunged in his flank. Ker parried at the last possible instant, carrying the point only just clear of his left ear.

They disengaged and circled, Ker reflecting that this Henshaw's sword-work was not only very fine, but that great power was behind his blows. Without the greatest luck on his part that thrust would have gone not past his ear, but into his eye or throat. His opponent was taller, and had a greater reach; he was a very good swordsman indeed and moved with the fluidity of practice, while he himself had not picked up a sword for months.

The Yankee lunged again, from a high *garde*, very fast, and Ker parried *en octave*, outside, with his wrist bent and sword-tip low. The tempered steel made a clashing audible even through the pop of firearms and the cries around them. Indeed they seemed to be isolated in a curved confining crystal of smoke and sound, alone together in the struggling throng. Ker changed *quarte* for *tierce* and lunged back, was parried, then once more fought off an attack that very nearly cost him a blade through the chest. A slip of the foot and he would have been run through.

A terrible consciousness of being overmatched assaulted him. Sweat burst under his uniform. He fought weakness and the foreknowledge of defeat to leap recklessly forward in a clashing of hardened steel. *Quarte*, lunge. *Tierce*, lunge. Demicircle, lunge. *Octave*, lunge. The tall Yankee met each advance and thrust as if they'd practiced it, as if he knew before Ker what was in his mind and telegraphed to his sinews. A stark smile had taken his features. Neither had spoken after the initial exchange, but from time to time a glance of those cold eyes met his own. Ker shook his hair back and returned the look, though not the smile.

—Your death, sir, the Yankee shouted.

Ker disengaged and fell back. He did not dare take his eyes from Henshaw's point to glance behind him. At any moment he could stumble over a body, a fallen spar, a dropped weapon. Yet he had no choice but to retire.

The silver-haired swordsman came on, sensing his weakness, pressing his attack with slashing speed. He doubled, passing his point in a complete circle, and Ker made the error of following the blade too closely. The thrust that instantly followed, fast as the strike of a rattlesnake, came through his guard and pierced his stomach before he could react.

He knocked the point away but too late. He'd been hit, though he didn't feel the wound yet. A stomach wound meant death, slow and agonizing. But why didn't he feel anything?

—A touch, I believe, the lieutenant called contemptuously. Ker had no breath to answer with. Dreadfully afraid, yet still keeping his guard up, he brought his left hand in to grope at his belly; to feel with relief and renewed fear the indented, ragged scar in the thick leather of his sword-belt.

Breath sawed in his throat, sucking in hot choking smoke. They circled between the mainmast and mizzen. Men were falling back past them, but avoiding them, streaming around them, as if their intense concentration on each other protected them from the attention or even the sight of others.

Ker was still alive, but only by the merest margin of accident. He kept his attention locked on his opponent's weaving point. The smile, the remarks were meant to distract him, anger him. But he was no longer angry. The passion of battle that had carried him onto the enemy's deck was gone. His guard was flagging. Harder to keep the point aloft. Harder to meet each advance. The wound flamed in his thigh. He was losing blood.

But one touch of that shining point meant death.

He did not fear it, in his mind and heart. He had long ago submitted his life to One who had vanquished death. But ah, the flesh was a coward. It shrank from the circling blade. It did not wish to die, but to fling down his weapon and cry for mercy. Surely he'd fought enough!

Gritting his teeth, he forced it to stand its ground.

The Yankee grinned triumphantly, guard high, then suddenly *moulineted* left and cut with terrific force directly at his skull. Forewarned by the glittering, showy swing, Ker parried *tierce* and deflected it with the forte of his blade with a resounding clash of steel, but could not muster the strength to riposte. He sucked air again and fought to disengage, then returned to *quarte*.

His opponent suddenly unleashed a flurry of energy, cutting again and again at his cheeks and flanks, seemingly trying to batter down his defense. Ker met each, then suddenly disengaged over his opponent's point when it dipped, instead of under, as he had each time before. He went to a high outside parry, and lunged.

This caught the other off-balance, but he parried and countered *en sixte* as well, without hesitation, though without flair. And with less force as well. Ker saw his forehead shining with sweat. The heat and smoke were taking its toll on his enemy too.

And just as he'd dared hope, his going over the point made the other raise his guard even more. As a tall man it was already high. And staking all on one lunge to *quinte* he dropped his point to the horizontal and went with every ounce of speed and force he could muster cutting under the man's point, under his hand, to bury the tip of his sword deep in the junction of hip and trunk. The pop and then slide of resisting muscle and then softer tissue beneath vibrated back through the blade. He fended off a vicious downward hack at his left cheek with his left hand, taking a cut, but driving still forward, pushing the blade through till he felt it emerge on the far side of the other's body; then changing as he withdrew to twist the point in the wound.

He disengaged and retired, returning to *quarte,* and suddenly the other man was on his knees, hands clamped to his side, cursing him with vicious oaths. Ker almost sabered him down but stepped back at the last moment, wheezing for air, supporting himself on his grounded weapon as if with a cane.

He looked about him. To see a semicircle of his men, blood-smeared, panting, but clearly ready for more. So that he forced himself forward once more, toward the flames, and the men desperately fighting them.

In the smoke he came suddenly face-to-face with a doubled, coughing Charles Reynolds. The soft cheeks hung flabby now, sagging with shock. His old Academy classmate carried no arms.

—Charles.

—Ker.

—Where is your captain?

—I am he. I have been in command since Brazil.

—Will you strike your colors, sir?

Reynolds stared at him, then bent again to cough so deeply Ker feared he would not live through it. When he lifted his head again he gasped, —We are afire, sir. I can spare no one to fight you.

—Do you surrender, then? I have no wish to continue this slaughter.

—What, will you saber my men in the back as they fight the flames?

—I must and shall, unless you strike at once.

—All right, then. But I protest this inhumanity.

—*A la guerre comme à la guerre,* Charles. They taught us that at Annapolis.

—They taught us honor too. All right, you have won, but you must take us aboard. She cannot live much longer.

Ker turned to the men around him. —They have struck, they have surrendered. Epping, haul down their flag. The rest of you, join in fighting this fire.

—Our own ship, sir—

—*Maryland*'s going down, Mr. Dulcett. This is our home now. We have won her. Now we must keep her.

A cloud of flame above them, descending; a scatter from beneath, and with an enormous fiery whoosh the topsails came down in a gusting roar of heat and smoke and fire. Shapes moved beneath its coating of flame, screaming shrilly. Ker snatched at the burning canvas, searing his palms. Others were hauling from the far side and for a moment they engaged in a ghastly tug-of-war before the burning fabric parted, revealing shrieking men with their clothing afire. The clank, clank of the pump resumed. The hose-spray doused the victims, and they were lifted and dragged off toward the bow.

Looking that way, he saw a mast tilted far over. *Maryland*'s. She was rolling over even as he watched. Then he saw she wasn't capsizing, as he'd for a moment thought, but going down by the head, and very rapidly. She could not have many more minutes to live.

A hand on his arm; it was Reynolds. —We don't have much time. We've got to get all my wounded into your ship.

—I am afraid we too are in some embarrassment, Charles. My command is beyond help and sinking; yours is afire. But if we work together, I think we can save her.

—Unfortunately it has proceeded even more rapidly below. The flames are next to the magazine. I'm ordering my men to abandon.

—You have surrendered, sir, you can order nothing.

—Sort it out your own damn way, we're taking to the boats. Stay and get blown to hell if that's what you want.

Reynolds turned his back and made for the launch, which fully twenty of his men were struggling around, trying to get over the side. Ker looked after him, then aloft, as his own lads straggled back from the corners of the spar deck, from pumps and hoses. Dulcett was among them. Ker looked past him, did not see the bushy black beard he wanted. —Where is Mr. MacDonnell?

—The exec's dead, sir.

—Dead, sir, no; I saw him a moment ago. He must be about.

Dulcett took hold of his arm. He said dully, —I saw it happen. He received a musket-ball in the heart, as we came over the bulwarks.

Ker stood bereft, unwilling to believe. The giant Australian, fallen? Somehow it seemed unnatural, beyond the bounds of possibility.

But he could not stand questioning for long. Action was called for, and at once. The entire fabric above them was afire now, the wind having blown sparks from top to top. Burning lines were falling, blocks crashed into the deck. The very planks were heating up beneath his boots. Thin ribands of smoke squeezed up from where the paying had melted. He didn't know where the magazine was, but it would be the sheerest folly to go below. Reynolds knew his ship, and he'd concluded she was doomed. Ergo, they'd best get off as soon as possible, and only one refuge remained.

He said tightly, —Back to *Maryland*, and into her boats at once. Mind the wounded are boarded first, Bo's'n, Mr. Osowinski. Tell Epping we shall want charts, navigational instruments, and the chronometers in the cutter with me. Check the water and harness-casks before you swing out, but do not dally, above all, do not dally.

Back aboard his own vessel, he descended at once to the surgeon's cockpit. It was empty save for the dead. He found Steele by the mainmast, having moved the wounded topside when water had begun flooding the central passageway. They lay on blankets, shivering in the icy wind. Ker shivered too, suddenly conscious he was soaked through with sweat and blood and seawater. On *Potomac*'s burning deck he'd forgotten how cold the winter wind and sea would be.

He made sure Kaiser had the boats in hand, those not too shot up to

be of use, then went below to his cabin. It took only moments to throw
what he needed in a valise: the ship's documents, his letter-book, the gold
and drafts from the safe. Romulus trailed him back and forth, wringing
his hands, getting in the way. At last Ker told him to put on his coat and
muffler and wait in the passageway. He left the safe open as the first
tongue of seawater welled under his door and lapped across the cabin
planks. If water had reached here, the engine spaces were flooded. The
long-drawn-out shudder that ran through her fabric, as if she too felt the
cold, confirmed the imminence of her end.

When he went topside again he was shocked to see how far she'd settled. Waves were washing through the forward gunports. Subsiding, she'd
slipped out from beneath the Federal's bowsprit. The Union cruiser lay
fifty yards off, burning so fiercely he could not face it full on. A sense of
danger and terror emanated from it like some mesmeric field. Her magazine could go at any moment. But already the launch rode alongside, Dulcett at the tiller. Steele was bundling the walking wounded into it. The
transfer was made easier by the raider's having subsided nearly to the same
level. The hurt men had only to step or be handed from the dropped gun-
bulwark across into the boat. The others were lined along the deck, carrying duffels and blanket-rolls like soldiers. Ker made a swift comparison of
their number to the capacity of the remaining boats, and sighed in relief.
Their casualties had spared them that horror, at least; every survivor
would have a seat. The dead piled on the stern would need no coins for
the ferryman, he thought. *Maryland* herself would serve as their ark across
the Styx.

The Federal was turning slowly, her whole length swinging into view.
The glare of the fire was terrific. He realized the early dark of winter was
approaching. Dark, and a gathering of winter clouds. He walked among
the men, alternately hurrying them into the boats and reassuring them all
would be well, as soon as they could get away from the burning Federal.
He couldn't help looking at her over his shoulder from time to time, expecting from moment to moment to be blown to vapor. From her sides
the last of her boats had put out. They were riding downwind, the faces
above their gunwales turned toward the abandoning Confederates. From
time to time a jibe or shout rang across the gray sea, but for the most part
they passed in silence.

Kaiser reported the launch full. Ker snapped to cast off at once, not to stand on ceremony, to get them all filled and to stand off downwind as quickly as possible. Moments later the port quarter-boat cast off. The one to starboard had been smashed to kindling by a shell.

The remaining wounded had already been loaded into the cutter; now the last unwounded hands aboard stepped into her as well. Ker told Romulus to go ahead, with the valise. He stood for a moment alone on deck.

The sea came rolling in through the hawseholes, the eyes of the ship, deepening from transparent to green. A barking protest came from the tilting foremast, an echoing complaint from deep below; a rumble, a boil of steam and foam erupting through the gaps blown in her deck. She was beginning her last long plunge. As the sea reached his boots he looked around one last time, glanced back at the sorrowful heap of dead; then stepped across as well, and settled into his place in the stern. —Cast off, Bo's'n, and make way.

—Out oars. Give way together.

They were half a mile distant when *Maryland*'s trucks disappeared silently beneath the gray sea; the bright colors at her masthead still fluttering as they descended into the embrace of the Atlantic. Nearly simultaneously with her foe's demise, the Union cruiser exploded in a column of fire that split the heavens, then branched outward into a great flaming tree from which debris and exploding shells rained down on the surrounding sea.

By then, driven down together by an icy wind on an ocean that seemed much larger now that they were so much closer to it—they could look up at the wave-crests as they passed—the seven small boats, three from the Confederate, four from the Federal, lay scattered in a rough circle. Perched in the cutter's stern, Ker snugged the lapels of his reefer-jacket close about his face. Realizing, with every other man in that voiceless ring, that they were adrift, cast away, three hundred miles from the nearest land, with the wind against them and the storms of a North Atlantic winter coming on. Silence lay among the bobbing craft. Not one of them, now, flew any flag at all.

Part V

Cast Away, January 10–17, 1862.

29

THE light was passing when Ker ranged the cutter alongside that of *Potomac*'s. He left Dulcett astern in the launch, in company with the quarter-boat. Already he doubted if the latter, little more than a skiff, would be seaworthy long; its occupants were already bailing, and the prospect of storm hovered in the darkening clouds. As the light sank the cold grew more intense. The men bent to the oars, blaspheming bitterly as a freezing spray burst up over the bow, flooding the length of the boat and wetting the wounded, who lay beneath the thwarts. When he was abreast the other Ker told Epping, who was acting as coxswain, to have the men lay on their oars. He shouted, —Ahoy, Captain Reynolds.

The enemy commander looked across, and his round face hardened. —Captain Claiborne.

—We seem to be in mutual difficulties. I came to propose we meet them together, rather than separately.

A murmur in the wind; Reynolds was consulting with someone, perhaps several someones. Finally he shouted back, —We are still enemies.

Ker shouted, —May I remind you that you have struck to me?

As soon as it was out of his mouth he cursed himself. It was exactly the wrong note to touch. The Union commander's response confirmed it. —No sir, you are mistaken. It was you who surrendered.

—Don't play at this, Charles. I hauled down your flag.

—You were played out, Ker. It was just bad luck that fire started back aft, or I'd have you all below in chains.

He took counsel of the necessity to tread lightly, and tried again. —As you say; as you say. Perhaps we had best leave all such questions in abeyance, until such time as we land.

After a little while Reynolds shouted back, —What do you propose?

—We are faced with sailing some hundreds of miles to the nearest land against an offshore wind. If we stay together, we can assist each other in case of need.

Another murmur; then a reluctant, —Very well; let us stay in company, if you like.

—And aid each other?

—Of course, of course.

He decided to rest satisfied with that for now. He nodded to Epping, and the men were lowering their oars again when he thought of one more point. Turned back and shouted, —And where shall we steer?

—I hold Nantucket as the closest land. A little less than three hundred nautical miles to the northwest.

—We won't get there. The Stream sets north along the coast, and the wind's dead in our teeth.

—You suggest?

—Canada. Nova Scotia, perhaps.

There was self-interest in this, since they would not be prisoners if they landed in English territory. But it was also true that heading directly for the New England coast was impossible in this wind and sea. After some discussion, he and Reynolds compromised for the time being on a course of north by west. This would point them into the Gulf of Maine, but the influence of wind and current would set them inevitably above that point.

Actually Ker thought reaching any safe haven would take an act of God, considering how far at sea they were, the harsh season, and how many wounded they had in the boats. But they had to make for somewhere, and without delay. The Federals must have felt the same, for a stumpy mast-pole was being shrugged aloft in the larger boat. —I wish you a good night, he called at last, and not hearing an answer, dropped astern.

When he rejoined his own little flotilla he found that Dulcett and Oso-winski, in the launch, had passed a line to the quarter-boat. He passed a line to them as well and lay to, the men dipping an oar from time to time to keep head to the wind, and set the two larger boats to making sail while he took stock of the situation.

The launch, the biggest of the three, was an open craft, twenty-six feet long, seven feet in beam, and about a yard deep. She was clinker-built and copper-fastened. She had a small mast and dipping lug-rig broken down under her thwarts for just such situations as this. She'd been cut about considerable by the shell-fire, but the carpenter had managed to hammer plugs into the worst holes and was working on the others. The cutter was somewhat smaller, though she also carried a lug-rig, and the quarter-boat, of course, was smallest of all. Dr. Steele and the worst wounded, both Confederates and those Yankees who had fallen in their attempt to board, were in the cutter with Ker.

As the stars winked into burning he asked the senior man in each boat to do a written muster and to inventory stores and water. He had his tally not long after. The boats together held fifty-nine men. They had eight breakers of drinking-water, at ten gallons each. The food situation was less happy. Only four boxes of English hardtack sealed in tins, the basic lifeboat stores. In addition they had what Uffins and Rom had tumbled into a wa-ter bucket from whatever lay to hand in their flooding galley: four small tins of preserved meat, a sack of potatoes, and a miscellany of beans, but-ter, molasses, a cooked ham, tea, preserved oysters, and whortleberry jam. He ordered nothing to be touched till morning, save that the jam, mixed with a cup of water, could be served out to such of the wounded as Steele thought could benefit by it.

He was happy to find Epping had managed a complete set of charts of the New England and Canadian coast, Ker's favorite Troughton & Simms sextant, two chronometers, a patent hand-log, the nautical almanac for

1862, and *Maryland*'s log, all wrapped snugly in oilcloth. The quarter-master inclined his head gravely when complimented on his presence of mind, and allowed it wasn't the first time he'd abandoned ship; he'd done so off Ceylon in 1853, with twenty men in two boats, and had been one of only eight survivors.

—Ready to make sail, sir, Dulcett shouted from the launch. Ker looked up at his own unstayed mast, nothing more than a light spar with a single hoisting yard, running on a rusty iron hoop-traveler; a halliard and mainsheet were all his running rigging.

—Hoist away, Mr. Dulcett. Our course is nor'nor'west, keeping in company with each other, and with the Yankees as well.

—It will be a cold night.

—That it will, but we'll survive it. If the sea should part our lines, maintain your course and we'll rejoin at dawn.

A wind-obscured aye aye, and Ker nodded to the boatswain. Hand over hand, with heave and ho, the yard climbed slanting aloft. Kaiser had double reefed, of which he thoroughly approved. But still, as the stained, long-rolled canvas shook itself out, caught the wind, and snapped taut, the cutter rolled so far they shipped a gray sea over the gunwale, a tiding, foaming, freezing flood that resoaked every man amidships. Those who were able scrambled for the weather side; the rest groaned and damned helplessly. The mainsheet chattered, running out, and young Prioleau be-layed it. Kaiser cuffed his head and shouted never to belay, to tend it with a weather eye aloft. Looking to leeward Ker saw Dulcett's sail bellying out as well, a pale patch against the darkening sea.

As the last of day faded a light glimmered out from ahead; a taffrail- or masthead-lantern, swaying on Reynolds's boat.

Ker sat shivering, filled with dread of what the oncoming night might bring. Then he remembered. They weren't alone on the great waters, in the falling night. One looked down who would always care for them, and never look away. He cleared his throat, and tired, frightened faces sharp-ened to hear what the captain had to say.

—Men, I've heard that when sailors pray, they have something to pray about. I think we might be in that kind of fix now. I propose we ask Di-vine blessing, here at the beginning of our voyage.

They bent their heads, and words came to him. Simple words, and he said them simply; asking for strength, for courage, and for mercy. And then someone else spoke up, and started the Lord's Prayer, and they all said it together.

The darkness came then, night so profound that save for their own lantern, and the distant spark of the Yankee's, all the world was black. The seas heaved endlessly, and from that darkness the wind came steadily, fresh and cold; and when at midnight Ker put his hand to the halliard, it was hard as iron, slicked with a freshly created coat of ice.

All of them knew the color of the sea. The dawn lit it around them, a wearying waste of black in the distance, gray closer in, and a coldhearted olive when the waves soaked them with generous impartiality and crystal rivulets of piercing cold swirled about their feet. The gunwales had gathered a translucent coat of rime. Those on watch bailed with hats and hands and tins. Those off sprawled in the ceiling boards, watching with fatigue-drugged eyes. Some of the wounded were barefoot. Their shoes had come off in the surgeon's cockpit, and *Maryland* had gone down so quickly they'd been left behind. Kaiser had wrapped oiled paper from the foodstuffs around their feet, but that did little to warm them.

Ker blinked around the heaving horizon, hardly believing light had returned to the world. The night past had been the longest of his life. He sat stiffly at the tiller. The launch carried a heavy weather helm, and an hour's trick was as much as a man could stand. Still, the exertion helped keep the cold at bay. He watched the main, the compass, lashed to a thwart, the sails around them and astern. Clouds hugged the waves, and he guessed they'd take rain or snow later in the day.

The bad news came when Uffins and Rom opened the hardtack for a first distribution. It was rotten with saltwater and worms. The iron containers had rusted through on the bottom, where the minute penetrations had been invisible to the eye. The good news came with Steele's crawling aft, clutching something swathed in burlap. He lowered his bulk awkwardly at Ker's feet, and undid the cloth to display a squat bottle.

—I took the liberty of rescuing a case of Calvados.

—Doctor?

—As medicinal stores, Captain. A sustainment salutary to health, a stimulant against the cold, a brace to the wounded and a stiffening to the weary. Really sir, one dare not abandon ship without it.

—I was not reproaching you. Not yet. I assume you'll serve it out, as you say, in the role of a medicinal stimulant. To the wounded only.

—And to the aged.

Ker coughed into his fist. —And to the aged; very well. But restrain yourself, Doctor. I'll need you available for consultation.

Steele grumbled that he'd never indulged beyond his readiness for duty. Which Ker did not care to contradict.

Potomac's launch altered course toward them. It gradually grew between the passing seas. At times they looked down into it, to see a sprawl of blue-clothed, sodden men like a reflection of themselves; at times aloft, as the waves careered it upward, silhouetting every line and strake and flapping reef-string against the lowering clouds. A seaman slowly hammered a board against the gunwales, smashing off ice accreted from wind-driven spray. Ker watched it approach without feeling, without expectation. He noticed, though, that someone had had the presence of mind to take up several floorboards, and extend the gunwales at bow and stern. A spare sail had been stretched to form a partial shelter. He beckoned Kaiser to him and pointed silently. The boatswain nodded and set to work.

—Captain Claiborne. The words carried across the wind.

—Captain Reynolds.

—Have . . . you . . . water? The words spaced out to carry across forty yards of heaving sea, through the rush of twenty knots of wind.

—Water? he repeated. Fatigued by the constant motion, without sleep all night, wet and frozen through, he did not at once grasp the question.

—Our butts have been stove and are fouled with seawater. Have you any drinking water to spare?

Ker was still turning this over in his head when Prioleau, beside him, whispered angrily, —Captain. We can't give them our water.

—We can't, Sam? And why not?

—Because they're Yankees! That's why.

—Yes, we have water, Ker called. Then he remembered the spoiled rations. —But we're a bit short on comestibles.

—Sir, you should not.

He restrained angry words, to the effect a ship's boy did not reproach the captain. Really, Sam was presuming on his family connection. But a lad was a lad, disposed to strong opinions; he'd not be worth a tinker's fart otherwise. So he just said, mildly as he could, —Think, Sam. Cold men, wounded men, need food as much as water. They need water, and we need food.

He added that even if they wouldn't benefit from the trade, he'd be bound still to go halves. The traditions of the sea went beyond the petty quarrels men conducted on its surface. The boy listened, but his intransigent scowl told Ker he hadn't convinced anyone.

They ran alongside for a few minutes, then Reynolds called across with a proposal. Ker agreed, and the two craft ran closer. They seesawed up, then down with dizzying speed.

Kaiser stood. A heaving-line uncoiled in the air, dropping across the Federal's flank. A grizzled long-beard bent, then signaled them to haul around. The cargo was a U.S. Navy–issue box of hardtack, a sight so familiar and yet so foreign now Ker blinked at it dumbly. Meanwhile a breaker of water was going back across. The lines tautened and slacked, the boats rolled and pitched, but eventually they completed the swap. The Yankee put his tiller over, and here and there one or two fellows lifted their palms. Others, however, gave them only hostile glares of unyielding hatred.

That day passed with all the boats in sight of each other. Ker tossed the log and consulted his chart; more he could not do, the overcast prevented a glimpse of sun. He judged they'd run fifty-four miles in the twenty-four hours past. Unfortunately, that did not equate to the same distance closer to land. On this tack they were paralleling the coast nearly as much as they were approaching it. Sooner or later, though, they must reach the Stream. The dreadful cold must moderate then. If they continued north into the higher latitudes, though, even it might not save them.

It all came down to the wind, and what disposition it would make of them. But as he glanced aloft he saw no sign of change.

And night came, and it was the second night.

At the second dawn the launch was no longer in sight. Ker stood and strained his eyes around the horizon; sent Prioleau shinnying up the mast-pole. The boy slid back down with a silent shake of his head. They were all growing silent, as much from the dryness of their mouths as a growing lassitude.

One of the wounded had died during the night. A shell fragment had shattered his upper thigh. Steele had amputated at the hip joint, but the old man said he wouldn't have had much chance even in hospital ashore. When they made ready to slide the corpse over the side, though, the men murmured, pointed.

Looking astern, Ker saw them too. A pair of black dorsals, stitching across their wake. When he ordered the body put over—naked, they could spare neither blanket, nor canvas, nor even clothing, it went to those who still shivered—the fins drew close together. They pirouetted where the poor pale corpse had disappeared. Their motion might have been beautiful had it not been so terrible. Then they vanished, simultaneously, as if sucked below the surface.

Ker looked away, swallowing, and met the others' eyes as each man in the frail wooden envelope that alone preserved them understood others would leave the same way before their voyage ended, that as far as the odds went, not one might ever see land again.

He slacked the sheets, and gradually the other sails drew ahead. They shrank to hull-less triangles, then specks, and at last vanished altogether save from the masthead. Ker held on as long as he dared, then past the time he dared. They plowed alone through gray seas, under low, dark, turbulent clouds.

He was rewarded at last by a cry from above. Prioleau, clinging to the very cap of the spar, had spotted the launch to the southeast. She altered course toward them as soon as she was spotted. Within a couple of hours Ker was able to sheet in again and run for the main body. And to his sur-prise they must have slowed, waiting for the laggards, for the lost sheep

made up swiftly on them. Before dark came again all seven boats were together once more.

Two more men joined the sea that day, one from the cutter, one, Dulcett reported, from the launch. The black fins, which had accompanied
them all day, performed their grave and chilling sarabande once more.
Following which Ker brought his three boats close together, and watching
his chances in sea and wind, divided the quarter-boat's crew into the two
larger craft. Then brought it alongside the launch, where the carpenter
hammered it apart down to its wooden ribs, and parceled it out between
the remaining craft to fabricate shelter.

It was as well they did. That night the wind rose to a frenetic crescendo,
and after hours of it the sea heaved in terrific billows that aimed the cutter alternately aloft and alow and in-betweentime on its beam ends. All
the boats had lowered sails and masts, and drove together before the fury
of the storm. Sea-anchors kept their bows to the wind, and the lowered
sails, bent over the built-up gunwales, kept most of the sea out; that
which still penetrated they threw overboard through a flap at the stern.
The sheer force of the wind seemed to keep ice from accumulating, or
they'd have capsized from its weight. In the middle of the storm, Ker became suddenly aware that the water which surged to and fro past his sodden body had changed. It had become warm, nearly as warm as blood.

They'd reached that river of tropic sea that stretched like a vine up the
western side of the Atlantic. With its roots in the Caribbees and its
branches at the far Arctic. Now the men did not bail quite as fast, and lay
with frozen limbs painfully thawing in its welcome warmth.

The storm endured through that day and all through the night. The
men endured too with stubborn suffering, lying in the near-dark beneath
the shielding canvas. They gnawed at hardtack and morsels of ham. They
sucked greedily at cups of water too scanty to blunt their thirst. Some lay
insensible for long periods of time, rolling to and fro in the bottom of the
boat.

They found Jacobs sightless and motionless in the morning. He
couldn't speak; an hour later he stopped breathing as well. The old sailmaker's aged body had given out. Ker read the Service over him, as he had

over each of the dead. The rolling seas seemed to have driven off the sharks, or some mysterious process of satiation had taken place; whatever the reason, they were gone, and the old man drifted away to his long home in peace.

The next day the wind lessened, and backed westerly. The seas were still mountainous, but by midmorning all six remaining boats had reerected their masts and resumed their port tack. The sun came into view for short periods of time between the lingering banks of cloud-wrack, but Ker was unable to hold it long enough for a line of position.

As best he could estimate, from the hand-log and his estimate of time run, they were roughly at forty-one degrees; about at the latitude of Long Island. For even as they lay to in the storm, the great stream had been carrying them northward. The wind was still freezing, but the warmth in which they lay gave them life and hope. The little flotilla surged together over long wastes, rising and dropping in turn as the seas swept under. Between noon and dark the wind backed even more, and they shook reefs from their sails and plowed nodding across water that was green, not gray, and speckled with the pale sprigs of sargasso weed.

The next day another man did not awaken. This time it was a younger fellow, a stout sailor who'd seemed perfectly healthy the night before. Ker had a long discussion with Steele over his body. The surgeon explained that when the life-force ran out, the human mechanism simply ran down. It was well known that many newly enslaved Africans, if allowed to withdraw into themselves, would simply draw up their legs and die without visible cause.

The old man pursed his lips, glanced round, and lowered his voice. Ears were all around, though heads nodded and eyes were closed. Ker thought of the raft of the *Medusa,* looking at the crumpled tumbled figures. The surgeon reached up and with a quick, furtive embrace drew him close. Ker smelled brandy as the surgeon whispered, —The fellow is young, and well set up.

—What are you saying, Doctor? He's dead, is he not?

—My point exactly. He is dead, and of no use to himself.

Ker blinked, still not comprehending. Till suddenly he did. He recoiled, pushing the surgeon's soft fingers away. —Such is beyond discussion, Doctor.

—I beg your pardon, Captain. It is well within the realm of discussion, given our circumstances. And soon will be within the realm of necessity.

But he shook his head again, pushing away even the suspicion of what Steele had so delicately proposed. Yet when he read the Service once more, from the wet translucent pages of his falling-apart Testament, he couldn't help noting the crew's whispering. The furtive way one of the men holding the corpse squeezed a meaty arm.

That night he was awakened by cries of terror. Starting up, he smelled a warm, fishy, barnyard-redolent aroma. A rushing hiss followed by the turbulence of water surrounded the boat. Pushing his head up, he found Epping intent on his course amid the sounds and cries.

—Whales, sir, the quartermaster said, not turning his head. Ker sensed them to port, to starboard; vast presences in the darkness. Were they aware of the fragile shells among them? One blow of a great fluke, one brush of a mighty flank would send all the men spilling into the sea. But not one creature so much as touched them. Only swam with them for a time, blowing streams of warm rain into the wind. Then silently sank from their knowledge, back into the immense and unknown ocean.

The next day the sun gleamed through just long enough for him to get a snapshot with his sextant. It placed them thirty miles north of his dead reckoning, meaning that the current was hastening them on all the more rapidly. But he knew that as they approached the vicinity of land, that current doubled on itself in gyring eddies that would carry them not forward but back. There was no help for it, he could not predict nor guess its direction, only sail on.

The wind backed and dropped to a fresh breeze. A shouted noonday discussion with Charles Reynolds brought them to compromise once more, and they took advantage of the wind to haul round more nearly to the west. They discussed the dwindling rations of water and food, and equalized them among the boats.

All that day they sailed in company, often within shouting-distance. By now the men knew each other on sight, and traded insults and banter until called to account by the petty officers. Kaiser shook the last reefs out and all hands lay out to windward.

Ker's heart lifted as they boomed along, sending a frothing bow-wave hissing out before them. The other boats sheeted in their lugs as well, and for that entire afternoon all was as gay as a yacht race. Lamb-white clouds tumbled about the sky, and from time to time the sun gilded the crests with brushfuls of purest gold. A song sounded across the fleeing waves; the cutter's crew called back a chorus. But gradually the launches drew ahead, faster by virtue of their length. To Ker's frustration his cutter proved slowest of all. He altered sail, sent men scrambling forward and aft, seeking the ideal trim, but in vain. But as night drew on again a clustering of canvas ahead announced the winners had shortened sail, to allow the sluggards to close up.

The next day proved just as splendid, with the cold air sharp as shattered crystal and the sky filled with sunlight and fleecy clouds. This time the larger boats did not sheet home quite so tightly, and all raced together across green swells that seemed to be turning darker, to be reverting to the dark blue of the mid-Atlantic. Toward afternoon Ker put his hand over the side, and felt the chill ache deep into tendon and muscle. From tropic currents, they were once more plunged into the depths of winter. The weather too was changing, the overcast thickening once more. The men responded, the transient gaiety of fine weather giving way to something resembling stupor. They lay for long periods motionless against the gunwales, staring into the passing sea. The wounded particularly concerned Ker, and not only those in the cutter. Dulcett reported those in the launch were weakening too. If they didn't make land soon more would die.

He passed hours going over his chart, attempting to fix a landfall. The days of fine sailing had put them nearly two hundred miles closer to land. But which land? Comparing results, he and Reynolds agreed they were at forty-three degrees north latitude, heading into the Gulf of Maine. The southwestern coast of this Gulf was the coast of Maine; the northwestern, that of New Brunswick; the northern, the island of Nova Scotia.

Through hours at the tiller he'd pondered their course once they closed. Any landfall would save their lives, but it would be better to step ashore under the Canadian flag rather than that of the Union. For that reason, he'd decided that once within the Gulf, *Maryland*'s launch and cutter would break off and make their own way north, trusting to Providence to throw them on friendly shores.

But against that intent he had to balance the condition of the wounded. For their sake, he had to make landfall soon. Only then could they receive rest, and food, and the medical care they so desperately needed.

Though he was not certain as yet they were fated to land in Maine. The longitude would make the difference, and his calculations were questionable. Both chronometers had taken shock and wet in the open boat. They now diverged by forty seconds, and he didn't know which was the more accurate. They could be twenty miles west or twenty miles east of where he estimated they were. He had to bear in mind the possibility of accident too. Both the launch and cutter had started planks. They'd managed to fix them with the carpenter's kit, but one brush with a floating log could founder them. In company with the Federals, they could distribute a boat's complement among the five remaining—overloading them, but they might just make it. With only two boats, the loss of one would mean the death of every soul in it.

He flexed his hands, examining the great raw weeping cracks that had opened at the joints of his fingers: saltwater boils from pulling at lines in the cold, then tearing them open again and again. Every muscle ached from bracing himself against the endless motion, and his thigh flamed where the iron shard had struck. Hunger growled like a wolverine in his belly. He'd made sure the wounded and sick got double rations, and the scarce tins of preserves. Only mouthfuls each of hardtack remained. Though the water, thank God, was holding out, eked out by rainwater caught in the sails.

As between Canada and the United States, it would be close. He could see that from the chart. They could make landfall either in northern Maine, in the vicinity of Matinicus Island or Bar Harbor, or in southern New Brunswick, Campobello Island or Saint John. If they fetched up in the Bay of Fundy he could part company then, and make for the eastern shore; that would put them ashore in Nova Scotia.

He sat for a long time, mind empty, looking not at the horizon, but at his suffering men.

30

Night and Snow ♦ A Union Lad's Request ♦ Breakers, Approached by
Line Ahead ♦ Landfall ♦ Insight into One's Fate

T HAT night the wind shifted to the northeast and blew up again,
this time with a polar edge that cut like blunt steel. It froze uncovered flesh to marble, and numbed the mind to an opiated
slowness.

Ker crawled to the tiller at midnight. He steered with hands that had
all the sensitivity of oaken blocks, and arms like levers of lead. The only
light was the distant winking of Reynolds's taffrail-lantern, rising and
falling on the chaotic, building seas.

Gradually his fogged brain became aware something was amiss. But
apathy was a warm cloak. Whatever was wrong, it didn't matter. All that
mattered was holding the dancing light fine on the bow. The wind, and
the savage luff of the reefed sail, like frantically beating wings, when he
steered too close.

So that when the prow came out of the night, and a warning scream
burst close beside his ear, he only slowly woke to realizing the cutter's frail
scantlings were about to be stove in. He shoved the tiller full over, sheering away. The sail flattened as they came beam to the wind. The cutter
reeled far over, throwing men bodily to leeward, nearly spilling them all
into the sea. He struggled to slack the main but it had fouled on something in the dark, it wouldn't run free.

A crashing surf rolled the length of the cutter from stern to stem, soaking every man in her to the bone for the thousandth time in water cold as ice. Solid sea tided in, rising to his boots, his knees, as he struggled savagely with the fouled sheet. Till at last it gave, came free. He slacked off hand over hand and ran heart hammering madly before the wind as every man bailed for his life in the wallowing, lurching, all but foundering shell. For long minutes he shook with fear. He'd all but capsized them. He saw again and again what would have happened to wounded and starving men, cast into that icy sea. Only gradually did he sense tiny moth-touches here and there on his upturned face, soft as a child's kisses, as his son's kisses had been when he crept into his parents' bed. . . . Touches that only when they struck his opened eyeballs became heavy, damp, accumulated snowflakes.

The morning dawned an opaque white. Thick towels of blowing snow flapped endlessly down the northeast wind. The boats sailed close together, keeping in touch with the thin gull-cries of boatswain's pipes. They sailed on a reach, heading west. Somewhere there lay land. Where, no one knew. But with this wind they'd strike on a lee coast. Maine and New Brunswick were rockbound shores. Their long sail might well end with breaking up in heavy surf, panicky struggles in the freezing surge. He had Kaiser make up the empty water casks into preserver-floats, but there weren't enough for everyone. He called the launch in and made sure Dulcett understood to round up at the first sound of breakers, not to stand in until they could see to steer for a sheltered cover or inlet.

Yet Reynolds was still running west, all out, even through the blinding snow. Did he have a better chart? He too had wounded aboard, was he risking all for the sake of a few? Ker took the tiller again, and sailed into the white blindness with every sense twisted to the snapping point. At last he told Kaiser to make up a line and sound, using a hammer from the carpenter's kit for a lead. No bottom, so they ran on. Into a sightless blizzard that covered the unconscious wounded with crisp white, that whirled in the belly of the sail and coated his bleeding fingers with smears of pink frost.

Later Steele dragged himself aft. —Are you holding out, Doctor? Ker asked him.

—With the help of Vergil.

—Indeed?

—*Forsan et haec olim meminisse iuvabit.* Perhaps you recall the passage. Aeneus and his men are being hurled about in a stormy sea. He reassures them with these words.

—I fear my Latin has not been overhauled in some time, Doctor.

—Dryden's rendering goes: "An hour will come, with pleasure to relate, Your sorrows past, as benefits of fate." I thought it appropriate to our present situation.

Ker wasn't sure if it was the numbed state of his mind, but the words didn't bring him the comfort they seemed to afford the surgeon. Steele snuffled, wiped spray from his sagging grizzled jowls. —One of the Yankee wounded. Whipple.

—Tell me what you must tell me, Doctor.

—He's very low. He asked for you.

The lad lay with his head pillowed in another man's midriff, brow pale as the snow, eyes closed. His thin chest rose with effort. He'd been bayoneted. Ker touched his hand, and after a moment his lids parted. —Captain, he whispered.

—How are you doing, my boy.

—I'm not cold anymore, sir. Or hungry.

—We're very near the coast, son. There'll be fire there and hot food. You must hold on till then. That's an order.

—There's a letter in my tunic here. For my father. Tell him I died game. That I gave you Rebels hell.

—Tell him yourself, Whipple. You'll live through this, and be a credit to him.

The boy didn't answer. Only closed his eyes. When Ker touched the blue still lips they were cold. He was still breathing, but only just.

—Doctor Steele; a dose of your special tonic here, at once. Ker looked about, searching for something to wrap the boy in; a scrap of fearnought, canvas; nothing offered. At last he pulled off his own reefer-jacket and pushed the boy's arms into it, buttoned it with wooden fingers. The bitter wind struck his soaked shirt, turning it the stiff creaking consistency of cardboard, penetrating it almost instantly with ice.

————

—Captain. Captain!

He rose with sluggish effort from vivid dreams of home. To find himself lying rigid as wood atop a snow-covered pile of corpses. Then another body jerked, and he sat up slowly; still dazed; perhaps not all were dead?

—Here, he whispered.

—Breakers ahead.

He pulled himself upright as rapidly as stiffened sinews would let him, and crawled aft. Propped himself up beside Kaiser. The German's once-heavy face was gaunt, his sodden whiskers silver.

Back from the foggy milling of miles of snow came a muffled booming like hundreds of distant kettledrums. Heavy surf on rock. Just from the sound he could vision the crags, the milky white of boiling sea waiting to tear and rend boats and bodies. If only he could see! He cupped his ears ahead, then to either side, straining to link sound with sense. The roar came from ahead, but also from starboard.

From the snow. —Capt-aa-in Claiborne.

—Captain Reynolds.

—Do you hear that surf?

—I do indeed.

—We can linger out.

—I have wounded and dying, Ker shouted. Most likely it'll still be snowing at nightfall. Another night out here will finish many of us.

—I'm in the same condition, Reynolds called back. —I shall proceed first, sounding with the lead, and attempt to find a passage. If you will second me?

This was a brave course, and Ker could only shout back, —I shall follow you in, and relay to the boats astern. Good luck, Charles.

—And the same to you, Ker.

He took the tiller again, unwilling to relinquish it at this supreme moment. Fortunately the wind was not totally unfavorable, being from the northeast still. They could wear round at the first sight of danger and perhaps make it back to sea. At any moment, though, some isolated rock could loom from the snow-fog, some barely submerged pinnacle could jackknife them open from below. Epping gripped the mainsheet, staring ahead. Kaiser fumbled his way to the prow, to provide a few more seconds of warning. Sam tried to shinny the mast again, but Ker told him brusquely to get down in the ceiling boards and hang on. He drew his sodden, frozen cap down over his eyes, blinking ahead.

The swells were building, a sure sign of a rapidly shallowing bottom. They lifted the cutter bodily and surged it ahead, rushing it through the air with a frightening speed, then dropping away to cradle and wallow before the next wave came rushing out from white obscurity. Even after days of storm the motion was giddying, vertiginous, unbearable to senses sharpened by terror and drawn fine by hunger and cold. His fingers would not close around the tiller-bar. He wedged his hands around it under his armpit, and vised them together as he would a clamp of soft copper.

A cry came from ahead. Of despair, or triumph? He could not tell. It came again, echoing from some unseen obstacle in the mist, but still he could not make out its import. Was it warning them off, or beckoning them on? From their tumbled positions the men stared up at him, eyes steady in the falling snow. He averted his gaze, blinking snowflakes from his lashes, concentrating on the milling whiteness ahead with all his force. His breath moved in and out like reciprocating iron.

—Py der mark four, said Kaiser.

—Very well, Bo's'n, Ker told him. Keep them coming.

The roar of surf resounded all round them now, from port, from starboard, from ahead, even, now, from behind them. He could hear the cries no longer. They were drowned out by continuous thunder. The swell lifted them again, stern first, much higher this time than before, and with a swaying motion to and fro, as if making sure of its grip, suddenly rocketed them forward through the snow-laden air. Ker caught pleading brown eyes fixed on him from a dark face: Romulus, clinging desperately to the gunwale. Prioleau. Kaiser. Steele. They were all watching him, at least those who could still lift their heads. So many eyes, so many unspoken appeals . . . he tried to smile confidently back, but feared the cold and tension made it a twisted grimace. His heart was squeezed tight with dread. He hauled the tiller this way and that as the rudder went sloppy, struggling to keep her head to the west.

Was that a gap, an absence of sound? A lacuna in the shaking thunder from one quarter of the compass? He cocked his head, concentrating all his will on the act of listening.

A thin high cry, as if from a fox dying in a steel trap, reached his ear.

—By der mark t'ree, shoaling fast.

He did not answer. His mind was groping through the opacity of the snow. His hearing reached for the very texture of the savage endless roaring that was their only clue to the danger all around. The snow whipped past, flakes rising, falling, colliding with the cresting seas, mingling with the icy breaths of spray that came to him now blown on the wind. Surf to windward, but an absence of sound just ahead of it. And one faint cry to go on.

He carried on for seconds, then suddenly threw his back into the tiller, yanking her head round to the northward, and in the same instant crying to Epping to sheet in. The block grated with ice as the lug-boom clattered against the mast, knocking down crackling white crusts of frozen spume. The cutter rolled sickeningly, making way slowly into the milling whiteness. He could barely breathe, his chest was squeezed so tightly with fear.

Slowly a darkness emerged ahead. To starboard, a ghostly pale glow, and the air-quivering boom of violent surf. To port, the susurrating hiss of a gravel beach. Ahead, a loom of shadow that as they wallowed forward became a curving hook of darkness, a strand of beach, a looming cliff.

Till the curtain lifted suddenly, the falling driven snow blocked by that cliff wall, to show a curving black-pebbled and startlingly close beach on which *Potomac*'s launch lay drawn up, sail cast free to lie in flapping folds. Its crew were dragging themselves over the gunwales to slip and drop heavily into thigh-deep water. Then lurching and staggering on, to reel and fall full length on a black, snow-spotted, shingle shore.

Now suddenly everything moved very swiftly indeed. The cutter scraped, yawed, then came to a violent rocking halt as floorboards gave way beneath their feet. Black water flooded up. Ker levered himself stiffly out and fell into a hole in the sea. His kicking boots found no bottom. His popping eyes searched a blurred bubbly greenness. He had no flotation. There hadn't been enough empty casks for everyone.

He came up gasping and flailing, arms clawing as if climbing a watery ladder, and got a death-grip on the gunwale. He hauled himself shoreward along it hand over hand, till his feet gained a jagged hardness of submerged rock. The others, those who were able, had rolled out too. Together, bawling in wordless encouraging discordant voicings, reeling as if drunk, they wrenched the sinking cutter free of the spur and ran it forward, sail flapping uselessly in the lee of the cliff, to ground beside the Yankee.

Ker was kneeling on the shore, gazing down at the priceless miracle of rounded pebbles shining with wet, when he became conscious they were not alone. Rough-looking men in slouch hats and worn oilskins had come from nowhere, it seemed. Till he noticed a path descending the strand, a gray weathered board-and-iron structure farther up the beach. He could not quite make out what it was; some sort of fishing station, perhaps, with wooden racks for drying nets. The natives surrounded them, and for a time the two groups regarded each other, those who kept the beach, those who'd suddenly appeared from the snow. Looking behind, Ker saw the *Potomac*'s cutter emerge into the little bay, and beyond it the shadow-outline of Dulcett's launch.

Finally an old man with sea-graven eyes and ragged grizzled beard drew a short pipe from his lips and spat on the shingle. —Wheah you fellahs drop from? Look like you had a pull to get heah.

—We are castaways from U.S.S. *Potomac*, sunk in battle at sea, Reynolds said. Ker struggled to his feet and went forward, intending to stand beside him and represent his own. —Where are we?

—Youah in Machias Bay; Cutler's a little up the way.

Ker asked him, his voice sounding strange to his own ears, —Are we in the United States? Or is this Canada?

The old man turned to him, running those far-off eyes up and down him. —Neethah, Mister. Youah in Maine. Canada's fourteen more mile up the way.

A chuckle from his fellows, but followed by a proffer of flasks and hands. The fishermen, for such they seemed to be, began helping weary men up from where they lay exhausted, stretched full length in the washing surf. One said he'd see to a fire, and began jogging along the beach. Ker was about to speak again when Reynolds turned, and their eyes met.

—Gentlemen, I have the honor to present the notorious pirate and marauder, Captain Ker Claiborne of the so-called Confederate Navy. He is my prisoner. There is a price on his head, and a hundred dollars of it in gold will be shared out among you if you find me a secure place to hold him.

—Charles, Ker said in a low voice.

His classmate smiled frostily. —It is the fortune of war, sir. Would you not do the same to me, if we had landed in Virginia?

—I am no pirate, nor are my men. My wounded need treatment. Some are Yankees; others Southerners. I treated all alike. They all need food, and fire, and dry clothes.

—And they'll get it. We're not savages. As to being a pirate, or not— your fate's not in my hands, Ker. You crafted it, by rebellion and treason to the flag we both once served together. It may be the gallows. It may be prison. That's up to the government. Not to me.

He stood without response. Reynolds nodded, and turned back to the old fisherman. —I should be indebted if you would carry word to your local militia, and have them send a guard. I shall also want a good legger, to run a message to the nearest telegraph office.

Reynolds turned away and began shouting, ordering the wounded brought up the beach to the house. Ker stood motionless on the shingle. Then, at last, turned away, and made his way back down to where his own men waited, pale, staggering, retching on hands and knees, but alive. They watched him with bright eyes, shivering.

Without words, he stepped into their embrace. They surrounded him, clapping him on the back with rough blows that went on and on. He felt tears sting his eyes, and did not bother to blink them back. The gibbet, prison, indignity, death; what lay ahead did not matter; he'd brought them through. Whipple smiled weakly as two burly Downeasters shouldered him up, carried him off between them toward a driftwood fire just beginning to roar and snap.

Ker started to follow, then his steps slowed. At last he halted. Though he was shuddering, soaked through, he lingered. Gazing not ahead, at the rising smoke, the gathering throng, but back, to the now-abandoned craft that had carried them so far, so faithfully, over so many miles of sea and terror.

It was suddenly given to him, freezing and in pain, hungry and nearly naked, to understand.

His preservation was not due to chance. A power greater than himself had brought him through battle and storm. Not for his own purposes, but for its own; for a reason he only dimly glimpsed now, shivering on a barren beach, but that would in time be revealed.

All will be revealed! All will be clear! Someone called to him through the very sigh of the wind, as if His tongue spoke with the pebbles that grated in endless sullen mutter with the rush and retreat of the sea.

He sank to his knees, there on the strand; and the men who stood with ropes in their hands waited patiently. Until at last he stood, and put out his hands to be bound.

ABOUT THE AUTHOR

David Poyer's many naval and historical novels make him the most popular living author of American sea fiction. *That Anvil of Our Souls* is third in his continuing novel-cycle of the Civil War at sea, following *Fire on the Waters* and *A Country of Our Own*. Retired naval captain and engineer, he lives on Virginia's Eastern Shore with his wife and daughter, who sail with him to research locales on their sloop, *Frankly Scarlett*.

Visit David Poyer's website at www.poyer.com.

Now available from Today's Master of American Sea Fiction

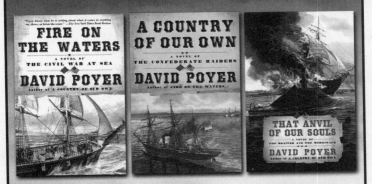

Available in paperback	Available in paperback	Available in hardcover
0-671-04681-0	0-671-04741-8	0-684-87135-1

In the opening volume of his extraordinary *Civil War at Sea* series, David Poyer introduces the characters through whose eyes we'll experience the greatest conflict in American history. The crew of U.S.S. *Owanee* witnesses the gripping and heartbreaking events that led to the battle of Fort Sumter and the breakout of the Civil War.

Lt. Ker Claiborne is no admirer of slavery, but he's also a Virginian. In *A Country of Our Own*, Ker "goes South," joining the Virginia Navy, then the fledgling Confederate States Navy. His command of the fastest, most dangerous raider ever to put to sea may even decide the outcome of the war.

North meets South in two momentous battles—one between the first ironclads, the other between two visions of America's future. Poyer's vivid characters return to re-create the bloodiest conflict in American history.

"Poyer knows what he is writing about when it comes to anything on, above, or below the water." —*The New York Times Book Review*

SIMON & SCHUSTER PAPERBACKS
A VIACOM COMPANY

www.simonsays.com